The PRIZE

RA GOFORTH

The Prize

Published by Wheatmark®
2030 E. Speedway Boulevard, Suite 106
Tucson, Arizona 85719 USA
www.wheatmark.com

ISBN: 978-1-60494-496-9
LCCN: 2010931233

FOREWORD

My Grandpa and Grandma are a family legend. Especially the stories of their travels and exploits throughout Europe. Their biggest family legend stems from how they first made their mark on history. It started back in the days well after World War II when the world was at peace and happy. There was no such thing as cell phones, self serve gas stations, and long before the world was ripe with terrorism. Hard to believe, but it was even before the ancient stories of how man first walked on the moon.

The adventure started for me about a year ago while cleaning out Grandma and Grandpa's upstairs attic in the house they spent their last few years together. My family had decided to liquidate their home and belongings after everyone had gone through and taken what they wanted. The final task of going through their more personal belongings fell on me. I had been the one who had spent the most time in the attic playing as a child, and about a year and a half ago my dad—their only child—had succumbed to his long battle with lung cancer. As I started going through the contents of the attic I was very surprised at the dust and piles of junk that had accumulated in what used to be a practically sterile upper room.

I was just about finished with the initial sort-by-sell and trash piles when I came across an old wooden footlocker-type trunk tucked under a tarpaulin. *Why not?* I thought. *It all belongs to us now anyway.* As I was searching through the normal old photo albums and European souvenirs it struck me like a lightning bolt. This must be Grandpa's chest. I'd heard, and even briefly glanced at the box in the past growing up, but was never allowed to be near it. At the bottom in the back right corner was snuggled that kind of gold nugget that seems to start all great journeys. The first thing that caught my attention was the bright brass-colored latch that went from back to front and snapped into a lock. A black leather-bound book! I could see no keyhole in the latch. But before attempting to unlatch the strap I hesitated, then picked it up to inspect it closer. Under better light I could tell that it was actually a very dark brown leather. A first glance over gave me the impression that it had been hand made of very high-grade quality leather. However, there was no inscription anywhere on the front or back.

So back to the latch. It was made of a brownish yellow metal of some kind. It had a square latch with a small round button sticking up in the center.

I stepped back a bit and with the kind of body posture that says, "Hmm . . ." I thought to myself. *Stands to reason this thing should either push or slide to unlatch the treasure within.*

Gently using my thumb, I tried to slide the button to the left. Like a shotgun blast in the attic the snap popped open and the latch fell loose.

As I opened the cover I realized that I had been holding my breath. The sudden exhalation of air exploded out of my lungs as I saw the words on the first page.

The Love, Woman ,and Money of my Life
by James Peterson

I plopped down on the floor next to the chest and started to read. What follows are his own handwritten words from start to finish.

CHAPTER 1

The rain was falling so hard and thick that I felt as if I were walking through a wall of water. But I didn't care. In fact, I welcomed the feeling. The weather matched my dark, gray mood as the thick clouds dumped their load. Tons of water fell on top of everything and anything. I wished I could do the same. I felt as if I were carting around a hell of a load myself.

It was late Friday afternoon. Another lousy workweek was done. I was heading home for a weekend full of quiet solitude so that I could wallow in my own world of doom and gloom. As I made my way down the sidewalk, I didn't even try to walk very close to the tall skyscrapers to try to block some of the rain.

So what. Who cares? I thought.

I sure didn't, and I knew nobody else did either. A Freudian intellectual would say it was a form of self-abusive punishment for which I held myself responsible for my current situation and problems.

Bullshit! I can't be to blame for everything. I was no longer just thinking but mumbling to the very buildings I was trying to not walk next to.

It just felt like a natural adaptation to my surroundings. The water was flowing down the gutter so quickly that the street drains couldn't keep up and the streets were flooding over the curb. However, when I came to the corner intersection, I didn't even slow down. I just stepped off the curb, right into the ankle-deep water. I kept going across the normally busy intersection to the next sidewalk. I didn't even look to see if any cars were coming. The way my luck had been going lately, I wouldn't have been so fortunate as to have a car hit me and take me out of my misery. Sure enough, I sloshed across the quickly building river without any high-speed boats running me over.

It's amazing how fate works. Now feeling a bit meek and humble.

It was only because I was feeling so down that I was walking hunched over with my head down. I wasn't looking where I was going. I was only looking down at the ground in front of my footsteps. I wasn't really looking at anything. I was just shuffling along and mumbling to myself about all the things that had gone wrong lately.

A few years ago, I had been a happily married insurance investigator. After twenty-five years of marriage with no children, my wife suddenly announced she wanted a divorce because I was a bum with no ambition who was going nowhere. She said she felt she deserved something better before she got too old to enjoy it. After all, she had reached executive secretary of a large accounting firm. I had only held the same position with the same company for twenty-two years. I'd gotten a few raises along the way, but I got no promotions. I had put on a few pounds since we were first married when I was twenty-four years old, but who hadn't? I still got out and played golf regularly. So I wasn't exactly a fat old couch potato. I felt I must be the one to blame for my wife feeling I was now beneath her. She wanted to get along with her life without me. I was the heavy anchor around her neck.

To be able to learn to live with all this, I had to mentally force myself to transfer the blame for everything I carried around that had gone wrong back onto her. I had been able to get away with it until other things happened. Last week, my boss had hinted

I was perhaps old and stagnant in my job. Perhaps a younger, newly trained person could do my job better. Yesterday, my car broke down, and the mechanic said it would take between $1,000 to $1,500 to fix or replace the transmission and brakes and do an engine overhaul. He had assured me that his quoted price was a very fair and inexpensive repair bill. What good did it do when I only had $28 to my name? My landlady was threatening to evict me because I was two months behind on my rent. Other than my ex-wife, I had no family to turn to for even friendship. I had never taken the time to make any real close male "buddies" over the years. I felt like I was basically all alone in the world except for one couple that I had become somewhat close to. Initially only because our business life bumped us into each other. Then over the years a love/hate relationship developed. When my marriage and life hit the toilet Mike really took me under his wing. I fought it at first, but I guess some day I will fully heal. Of course, I felt like it wasn't ever going to get any better. So, I felt I just didn't care anymore. It just didn't matter. One could say I was becoming very pessimistic. I didn't know about that, but I felt that, if something bad were to happen to me, it wouldn't surprise me.

To top it all off, I broke both shoestrings this morning while I was simply trying to tie my shoes. When the second shoestring broke, I felt all the remaining will, desire, and hope drain right out of my body. Nothing was left.

I trudged along through all the water at the next curb. If I hadn't kicked it and heard metal bouncing along on the concrete sidewalk, I would have totally missed it. Even still, I almost didn't pay any attention to the noise. I came out of my blue funk trance just long enough to notice that I had kicked a key. I started to return to my previous state, but something made me stop and take a second look. When I had kicked the key, it had fallen off the sidewalk. It was being washed away down the gutter and toward the drain, about to be lost forever. I practically dove headfirst into the gutter river to barely catch the key before it fell past the bars of the street drain.

The hell I went through makes me almost wish that I had not been so aggressive for once. If I hadn't, then the key would have been washed down the drain. I would have gone on with my miserable, but boring, simple life. But I made that little extra effort and barely caught the key with my fingertips. At the time, I stood up and cheered my gallant effort.

My celebration was short-lived as my curiosity took over. As I looked closely at the key, I could tell it was to some form of locker. It was like the type located at an airport or train depot. It had a number on it, 179, but no name to indicate where the locker might be located. I started to think about all the possible locations that might have storage lockers.

Independent mental brainstorming is wonderful as I started down the first bunny trail. *There must be several. We have an airport and train depot in the city. Bowling alleys also have lockers. A dozen alleys are probably located throughout the city.*

I was sure several other places had lockers, and I hadn't even begun to think of them yet. The way my luck was going, I was sure the key fit one of the lockers in some obscure place. But the number gave me hope that the place might have many lockers.

The next idea momentarily brightened me up. *Who knows? It probably belongs to some exclusive health club.* Then I fell back down as I reasoned, *I'll never get to that locker.*

I started to throw the key back down. Instead, I stuck it in my pocket and headed back off down the street through the rainstorm.

CHAPTER 2

I walked into my small, one-bedroom apartment and immediately stripped out of my sopping wet clothes, leaving them piled in a corner of my bathroom. I didn't even empty out my pockets. I went into the kitchen and put on a coffeepot. While I was putting the water into my auto-drip coffeemaker, I stood there completely naked.

I chuckled to myself and said out loud to the coffeemaker. "Well, this is one thing I never did the whole time I was married."

For twenty-five years, about the only time I stood anywhere completely naked was in the shower. As soon as I had the coffee started, I headed off to take a shower.

I must have stayed in there for a good twenty minutes as I let the steaming hot water beat down on my back. My body core temperature felt as if it were ten degrees below normal, so the hot water felt as if it were doing miracles. I shut my eyes. For a few minutes, I left the harsh world of troubles outside of the shower. I finally reluctantly left my small cubicle of escapism and walked back out into the world of reality. I slowly dried myself off and then wrapped the towel around my waist. More than anything else, it was probably out of habit because there sure wasn't anyone around for me to cover up for.

I stood before the mirror above the sink, now completely steamed up. As much as a steam-filled bathroom would allow, I wiped away the condensation. It was a good thing that the mirror wouldn't come completely clean. With the mood I was in, I probably wouldn't have been too happy with what looked back at me. No longer was I Jimmy Peterson, the eighteen-year-old, six-foot-tall, one hundred and eighty-five-pound swift running back for Mason High School. Instead, I was Jim Peterson, a forty-nine-year-old, six-foot-tall, two hundred and eighteen-pound, partially bald, out-of-shape, divorced insurance investigator who was going nowhere.

As that thought passed through my tired brain, I went into my bedroom to get dressed. I really wasn't an exhibitionist, and I felt more comfortable with clothes on. I got out a clean pair of jockey shorts and clean, white socks and put them all on. I threw my towel in the direction of the bathroom. It landed on top of my wet clothes.

"Good shot!" I mumbled sarcastically.

It didn't take long to select a comfortable pair of pants and shirt. After some mental debate, I decided to put on my slippers instead of shoes.

What am I going to have for dinner?

It wasn't a hard decision to make. All I had in the whole place was a frozen dinner. I set the stove to preheat at the correct temperature. Then I poured myself a cup of coffee. I went over and sat down in my old, beat-up chair, my one prize possession that my ex-wife let me have. She probably felt more like she was getting rid of what she considered an eyesore. I didn't care. It may have been beat up, but it was my chair, and it was comfortable. Plus, it fit my butt perfectly.

I reached over and picked up the TV remote control. The six o'clock news was just about to come on. I always watched it to see if anyone had blown up the world. After all, it wasn't official until you saw it on the TV news. I turned on the TV to my favorite news channel. I tossed the controller on to the table and turned on the table light. I was just in time. The local news was just coming on.

I started to take a sip of coffee, but I didn't get very far. I froze in mid-sip. The lead story was about a murder that had happened downtown earlier today.

The story wasn't unusual, but the location caused my reaction. The very spot where I had taken my headfirst dive into the gutter after that damn key was being shown on the TV. So far, I had only been halfway listening to what the broadcaster had been talking about. He now had my undivided attention.

The talking male head pronounced, "A prominent accountant from a very large investment firm, Browning Investment Group, had been gunned down early this morning as he walked down the street. Officials are stumped as to who was responsible." The broadcaster said, "No reason had been found as to why the accountant, Joseph Branning, was even in the neighborhood. He had no known business or personal reason that would have taken him into that part of town. " They showed a short interview with his wife. He had a young wife and two small children.

Through the tears, all she was saying was, "Why was he in that part of town?"

I had a thought. I looked over at my wet clothes that were lying under my bath towel.

"No. It couldn't be. Could it?" I said aloud to myself.

The more time that went by since my divorce, the more I found I was talking to myself. I shrugged my shoulders and put down my coffee cup. I got up and went over to my clothes pile. I sorted through the wet clothing until I found the locker key. While I was going through the clothes, I went ahead and emptied out the rest of my pockets onto the top of my dresser in the bedroom. I went back to my chair and examined the key as closely as possible. I found nothing new. Still, the only markings on it were the number 179. I held up the key in front of my face, slightly waving it back and forth as I stared at the TV screen as if the murder story were still being broadcast, which it wasn't. I was so absorbed in my thoughts that I didn't even notice what story was being reported.

Suddenly, the twenty-two years of insurance investigator took over. I started to form a plan of how to look into things. I knew instantly that I had to find out two things: find out where locker 179 was located and determine if that locker had any connection with Joseph Branning. After I found out the answers to those two questions, then I could make further plans. If I couldn't make any connection, then it would be a moot point.

Boy, how I hate dealing with moot points.

The part about the locker was simply just a matter of legwork. The second part would be tough because it was going to take other people opening doors and talking to me. Some of it was out of my hands. I was going to need a little old-fashioned good luck. The way things were going lately, maybe I was due some. *Well, maybe just a little.*

Sometimes, just a little luck was all we needed. Plus, the very people I needed to contact to find out any of the answers owed me a few favors.

I leaned back into my chair and casually flipped the key in my left hand. After a few minutes of letting my mind wander, I dropped the key into my catch-all glass on the table and went into the kitchen to make my TV dinner.

Right then and there I made myself a private vow, *I'll start my private investigation the first thing tomorrow morning.* Maybe on this one I would follow through.

Even though tomorrow was Saturday, the police would be working.

CHAPTER 3

As I walked into the police station, I first noticed the quiet. Ten o'clock on a Saturday morning was a slow time for crime. I knew several of the police here at this station. I was close to being friends with a couple detectives in the criminal investigation division. Some of my work took me in contact with them on a regular basis. When I walked past the dispatch sergeant's desk, I waved my hellos.

"Hey, Peterson. How's it going?" Sergeant Howitz said.

"Not bad. A whole lot better day outside than it was yesterday."

"No kidding. I thought the whole damn city was going to wash away."

"Too bad it didn't wash away the garbage."

I didn't hear if he gave any further comment. I turned down the hallway to the detective bureau. The hallway was supposed to be all white, but this individual station was old. The color had long ago faded to a dingy gray. Three doors down on the right was the one I wanted. I slipped in front of the door. The words "Detective Division" were written in simple letters on the foggy, glass door.

Without knocking, I opened the door and walked in. The detective division was just a one-room office with five desks and several filing cabinets spread throughout the room. There wasn't much room for the detectives themselves. Only two of the desks were occupied. One of the occupants was Lieutenant Mike Glosman, whom I had known for almost as long, as I had been in the investigation business. We had first met during my second case, an arson investigation. I was eager and still full of the enthusiasm of youth. All the officials were convinced the owner of a small laundry business had burned down his building to collect the insurance money. Because of my youth at the time or because I hadn't yet learned to conform to the system, I set out to prove that he hadn't started the fire. I was determined to get to the truth. Patrolman Mike Glosman was the only one who would even listen to me, less believe that I might be right. For the same reasons I stuck to my guns, he was willing to stick out his neck and help me, even though I was a stranger initially. With his help, I was able to prove that the owner's wife's boyfriend had actually set the fire in order to discredit and destroy him. The insurance company wasn't all that thrilled because it meant they had to pay out the claim. They publicly stated they were glad an innocent man wasn't prosecuted, and justice prevailed. Even though nothing was actually said to me, the atmosphere around the office told me that the top shitheads, as I called them, weren't happy that I didn't go with the flow. I was to process the case and save the insurance company, their client, lots of money, regardless if an innocent man would have gone to prison. Thus, that was the real reason why I hadn't progressed further in my career. Only when they were in a position of no other choice was I ever given a case that would warrant a promotion if solved.

On the other side of the coin, my new friend, Mike, received nothing but accolades for his part in solving a criminal investigation that prevented an innocent man from going to prison. This would have made for bad publicity. The night we solved the case, we drank heavily but peacefully until the daylight hours. He was in celebration mode; I was to drown my sorrows. Mike wasn't married then, so he had no one to answer to at home. I had a terrible time explaining why I stumbled through the front door while daylight was poking its way through the bedroom window. My career and my marriage were never the same from that day forward.

As I walked over and sat down next to Mike's desk, he briefly looked up, saw it was I, waved hello, and kept reading the report he had lying in front of him. I took his cue and sat there silently until he was finished. It took about five minutes, but he finally put the papers into a manila folder and slapped them into his case basket.

"What's up, James?" Mike leaned back in his chair and put his feet up on his desk and his hands behind his head.

He knew I didn't really like "James." He was the only one I let call me that. But he usually only called me "James" after he hadn't seen me for a while, but not always. That was sometimes all he called me. So, I didn't object.

"I haven't seen you in a couple months."

"Not a whole lot going on. I'm just trying to stay out of trouble."

"Since when do you stay out of trouble? I don't think you know how to do that."

"Sit on it, asshole. Not everyone can fall in a pile of shit and come out smelling like a rose like you always seem to do."

"Yeah, some of us do seem to be able to fall in a bed of rose petals and come up smelling like shit." He laughed.

We had been friends long enough that this banter was our normal way of saying hello. I waited patiently until he stopped chuckling.

"Okay. What can I do for you? I know you well enough to know that you wouldn't be down here early on a Saturday morning unless there was a good reason or you want something."

"As usual, you got me pegged. There is something I'd like to know about."

"How did I know that you'd say that?" he asked with very deep sarcasm.

I ignored it. "What can you tell me about that accountant who was gunned down over on Madison Street?"

He sat up in his chair. His sudden ridged posture and hard stare indicated to me that he was suddenly very serious.

"Why do you want to know?"

I had played this game several times before, so I wasn't intimidated. I allowed enough a pause to show that my question wasn't really critical.

"Oh, I'm just curious."

The look on his face told me that he wasn't buying my nonchalance. But he trusted me enough not to push.

He relaxed a bit more back in his chair. He was becoming like a yo-yo. Back and forth in that chair. "We don't have much on it. All we know is that, as he was walking along, a late model, black or dark blue sedan pulled up alongside him. A window rolled down, and an automatic weapon basically cut him in half. Then the car casually drove off."

This time, it was my turn to sit up a little straighter in my seat. "You must have had a witness if you know that much. Who is it?"

"Actually, we do. It's not a very reliable one, but one nevertheless." He paused long enough to see if I were anxious enough to squirm while waiting for an answer. It took every bit of self-control I had to seem to remain calm as I waited. "One of our city's homeless drunks just happened to be across the street in an alley, looking through the garbage for something to eat when all hell broke loose."

"You're right. Not a very good witness."

"Not in court, but good enough to let us know what really happened."

"Did he happen to get a license number?"

"No. He was a few feet back in the alley and only saw everything from the side of the car. He didn't get a look at the front or back."

"What do you have on the Branning fellow? And what was he doing in that part of town?"

"All right, Jim. It's time to come clean. What's your interest in all this?"

"I told you. Curiosity."

"Bullshit!" he snapped.

He sat back up and gave every indication of being tight-lipped. In fact, I became sure of that when, after a few moments of my silence, his jaw looked as if he were clenching his teeth tighter and tighter. The look in his eyes was getting angrier and angrier.

"Look, Mike, you know that I'd tell you if I really had something. You're going to have to trust me on this one."

"Yeah, and the check's in the mail. I've heard that one before." He started shuffling the papers on his desk.

I figured this was just a stall tactic while he made up his mind, so I kept quiet. As soon as he finished the first sentence, I knew he was going to help me.

"Look, you didn't hear this from me, or I'll cut out your heart. Over the last few months, there have been some very loose ties between Branning and the local member of organized crime here in town. It's nothing concrete or solid that we could build an investigation on. There were just rumors and innuendoes. You know the kind of thing."

"Yes, I know. But, usually, where there's smoke, there's fire. What are the rumors?"

"Well, like I said, nothing solid. Even though he was married with two children, rumor has it that he had a weakness for women and gambling."

I thought he was going to say more, but he just sat back and looked at me instead.

"Is that all you've got?"

"That's it." He sat forward slightly as if to challenge me for questioning him.

The alarm bells went off in my head telling me that this must be something big for him to be so defensive.

"Figure it out for yourself. The man liked fast horses and hot women. Then he's gunned down without a clue, obviously by a couple of pros. What do you think?"

"Sounds like you picked the right scenario to me. You say there's nothing else? Does his wife know anything about his extra activities?"

"No, nothing else."

He sat back and let out a deep breath. He also let his shoulders slump in an obvious sign of frustration and helplessness. "Look, we are able to get any more clues, we might as well file this case under the unsolved and save themselves the time and money. We weren't going to get any further." He went on hardly taking a breath, "The man led an ideal life. Young, pretty wife with two kids. He had a good-paying job and made promotions ahead of schedule. We can't find any outstanding bills except for a couple of small charges on his credit card that he could have paid off with only a single check from his checking account balance. Who would want to kill him?"

"Where do the rumors about women and gambling come from?"

"His coworkers say he was a flirt with every good-looking woman who came into the offices, whether they were customers or employees. They also say he always ran and pushed all office betting pools."

"Flirting and office pools are a far cry from fast horses and hot women." I suggested.

Then he got a shit-eating grin. "One of the office secretaries told us in strictest confidence … and I'll kick your ass if you let this one out … she hinted very strongly that they had an affair, and she knew he liked to go to the racetrack over in Culvert."

"Does his wife know about his extracurricular activities?"

"Not that we can tell. Because they are unfounded rumors, we didn't tell her. We had to be very careful to tap-dance around it."

I paused a while to give the appearance of being casual. "What's the bit about loose ties with organized crime?"

"And you call yourself an investigator. Use your head. Gambling debts. You know, loan sharks to pay off his losses."

"How do you know about that? What's your proof?"

"Oh, come on, James. Use your head for something other than hanging your nose on. Nobody wins at gambling over the long haul. He must have had gambling debts and gone to loan sharks to pay off those debts."

Mike was normally very good, but those same alarm bells and now sirens were telling me that he was way off on this one. Then again, he didn't have the theory of the locker key to add to the situation. But then again, I didn't know for sure that the key had anything to do with Branning. It was just my gut feeling to keep quiet about the key. So, I did. In fact, I felt as if I had reached the end of anything I was going to get out of this one. I changed the subject.

"Can you tell me about the secretary? What did you say the secretary's name was?"

"I didn't!" He sat and glared at me for a minute.

"What can you tell me about her? I probed harder.

Mike's voice got even harder and colder for just a second. "When all this is over, you had better have a damn good reason for not telling me any more than you are."

I started to give him a smart-mouthed answer, but, before it came out, I realized he was very serious. I backed off and played the passive role. After all, we were friends, and I didn't want to ruin what little friendships I had left in this world.

"Mike, please. I'm not holding out on you."

He picked up a pencil and thumped it a couple times on the desk. His expression softened just a little. "Marci Ann Johnson, and she lives in the Woodward District. I figure even a bright you kid like you can find her with that much information. Now get out of here and let me get some work done."

"Sure thing, Mike. Have a nice day." I got up out of my chair.

He just mumbled a sound as he dove back into his paperwork. As I got to the door, I stopped short and turned back.

"Thanks, Mike. I appreciate it."

He waved a hand in the air and went back to what he was doing. I walked out the door and stopped for a moment's reflection.

"What I have just learned from Mike? " I asked myself in my own special mental style. "Well, you haven't learn a lot, but you have discovered something."

I tugged on my right earlobe as I am sometimes prone to do when in serious mental problem-solving mode. "I have made progress by coming here. Next, I have to decide on where I went from here." I decided I had progressed well on part two of my major two-part plan. *Maybe I should let that simmer a while.*

I didn't want to press my unusually good luck. So it was time to do some work on part one, finding what locker the key might fit. The obvious place would be to start where I found the key.

CHAPTER 4

As I walked out of the police station, I stepped into a beautiful, warm day. The sun was shining, and not a cloud was in the sky. For the first time in quite a while, I felt good. I welcomed the day because I felt I had a solid purpose. That hadn't happened very often lately. I had a case to solve, and it was all my case. So, as I stepped off the last step and headed down the street, I had a spring in my step that, until now, had long been vacant. After I had walked a few blocks, I decided to splurge for a taxi.

To hell with walking. I'm on a roll, I growled to myself.

It was only a couple miles away so I knew it would only cost me a few dollars. Plus, I was supposed to get paid on Monday. Thirty minutes later, I was standing on a familiar but dry street. I looked around to see where I was. Apparently, this was the first time I really looked at this area, considering how I had traveled down this street twice every day since I had moved out of my ex-wife's house. I traveled it once into work and once on the way home, but I had never taken the time to really look at the surroundings. I saw things I didn't know existed. I made a mental note to be more aware of my surroundings.

I decided to walk to the drugstore that was around the corner from the place where Branning had been shot. As I entered the store, I saw a clerk and pharmacist were on duty. There weren't any customers in the store. The pharmacist was probably in his mid-thirties. The clerk was about my age, maybe even a little older. The clerk noticed me right away because the cowbells on the door practically screamed at my entrance as I opened the door.

She waited until I was within a few feet from the counter. She smiled. "Good morning. May I help you with something?"

"Yes, as a matter of fact, you can. I need a little bit of help."

"Sure thing." She had a very warm and friendly smile, a welcome sight.

"Well, I'm relatively new around here. I don't know my way around very well. I'm looking for someplace in particular."

"Where might that be?"

"This is kind of difficult to explain. I have to leave town for a while, but I have to leave a package for my brother who won't be in town for a few days. I'm looking for some kind of small locker I can put a package in so that, when he gets into town, he can pick up the key and get the package. You know, the kind of public locker where you put in a couple quarters and then remove the key?"

"Well, yes, I know what you are talking about. They used to have those at the airport and train depot."

"I was hoping you might know of some places around this neighborhood."

"No, I can't say I do."

"Thank you very much. You have a nice day."

I walked out a little down, but not too much. I didn't really expect to find it right away. By two o'clock in the afternoon, I was really depressed. Everywhere I went in the neighborhood, I had the same results. There was no known locker. So I figured it was time to change tracks again. I found a local mom and pop deli and convinced them to loan me their phone book. "Marcie Johnson", in The Woodard District of town was listed. I looked up the address and phone number of the secretary that Mike had told me about. I still had some luck left. She lived within a five-minute walk from where I was. Then it dawned on me. She lived within one block from where Branning was killed. I quickly put a quarter in the pay phone slot and dialed her number. I didn't want to spook her.

When she answered on the second ring,

"Hello." She answered with a very soft but sweet-sounding voice.

"Is Jeremy Logan there?" I asked for some bogus name.

"I am sorry, but you must have the wrong number. There is no one here by that name." At first, I was stunned by the soft velvety music in her voice.

After a few quick gulps I managed to say apologetically, "I am sorry to bother you. Good Bye." What I really wanted was to try everything I could think of to keep her on the line so I could hear more. Before I could come up with anything I heard the click of her phone hanging up.

I practically ran to her residence because I knew she was home. I didn't want her to leave before I got there. I made it in nearly three minutes. I walked up the steps of the brownstone, two-story, fourplex to the mailboxes. I looked and saw that the secretary lived in 2A. I tried the front door. It opened easily. This somewhat surprised me. I figured it might have been a security building and would require someone in one of the apartments releasing the lock electronically to let me in.

I opened the door slowly because I had no idea what I might find on the other side. I didn't find much except two downstairs apartments. Back away from the front door, going up the right side of the entrance hall, were stairs. The left side of the entrance hall led back behind the stairs. I took a quick look back behind the stairs and saw that this area led to a washroom at the back end of the hall. I saw two washers and two dryers.

The thought quickly went through my head, *Not too bad for a fourplex.*

I cautiously climbed the stairs. I wasn't in that big of a hurry now. I figured that, if she left now, she would have to pass by me. Even if I didn't know what she looked like, I could tell if she came out of 2A. But I didn't pass anyone on the way up the stairs.

I got to the top of the stairs and walked around to my left and down the upstairs hall until I was standing between 2A and 2B. In front of me was a window, which let out over the street. I stood in front of 2A for a few minutes and listened. At first, I didn't hear anything. I was slightly disturbed that I might have missed her in the few minutes that it took me to get here. Then I heard some kind of noise from inside. It sounded a lot like pots and pans or dishes. So, I knew she was still home.

I knocked on the door. I wasn't prepared for what I saw when the door opened fully. She stood about five-foot-five, and she was dressed in a comfortable pair of blue jeans, a loose gray sweatshirt with the sleeves pushed up to her elbows, and a pair of tennis shoes. She had little, if any, makeup on. Pulled back in a ponytail, her hair was a very light brown with red tints that I liked so much. She absolutely astounded me. I was totally speechless. She was gorgeous. Even with the loose-fitting clothes, I could tell she had the perfect hourglass figure, a body that would stop the whole 1st armor Division dead in its tracks. She had a nice, trim waist with luscious hips. From the front, I could only imagine that she had a nice ass to match. She had big but not overly large, firm breasts. Because of my work I had learned to become a pretty good judge of people's age by just their appearance, mannerisms, speech patterns and body language. So, she seemed to me like she was only about twenty-four years old. Her breasts stood out straight.

Even with that extremely sensuous body that instantly gave me an erection, the part of her that actually drew most of my attention was her beautiful sky-blue eyes and lovely mouth. If I could have gone through a police ID kit, I couldn't have picked a better facial structure for my tastes. Her cute, little nose was in between a pug and a ski jump, but not really either one. It just completed the picture as if she was one of God's very own angels. That he had personally sculpted her face.

She started to close the door. I had only stared at her when she opened it. I finally came back to reality as the door started to close in front of her. I was losing sight of her.

"Wait a minute. Excuse me. Marci Ann Johnson?" I blurted out.

She opened the door a little and peeked around the side. "Yes, I am. Who are you?"

"I'm sorry. My name is Jim Peterson. I'm with the Wheaton Investigation Company. Mr. Branning had a life insurance policy, and I'm investigating the claim against his policy. I'd like to ask you a few questions concerning Mr. Branning and his untimely death."

"May I see some identification, please?" she asked cautiously. She still hid her body behind the door. Only her pretty face was poking around the edge.

"You certainly may."

I reached inside my jacket pocket to pull out my ID. Thankfully, I had actually blurted out my real name and job. My ID matched who I said I was. I normally didn't tell people the truth so rapidly about myself when I first met them on an investigation. It was part of my built-in negativism and self-doubt that I didn't want to admit to anything until I knew I wasn't going to get into any kind of trouble or suffer any due hardships. This time, I had just opened my mouth, and out it came.

I held up my ID in front of me. From where she was standing, she really couldn't make out much. She slowly reopened the door, stepped forward, and looked closer at my picture. I held out my ID for as long as she wanted to look. Finally, she must have satisfied herself that I was who I said I was.

She looked up. "How may I help you, Mr. Peterson?"

"First of all, you could start by calling me Jim. Second, if it is possible, could you invite me in? I only have a few questions, but I don't feel they are for public knowledge."

"When the police questioned me at the office, they said they probably wouldn't need to ask me anything else."

"They questioned you at the office?"

"Well, yes. They talked to everyone at work."

"I'd still like to ask you a couple questions. Just to clear up a few areas I'm confused about. Please?"

"Of course, you can." She showed an extremely warm smile. "Please come in." She stepped aside and indicated with her arm that I should enter.

When I walked in and looked around, I saw she had a very warm and comfortable-looking apartment. I entered a living room/dining room combination. Off to one side was a kitchen with a counter separating the kitchen from the other rooms. She had a nice sofa and a couple chairs set around a console TV and stereo. A door was close to the front entrance. I assumed this was a coat closet. Because I didn't see any type of bed, I figured the door on the opposite side of the room led to the bedroom.

She led me to the couch. "Please have a seat. Can I get you something to drink?"

"Just the answers to some questions will be all. Thank you." I sat down.

She sat in a chair about ten feet away. She had a very pretty smile. I found myself staring at her and those beautiful eyes.

Stop it. I'm old enough to be her father.

But I couldn't stop from admiring her. I suddenly realized that she was looking back.

Then my thoughts took another 180 degree turn. *Does she find me attractive? No, I'm just being an old fool.*

She was smiling and looking at me out of common decency and manners. I didn't know though. Something electric did seem to pass between us.

No, it's just my imagination and wishful thinking.

I finally came around. "Marci. May I call you Marci?"

"That is my name, Mr. Peterson. People who know me call me Marci."

"It's Jim." I looked down shyly.

"Excuse me. What did you say?"

"I said that people who know me call me Jim, Marci."

"Okay, Jimmy."

I looked up at her quickly. Nobody called me Jimmy. Her sweetness melted me. This lady could call me anything she wanted.

Some more roller coaster thought patterns. No one has ever affected me this way and sent me in such a tizzy. *What am I doing? I'm a professional, and I came here to ask her some questions.*

"How well did you know Joseph Branning?"

At the mention of his name, I saw a slight cloud pass over her lovely blue eyes. I hated myself for asking, but I had to get on with this.

"I knew him pretty well from work. In fact, we even had dinner a couple times after work."

"You know he was married, didn't you?"

She chuckled lightly. "Our dinners were never those kinds of dinner dates. They were basically convenience dinners after we had both worked late. We were good friends, even though we both flirted with each other as a joke. He flirted more than I did, but then that was natural for Joe."

"He'd flirt a lot?"

"He'd flirt with every female who walked into the office, no matter if she were old, young, fat, thin, pretty, or ugly. It didn't matter. He flirted with them all, except when his wife was in the office. Then he was a very straight arrow. She's a very intelligent woman. I got the feeling that she not only knew and tolerated his actions, but almost encouraged him. But he felt he had to maintain the appearance of fidelity around his wife. He once confided to me that he felt it was his curse that he appealed to all women in a sensuous way. He said he couldn't go anywhere and not run into a female who would have a small relationship with him. He used to complain he had lots of lady friends because of it, but no male buddies he could get along with. Somehow, he and I had a very different kind of relationship. We were actually friends. Other than an occasional light sexual comment or even a rare pat on the rear, there was nothing more than a warm friendship."

She seemed to be relaxing. She even pulled her feet under her in her chair.

"You mentioned he was a straight arrow when his wife was around. Was she around very often? What kind of relationship did he and his wife have?"

"Actually, she was around quite often. It was an office joke that she was there so often that she should draw a paycheck. As for their relationship, no matter what he did with other women, he really did love his wife. From what I could tell, she loved him. They seemed to have a good marriage."

"What do you mean? No matter what he did with other women?"

She had a slightly perplexed look on her face. "I don't know for a fact that he cheated on her. But someone who had that kind of an effect on very pretty women and liked women as much as he did, I'd find it surprising if he didn't."

She paused. I watched as she looked down at her hands as she fidgeted. I took the opportunity to look at her lovely chest. I watched hypnotically as she breathed. I somewhat felt ashamed. I couldn't tear my eyes away. I finally forced myself to look away before she caught me. I lucked out. Just after I looked up at her face, she raised her head and looked at me. I could see the sorrow for a lost friend in her eyes.

"I'm sorry for your loss. It isn't easy to lose a friend."

"Thank you."

I could see just a trace of moisture in her eyes. Then it was gone. The smile was back.

"Only a few more questions. I won't trouble you with anymore of this pain."

"That's okay. I want to help Joe anyway I can," she said softly.

Our eyes locked. This time, I knew something passed between us. I felt emotions stir in me that I hadn't experienced in a very long time.

Sometimes I am surprised how my brain works. As I sat there watching her I couldn's help but feel, "Here's this woman sitting in casual clothes, but she appears to be the sexiest woman I could ever remember seeing. She isn't all dolled up in fancy clothes and makeup. She's all completely natural."

Suddenly, it was as if she read my mind. She got a very definite gleam in her eye.

Could she like me despite our age difference?

I didn't have the guts to pursue that any further. I shifted in my seat and looked away. I had to do something to get my mind back to the subject at hand. I had to shake the previous thoughts out of my head and be very careful handle the next area of information that I wanted.

"I understand Joseph Branning usually ran most of the office sports pools. Do you know anything about them?"

"Not most of them. All of them. Not only was Joe a sports nut, but he loved to bet on them. To the best of my knowledge, he never bet very heavily. With him, it was more like the enjoyment of the betting than the money."

"Did he bet anyplace else in particular?"

"I don't know. He did go over to the horse track every so often, but more often than occasionally."

"Do you know if he owed anybody any money?"

"If he did, he didn't say anything to me. His wife always gave him enough money. He didn't seem to have any problems. He was always happy, especially lately."

"Why?"

"I don't know. He just seemed to be on top of the world for the last couple weeks."

Suddenly I had this feeling that Marci was more involved in what happened to Branning then she was letting on. I had a huge hunch that I needed to press this line of thought a bit further.

"How long have you worked there?"

"A few weeks short of a year."

"What do you think of your company?"

"I like working there very much. Everybody is friendly and gets along great. The work is challenging, but not hard. They pay me decently with good medical benefits. I only work eight to five Monday through Friday. What's not to like?"

"What kind of work do you do?"

"I mostly do standard secretarial things: typing, filing, and office management. Nothing very special or hard. I'm just one of a crowd in the office."

"I find it hard to believe that you could ever be lost in a crowd. I'd tend to believe that you'd always stand out."

I had meant to think that thought, not express it orally. Right after I said it, I initially thought that she took it wrong. The surprised look on her face put me on the defensive.

I started to apologize. "What I mean is that you are a very pretty lady. Someone who looks as good as you wouldn't just blend in. You'd stand out as something better than the rest."

The more I said, the worse I put my foot in it. The appearance of a smile on her face halted my mumbling.

"Thank you. You're very sweet to say that."

"No, I'm not. It's the truth."

I was next treated to the sexiest smile I had ever seen. The corners of her mouth just slightly turned up. I saw a hint of mischief in her eyes. Her head was slightly cocked down and to the side. I could hardly believe it was directed at just me. I had to get a grip on things. She was making me feel like a bumbling schoolboy. I was too old for her. But I still couldn't mistake what I was feeling.

I knew it was very close to being just plain old lust. But I was feeling more than physically attracted to this lovely lady. She was intelligent, well-mannered, well-spoken, and incredibly beautiful.

She started to say, "I think you are…" I didn't let her continue with that thought, I cut her off. I didn't want to hear her being forced to return a compliment that she really didn't mean out of good manners.

"Marci, is there anything else you can tell me about Joseph Branning or his personal life?"

"No, nothing I can think of right now."

"If you do remember, please give me a call."

I started to get up. I handed her one of my business cards. It had both my work and home phone number. But, instead of walking to the door, I sat back down.

"You obviously aren't married, but are you seriously involved with anyone at this time?"

Asking personal questions was something I made a strict rule of never doing. I felt like I was sitting here and watching someone else. It was an indication of how much this woman affected me.

Her expression changed to a little more serious. She snapped, "What does that have to do with Joe's death? That's a little personal."

"You're right. It has absolutely nothing to do with the case. I'm just wondering. I'm sorry. I withdraw the question."

I suddenly felt put in my place. I somewhat felt like she had burst my bubble. I stood up to leave.

"Thank you very much for your time. I won't bother you any longer. Have a nice day."

I got as far as the front door when I heard her soft feminine voice right behind me.

"Jimmy?"

It was enough to stop me in my tracks. I wasn't sure what to expect. I finally faced her. She was standing barely five feet behind me.

"I'm the one to apologize. This whole situation has me on edge. I'm sorry."

"No, don't be sorry. I had no right to ask you a personal question during an investigation."

"You know, you didn't tell me precisely why you are investigating his murder. It seems to me that it was pretty obvious that someone killed him."

I stammered for a while until I could think of an appropriate answer. I sure didn't want to lie to her. "Any time there is a murder, it's standard for an insurance investigator to conduct an investigation to ensure all the facts are straight." That part was true. I just didn't tell her that the insurance company hadn't appointed me to do that job.

"I understand." The smile was back in her eyes.

"I have one last thing before I leave and stop bothering you."

"You are no bother. In fact, you're a very nice person."

I blushed slightly. "Thank you."

I looked at her. She wrinkled her nose slightly and let out a little giggle. If I had seen most females do that, I would have thought they were either airheads or stupid. On Marci, it looked cute. I didn't know what caused the difference, but it was there.

"You were going to ask me one last thing," she said softly.

"Well ... ah ... yes. Oh, yeah. Now I remember. The day he was killed, was he over here?"

She had a shocked look on her face. "How did you know? The police never asked me about that."

"He wasn't far from here when he was killed. From all indications, he had no other business in this neighborhood. Why was he here?"

I was suddenly very suspicious of their relationship, and it showed on my face. She put her hands on her hips, pulled her shoulders back, and raised her head in defiance. I almost didn't hear what she said because her posture pulled her sweater tight against her perfectly round, large breasts. They not only stuck out further, but I could see her erect nipples very distinctly. I couldn't help but stare at them. I knew she could tell where I was looking, but it didn't seem to bother her. Or at least she didn't give any indication that it bothered her.

She stated sternly, "His visits were always strictly about business!"

"What business was that?" I looked up at her face.

She relaxed slightly. "Friday was the last day of my vacation. Because I hadn't been to work for a week, he came by to ask me some questions about one of our accounts."

"Why did he come all the way down here when he could have asked you over the phone?"

"Well, his questions pertained to some files that I had to see to answer."

"What files would that be? According to the police, when they found him, there weren't any files on his possession."

She wrinkled her forehead and looked extremely perplexed. She crossed her arms, turned away, and walked a couple steps away. "I know he had them with him when he left. He had them in a manila folder under his arm."

"What did the files pertain to?"

She turned to face me. "One of our accounts. He seemed to think that a part of them had been changed or something was missing. Because I had typed the final draft, he wanted to know if I could tell."

"Could you?"

"Not really. When I usually type routine account information, I just type what I hear on the recorder. I don't really pay any attention to what is actually said."

"Which account was it?"

"That's supposed to be privileged information."

"I know. But I'm not asking any of the details of the account. Just which one it was. Besides, if it turns out to be relevant, then it will all become public knowledge."

"I guess you are trying to help find who killed Joe. And it won't hurt anyone." She paused. "The Gionetti account."

"Was it raining when he left?"

"No, but it was sure getting ready to."

"Okay, one more thing."

"You said one more thing before."

"Yes, I know, but your answer prompted another train of thought. Did he say anything about storing anything?"

"Not exactly."

"What do you mean?"

"He sometimes used to keep things in his bowling locker that he didn't want his wife to know about."

It was all I could do not to scream. I asked a question to try to hide my real interest. "Did he often hide things from his wife?"

"I don't think so. It was just small stuff. He didn't really need to. I think he kind of enjoyed getting away with something on the sly."

"What kind of things would he hide?"

"Oh, I don't know. Birthday cards and gifts for the ladies at the office. Things like that."

"Which bowling alley did he use?"

"Broadway Lanes down on Broadway Street."

"I'm familiar with the place. Did he ever leave anything with you?"

Her definite awkward pause told me that the answer to my question was yes. "No, he sure didn't."

I was disappointed. I didn't like anyone to lie to me.

She sensed my mood change. "I can't help you any more at this time." She emphasized "at this time."

So, I was now confused instead of disappointed. Still, I had gained a lot. Plus, I had the pleasure of spending some time with a very lovely lady.

"That's all right. You have helped me a great deal. If I have any further questions, may I call on you again?"

"Of course, you may." Then she added softly as if in a little bit of shyness, "Or perhaps you could call back, even if you don't have any further questions."

"I will. You can count on that."

I beamed inside as I realized she might like me. I was amazed. Now I didn't want to leave. But I knew I had to go.

"Good-bye, Marci. I'll be looking forward to seeing you again."

"So will I, Jimmy."

I reluctantly turned and opened the door. I stepped into the hall and looked back. Marci was standing in the open door and smiling. I waved. She waved. I turned to go down the hallway. I heard her close the door behind me. Even though she closed the door softly, the sound rang loudly in my ears. I walked downstairs and out into the street, like I was in a daze. I stopped on the sidewalk in front of the brownstone in an effort to clear my head and absorb all she had told me. I needed to decide what to do next. The bowling alley would be the next logical place. I turned right and started down the street. As I took my first steps, I looked up at the second floor of the brownstone. Marci was looking down at me through the window. When she saw me look up, she smiled and waved. I waved back and kept going.

I'm going to have to figure this one out. Why would a gorgeous twenty-four-year-old even show any interest in a nearly fifty-year-old fart like me?

I enjoyed the possible flirtation. My ego sure could have used the boost, but I had been around for a while. I was suspicious of things too good to be true. Things like this only happened in fairy tales. And fairy tales didn't ever come true.

CHAPTER 5

I debated whether to walk or take a taxi. I didn't have a lot of cash left, but I sure didn't look forward to walking. I didn't think I'd be able to catch any buses going my way. I was going to have to do something about this car situation. I stopped at the first pay phone I came to. I fished out a coin from my pocket and inserted it into the pay slot. Then I hesitated. *Who am I going to call?*

I hung up and retrieved my coin. After I thought for a while, I pulled out my little address book, looked up a guy I work with, and dialed his number.

After about three rings, a young voice said, "Hello?"

"Is George Redus there, please?"

"Just a moment, please."

A few minutes later, I heard George's voice on the line. "Hello."

"Hey, George. This is Jim Peterson."

"Hello, Jim. How are you doing?"

"I'm doing fine. And you?"

"Okay, I guess. I was just washing my wife's car."

"Sorry to bother you, but I need to ask you a favor."

"Sure. What do you need?"

"Remember I put my car into the shop yesterday morning and they said it was going to take major repairs?"

"Yes, I remember you complaining about that. Transmission wasn't it?"

"That's correct. Well, I'm in a kind of a predicament. I'm without a vehicle this weekend, and I'm in a definite need of transportation. I remember you saying you might be able to help me out if I needed it. Do you have or know of anyone who might have a car I can borrow for a few days? I'd rent one, but I'm a little tight on funds right now."

"Boy, I know that feeling. Let me see. My boy broke his foot in a basketball game last week. I don't think he'll be doing much driving this weekend. I'll check. Hold on."

I heard him lay down the phone. Then there were several minutes of silence. I finally heard the phone being picked up.

"Not a problem, Jim. Do you want to come by and pick it up, or do you want me to meet you somewhere?"

"You're being good enough to loan me the car. I don't want to put you out by having to deliver it, too."

"That's not a problem. Part of the deal I made for washing Martha's car was that she was going to drive me into town to the sports card show I want to go to. I'll just have her follow me. Then we can drop it off. Where do you want to meet?"

"That's great! How about meeting in front of the office?"

"Sure thing. How about forty-five minutes? That okay?"

"You bet. I'll see you then. And, George, thanks."

"No big deal. I owe you one anyway." He laughed and hung up.

I didn't know what he owed me one for, but I wasn't going to argue. Instead, I headed for the office. I got there in about twenty minutes, so I decided to go inside. We didn't have any kind of alarms on the place. There wasn't much to steal, and investigation sometimes required us to work all kinds of hours, weekends or nights. We had to be able to come and go at will.

I walked over to my little cubicle and sat down at my small desk. I pulled out a legal-sized notepad and started to write down everything I knew about this case. This practice sometimes helped me to see the broader picture. Within about fifteen minutes, I had everything I could think of listed, edited, and relisted. It somewhat put everything into perspective. No new startling realization appeared. If Joseph Branning had a large gambling debt, then there would be motivation for a loan shark to break his kneecaps, but not kill him. Or perhaps his flirtations had gotten out of hand with the wife of a jealous man. Then he would have gotten a beating, not an execution. Frustrated, I tore off the paper from my notepad, folded it up, and stuck it in my pocket.

As I was walking out the front door of the office, right on time, George was driving into the parking lot. A few seconds later, his wife pulled in behind him. He got out of a small, compact Japanese car. I headed around to the front of the car, right next to the driver's side. When I was a few feet away, he tossed me the keys. I caught them and walked up to him. We shook hands.

"Get it back when you're through with it. No hurry. He isn't going to be driving for a while."

"Thank you, George," I said to his back as he walked away.

He raised his hand and slightly waved. He got back in his wife's car and smiled at me. They backed off and drove away. I didn't even get to say hello or thank you to his wife. Even though I had met her once or twice, I really didn't know her very well.

That sure was painless.

I opened the car door and got in. It was an automatic, and it had a full tank of gas. George was wrong. I owed him one.

Fifteen minutes later, I was pulling into the parking lot of Broadway Lanes. I had never been in here before. I was only familiar with it because I had driven past it several times. The parking lot seemed to be full, so I couldn't find a parking space close to the entrance. I finally found a spot about half the lot away. I nervously kept looking over my shoulder as I crossed the front of the lot, headed for front door.

As I entered the building, all the noise assaulted my ears. I didn't know how many lanes there were, but every single one seemed to be in action. Several kids were making a tremendous amount of noise. The adults who were bowling weren't making much noise, but the pin-setting machines were adding to the decibel level. I walked in far enough to be able to look up and down the length of the place. A long, straight lobby ran the whole length from behind the first lane and went all of the way to the last lane. There were enough lanes that the last one was too far away for me to see the number. I was standing behind what looked like the center lane. It said "number twenty."

I surmised that there must be forty lanes.

I used to bowl when I was a kid, and I occasionally watched bowling on TV during the weekends. This was a large-sized house. I turned left, headed down the lobby, and walked toward lane number one. The lanes were on my right. The lobby was a few feet higher than the bowling areas themselves. In fact, I had to walk down three steps to get from the lobby level to the settee area of the lanes. A counter ran behind the lanes between the lobby and settee area. Steps led down to the bowling area behind every set of lanes. Along the left side of the lobby were a few offices and then some restrooms. At the end of the lobby was a combination lounge and snack bar. Some video games were inside the snack bar. I turned around to head back down the other direction of the lobby. Obviously, the lockers weren't down here.

As I passed the entrance, I came alongside the control desk. After the desk were the bowling pro shop, a few more offices, and then an open doorway to a large room. As I looked inside the doorway, I saw several lockers. The lowest number I could find was one hundred. So I started down the rows, one hundred and twenty, then one hundred and forty, and then one hundred and sixty. I was getting close. I turned down that row. There it was, about waist high: Number 179.

My heart rate quickly sped up as I pulled the key out of my pocket. Sure enough, it still read number one hundred and seventy-nine on the key. I held my breath as I brought the key up to the lock. I hesitated and then carefully tried to insert it into the lock. It slid in easily. I let out my breath. I puffed a couple times as I wiped the sweat off my hands and onto my pants. I held my breath again as I reached up and tried to turn the key. The sounds of the tumblers clicking were as loud as an explosion. The locker door popped open. I started to breathe again. I looked inside the locker. There was only a single bowling bag and nothing else.

This time it came out vocally. But no one was near to hear. "Shit! That's it?"

Attached to the handle of the bag was an ID tag with his name and address. I copied the address down on a piece of paper I had in my pocket.

Well, maybe there is something inside the bag beside a bowling ball.

I unzipped the bag. A pair of bowling shoes was on top. I took them out and looked inside each shoe. Nothing was there. Next, a bowling rag was on top of the ball. I pulled this out and set it aside. The ball was inside some kind of a cloth pouch with handles. I used the pouch handles to pull out the ball. I set this down on the floor. I looked inside the bag. I didn't really expect to find anything. I was slightly surprised when I found a small notebook lying inside. I pulled out the book and opened it. Across the front of the first page, I saw several numbers in a sequence that looked like an account number. Inside on the preceding pages were someone's bookkeeping. Down one side of the page were people's names. Across the top were dates. Across from each name and under each date was what looked like a dollar amount.

I examined every inch of the inside and outside of the bowling bag. Nothing else was there. I put the notebook in my pocket. I stopped when I realized I had forgotten something. I pulled back the pouch on the ball and looked inside the finger holes of the bowling ball. Nothing was in the finger holes, but some rolled-up paper was inside the thumbhole. I pulled them out and unrolled them.

A one-way trip airline ticket to Zurich, Switzerland. My, my. Isn't that interesting?

I looked closely at the ticket and saw it was an open ticket with no date. I pulled out the notebook and put the ticket inside. I stuffed them deep inside my pocket. I replaced everything else back inside the bag, just as I had found them. I placed the bag back into the locker. I closed the door and put the key inside my pocket. I walked slowly, even though I wanted to run out of the bowling alley. I walked across the parking lot and headed toward the car. I felt sure that at least a hundred pair of eyes was on me and watched my every move. I reached the car without an incident, except I fumbled with the car keys for at least three minutes until I was able to unlock the car and climb inside.

I started the car and slowly pulled out of the parking lot. I constantly scanned all my mirrors. What I found in his bowling bag wasn't only very important, but also very possibly the reason he was killed. For the next thirty to forty minutes, I just drove around. I didn't have a clue where I went. My mind was racing at the speed of light.

When I get into that problem-solving mode I quite often think out loud to myself. People that can see and or hear me swear I am talking to an imaginary person. I find it quite soothing and an effective way to process through all the evidence before me to reach some sort of a conclusion. I am quite aware that I do it, but I have worked through problems that way for as long as I can remember. I have long gotten past strangers looking at me as if I had lost my mind. I didn't give a damn. It worked!

"Joseph Branning was an accountant for a large investment firm." I said out loud as I checked this off my mental checklist by lowering one finger on my right hand. "Two, he may or may not have been having several extramarital affairs." I lowered another finger. "He definitely bet on horses and other sporting events." Number three went down. "He had an accounting notebook and an airline ticket to Switzerland stuffed in his bowling ball." All I had left was my thumb. My left hand was busy steering the car. "This might or might not have led to his being gunned down execution style." I couldn't add any more topics to the discussion because I had run out of fingers.

Something was brewing here. I needed to talk to his wife. I took out the piece of paper with his address copied on it. It was a good thing I had this car. The address was clear across town, sitting on the outskirts.

I turned on the radio, and some teenage boom-boom rocketed out of the speakers. I quickly turned down the volume and changed the radio station to something I could listen to. Somewhere along the way to the Branning house, the radio station broke for the hourly news broadcast. I turned up the volume slightly so I could clearly make out what the newscaster was saying. The second story really caught my attention.

"Friday's execution-style murder of accountant Joseph Branning still has police baffled as no clues or witnesses are available. However, reliable sources have told us that Branning had been known to associate with known gamblers. Possible ties with organized crime may be indicated."

"Oh shit!" I slammed my fist down on the dashboard. "That sure as hell didn't need to get out."

As the news went on to other stories, I turned down the radio. Momentarily lost in a train of thought, I drove along.

How did that get out? "The police wouldn't have let that leak." I said loud enough that I am sure if I had the windows down anyone near would have heard me because I also slammed the steering wheel with the side of my fist. "I knew I haven't talked to everyone, but, so far, based on what Mike had told me, Marci would be the most likely source of the reliable information." I shook my head as I had to admit. "I am going to have to call her and let her know that it might be prudent if she didn't let many people know what she knew. "That momentary thought of hearing her voice again initially brought a brief smile to my face. Then the primary reason for the call turned my stomach upside down.

I was getting close to the Branning house. I forced myself to get into a train of thought to form a line of questions for Mrs. Branning. My initial approach was going to have to be very delicate. She most definitely knew the name of their insurance company. Because I didn't, I couldn't use the same approach I had used with Marci. I pulled up in front of the house, but I still hadn't decided on the best approach. So I decided to play it by ear. Three cars were parked in the driveway; two were parked in the street in front of the house. I hadn't stopped to think that she would have visitors. It, of course, would be natural for her to have family members there to comfort her and the children.

I mumbled to myself, "Should I just drive off? No, I'm here. I might as well knock on the door. If the situation isn't right, I could always leave and try later."

I parked two houses down the street. It was the closest I could park because of all the cars parked in front. The neighborhood was like any other suburban area in America. All homes were three to four bedrooms, a two-car garage attached to a driveway, and small, grassy front yards with one or two shade trees, a perfect example of the American dream.

Yuck, not my dream! Give me the concrete jungle anytime.

As I approached the house and headed up the walkway, through the window, I could see movement inside the house. I couldn't hear a lot from the obviously subdued household. I chose to knock on the screen door instead of ringing the doorbell.

A few seconds later, a middle-aged woman opened the door. "Yes, sir. May I help you?"

Unless I was dead wrong, I knew this couldn't be Mrs. Branning. She didn't even come close to the lady I saw in the interview."May I speak to Mrs. Joseph Branning, please?"

"May I say who's asking, please?"

"Yes, my name is James Peterson."

"Hold on one moment."

She disappeared into the room. She didn't close the door behind her. I could hear some discussion within the house. Finally, a young, attractive lady dressed in black came to the door. "May I help you?" She had obviously been crying lately. Her eyes were very red.

"Mrs. Joseph Branning?"

"Yes, I am."

"First of all, may I offer you my condolences for your loss? I know this is a very painful time."

"Thank you. Do I know you, or did you know my husband?"

"Actually, neither one. My name is James Peterson. I'm an insurance investigator. I know this may be a very bad time to come to you so soon after your husband's untimely death, but a few matters must be settled as soon as possible. So that at a time of such great grief, you won't have to be bothered any more than is absolutely necessary."

"That's quite all right. I understand perfectly. Please come in." She opened the screen door.

I stepped in and shut the door behind me. As I stood in the foyer, Mrs. Branning stepped into the living room. Without permission and not necessarily with denial of entry I crept closely behind her but not coming completely into the room. I could clearly hear her explaining to her family members. "His name is James Peterson. He is an insurance investigator handling Joe's life insurance policy."

I heard a couple disgruntled voices. One male voice was particularly loud and abrupt. He has a lot of nerve showing up here before poor Joseph was even put in the ground." She silenced those voices quickly, "It is perfectly all right and acceptable to me. Life goes on, and Joseph would want me to be strong enough to take care of business."

A quiet fell over the room as she continued, "I know this may be a very bad time for him to come bye so soon after Joseph's death, but a few matters must be settled as soon as possible." This last part was like a challenge to all of them, defying them to deny her the right to be strong. I liked her spirit. If she didn't know what her husband had been up to, I sure didn't want to be the one to tell her. I noticed that the TV was turned off. I couldn't hear any radio playing. So maybe she hadn't heard the latest about her husband's indiscretions.

I took a momentary sigh of relief. *That will make it a lot easier on me.*

She turned so fast she almost ran into me as she come out of the living room.

I muttered the first thing I could think of. "At a time of such great grief, you won't have to be bothered any more than is absolutely necessary."

She came back to the foyer and led me into another room. This room was clearly her husband's study. There was an office desk, a wall full of books, and a chair. She led me over to the couch.

"Please have a seat, Mr. Peterson. May I offer you something?"

"No, thank you. I'm fine. My name is Jim, please."

"Only if you call me Anne." She gave me a weak smile.

"Okay, Anne. That's a deal."

"You mention that a few matters needed to be cleared up. Which ones?" Mrs. Branning was a strong woman. She was almost intimidating and a far different cry from Marci.

I decided not to pull too many punches. "Do you have any idea who might want to kill your husband?"

She only gave me the slightest bit of a reaction. She held her head a little higher and lifted her shoulders slightly. "No, my Joseph was a very well-liked, popular man who got along with everyone. Prior to yesterday, I would have sworn he had no enemies."

"Anne, I have to ask a few questions because of the way he died. They by no means imply that your husband was anything but an upstanding member of the community. They are questions that, because of formality, must be asked so all the negatives can be put to rest."

She took a deep breath. "Certainly, I understand. If you are as sensitive a man as you appear, then this can't be easy for you either."

"No, it really isn't." I hung my head slightly as if in embarrassment. I did feel a little bad having to lie, but I had some satisfaction that I was quite convincing in my act.

"Please, Jim, continue with your questions. Life goes on, and so do I."

I looked at Anne. She looked back at me.

"Did your husband like to gamble?"

"He was always very athletic and competitive. He'd buy a few squares in the office sports pools, occasionally nothing really serious or often."

"Did your husband ever do any traveling or go off on any business trips or weekends?"

"As a matter of fact, he did, but not on any kind of a regular basis. Once or twice a month or maybe once every couple of months, he'd be gone for a couple days. He was never gone any longer than that."

"Do you know where he'd go?"

"He'd usually inform me where he was going, but very seldom would he go to the same place twice."

"Where were these places?"

"He'd travel all over the country to all the large cities."

"Would you hear from him while he was away on these business trips?"

She gave me a strange, quizzical look. "Sometimes I would, but not always."

"The next couple questions may seem a little strange, but it will help clear up some things. Did you ever call him while he was gone?"

"No, as a matter of fact, I didn't. He wouldn't let me. He used to say it was a waste of long-distance charges. His schedule was such that I wouldn't be able to catch him in his room."

"Even in the early morning hours? Like two or three?"

She got a slightly troubled look on her face for just a few seconds. Then it was gone. An expression of surrender took its place. She looked down. I didn't hear what she said.

"Excuse me, but I didn't hear what you said."

She looked up. The well-put-together lady expression was back. "He always said he'd be working late. And he never knew where he could be reached."

I felt I had pursued this issue enough, so I moved on to something else. "Do you know if he had any gambling debts?"

She didn't handle this one very well. The obvious shock on her face told me that she wasn't ready for that question. "No, absolutely not!" She tempered her voice. "I mean, I know he liked to make bets, but only for enjoyment. Not like an addiction. He was above that."

My inner voice was laughing. *Boy, lady, are you in for a shock if any of what I've heard is true and all hell breaks loose!*

"Once again, I'd like to offer my sympathies for your loss and apologize for my intrusion during your time of grief. Thank you for allowing me to ask you these most important questions."

I stood up. She also stood. She escorted me to the front door. I reached out and shook her hand.

"Thank you for your cooperation."

I walked out the door. I could hear family members asking her who I was. I didn't get to hear her response as the door closed behind me. I walked to the car, got in, and pulled away.

Searching for something to listen to on the radio as I drove I mumbled, "Well, not much help there. Some confirmation of what I already knew or suspected."

Joseph Branning was into something or somebody he shouldn't have been. It was getting to be about dinnertime, so I thought I'd head for home. I'd get something to eat and take a few minutes to try to put together what I had learned.

But of course, I didn't have anything to eat at home.

I made a quick detour by a corner store near my apartment.

I pulled into the parking lot, parked the car, and went inside the store. As I walked up and down the aisles, I realized how hungry I really was. Because I didn't feel like cooking, nothing looked good. So I finally settled on a TV dinner of a large Salisbury steak with corn, potato, and apple pie dessert. I also grabbed a quart of milk. Not many people were in the checkout lane, so it didn't take very long to pay for my groceries. The checkout clerk put the two items in one bag, and I was out the door.

The second I was outside, I could see two individuals doing something to my borrowed car. I played it cool and walked out into the parking lot, heading in the general direction of the car, but not directly at it. As I got closer, I watched to see if they recognized me as the driver of the car. I also wanted to see if I could tell what they were doing. Even though they saw me coming, they kept on doing whatever they were doing. They obviously didn't recognize me. When I got about five feet from the car, I could see one more person on the ground, lying underneath the car. The other two were just fiddling around and trying to hide him. I could tell they were all in their early twenties and dressed alike in jeans and leather jackets.

I asked, "What in the hell do you think you are doing?"

"Move it along, Pops. This is none of your business," the one with the greased-down, brown hair said.

"It is when that is my car, Puke Face."

"Puke Face?" He shouted with such anger that he was spitting as he was talking.

He started to come toward me. The other one standing up, the one with white sidewalls and a small tuft of orange-blonde hair on the very top of his head, grabbed Puke Face's arm.

"Remember what we were told?"

Puke Face stopped short. He just stood there seemingly frothing at the mouth and breathing quickly and heavily. By this time, the guy on the ground had gotten up. He didn't seem to have anything in his hands. So I couldn't tell what he had been doing under the car.

I'd had enough of the bullshit that had been happening lately so I decided to push back a little. "What's the matter, Puke Face? Pussycat got your leash?"

It was enough to break him. He came at me. I stepped forward to close the gap before he was ready. I kicked him as hard as I could in the balls. He crumpled like a paper doll. The other two rushed over and picked him up. Puke Face couldn't even move, walk. The other two carried him off in a frozen, bent-over position. I didn't follow. Instead, I placed my grocery bag on the hood and got down on my hands and knees. I looked up under the car, where the hoodlum on the ground had been messing. I searched the whole underside of the car. I couldn't seem to find anything. He had been down there doing something, but I'd be damned if I could find what it was. I crawled on my hands and knees for a good thirty minutes. I looked from bumper to bumper and couldn't find a thing that didn't look like it belonged there. Apparently, George's son had always drove this car around the city. There wasn't very much dirt or mud caked underneath. So, I could see everything real clearly. Twice, while I crawled around on my hands and knees, some shoppers stopped and looked at me as if I were nuts.

One sweet elderly lady asked, "Young man have you lost something? Maybe I could help you find what you are looking for."

I answered, "No thank you ma'am. I thought I had an oil leak and I was trying to find where it might be coming from. This seemed to pacify her. As she nodded, smiled, and moved along.

I finally gave up and got to my feet. After brushing myself off, I grabbed my grocery bag and very cautiously unlocked the door. Slowly I opened the door. Nothing happened so I got in and set my bag on the passenger seat. I stuck my key in the ignition and held my breath as I turned the key. The motor kicked to life on the first turn. As the car sat there idling, I breathed a lot easier. Then I noticed the sun starting to set. It was beginning to get dark. I turned on the headlights and pulled out of the parking lot.

By the time I got home, it was dark. I pulled my borrowed car into the parking garage that was underneath my apartment building. I found my assigned slot. I got out of the car and shoved the car keys into the opposite pants pocket from my apartment door key. I grabbed my dinner and slowly dragged my tired ass over to the elevator. The door was over against the wall, on the opposite side from my parking slot. The garage was about halfway full, so I didn't have too many cars to detour around. When it was full, the supervisor said the place held twenty-three cars.

Why twenty-three? There were five floors of four apartments. One slot per apartment came to twenty. So why the extra three slots? Who knows?

The supervisor claimed visitor parking wasn't allowed. So, alas, it was another one of life's great mysteries that I wasn't going to solve. I pushed the up button, stepped back, and waited.

I never heard them walk up behind me, but I sure did feel them. The blow to the back of my head made me see lots of stars. I didn't think I completely blacked out. My knees hit the floor. Of all the stupid things, I tried not to let my dinner hit the ground and spill. I didn't know what they hit me with, but it sure did buckle me. I lay on the floor in front of the elevator like a used pile of rags. I kept my eyes shut. Simply, I knew it would hurt less that way.

I heard Puke Face's voice in my ear, "Stop investigating Joseph Branning, or you'll beg for what happened to him to happen to you to stop your suffering."

I felt the most awful pain in my lower back and rib cage. Someone kicked me extremely hard. Even with my eyes shut, I saw nothing but blood-red. When I heard the elevator door open, I used up almost everything I had left to crawl inside, as if the inside of the elevator were somehow a safe sanctuary. It seemed like an eternity before the doors closed behind me. After I heard them come together, I opened my eyes enough to see the floor buttons. Somehow through the pain and agony, I was able to reach up from the sitting position and push the button that corresponded with my floor before the door would reopen on the garage. When I felt the elevator start to rise, I felt a lot safer and let out a held breath. That was when the real pain started. I just knew I had a five-inch hole in the back of my head. That was the only way it could possibly hurt this much. I started to reach up my right hand to feel the back of my head. The resulting pain in my back made me stop instantly. After the few stars of pain had subsided, I continued to raise my hand slowly to feel my head. The pain was at least tolerable this way. I could feel a tremendous bump already starting to rise. I knew it was going to be sore as hell later. As I brought my hand down, I was relieved to see only a very small trickle of blood. That meant that there wasn't any serious cut or abrasion, just a large goose egg.

The door to the elevator opened, and I realized I had reached my floor. I tried to stand, but my head and body wasn't ready. I crawled out. The door wasn't timed for a beat-up, old man on his hands and knees. It started to close before I got out. I couldn't react quickly enough to get out of its way. Plus, I knew that, when it found that it couldn't close, it would just open again. But I hadn't planned on it trying to close on my lower ribs. When the sensors were against my sides, I was momentarily pinned. I must have been a hell of a sight. For those long, eternal seconds, I was writhing around in extreme agony. I might have even screamed out in pain. Finally, the doors reopened, and I fell to the ground, halfway in and halfway out of the elevator. I lay there for a few seconds while trying to recover. I heard the doors start to close again. It was amazing how much strength one gets from a sudden surge of adrenaline just to avoid pain. I didn't try to get up though. I simply jerked the lower half of my body out of the way of the ensuing jaws of pain. At this point, I lost interest in everything except lying perfectly still. Waves of nauseating pain continued to wash over my entire body. I didn't know how long I lay there, but the pain eventually decreased enough so I could stand up and walk. I was hunched over slightly, but I could walk. What normally took me about forty-five seconds to reach the door of my apartment took five long, agonizing minutes because I had to stop every few steps to catch my breath. When I reached my door, I started to dig into my pants pocket for my door keys. I realized I still had the paper bag with my dinner still clutched in my hand. It appeared to be completely intact.

"I'll be a son of a bitch!" I started to laugh and stand a little taller at my moral victory, that is, until I suddenly came to grips with the old expression, "It only hurts when I laugh."

The sudden, stabbing pain quieted my laughter slightly, but it in no way dampened my spirit. They might have kicked me while I was down, but they couldn't take away what I was made up of inside.

After all, my mother always said, "You are what you eat."

All this silly shit went through my head as I stood there and fumbled for my keys. Just as I was about to insert my key into the lock, I heard a noise from behind me and to my left, from the direction of the elevator. My head jerked up and looked left. The pain nearly sent me to my knees. The momentary reaction of fear of being beaten again turned to relief. I saw it was Mrs. Grover, who lived a couple doors down. She was also just getting home. Her husband was retired. She worked a part-time job in the afternoon, strictly for something to do. I envied them. She smiled and waved. I smiled back, unlocked my door, and went inside. I stood with my back against the door and took a moment to breathe a sigh of relief. I was home, safe in my own castle, so to speak such as it was.

CHAPTER 6

It was amazing how an extremely hot shower and a meal could miraculously make a person feel a lot better. I was sitting in my chair and drinking a cup of coffee after just having taken the miracle cure. I was still sore, but I felt a lot better. I reached over and picked up Branning's notebook off the table next to me. This was going to be the first chance I had to study the book in detail. There was nothing unusual about the cover. I opened it up and looked at the first page. Both sides were blank except for the one long sequence of numbers. The more I looked at it, the more I was convinced that it was an account number. *But to what?*

I looked over at the airline ticket to Zurich that lay on the table. I whispered softly, "A numbered Swiss bank account? It fits, and it would explain things."

I wondered if I was trying to reshape the facts to make them fit the apparent situation, or am I uncovering the situation that fit the facts? The former assumption is quite often the reason good investigators never becomes great investigators.

I turned the first page and started to look at the rest of the book. Down the left side of the page were people's names. Across the top were dates. Down the right side were letters. Where the columns intersected were numbers, either two- or three-digit numbers with a dollar sign in front. I got up, went over to a cabinet, and grabbed a legal pad of paper and a pencil. I stopped by the kitchen and refilled my coffee cup. I usually didn't drink two cups of coffee back to back. The first one tasted so good that I figured one more would also taste good. Plus, I knew I was going to be doing paperwork. Somehow, it just seemed to be appropriate to have a cup of coffee sitting there while doing my paperwork.

I walked over to my chair, put my cup of coffee on the table, and flopped down. I stretched out my legs and just sat there relaxing, both mentally and physically. A few moments later, I picked up the notebook. I started to list the entries from the notebook on the notepad. When I got to the next-to-last page, I found a list of letter codes and their meanings. They corresponded to the codes listed on the right side of the previous pages. These codes were all names of what looked like investment groups or companies. Then, as sudden as a light being turned on, it became all clear.

This is a record of several people's investments, their investment dates, and their investment amounts.

I sat back and let out a deep breath as I realized what I had. I took out a separate sheet of paper and listed down all of the names in the notebook. Next, I did some very hard thinking. After some extreme brain-rattling thoughts, I made a decision.

I went to my utility drawer and got out a very sharp X-Acto knife. I went back and sat in my chair. I opened the notebook to the first page and studied both sides near the bindings. If I was really careful, I could accomplish the task at hand. I turned sideways in my chair toward the table and pushed the lamp and my coffee cup to the backside of the table. I needed a clear, flat surface on which to work. In an effort to expose as much of the first page as possible, I very carefully folded back the cover as far as I could without breaking the bindings. I laid the notebook down flat with the first page facing up. I took the first page and turned it over so it was lying facedown on the table. With the X-Acto knife, I made a cut the entire length of the first page, as close to the binding as I possibly could. The first page came loose. I looked very closely at the book where I had made the cut. Very little of the page remained in the book. So little in fact that I felt very comfortable that, unless one knew the page had been there, one wouldn't know there had ever been a first page.

If this was indeed a Swiss-numbered account and the notebook did fall back into the wrong hands, then at least they wouldn't have what was in the bank because they wouldn't have the number. Deep down inside, I knew I'd cut it out so that, if there were anything in that account, then I'd have it all to myself. I didn't know if I were going to follow up on that premise, but that thought was in my head.

I took the notebook into the kitchen and stuck it inside a plastic sandwich bag and then inside another one. I went to my refrigerator and opened the door. Not much was inside. Corn filled a large food storage container. I opened the lid. The smell nearly knocked me over.

"Perfect!" I said smugly.

I stuck the notebook inside the corn and put the lid back on. I shook the container. I couldn't see the book within the corn. I put it back on the shelf and shut the door. I sat back down in my chair and looked at the account number further. The last three digits of the number were "ZNB." The rest of the digits were numbers.

I surmised that ZNB must stand for Zurich National Bank.

I folded the paper and started to stick it in my wallet. Then I had an idea. I got out my phone book and opened the white pages to the Ms. I got a pen and copied the account number in its entirety under someone's name of "Money." Then I folded the page, along with the airline ticket, and placed them inside my wallet. About ten minutes later, I was finishing my cup of coffee when the phone rang. I looked at the telephone quizzically.

I spoke to this stupid inanimate telephone as if it could actually listen to me. "Who's calling?" Genius that I almost sometimes can be, I finally realized there's only one way to find out.

I picked up the phone. "Hello."

"Jimmy, this is Marci Johnson."

I was shocked out of my skin. I couldn't think of anything intelligent to say.

But she apparently did. "How are you doing this evening?"

"I'm doing fine." I managed to stutter. "How are you doing?"

"I'm just fine. When you gave me your card, you said I could call you anytime."

"Yes, that's why I gave it to you."

"Ever since you left, I have been going over and over our conversation in my head."

I thought back to my visit with her. Our conversation wasn't the foremost thing I remembered. The first and only impression I recalled was her out-of-this-world, gorgeous face, luscious hips and ass, and those large, sensuous, pointed breasts. The sound of her voice just served to enhance the vision. The picture in my mind was so real that I began to get an erection. This was amazing me. Even over the phone, this woman was stirring feelings in me that I hadn't felt in a very long time. Granted, my wife's and my sex life had been pretty good for two dump kids who really didn't any better or what the hell they were really doing. But over the years our sex life had dwindled to barely above nonexistent. But I hadn't felt like this in years. I was getting horny as hell.

I heard her soft voice. "Excuse me? Hello?"

I literally shook myself back to Earth. "I'm here. I just dropped the receiver for a moment."

"You dropped the receiver? Funny, I could hear you breathing the whole time. I might add that it was slightly heavy. Are you all right?"

"I'm fine. You're quite right. I didn't drop the receiver."

"Then why did you say you did?"

It was a good thing we didn't have television phones. Or else she would have seen me blush very red.

"Ah ... Well ... It's a little embarrassing. I'm not sure how I could tell you."

"There's nothing to be embarrassed about. I'm a big girl. I know you're a big boy. Is something wrong?"

"No, nothing is wrong. I ... ah ... was also thinking of our conversation. But I wasn't actually thinking about what we were talking about." I paused.

"Then what were you thinking about?"

"Are you sure it won't embarrass you?"

She got a suspicious sound to her voice. "Why would it be embarrassing to me?"

"Well, I was remembering what you looked like." I paused for about three seconds. "And I found that experience quite stimulating."

I heard a soft giggle. "Why thank you very much. That is quite a compliment that I could have that much of an effect on you from just a memory. But I still don't understand why that's embarrassing."

"Honest answer?"

"Yes, absolutely."

I went ahead with my answer before cowardliness stopped me. "Because I'm so much older than you, I'd be out of line."

"Come on, Jimmy. Nowadays, age really is an irrelevant issue. Besides, you aren't that much older than I am."

"Marci, you're in your early twenties. I'm forty-nine. That's over twice your age."

"Well, you may have been on this Earth for forty-nine years, but you sure don't look that old. Judging by the sound of your breathing a few minutes ago, your bodily reactions tell me that you're not too old. There's still plenty of life left in you. Besides, that's quite a compliment that I should have that kind of an effect on you."

"No, Marci, thank you. I haven't felt those kinds of ... excuse me ... urges in a long time. It has been so long in fact that I had forgotten that I missed them."

"It's my pleasure, Jimmy. I mean, it's my pleasure to be the cause of those feelings. I have to admit that I've felt an attraction for you."

I didn't know what, but something in her voice said this wasn't a come-on or con. It was more like a shy admittance of the truth. It was kind of like she was able to say those things over the phone only because we weren't face-to-face. She showed only some of the same shyness that I noticed when I was questioning her at her apartment. Then I realized that neither one of us were talking.

"You were saying something concurring your thinking about what we were discussing earlier today."

"Yes, I was. Uh, you asked if Joe ever left anything with me to hold. I said no. Well, that isn't exactly accurate. I also didn't tell you that he wasn't going to the office. He was on his way to the airport, and he wouldn't be back for several days."

"Wasn't that unusual?"

"No, it really wasn't. He used to make several business trips. Some were real spur-of-the-moment things. The unusual part was what he told me the second reason why he had to speak to me. He said he was expecting a letter to be mailed to him at my address."

"Say what?"

"That's about the same reaction I had. He said there were several reasons why he was having it mailed to me. The first one he said was because it was a business letter, but it had nothing to do with the company. It might be considered a conflict of interest to have it mailed to the office. Second, he said his wife always backed him as far as work was concerned. If she thought for a minute that he was doing anything financially of a personal nature, she would jump all over him for risking their money. Finally, he said his kids sometimes got a hold of the mail, and he wouldn't always get everything. Because this was very important, he knew he could count on me to get the letter to him."

"Why didn't you tell me about it this morning?"

"He had asked me a week or two ago, and I hadn't received the letter yet. What with all that happened yesterday and all the questions I've been asked, I just plain forgot all about it. I guess I must have figured that it wasn't that important."

"Well, what made you remember now?"

"I received the letter in the mail this afternoon. I've been debating all afternoon and evening whether to call the police or you. I finally decided to call you because you seemed to be the nicest. You were the only one who asked if he had left anything with me."

"What was in the letter?"

"I don't know. It isn't addressed to me, so I didn't open it."

I didn't want to seem too anxious to get my hands on the letter, but I was desperate to see what was in that envelope.

"What are you planning to do with it?"

"I don't know. That's why I called you."

"I'll tell you what. Put it somewhere safe until I can get over there. Then we'll decide what to do with it."

"Okay. That sounds all right to me. I'm sure it isn't going to go anywhere tonight. If you can get over here sometime tomorrow, we'll take care of it."

As badly as I wanted to see the contents of that letter, I didn't feel like going anywhere tonight. But when she said tomorrow and not tonight, that was like a challenge. I was now willing to walk barefoot over hot coals to go over there tonight.

"Tomorrow? What's wrong with tonight?"

"Well, it's getting a little late. I didn't figure you'd want to be driving clear across town this time of night for just a business letter that didn't mean anything now that Joe is dead."

I looked at the clock. It was nearly nine thirty. I was beat tired. But everything considered, I had to know what was in that letter before anyone else found out. Plus, I wanted another look at this good-looking lady.

"It's not that far to drive, and I won't stay long. I'd stay just enough to see what's inside that envelope. Then I'll leave and be out of your way."

"Silly, you won't be in my way. I was just planning to sit up and watch some late-night TV."

"Give me a few minutes. I'll be right over."

"Okay. I'll see you in a little while."

"I'm looking forward to it."

"So am I."

"Bye."

"Good-bye."

I didn't mind hanging up and not hearing her voice anymore because it meant I'd get to see her sooner. I decided to take a few extra minutes and shave, brush my teeth, and put on some fresh clothes. The ones I wore were okay for lying around the apartment, but I sure didn't want to show up at Marci's place looking like a bum. So I put on a nice shirt and sweater with matching pants.

I must have made record time getting there. I made all the lights without hitting a single red light. I was soon knocking on her door. When the door opened, she was standing behind it. Only her face was poking around from behind the door, much like the first time I met her. The only difference was that it was night. Because she had the lights turned down in her apartment, I couldn't see her face that clearly.

"Come on in, Jimmy."

"Sure thing."

I walked in until I heard the door close behind me. I stopped and turned around. If I had been impressed with Marci the first time I saw her, then, this time, I felt as if the full shock wave from a nuclear blast had hit me. Marci stood slightly against the now-closed door with one leg slightly bent. She had both of her hands behind her. They were about waist-level so as not to block any of the view of her. She had on a very short and tight, black skirt, which showed off a heavenly pair of legs with flesh-colored hose. The bottom of the skirt came to about two inches below the top of her thighs. I could see the shape and curve of everything below her waist. The high heel, black shoes helped emphasize her already nicely sculpted calves and thighs. I didn't like skinny legs on women. Hers had just the right amount of muscle tone to them. I was experiencing an overpowering desire to bury my face between those luscious thighs. Above her waist, the skirt came up to just below her magnificently round breasts that were pointing straight at me. Black suspenders went straight up over the points of her boobs and shoulders. I couldn't tell if she had erect nipples or not. Only for a split second I felt slightly disappointed. The way the suspenders over her sweater emphasized the shape and size of those magnificent round mounds that I was rapidly becoming hooked on overshadowed my hurt. I was normally a leg man. Lord knows she had what I'd consider the perfectly shaped feminine legs. But her chest was so magnificent that I was hooked. Her skintight, very thin sweater made it look like it was painted on her instead of being a clothing garment. It clung to and detailed every inch of her body and breasts.

As I looked closer, I suddenly realized by the shape of the bulges under the suspenders that she wasn't wearing a bra. Yet, her breasts still stood completely up and straight out. The V-shaped neckline came down low enough to expose about four inches of cleavage. She was quite a sight.

She said, "It's good to see you again."

I looked up at her face, and I could see her features very clearly. She was lovely. Without a doubt, she had the prettiest face I had ever seen. It was also obvious that she was happy, pleased, and not at all shy about what she was showing and sharing with me. She had put on a little makeup, and she had her hair down. She didn't have a lot of makeup on, just enough to highlight and emphasize her beautiful facial features. She had on just a hint of mascara and the slightest trace of blue eye shadow. Her full lips had just a hint of red coloring. She was even lovelier than I remembered her. The way her reddish brown hair rested on her shoulders helped to complete the picture. My heart started to beat so hard that it hurt my chest.

If this keeps up, I'm going to have a heart attack. But what a wonderful way to go!

At the same time, I could feel I was getting the biggest and hardest erection I could remember having in a long, long time. What amazed me was that too felt complete openness and no shyness as I noticed her short casual and pleased glance at the obvious bulge that was showing in the front of my pants. Every inch of my penis was throbbing so hard that it hurt. I was in great shape. Here was the prettiest and sexiest woman I had ever seen standing here for me to look at, and I was in pain. I continued to look. Obviously, she intended to let me. So, I did. First, I'd look at the whole woman as a complete picture. Then I'd look slowly, but closely up and down every inch from head to toe and then back up again. Marci must have been paying very close attention to my eyes and what I was looking at. As my eyes would briefly come to rest on each and every celestial wonder woman part of her she would just slowly adjust said part. The erotic movement was just enough to move, flex or emphasis sexually the part I was enjoying. I was beginning to get weak in the knees.

Marci must have seen the little shake I had in my legs. She seductively moved away from the door and headed across the room. "Let's have a seat on the couch, and I'll show you the reason I called." She had a slightly embarrassed grin that said she wasn't very good at double meanings, but she was trying.

"I think you already have."

She stopped dead in her tracks, looked over at me, and blushed bright red. "I must say I couldn't think of a better reason." Her expression slowly changed to one of a small child who finally realized she was being complimented and not criticized. Her smile of innocence was refreshing.

She walked over to the couch. As she walked past me, I smelled the most stimulating perfume scent I could imagine. Its effect was almost intoxicating, like a drug. After she passed, I took a moment to study her ass. Her skirt clung to her checks so snugly that it was as if she were wearing nothing at all. That was when I remembered why I was a leg man. Legs like those always seemed to end up connected to an ass like that, perfectly round, plush cheeks that I just wanted to walk up behind and fondle for hours. As she reached the couch, I hustled over to be beside her as she turned around to sit down. She sat down at the end, near a table and light. She crossed her legs, which pulled her skirt even a little higher up her legs and completely exposed her thighs. She patted the cushion next to her.

"Have a seat, and I'll show you the letter."

I sat down. She reached to the left, over the end of the couch, to open the drawer in the end table. She was slightly leaning over the end of the couch in order to reach the table. I couldn't help but notice that the back part of her skirt pulled up to expose the cheeks of her raised right buttocks. I hadn't had much opportunity to witness such a heavenly sight, but I could have sworn that she wasn't wearing underwear underneath her skirt. I could clearly make out almost her entire right ass cheek. Right then and there, I almost had an orgasmic experience in my pants. Much to my dismay, she found what she was reaching for and sat back down completely. As she lowered her buttocks back down on the cushion, the skirt slid back down into place.

She handed me a still-sealed envelope. "This is the letter I received in the mail."

I suddenly started thinking with my head instead of my loins. Although, I understand the phrase these days is, "I stopped thinking with my little head and started thinking with my big head." I very carefully looked over the envelope. It was addressed to Joseph Branning, in care of Marci Johnson. The postmark was dated from yesterday morning and sent from the downtown post office. No return address was listed. I turned it over and examined the sealed side very closely.

"It wasn't actually addressed to me, so I didn't open it," she said a bit defensively.

I looked at her briefly. I had a quick passing thought. *"God, you are beautiful."*

I forced my attention back on the matters at hand. I tore open the envelope.

Marci excitedly said, "You can't do that! It's against the law to open someone else's mail."

"Well, Marci, I don't think Joseph Branning is going to be around to press any charges."

"No, I guess he won't," she admitted.

I pulled out a two-page letter. I was trying with all my might not to look at her. I knew that, if I looked at her in my current aroused state, I'd lose control once again and be lost in her beauty. Right then, I needed to read this letter and not be caught up in all her splendor. I started to read the letter quietly to myself.

Marci quickly said, "What does it say? Here let me read it, too."

She scooted right over next to me. Her hip pushed right up against mine. She reached up with her left hand and slightly turned the letter, so she could read the it at the same time I did. But I was having difficulty concentrating on the paper. Her right breast was solidly pressed against my left arm, and I could faintly smell her perfume, which was almost bewitching in its arousing aroma.

I mentally pulled myself back to the letter as I heard her say excitedly, "Would you look at that? It's Joe's handwriting."

The letter was handwritten and addressed to Marci. Even though she was also looking at the letter, I still read it aloud. The very first thing written answered some questions.

Dear Marci,

The times we have spent together have meant more to me than I could ever explain. Your friendship, genuine kindness, and understanding mean more to me than any wife or other family member could. You were a good friend.

If the day comes where you are reading this letter it would mean that I am gone. Because of your efficient and professional manner I know you would hold on to this letter and only open it as I had asked. By now, you know have left town and can't be found. Interested parties shouldn't try to look for me because my disappearance was a planned event. Certain interest had come about in my life that precipitated this sudden departure. It would be highly unlikely that anyone should expect me to return. This was the only written or oral statement anywhere as to any kind of an answer to my disappearance. I haven't written to my wife because she was part of the reason why I was leaving as unexpectedly and secretly. But I feel as if owe you an explanation. You had been a real friend who had cared. I wish he I had you for a sister.

Your best friend for life and beyond,

Joe

I felt her slightly pull away. I had stopped reading and looked at her. She was making a gallant effort not to cry. In fact, she had gotten a tissue out of a box on the table, and she was lightly dabbing her eyes.

"It sounds like he was a close friend."

"Yes, but I don't understand why he was running away. He seemed to be on top of the world, and he had everything going for him."

"Apparently not. Maybe he was trying to get out of town because he knew someone was looking to kill him."

The surprised look on her face told me that she hadn't put that together as of yet. She was still awfully pretty, but the sexual electricity was gone out of the air. As she sat back, her head slumped slightly. She was visibly upset about all that was happening. My heart went out for her. She looked so frail and vulnerable. I just wanted to hug her and comfort her that everything was going to be all right. But I didn't think I knew her well enough for that.

"Do you want me to stop reading?"

She sniffled a couple times. "No, Joe wouldn't want me to fall apart. He'd say something silly like, 'Just as show business, life must go on.'"

I watched her face closely. She lifted just her eyes slightly. Just for a few seconds, she looked at me. Then she looked back down. Then she couldn't hold it any longer. She started to giggle. It was light at first. Then it turned into a healthy laugh.

"Damn him. Why did he have to go and do something stupid? He was such a nice, likable person who always seemed to land on his feet. Not this time though." She had a weak smile.

"You sure have a pretty smile. It makes me feel warm all over to see happiness on your face."

Some of that gleam and sparkle had come back into her eyes. "You certainly make me feel good all over, too."

As we stared into each other's eyes some, more of that electricity passed between us. My lack of confidence took hold as I broke the stare. I looked down at the letter I was still holding. I fumbled with it for a short moment.

"Let's see what else he had to say." I tried to find where I had left off, but I couldn't seem to find the right spot. I kept turning one page after another over and over.

"How could I be so clumsy with only two pieces of paper?" I turned slightly away and said softly to myself.

I felt her hand on mine. She was gentle at first and then a little firmer, like she was reinforcing me. I looked at her hand on mine and then up at her face.

"What's bothering you, Jimmy? Everything is okay."

"I know, but it's just that—"

"What?" she asked softly.

The sadness was gone. Now there was only concern in her very feminine voice.

"It has been a very long time since a female has shown genuine interest in me. That's one area where I don't have much confidence. I may be way out of line here in assuming you have an interest in me. Lord knows I'm not a very good judge in that area. It makes me very nervous. My natural defense mechanism snaps into gear. Why would someone as young, pretty, and vibrant as you want to show any interest in a middle-aged fart like me?" She started to answer, but I held up my hand to stop her. "Don't get me wrong. I find you very attractive and extremely desirable. However, we only met this morning, and you hardly know me. Believe me, if anybody knows, I know it's not because of my good looks. Also, when you have been in this business as long as I have, you become naturally suspicious of anyone trying to get close to you. Now I may be shooting myself in the foot or, as my mother used to say, cutting my nose off to spite my face. But if you knew what I have been through lately, you'd understand."

I was about to run out of breath as I felt I had just given this long speech on one lung full of breath. So, I stopped talking. I expected a backlash or something from her. I mentally braced myself for the impact. When it didn't come, I looked at her. She was just sitting there with a small, shit-eating grin on her face.

Oh, great! I sure nailed this one correctly.

In case you haven't figure it out yet, I often talk to myself. I feel like sometimes it is the only way I can get an intelligent answer back without any extra crap. And of course, I always like the suggestion that is made. It does have that extra bonus.

After what seemed like an eternity, she finally spoke, "You're absolutely correct. I don't know you very well. But I do know that you are browbeating yourself far more than you deserve." A little bit of anger appeared in her eyes. "She must have been a horrible person to have hurt you and belittle you to the point that you have very little self-esteem. I also have not been very lucky in affairs of the heart."

She saw the look on my face that said I found that hard to believe. "It's true. I have only been with ..." She momentarily lowered her eyes in embarrassment. "I had a serious relationship with two men in my life. One when I was seventeen and in my senior year in high school. The other was about two years ago. Both ended in failure. The boy in high school wanted only one thing. Once he got it, I was like a trophy on his wall, and he was off to other conquests. The other one lasted about six months, and it was great until I found out he was married. I understand how you feel. Why am I showing interest in you? Maybe you are the first good-looking male I have ever met who didn't try to hit on me from the time we met. What little we have talked, I have found you intelligent. Even though you try very hard not to let it out, you do have a good sense of humor."

"I've spent my entire adult life hiding from men because they are generally a bunch of animals who only think with their little head, not their big one. But from the moment you walked in here this morning, I felt like you were different. You were actually a very sensitive human being under that rough exterior. When I look at you, I don't see a middle-aged fart. I see a sexy, lovely man, whom I'd like to get to know better. I can't explain it. You're right. We just met. I don't know what's gotten into me for being so forward. I was doing something I hate for men to do to me. I was coming on to you like a cheap whore."

I could see the change literally taking place before my eyes. She was going from a sexy flirt to a defeated, little girl.

"I'm sorry. Now if you'll excuse me for a few minutes, I'll go and change into something that's more like the real me."

She stood up to leave the room. I reached up and gently grabbed her by the wrist. She hesitated and then turned to face me. Tears were really in her eyes.

"Please don't. Not right now anyway. I really like this part of you. I don't look at you as a cheap whore. I look at you now, and I see more woman than I know ever existed. If you change out of this woman, then you'll be taking a part of my dream girl away from me."

"But this isn't the real me."

"I think it's more a part of you than you know. It's at least a part of the real you. A part that has been submerged and buried because of what a couple beasts did to you."

She stood there and looked at me. She shifted her hand, so we were now holding hands.

I tugged gently on her hand. "Come on. Sit down, please."

She hesitated, as if she were deciding. She sat back down. Marci sat on the front half of the cushion, angled toward me. I reached over and took her other hand in mine. I sat forward so we were actually facing each other and holding both hands.

I asked, "Do I really appeal to you?"

Through sniffles, she nodded her head. "Oh, yes, you do."

"Why?"

"I don't know." She squeezed my hands tighter. "Maybe it's because you're handsome."

I started to protest, but she wouldn't let me. "But you are! You are also sweet, considerate, and sensitive. Most importantly, I like you. I'd bet that, if we took the time, we'd find we have a lot of the same likes and dislikes."

"But what about our age difference?"

"Will you stop with that? It doesn't matter anymore. It might have twenty years ago, but it doesn't now. Besides, because of everything you've gone through, you're the one person who is likely to understand me and how I feel."

"I'm trying to."

"I know you are. That's exactly what I mean about you being sensitive. You seem the type that would actually care about how I feel."

"I do. But let me ask you a question."

"Okay."

"What made you dress the way you did?"

"I knew I liked you. As I said before, I haven't had much experience with relationships. I figured the best way to attract you was through what I thought was the basis for attracting all men. Through their … you know … sex glands. Plus, I saw the way you looked at me when you were here this morning. When men usually look at me like that, it disgusts me. For some reason, when you did it, it not only didn't bother me, but also actually made me feel good, both inside and out. I didn't really understand it, but I didn't want to question it. It felt right."

"You mean you were willing to lower your standards just to attract me?"

"You're a man. I thought it would be what you would want."

"Yes, I am a man and of course I would want that for us. But not that way. Honey let me tell you something. Don't ever compromise your standards for anyone. If that is what it takes to get a man's attention or approval, then he isn't worth attracting."

"Then you did think I acted like a whore." She started to feel hurt again.

"No, you were just very sexy. Can I tell you a secret?"

"Sure." Her spirit lifted slightly because I cared enough to reveal a confidence with her.

"In a lot of respects, I'm just like every other man. Only I'm secure enough to admit to my own emotions and desires. The secret is that I, as with most men when looking for a woman, am looking for a woman who is a lady in the streets, but a whore in the bedroom. That's the perfect woman."

She looked at me and started to grin. "I think I understand what you mean. Then you like this outfit and the way I acted. You don't think I was acting cheap?"

"Like it? As a matter of fact, if we are going to keep on seeing each other, I must insist you keep it, along with some others for the bedroom, of course, but not the streets." I couldn't believe the words that came out of my mouth as the came out.

I had never been so assuming and forward in my life. I hardly knew this lady. Here I was trying to talk her into wearing sexy clothes and talking about being in the bedroom with her. "Marci, I… I mean I want…I need…I am sorry I don't mean to assume." I started to apologize for my outlandish statement.

A big grin came across her face as she sensuously purred, "You can count on us keeping it and enjoying it many times, lover."

We looked at each other. All that electricity was backflowing even more intensely than before. Then quite naturally, I leaned forward and kissed her softly. After only a few seconds of looking deep into each other's eyes from only inches apart, I again kissed her. This time, it was deeply and very passionately. She kissed back with equal feelings. We were soon in a tight embrace with my face snuggled into her neck and her large breasts pressing hard against my chest. I was becoming intensely aroused very quickly.

Not only my erection but my whole body was surging with passion. *Don't make her think I feel she really was a cheap whore,* I told myself.

I had to do something quickly, or I wouldn't be able to stop myself from trying to rip off her clothes and ravage her heavenly body. As I kissed the base of her neck, I felt her whole-body shudder. I reluctantly broke off the embrace and sat back a little from her. I wasn't surprised to see we were both very much short of breath.

I took a few moments to stop gasping. "This is happening too fast. Before we get too carried away, perhaps we ought to finish Joe's letter."

She panted, "Fast, yes. But you can't say it doesn't feel right, although perhaps you're right."

She reached up with her shaking right hand and caressed my left cheek. She looked deeply into my eyes. She smiled. "I haven't felt like this for such a very long time."

I leaned forward and kissed her lightly on the lips. She even tasted good. She smiled very sweetly at me.

I sat back and picked up the letter. "Let's see where we left off."

Marci scooted into place and snuggled against me. She put her right arm up along the back of the couch. This allowed her to press her breasts against my arm. I cuddled back with my arm and shoulder just enough to let her know that this wasn't only acceptable to me, but also wanted very much. I looked at her. She smiled and nestled back.

I had no trouble finding where I had left off. After the part about being a sister, the letter said, "Things at the office could bust loose if anyone official decided to investigate the company in connection with my disappearance. You aren't to worry for two reasons. First, you have done nothing wrong. Second, I have taken all necessary steps to ensure that those who were guilty of the money laundering and other crimes would catch all the heat." He didn't go into detail in the rest of the letter, but something was obviously going on at the investment firm. The letter finished, "Marci I will always have a brotherly love for you in my heart. Joe."

After reading the letter, I had many mixed feelings. The good feelings were because it was right there in black and white, the confirmation that nothing romantic had been going on between Marci and Branning. The letter also gave me feelings of anxiety because it explained the notebook. Branning was an accountant. The bookkeeping portion was just that, recording of the money laundering going on at his office. Now it all made sense. The account number really was a Swiss-numbered account, probably filled with organized crime's money. The plane ticket said that his out-of-town trip was a plan to empty that account and spend the rest of his life in luxury while hiding from the Browning Investment Group. My mind was racing at top speed about what I was going to do next. In the last twenty-four hours, so much had happened that life yesterday wasn't the same as it was today.

"Jimmy are you still in there?" Marci gently touched my face.

"Yeah … ah … yes, I am. I was just trying to put together all the pieces of the puzzle. What do you know about all this?" I tapped the letter.

"Nothing really. I mean, I felt an awful lot of money was flowing through that company. But everything always seemed on the level." She had a wide-eyed expression of innocence.

"Did you ever see any men there who looked like just maybe they didn't belong?"

"Well, there were always closed-door meetings going with lots of men in business suits. They must have been very important men. There were always lots of big, mean-looking bodyguards whenever they were there."

"Do you have any idea what those meetings were about?"

"I'm just one of the office secretaries. Those meetings were always above my level."

"Was Joe ever privileged to any of those meetings?"

"Oh, always! I got the feeling that he was their personal accountant. I don't think he actually worked on any other accounts except those of the ones that went on behind the locked and guarded doors."

The picture was becoming brighter and brighter.

"Jimmy, what's going on? Not only was Joe involved in something very large and crooked, but you know about it and aren't telling me everything. After all, Joe is … I mean … was my friend."

"Yes, he was that." I was about to lie to her again. I decided not to stall this time. I figured I might as well get it over with.

"I don't know that much, just what I have learned in the last twenty-four hours. Joseph Branning was an accountant for a large investment firm. He was gunned down execution-style yesterday, only a couple blocks from here. Actually, apparently shortly after leaving here. Police have no clues as to who the perpetrators were. Joseph was a friend of yours from the office where you worked. He liked to flirt with all the ladies, and he enjoyed gambling.

These two habits may or may not have caused him problems. He made many business trips. Some of which might have been legitimate business, but I'm sure some were actually excuses to cover up whatever he was really doing. Joseph was involved in closed-door meetings with men who appeared to be members of organized crime. For some reason, he felt the need to leave town and not come back. He ran out on not only his friends, but also his wife and kids. Which, I might add, is reprehensible. How could anyone run out on his own children?"

"I guess he must have had one heck of a reason."

"Well, we know one thing."

"What's that?"

"It cost him his life."

She put her head on my shoulder. I leaned my head lightly against the top of hers.

"I'm sorry to be so hard on him, but I can't change the facts."

"I know you can't," she said very softly. "Joe is the one who did all that."

We sat there and snuggled for several minutes. I reached up with my right hand and gently stroked her hair. She put her left arm over my belly and around my waist. While we sat there, I looked down at her lightly tanned legs. Her skirt was about halfway between her thighs and her crotch. Both of her lovely thighs were completely exposed. It was hard to be sad when such a stimulating sight was before me. She sat with her legs held loosely together.

I just knew I must be a real slime ball to be looking at Marci's legs while she's feeling so down about losing a friend. It was that I just couldn't pull my eyes away. *Am I terrible or just horny?*

Marci said, "Jimmy, what happens next? Who do we check with next?"

"What do you mean?"

She sat up straight and pulled a little away from me. I looked straight into her eyes. She had that "I'm going to do what I want" look.

"I mean, we can't let Joe's murderer get away with this. So where do we check next?"

"I was afraid that's what you meant."

"Why? Don't you think I can help you?"

"I'm sure you can. Although, remember we are dealing with people who are quite capable of murder, especially when a great deal of money is involved. This is big-time organized crime. You know, the mob. If they thought you were in their way, they wouldn't hesitate to hurt or kill you just because you're a sexy, beautiful woman. They'd waste you." I said that with as much seriousness as possible. I wanted to scare her into letting me handle this.

"On the same token, how can I let you go out there all alone and deal with them?"

"First, it's my job. Second, I won't be alone."

Marci got a puzzled look on her face. I read that as to say, "Who else is out there with you?"

"I know a few members of the police department. They'll be out there with me."

"But, Jimmy!"

"No buts about it. I don't want you to get hurt."

"Now that I've found you, I don't want anything to happen to you." She had a lot of concern in her eye, and she was holding my face with both of her hands.

"You got it halfway right, sweetheart. You've found me, and I've found you. Nothing is going to undermine that except you and me."

"Do you mean that?"

"Of course, I do."

She took back a hold of my hands. "Oh, baby, please take care of yourself."

"I will. Speaking of which, I must be going. It's getting awfully late. I've had a long day. Tomorrow promises to be even longer."

She sounded genuinely depressed. "Okay. I guess you're right. But please call me tomorrow as soon as you can. I already know I'm going to miss you the second you walk out that door."

"I'm going to miss you, too. I'll call as soon as I can if you promise me one thing."

"Anything. What is it?"

"Don't throw away this outfit. Save it until we're ready to use it at another time."

"I promise. Oh, I promise. Do you truly like this outfit and don't think it's too much?"

"Marci honey, to say I like it would be a gross understatement. No, I don't think it's too much. When I walked in here and saw you standing there, I thought I was having a vision from my best fantasy. Just don't you dare ever wear it for anyone but me!"

That seemed to act as a shot of adrenaline or perhaps acceptance. She just seemed to bubble over with a sudden happiness or maybe self-confidence.

"Don't worry about that. I know you're the only one I could ever wear this for and not be totally embarrassed. Considering the reaction, I got and what you said, I think I should pick up a few more items along the same lines just for you. You sure make me feel like a real and sensuous woman. I don't know how or why you've done it so fast. But I feel as if I've known you for a long time. Maybe that's why I feel so comfortable revealing some of my inner self to you that I've never let anyone else see, like wearing this outfit. In public, I'm very shy and timid. But I've always had this hidden desire down deep to be outgoing and openly sexy. I've even gone so far as to have bought other revealing and sexy clothes besides this one. I even put on one outfit once. Then I wore an overcoat until I got to a nightclub that I heard people around the office talk about. After I got there and walked in, there were actually people to look at me. I got scared, ran out, and came home. I cried all the way home because I didn't have the courage to be a woman." She hung her head slightly as if to hide her shame.

"Why? Because you didn't go to some bar, flirt, dance, and pick up some stranger?"

"Well, yes."

"That wouldn't necessarily have been anything ladylike. That sounds more like a whore than anything you've done with me here tonight does. Remember what I said was the perfect woman?"

"Yes, a lady in public and a tramp in the bedroom."

"Close enough." She looked up at me. "You, my dear, are every bit of a lady. You are far more woman than any female I have ever known."

She giggled lightly. "I'm going to have to keep you around. You're definitely good for my ego."

"You're going to have a hard time keeping me away."

"Good!"

We sat there and looked into each other's eyes. We held hands and smiled. I suddenly realized all the things I had said to this lady who I had only known for about twelve hours. I had virtually made a commitment. It was something I had sworn to never do again after my divorce. At this rate, I'd be proposing marriage to her by Monday, if not sooner.

There I went again, trying to second guess life by wondering if I was thinking with my big head, or was I thinking with my little head. *Confidence boy. Confidence.*

I had to get out of there to give myself some time to clear my mind of the lust I was feeling. I needed to analyze and evaluate the situation logically, not just emotionally and or physically.

"Jimmy, what's wrong?" Marci was getting to know me too well and too fast.

I had to think fast. "It just dawned on me. I think I know a possible lead to follow. I don't know why I just thought of it. It just popped into my head."

"What's that?" She was full of excitement.

"Just someone I know who might have some information about Joe's possible betting habits."

"Oh, do you think he could help?"

"Anything is possible. It's worth the effort to pursue."

"Are you going to go and talk to him tonight?"

"Well, considering this is Saturday night, it probably would be the best time to get a hold of him."

"Why? Where's that?"

"At a pool hall on the other side of town."

"If you give me a few minutes, I'll change and be right with you." She started to get up, but I wouldn't let go of her hands. She sat back down.

"No, Marci, this is something I have to do by myself for several reasons."

The look in her eyes told me that I had hurt her feelings.

"What reasons?" she asked meekly.

"First, this pool hall is not a nice place for pretty, young ladies. A bunch of very rough, dirty men is there. They'd like nothing better than to get their hands on someone like you."

"But they know you, don't they? They wouldn't do anything if you were there."

"That wouldn't stop them for a second. I tell you, those guys don't have any morals. Second, my contact would not talk to me if you were there. He doesn't like strangers, no matter how pretty they are."

"Okay, okay! I get the message. But you're sure it has nothing to do with not wanting to be seen with me?"

"Absolutely not! But I'm still trying to figure out why you'd want to be seen with me."

"Because I—" She hesitated.

I knew she wanted to say something more. "Because why?"

"Because I like you a lot, and I just want to be with you."

"I like you a lot, too. Because of that, I can't let you go with me. It wouldn't be safe for you, and I'd never forgive myself if I let something happen to you."

"Just don't let anything happen to you. I'd be awfully angry with you if you did."

I chuckled lightly. "It's a deal."

"It's not funny! I mean it."

"I'll bet you do."

"You're darn right."

"Well, I'd better get going."

I rose and picked up Joe's letter and envelope. "Can I hold on to this for a while? I want to reread it a couple more times to make sure I understand it."

"Sure, I certainly don't have any use for it."

I put the letter back in the envelope, folded it, and stuck it in my back pocket. As I headed for the door, Marci jumped up and followed right behind me.

As I reached for the doorknob, I heard her say softly, "Jimmy?"

I stopped and turned. As soon as I looked at her, I knew it would be hard to leave. Neither one of us said a word. She just stepped forward into my waiting arms. When we kissed this time, it was still deep, but it wasn't passionate. It was emotional. There was a difference. In the short time I had known Marci, she had taught me several things I hadn't known, even after all those years of marriage.

After our kiss ended, I still held her in my arms.

"I'll definitely see you later."

Without waiting for another word, I turned and opened the door. I didn't even want to hesitate. I walked straight out. I didn't hear the door close behind me. When I turned to go downstairs, I looked back toward her door. Sure enough, she was standing in the doorway, just as seductive-looking as she had all evening. Right then and there, as I slowed to wave to her as I started downstairs, I decided why she was so sexually alluring to me. Other females had not been, even though a few had tried since my divorce. Even though Marci had gone to the effort to dress the part of a seductress, her sexuality had just come natural to her. It was just the way she was. It wasn't an act or put-on. It was just her.

I must have lost twenty years somewhere. I had a bounce in my step as I walked downstairs. I reminded myself of someone in his twenties. I even started to whistle as I left the building and headed onto the street. This was something I didn't do.

I stopped on the sidewalk at the base of the stairs. I looked around. This time of night, not much was going on around here. It was pretty quiet for a block full of fourplex apartments in the middle of the city.

I turned and took my first step toward the car. My first impression was that I had run into a pole or something. But as I was spun to the ground, I heard the loud bang. Then I knew I had been shot.

I have my good sweater on, and this is going to ruin it.

CHAPTER 7

When I came to, the first thing I noticed was all the flashing red and blue lights.

"Who's having the party? And whoever it is, I wish he'd take those drums out of my head."

I tried to sit up, but, between my head spinning and the paramedic pushing me back to the ground, I didn't try too hard.

"Just stay down for a while," he said.

"What happened?" I asked.

"Apparently, you took a round in your upper left shoulder."

Then I felt the pain, and the memory came back.

"You were quite lucky. The round only grazed through the fleshy part. You have a nice half-inch groove carved through your shoulder. It's quite bloody and painful, but is nothing serious. It was a powerful enough round that, if it had hit you in the chest, you would have had a manhole-sized hole coming out of your back. Witnesses say that, just as the shot was fired, you had turned to your right and started to walk. That's what saved you. When you did that, your shoulder came across in front of you and blocked your chest. This made it a glancing blow instead of an impact. I've got the bleeding stopped, but we're going to send you to the hospital to check you out."

"Why did I pass out? Why does my head feel like a smashed watermelon?"

"The impact was strong enough that it spun you. You hit your head on the cement step of this brownstone. That's what made you lose consciousness."

"Thanks a lot. That makes me feel a lot better."

"You asked."

I gave him a dirty look. He laughed as he got up. I saw Marci talking to a uniformed police officer. She still looked great, but something different was about her. I realized she wore a full-length overcoat that reached just above her ankles. When she noticed the medic had left my side, she came over quickly and knelt down beside me.

"The medic said you should be all right. I've never been so scared in my entire life as when I saw you go down."

"You saw what happened?"

"Right after you started down the stairs, I went right to my window that faces the street. I wanted to watch you leave. I saw you stop at the bottom of the steps and then look around. Just as you turned to walk to your right, you were shot."

"Did you see who?"

"Yes. It came from a parked car on the other side of the street."

"What kind of car?"

"You sound just like the policeman. I don't know, but it was a dark color. Nothing fancy. Just a car."

"Was it a black or dark blue sedan?"

"Yes, I suppose so."

I sat up slowly. I wasn't trying to make any quick movements. This time, my head didn't spin quite so badly. I first went to my knees and then to my feet.

"Are you sure you should do that? They said you should keep still until they can get to the hospital."

"I'm not going to the hospital."

Marci was right beside me and holding on to my arm. "Are you sure? You've just been shot and knocked unconscious. You should let a doctor check you out."

"I'm fine. The medic said the bleeding has stopped, and I just have a bump on my head."

The policeman came over. "Mr. Peterson are you able to give us a statement?"

"There's not much to say. I have no idea who shot me or why. I was visiting a friend tonight. As I was leaving, someone took a shot at me."

Because I saw Marci talking to the policeman earlier, I held my breath and crossed my fingers that she hadn't told him about why I had really been visiting her.

"Miss Johnson said she also knew of no reason why someone would want to kill you."

When he said, "kill you," it really sunk home as to what had really happened.

Marci asked, "Are you all right? You just turned all white. You had better sit down."

I didn't say a word. Instead, I dashed to the curb. I proceeded to vomit everything in my stomach into the gutter. After a few thousand head spins and several drumbeats in my head, I felt much better. I walked over to Marci.

"Sorry about that. I couldn't help it."

"Do you feel better?"

"Much."

"I guess you were just going through shock."

"I suppose so. But I feel okay now." She came alongside me. I put my arm around her shoulder. She put her arms around my waist. "I'm glad you took the time to put on that overcoat before you came down the stairs after I was shot."

"Well, I initially didn't."

"What did you say?"

"When I first saw you go down, I could only think of you. I flew downstairs without stopping. I didn't take time for anything."

"You mean you went out in public in our outfit?"

"I was worried about you. I didn't think about anything else except you. I'm sorry."

"Don't be sorry. Under the circumstances, I certainly understand. When did you get the overcoat?"

"After I ran down here to you, some other people also showed up. I sent one of them to call the police. I stayed with you until they arrived. My neighbor, Mrs. Wilkerson, brought her coat down to me. She was a little shocked to see me dressed like I was. But she never said a word. Wait a minute. Did you say our outfit?"

"Ah, as a matter of fact, I did. I'm sorry. I didn't mean anything by it. It's just that I felt something special about it."

"Oh, don't apologize. I think that's wonderful you'd feel that way. I've never worn this outfit in front of anyone before. In a way, I think it might have helped in bringing us together. It will always be ours." She hugged me even tighter.

I said, "Come on. Let's get out of here."

"You're going to the hospital."

"No, there's no need."

"What do you mean? You've been shot," she said quite angrily.

"The medic said it was just a graze. More messy than damaged. I'm just fine."

"What about your head? You took quite a blow."

"It's going to take something a lot harder than a brownstone step to hurt this head." I lightly chuckled. I was trying to put a bit of humor into the situation.

"Then at least come upstairs long enough to sit down and have a cup of coffee. Give yourself a chance to make sure there's no damage."

"Marci, I can't. There isn't time. I must push on to find the answers."

Then I heard anger come out of her that I didn't know she possessed. "Fine. Then go on out there and get yourself killed." She stomped off quite mad.

I saw an older woman standing there and listening to us. She walked up to me. "Excuse me, I'm Mrs. Wilkerson. You must be Jimmy Peterson."

"I am James Peterson."

"Well, Mr. Peterson, I'm not sure what there is between you and Marci, but I've never seen her act like this. We spent the entire afternoon talking about you. I guess I'm her surrogate mother."

I stared at her and didn't say a word. I didn't really want to take the time to talk to this old lady, but it involved Marci, so I was willing to listen to her for a little while anyway.

"She said she had met this wonderful man just this morning. She was extremely confused. As pretty as she is, I've rarely seen her ever date anyone. Marci wondered what was she to do? She knew she liked you almost too much from the minute she'd met you. Therein lies the problem. How could she care so much for someone she'd only just met and didn't know? I told her that sometimes the head doesn't know shit from shinola when it comes to affairs of the heart. If it feels right, go for it. Judging by the way she was dressed tonight, I'd say that's exactly what she did. When I came down the stairs, I didn't recognize her at first."

"Did she happen to mention our age difference?"

"Yes, she said she really didn't even notice or care, but it bothered you quite a bit. She wanted my opinion."

"What did you tell her?"

"I told her that it wasn't worth a hill of beans to worry about. It was between you and her. If it didn't matter to the two of you, then everyone else could just stuff it. That sweet, lovable, quite shy, young lady is extremely upset. She must really care about you to let you affect her like this. I didn't mean to eavesdrop, but I couldn't help but overhear. She's concerned about you and your health. Don't push her away. You'll never find another as kind as she is. Go after her and apologize. I've known her for quite a while. She really cares for you." Mrs. Wilkerson turned and walked away.

I knew she was right.

I started toward Marci's apartment, but the police officer stopped me. "Excuse me, sir. But you need to go to the hospital. I also need to get your statement."

"Look, Officer Jones, is it?" I read his nametag. "I'm fine. I don't need to go to the hospital. You heard the medic. I was just grazed in the shoulder. I only bumped my head when I fell."

"Yes, sir. I heard the medic. He said you should go to the hospital."

"They always say that to cover their ass. Honest, officer, I'm fine. I'm not going to the hospital. Now if you excuse me."

I wanted to get away from here. I had to explain to Marci.

But the cop wouldn't let me go. "There's still the matter of your signed statement."

"Look, young man, what precinct are you with?"

"The ninth."

"Do you know Lieutenant Mike Glosman at the downtown precinct?"

"Yes, sir. I know him."

"I have no idea who shot me. You know more about this incident than I do. However, Lieutenant Glosman is not only a business colleague but a personal friend. I'll get in contact with him first thing tomorrow morning. I'll give him my written statement and have him transfer it over to you at the ninth precinct. I'll tell him you tried to get it from me. It will be on my head, not yours. Now if you have no further questions, I'll be on my way."

I didn't give him the chance to have any further questions. I turned and walked away before he could say a word. I had to talk to Marci. I couldn't let it end like this. Mrs. Wilkerson saw where I was headed. She caught up with me as I was just entering the building.

"This isn't going to be easy. Remember, you've just hurt her pride and feelings. Be apologetic but strong."

She went back outside, maybe to gossip with the neighbors. I didn't hesitate as I walked straight up the stairs and knocked on her door.

She said, "Who is it?"

"Marci honey, it's me, Jimmy. Please open the door. I'd like to talk to you."

There were a few moments of silence. Just as I was about to knock again, I heard the door being unlocked. She opened it just enough for her to stand between the door and the frame.

She said coldly, "So talk."

Except for the makeup she still had on from earlier, she was dressed exactly as she had been this morning when I had first met her, specifically in her sweatshirt and jeans.

"Look, couldn't I come in? It's kind of public out here."

"For now, right here will be just fine."

"Marci, I'm not very good at this. I don't know how to share things with someone. I'm sorry I hurt your feelings and made you angry. I was wrong. But it's getting dangerous out there, and I care about you. I don't want you to get hurt."

"Don't you think I feel the same way about you?"

"Yes, I know you do."

"Then why wouldn't you let me help you when you were hurt?"

"Because I'm just a stubborn, old—"

"Don't you dare say it! Don't you dare! Do you understand? I won't tolerate you trying to put one foot in the grave before your time."

"Yes, dear."

I loved it that, when she got mad, her breasts stuck out even further and heaved up and down with her breathing.

She opened the door all the way. "Now you get your butt in here and let me make sure you really are okay."

I stepped in without saying a word. She closed the door and pointed at the couch. "Sit! And what are you grinning about?"

"You." She softened her tone a bit. "What about me?"

"It may be an old cliché, but you sure are cute when you're mad."

I was trying very hard to stifle a giggle. Marci at first looked very stern. Then, as my laughter slowly leaked out, she started to laugh. We were soon both laughing forcefully so hard that we both had tears in our eyes. Soon thereafter, we were embracing and kissing furiously. At first, as our passion was growing by leaps and bounds. We kissed hard as if we were two starving people who finally got something to satisfy our appetite. That wasn't too far from being accurate. We had both been without sex for so long that one could call us sex-starved. We kissed so hard that I was sure we bruised our lips. From the start, our lips were apart, and our tongues were extremely busy dancing with each other. For a while, we'd lick tongues. Then our tongues would play chase back and forth between the inside of her mouth and then mine. Occasionally, we'd gently caress not only the other's tongue, but the inside of the other's teeth and gums.

While all of this was going on, our hands were also very busy. At first, I had been rubbing my hands all over her back on the outside of her sweatshirt. I rubbed and caressed her shoulder blades and then down to her lower back. As she had her hands up on my shoulders or on my face and head, her sweatshirt would rise at the bottom, exposing her lower back and stomach. It had been a long time since I felt bare, soft, female skin.

As the sensual sensation vibrated up through my fingertips to my heart and soul I'd realized I had forgot how wonderful it felt. Then as passion over took me and I was lost from thinking to much I remember feeling or thinking, *No, it had never felt this right and intense before.*

I ran my hands as gently and caressing as I could, considering how turned on I was, over and over her bare back. I reached up on her back far enough under her sweatshirt to realize she indeed had no bra on. There was nothing but bare skin all the way up to her shoulders. As I stroked and caressed the skin on her back, she shuddered and quivered as I passed over sensitive areas. Because the front of our bodies was pressed tightly against each other, every time she shuddered, I felt her breasts move against my chest. Also, the movement of her hips served to heighten the arousal of my now-hard erection. I was soon able to anticipate this, and I'd push slightly forward as it happened. Marci was also getting quite stimulated as she started to involuntarily move her hips to press and stimulate her crotch against the now-large bulge in the front of my pants. When she started to do that, I brought my hands down to her ass. As I squeezed and pulled myself toward her ass cheeks, I was able to assist her motion. It wasn't hard to tell that she was getting very turned on. By now, Marci had both her hands on my ass. She was also squeezing and pulling.

No woman had ever gotten that involved with playing with my ass. It felt good.

I brought my hands up to her lower back. Then I slid my hands under her sweatshirt. I lightly rubbed her lower back. Our mouths and tongues were still very busy dancing. We kept on licking and kissing each other's lips, cheeks, necks, and face. As I was nibbling, licking, and kissing her neck, she was performing oral sex on my ear. I slipped both of my hands inside the back waistband of her jeans and underwear as far as they would go. Marci sucked in her stomach slightly to give my hands more room inside of her waistband. This allowed me to slide my hands all the way in until I had those lovely, bare ass cheeks in my hands. I heard her have a sharp and sudden intake of breath. As I started to fondle her bare ass, she seemed to get even more aroused. It also had the same effect on me. The more I fondled her ass, the tighter she squeezed my ass and the harder she pulled my hips toward her.

I felt myself getting close to that first stage of orgasm. I stepped back with my right foot. I took my hands out of the back of her pants. Judging by her reaction, it was much to her dismay. Without breaking the oral stimulation that both of us were frantically doing to each other, I reached down with my right hand. I put it behind her knees and swooped her up. I broke my attention away from her long enough to find the direction to what was obviously the bedroom. As I walked in that direction, I looked at her face. Even though she had that obvious look of a woman who was extremely sexually aroused, her smile was one of warmth and tenderness. It wasn't just wanting.

Just as I got to the door, she said in between deep pants, "Oh, Jimmy, I want you so bad that I need you."

"Me, too, Honey. Me, too."

I stopped at the door long enough to kiss her wet lips more tenderly than passionately. When our kiss ended, Marci reached out with her left hand and opened the bedroom door. As we went through the door, she put her left hand up and around the nape of my neck and grabbed hold of her right hand. She laid her head down on my left shoulder. Unbelievably, I felt no pain in my fresh wound.

The only light turned on in the room was a very soft nightlight on her night table on the right side of her queen-sized bed. It was bright enough that I could still make out things. In fact, I saw our outfit crumpled up and thrown in a chair by the closet.

I felt the pang of anguish as the sight of that hurt a little. How much I would have liked to watch her take it off. Oh, well. Maybe someday.

I walked around to the left side of the bed and gently set Marci down lengthwise on the bed with her head on the pillow. I sat down next to her and faced the headboard. I was about even with her stomach. I leaned over her and braced myself with my forearms, one on each side of her. She put her arms up around my neck. Our faces were only inches apart.

"Marci, this is happening awfully fast. I want you so bad that I'm about to burst out of my pants."

"I noticed."

"Oh, you did, did you?"

"Uh-huh. And I couldn't have asked for a larger compliment." She grinned at the pun she had made.

I wasn't going to touch that one, even if my pole felt like it was ten feet long. Instead, I continued with my original thought, even though she sure did look good lying there.

"Are you sure this is what you want? Once we've gone past that point, there's no going back."

"I've never wanted anything more in my entire life. Now can we get out of our clothes and make wonderful love like I know we can?"

"Oh, baby, I just wanted to make sure."

"I'm quite sure."

"Then let me help you. Sit up."

I sat up. With her hands still around my neck, I pulled her up to a sitting position. I reached over and took hold of each side of the bottom of her sweatshirt. As I started to raise the bottom of her sweatshirt, she put her hands straight up in the air. When her naked breasts became exposed as the bottom of the sweatshirt passed by them, I was treated to a wonderful sight. They were just as I figured they were, large, round, and sticking straight out. Her erect and hard nipples completed the picture. They poked out somewhere around a half-inch. The area around her nipples, the areola, was at least the size of a half-dollar or maybe even larger. They were slightly swollen from her excitation. I probably could have been totally turned on by just staring at her nipples and areola. As soon as I had her sweatshirt over her head and off her arms, I threw it somewhere off to the side of the bed. She kept her hands straight up in the air. I took a moment to enjoy the view of her sitting there topless. She grinned from ear to ear as she straightened her hair from where the sweatshirt coming off had messed it up. The raising of her arms served to tighten and even more enhance the firmness and shape of her breasts. I couldn't stand it any longer. I reached up and placed my right hand on her left breast. I felt her nipple slightly quiver as the palm of my hand softly rubbed the tip. As best as I tried, my hand couldn't completely cover all her breast. There was enough left that it would have taken both of my hands to surround the one breast. This was exactly the size I liked. I leaned over and placed the nipple of her other breast completely in my mouth. As I sucked firmly on her nipple, I flicked the tip with my tongue. Marci let out a moan and arched her back further, pushing her breasts both into my hand and mouth. I sucked even harder. She reacted even more excitedly. I placed my left hand around as much of her breast that was in my mouth as I possibly could. She placed her right hand on the back of my head. Her left hand was on top of my right hand. She caressed the back of my head and squeezed my hand as I continued to play with those lovely mounds. She lay back down and pulled my head and hand with her, refusing to let me take my mouth and hand off her nipple.

As I continued my sucking and squeezing, she began the wiggle of ecstasy. Her moans were becoming more and more often. As I finally reached the level of stimulation I felt I could from this part of foreplay, Marci let me pull away. I stretched up and lightly kissed her several times on the lips. Then I moved left to her right cheek. I then went to the left side of her neck and shoulders. Marci continued to show signs that this further excited her as I kissed down her chest and went in between her breasts. I did stop to kiss each nipple, and she quivered again. Then I went back to kissing her chest, but, this time, I continued kissing down toward her belly. There was no mistake that Marci was enjoying this. As I got to the waistband of her jeans, I kissed all over her belly. When I did this, I reached over with both of my hands and unsnapped the top of her jeans. It was amazing how big a part psychology was of sex. I nearly had an orgasm shudder when I unzipped her pants. The sheer thought of exposing her womanhood caused my near ejaculation. I pulled down the top of her underpants a couple inches to the bottom of the zipper of her jeans to expose the top of her pubic hairs.

She said, "Oh, yes. Oh, yes."

I kissed her lower belly that I had just exposed. I looked at her face. She had the combined look of happiness and agony that only a totally awesome sexual experience could cause.

She was caressing her own breasts. "Please don't stop. Please don't stop."

I didn't. I placed my fingers inside the waistband of her panties and jeans on the top of her belly. I separated my hands and slid them under her panties until I reached her hips. As soon as I applied some downward pressure on her panties and jeans, she raised her hips and ass to allow me to pull her panties and jeans down easier. As her jeans and panties passed below her crotch and exposed all her pubic area, I saw nirvana. I hadn't seen too many pussies up close, so when Marci's was only a matter of inches from my face, I started to quiver and shake as I knew I'd cum in my pants.

I had seen my wife's while we were married mainly only when she was bathing. She was never very open and willing to share herself. So therefor it was never very impressive. But then again, even the ugliest pussy was pretty compared to no pussy. Marci's, on the other hand, was gorgeous, just like the rest of her. Just a little tuft of coppery-colored pubic hairs was just above her vagina. I regrettably drew my gaze away from the copper-colored honey pit, so I could further uncover the delight. I quickly pulled off her shoes and socks. Then I removed her panties and jeans the rest of the way and threw all her clothes on the floor by the end of the bed. Then lo and behold, I had a completely naked and beautiful woman lying on the bed next to me. I started to kiss her ankles and work my way up.

But Marci stopped me. "No, wait, please. Your clothes must come off first."

She'd gotten up on her knees, kneeled beside me, and removed my sweater by first pulling my right arm out of the sleeve and then carefully removing my damaged left arm out. Then she grabbed the bottom and pulled up my sweater until it cleared my head. Then she threw it on the floor in the same general direction of the rest of the clothes. As she started unbuttoning my shirt, she looked me straight in the eye and smiled. After every button on my shirt she undid, she would seductively kiss me. After she unbuttoned the last button, she removed my left sleeve. The medic must have had my shirt off because my shoulder was heavily bandaged. Marci didn't pay any attention to my bandages as she removed the rest of my shirt.

"Stand up, lover, so I can remove the rest."

"Of course, baby."

I stood up on the floor and turned to face the bed. Marci walked over to the edge of the bed on her knees. I loved the way her breasts bounced. When she got close enough, she sat down on her heels. Then she reached up and undid my pants. She did as I had done. She grabbed both my pants and underpants and started to pull them down. She had to stop pulling them down from the side as the front of my underpants hung up on my hard erection that was now sticking straight up and out. As she pulled my underpants off the head of my erection and down to thigh level, my manhood sprung into view. When Marci saw the full view of me, her eyes opened wide, and her lips parted slightly. She just stared at my throbbing muscle, and I didn't stop her. A few moments later, she slowly raised both her hands and took the full length of me between her hands. Only the head of my hard, throbbing erection was left exposed.

As Marci still held me gently in both hands she looked up at my face with a big smile. "It's beautiful."

She looked back down at the prize in her hands. She looked at my hard dick for what seemed a long time. But I knew she was enjoying herself so I just enjoyed watching her. That vision brought immense pleasure to my soul. The she leaned forward, and lovingly kissed the end several times. Then I couldn't believe it. She stuck out her tongue, licked the now-building moisture off the opening at the end of my dick of pre cum, and swallowed it greedily. Then she opened her mouth and put the full head of me inside. At first she didn't fully close her mouth or lips on my erection. She closed them just enough that their nearest could be felt and her warm breath over my dick head sent wave after wave of sexual sensations over my whole body. After several tantalizing teases with her mouth and warm breath she closed her lips on me firmly. I thought my legs would collapse. As she slid her lips slowly up and down on just the head of my manhood, she also sucked as if she were trying to suck me dry. When I started to throb, signaling I was about to ejaculate, she removed her mouth and squeezed me with her hands at the base of my penis, just tight enough to stop the process.

She looked up at me and said with just the slightest of devilish grin and tone to her voice, "You'll get to do that later. I promise. This time, I want you to be inside of my pussy when you do that. The first time I want all your love to blend with all of my love together where I can hold on to it and love it." I had never heard this before but with Marci it sounded so right.

Marci was still sitting on her heels as I removed my pants and shoes. I sat down beside her on the left. I reached up with my right hand and started fondling her left breast while I started nibbling on her neck.

"Oh, baby, that feels so good."

As I kissed and fondled, the passion pitch built up again. Marci started to squirm and wiggle. I placed my right arm around her waist. I gently lifted and laid her back down on the pillows. Once again, I started kissing her neck, first one side and then the other. After a while, I started kissing back down her chest. After a few light bites and sucks on both of her nipples, I started kissing toward her belly. But I didn't stop there. I crawled over and lay down between her legs, which she willingly opened. I positioned myself, so my face was just above her crotch. But I didn't go to the garden spot right away. I kissed and lightly licked across the top of her coppery pubic hairs. Then I kissed the inside of both thighs. As I kissed her thighs, she spread her legs even wider, so I had a complete view of her pussy. I was amazed. Everything about her was pretty, even her pussy. She didn't have a large growth of pubic hairs. It was just enough so a small patch was above her vaginal lips. Yet no hair covered any part of the pussy. I could completely see the lips and clitoris. I stuck out my tongue and lightly licked the complete length of both lips. I next started at the bottom of the vaginal opening and slowly brought my tongue up deep inside of her pussy, splitting the lips as my tongue worked its way toward her clitoris. The closer I got to the clit, the more Marci shuddered and shook. When my tongue finally met her clit, I thought she was going to explode. The more I flicked and stimulated her clit with my tongue, the more she gyrated and moaned. I stopped flicking and started sucking and lightly biting that lovely little button of pleasure.

"Oh, baby, what you are doing to me? Oh, God, baby." I heard her gasp in between erotic moans.

I brought my tongue back down just slightly, so it was in between her pussy lips, but just above the very opening into her womanly depths. I stiffened my tongue as hard as I could make it and drove it into her pussy. I made sure my upper lip bumped into her clitoris and my tongue reached its fullest penetration. I brought my tongue back out almost to the very end. Then, with just head and neck motion, I drove it back in and out over and over. As I kept up this motion, I made sure my upper lip contacted her clit. I was tongue-fucking her as if it were my dick. Then without hesitation, she erupted in spasm after spasm of orgasm as it washed all over her. Somewhere in the middle of her orgasms, I stopped my motion with my tongue fully in her. My now-open mouth surrounded her pussy. I sucked it all in and closed my mouth around her. Not losing a drop. I worked my upper lip on her clitoris and sucked hard on the rest of her pussy lips as I wiggled my tongue around inside of her. I could feel her pussy contracting over and over in my mouth.

I gloated inside as I thought, *I just finally proved to myself that whoever said a woman didn't produce a fluid when she orgasms was dead wrong and never fully appreciated the pleasures of a woman.*

Her pussy liquid filled my mouth. As Marci continued to erupt in orgasm after orgasm I eagerly swallowed every sweet, delicious drop she could give me. She really tasted very good. I kept her whole pussy, lips, clitoris, and all into my mouth and tried to suck it all in. Pussy and all. This brought Marci back up to more and more orgasms. Finally, after a period of time when I thought my mouth and tongue would wear out, she finally slowed and then stopped moving and gyrating her pelvis and hips. She lay still, apparently too drained to move. I quickly bent over and used the edge of the sheet to wipe the excess saliva off my mouth and face.

I somehow didn't think she'd want it on her face. Now it was my turn. I raised myself up on her, so the head of my hard, swollen penis just barely touched her dripping wet pussy. Marci didn't move a muscle except a small grin on her lips appeared. I slowly wiggled my cock and just gently rubbed the head on and just slightly in her pussy lips. It felt so good that I almost lost track of everything as I brought my hips slightly forward, it somewhat took me by surprise. My penis easily found its way between her vaginal lips without any kind of guiding by either of us. The end of my penis slid right into her vagina. It was as if we had been made as a perfect match. As I fully entered her she slightly arched he hips and ass in total acceptance of me. A very deep, husky and pleasurable moan escaped deep from her throat.

While I kissed her face and neck I pulled out of her until just the tip was still in her. She urgently moaned, "Don't leave me." I didn't. Instead I started very easy and slow with forward and back hip thrusts. Each time I'd thrust forward, the end of my penis would separate her pussy lips as it slightly penetrated her vagina and gently rubbed against her clitoris. As I slowly got into a rhythmic pattern of in and out with just the head of my penis, Marci started to move with me and quickly got into my rhythm. After a short while, I slowed down. I didn't want to cum quite yet. Marci was a good lover. She followed my lead as she also slowed her rhythm to match mine. Then as we slowed to just barely moving, I raised my head, so I could look at her face. She barely opened her eyes.

She looked at me and smiled. "Oh, Jimmy, you make me feel so good."

I propped myself on my forearms to hold up my upper body. I wanted to watch her face. She still kept a grin as she also occasionally would appear to tighten her face muscles as I'd rub her clit just the right way with my slow, inward pressure. Then on one inward pressure, I didn't stop. I just kept on slowly pushing forward. As my penis slowly entered further and further into her pussy, I could feel the lips of her pussy being pushed apart to warmly accept what was being offered. Then I could feel her vaginal muscles tighten around my penis as if to say, "You can come in, but you're not leaving." As I reached about half the length of my manhood inside of her, I firmly shoved the rest in deeply. Her face went through multiple expressions. She let out a loud moan as her pussy tightened with a firm grip on my whole penis. She had her hands on my back under my arms, but, when I thrust home, she grabbed two big hands full off my back about shoulder blade high. I didn't feel any pain, so I had to figure she didn't dig in any fingernails. As I pulled out all but the very head and then shoved it back in, she brought her legs up and wrapped them around my legs. Her hands came down to my ass and held my cheeks. Our rhythm matched perfectly, and we became as one. No matter how fast or slow I pumped, Marci matched me exactly, like two bodies and one mind. As we started to pump faster and harder, I knew that my time had come, so to speak. What felt like gallons erupted out of my penis and went deeply into her. Marci started to quiver once again as one orgasm after another took over we both seemed to erupt in simultaneous pleasure. I had no earthly idea how fast or how many strokes I lasted as I lost consciousness of this world. When I erupted in orgasm, I left this plain of existence. I have no idea where I went while in that other plain, but, wherever it is, it's the land of pure ecstasy and pleasure.

I felt wave after wave of that pure ecstasy and pleasure pass over and over my entire body and mind. Marci was apparently experiencing the same type of thing. As I came back to reality, she was still shaking and making little love sounds deep in her throat. They were the ohs and ahs of an ending orgasm.

We slowed our thrusting hips until I was just barely moving in and out of her. It was more like the tender post-orgasmic stroking and tender caressing of each other's love muscles than any other type of stimulation. I laid my chest back down on her chest. She brought up her hands through my arms to lie on top of my shoulders. She was stroking my hair and head as we both kissed each other all over the face and neck with light, little kisses. I had my arms kind of under her shoulders as I played with her long hair and ears.

This went on for several minutes until I finally laid my head on her right shoulder. She hugged me tightly, and I hugged her back. Neither one of us moved nor spoke. We just lay there and held each other tightly. I was still deep inside of her. I was a little concerned that I was too heavy on top of her, but her breathing was easy and unrestricted. She seemed to be completely relaxed. I just lay there and enjoyed the comfort of her embrace.

After quite a while, our breathing had finally returned to normal.

She started to stroke my hair. "Jimmy are you awake?"

"Yes, honey, I am."

"Baby, I've never experienced anything like that before. Ever."

"It was good, wasn't it?"

"Oh, it was way beyond good. No words could describe how far beyond it was."

"It was all because of you."

"No, Jimmy, it was all because of us! I told you I haven't had that much experience, but I don't need much to know that we matched perfectly."

I rose up on one elbow and propped my head on my hand. "I noticed that. No matter how fast or slow we went, we never missed a stroke together. I felt as if we had one sexual mind take over both of our bodies."

"I hope it will always be like that." The look in her eyes was just a momentary flash of fear. "Now that we've made love, is this going to be a wham-bam-thank-you-ma'am one-timer and off you go?"

I instantly reassured her. "It may or may not always be as passionately wild with us as this time, but every time we make love will always be the best one yet." She grinned from ear to ear as she understood my meaning. "How do you feel?"

She shut her eyes and moaned. "I have never felt so completely satisfied. My body feels absolutely numb and drained of all desire."

"Oh, does that mean you're done for the night?"

Her eyes popped wide open. I saw the defensive look on her face. "Oh, no. That's not what I meant. I mean I'm completely exhausted right now. But, if you give me some time, I'll be ready to do whatever you want. I don't think I'll ever totally get enough of you. I'll always want more of you. Right now, my body is physically too weak to obey what my mind would want it to do."

"Relax, honey. I was just teasing you. I feel the same way you do. I'm so completely drained that I think I'd find it difficult to walk."

She lightly punched me in the chest, but she had a smile on her face. "You silly nut. Hey, do you want to join me in a shower?"

"I'd love to."

We weren't quite as exhausted as we both claimed. We got off the bed, feeling a little stiff in the joints at first, but, as we started to move, we walked just fine. She led me by the hand to the bathroom. I enjoyed this as I got to watch the lovely, naked woman with a great ass walk in front of me. When we got in the bathroom, Marci turned on the light and shut the door. She opened the shower door and turned on the water to get it warmed up.

"How warm do you like the water?" she asked.

"As hot as you can stand it."

She looked at me and grinned. "Me, too."

She adjusted the water and shut the door to give it time to stabilize at the desired temperature. She turned toward me and came into my arms.

"Jimmy, just hold me tight for a minute."

I wrapped my arms around her and pulled her securely against me. She hugged back for all she was worth. She started to shake a little.

"Honey, what's the matter?"

"Just a little post-climatic shock, I guess. Jimmy are you sure this isn't just a one-time thing and you're not going to leave here, and I won't see you again?"

"So that's what's wrong. No, Marci, I'm not like that. For me, lovemaking is something special. Yes, we just had wild, passionate sex, but we also made love. Besides, I couldn't find anyone better suited for me. After what we just experienced, any other experience wouldn't even come close. We, on the other hand, can only get better. Right now, I find myself wishing it was tomorrow, so we could start all over again."

"Tomorrow? What's wrong with later tonight?"

"Oh, you little, sexy vixen." I lightly popped her on the ass with my open right hand.

She giggled as she separated from my arms in a mock attempt to escape my further spanking. Then she stood a few feet away from me. She held both my hands and looked deeply into my eyes.

Quite seriously, she said, "Thank you." She paused. "Jimmy, I think I'm falling—"

I grabbed her and kissed her to stop her from finishing that sentence. When we separated our lips, I said, "Baby, I want that, too. But don't say it right now. Let's wait until we are saying it based solely on emotion."

She had a confused look on her face. We stood in the middle of the bathroom with our hands loosely locked around and behind our backs and with our legs and hips pressed together. Her breasts were firmly brushing my chest, and our faces were about a foot apart. Her expression changed to one who looked like she just discovered the answer to a perplexing problem.

"Well then, Mr. Jimmy Peterson," she said sternly as she pulled me slightly tighter against her. "I certainly am in lust with you!"

I grinned. "I'm in lust with you, too. Now how about that shower?"

She started to say okay and then noticed the bandage on my shoulder. "What about that? I'm sure you aren't supposed to get it wet."

"Do you have any gauze or anything here?"

"As a matter of fact, I do. I keep a first aid kit in the kitchen."

"Then if it gets too wet, we'll change it. Now let's get in the shower before we run out of hot water."

"Okay." She giggled.

She opened the shower door, and we stepped in. I pulled the shower door closed behind me. Marci was under the water. I was close to her, as this wasn't a large shower, but I was far enough away from her, so I could enjoy watching her. She was standing with her back to the showerhead. As she leaned her head back under the water, she raised her hands to push her wet hair off her face. When she did, it caused her breasts to flatten slightly, but their shape and her pose was extremely striking. I stepped closer, leaned over, and kissed her breasts. I stood up straight and embraced her. The warm water felt good until it hit my damaged shoulder. It stung like hell. I involuntarily backed up a step quickly.

"Jimmy, what's the matter?"

"The water stung my wound."

"I'm sorry, baby. Do you want me to turn it down some?"

"No, it will be all right if I keep my shoulder out of direct line of the water."

She reached over and grabbed a bar of soap. "Here. Let me take care of you. I know it will make you feel better."

She stepped forward and began to lather soap on me. She started with the base of my neck and worked her way down. She completely lathered every inch of my chest, belly, and underarms. As she reached my waist, I was beginning to anticipate her lathering the entire area between my legs.

She stunned me. "Turn around."

At the same time, she grabbed my good arm and pulled it toward her while she pushed lightly on the inner part of my left shoulder. I obeyed obediently. I was too surprised to object. She started on my back about the same level that she started on my front. My surprise soon turned to enjoyment. I had never experienced this luxury before. I closed my eyes and sank into the world of pleasure. When she reached my waist this time, she didn't stop. She lathered on down to my buttocks. She slowed her pace as she soaped and squeezed both cheeks of my ass. The feeling intensified as she began to place soap in the crack of my ass and directly on my anus. As she lathered a little longer there, I parted my feet slightly. I put my hands on the shower wall in front of me, and I leaned forward slightly. She lathered even a little forward of my anus until she was just barely touching my testicles. Then she lathered back and forth between my anus and my balls. Because this was a new experience, I had no idea how sexually stimulating it could be to have someone caress my anus. I felt the beginning growth of an erection. It felt great, but it ended as she soaped down my inner thighs and legs, all the way to my feet.

She stood back up. "Okay. Turn around and face me."

I did as I was told without argument. She started at my belly and started soaping down until she reached my mostly erect penis. She teasingly soaped all around it, yet never directly touched it. Then she started to soap under and behind my testicles. A couple times, she brushed my anus again. I felt shudders all through my genitals. Then she came forward with her hands and gently soaped and played with my balls. I started to get a harder and harder erection. It came into a full bloom as she finally took my penis into her soapy hands and cleaned every throbbing inch thoroughly. I closed my eyes again and experienced the truly pure sexual pleasure. She stopped before I became overly excited. She stood up and waited until I opened my eyes.

With a very seductive grin, she handed me the bar of soap. "Your turn to do the pleasure."

We changed places in the shower. I had never soaped down a lady before, so I figured I'd do her the same way she had done me. I lathered up the soap some between my hands and then started with her neck and shoulders. The white foam from the soap seemed to highlight her lightly tanned skin. I applied soap all over first her right arm and hand and then her left. After I soaped under her arms, I came across to her breasts. I took a little extra time to make sure I completely covered both breasts and nipples. I was rewarded with two very hard and erect nipples. I stared back and forth between them for a while as I rolled first one and then the other between my fingers. I looked up at Marci's face.

She said, "I think you like that about as much as I do."

"Watching you and your body react to being turned on seems to have a hell of an effect on my arousal."

"It does? How wonderful."

I made sure I soaped up under her breasts. Then I proceeded down her sides and belly.

I was watching the whole Marci as I washed parts of her. My attention was so riveted on total lovely figure that stood before me. I must have slowed down wash as Marci said, "I trust that you are enjoying the view." As she went back to her closed eyed smile enjoying every second of this shower.

Quickly, I soaped in at the waist and then back out at the hips. I lathered up all over her hips and pelvis. I covered the area above her pubic hairs. Then I soaped the hairs themselves. I was very careful not to touch any of the pussy parts. I remembered the effect that had on me when she had teased me. After I had the pubic hairs completely sudsy, I turned her around, just like she did me. As I lathered her back, I also massaged her shoulders and the muscles on her back. As I came to the top of her ass, she bent forward slightly at the waist, separated her feet, and raised her buttocks. I gladly took them in my soapy hands. After I had both cheeks completely soapy and squeezed, I put the soap in the dish and moved my right hand between her cheeks and into the crack of her ass. When I encountered her anus, she moaned. I rubbed and soaped that round spot tenderly. She started to move her hips back and forward. At one point, I was gently probing her anus with my fingertip when it seemed like it opened slightly, and my finger easily slid into the first joint of my finger. This time, she let out a louder moan. As it looked like she was about to fall, she placed her hands on the shower wall in front of her. I tried to help by putting my left arm around the front of her waist across her belly to hold her up. The whole time, I kept on easily moving my finger in and out of her anus. She gave a few shakes and shudders and emitted a low, final gasp and moan. This new experience brought my manhood to an erect state. I'd heard of anal sex, but I didn't know that someone could orgasm from it. When I thought she seemed finished, I gently pulled my finger out and picked up the bar of soap. After washing my hand, I started to soap down her legs.

"Oh Baby, what wonderful lovely legs you have." I breathed softly into her ear.

She purred back her thank you.

When I got to her ankles, I stood up and turned her around to face me. She had her eyes closed. She obviously enjoyed the situation. I went to her upper thighs and worked my way inward. As I reached her inner thigh, she eagerly spread her legs to allow me easy access.

My ex-wife said how too much soap in the vaginal tract would cause female problems. With as little soap suds as I could, I caressed and cleaned her lips, clitoris, and vaginal opening. But I didn't penetrate her vagina. I stroked in and out between her legs, occasionally rubbing far enough back to pass over her anus. But I mainly concentrated on her clitoris and pussy lips. Once again, she started to move her hips in rhythm with my strokes. She reached up and put her hands on my shoulders, as her now-familiar orgasm signs were very evident. As she reached her peak and virtually came in my hand, I thought for a second or two that her legs would give out and she would collapse. I felt as if I were literally holding her up by her crotch as I continued to stimulate her. Finally, after her last shudder, she moved into my arms and held me tightly, as if her life depended on staying in my arms. As her breathing and heart rate slowed and came back to normal, she realized I had a very hard erection. She backed up against the shower wall and pulled me with her.

"Put this lovely muscle in my pussy." Marci stroked me.

I eagerly obeyed. I stepped over, bent my knees to get low enough, and very easily slid my penis into her waiting pussy. I started to pump my hips, causing me to push and pull my erection in and out. It didn't take too long as I had my hands on the back of her hips, helping to keep my rhythm, before I felt that feeling of the beginning of my orgasm.

I could barely hear Marci whispering in my ear, "Oh, yes, baby. Yes. Cum in me hard."

I did, and so did she. Because of exhaustion, I couldn't keep the motion up too long after I came. After a few minutes of both of us being frozen against the wall, we finally separated. I was finding it hard to believe that anyone could orgasm as much as Marci had. If I hadn't been there to see it, I wouldn't have believed it. But what really shocked me was how much Marci got me to cum.

We both soaped our genitals and rinsed off completely. Then Marci turned off the water, and we climbed out of the shower. Without saying a word, we dried ourselves off with the towels that were hanging on the racks. We continued to look at each other and smile. More was said with those smiles and looks than we possibly could have spoken with words. We weakly walked out of the bathroom and headed for her bed. Marci pulled back the covers. We crawled in bed and pulled the covers up to our chins. I lay on my back. Marci tucked herself in next to me on my right side. She had her head on the upper right side of my chest. Her right arm was draped across my lower chest. She had her right leg over my right leg and wrapped around it. I softly and slowly rubbed her right arm with my left hand. I occasionally kissed her forehead. Then just as I was feeling sleep coming on, Marci rolled over onto her right side and gently took my left hand and arm with her across her chest. This caused me to roll onto my right side as well and fit up next to her, like we were two spoons. Her ass was snuggled into the front of my crotch. She held my hand firmly on top of her breasts. I fell asleep with a smile as I thought of the angel in my arms.

CHAPTER 8

I awoke to the smell of fresh coffee and food being cooked. When I opened my eyes, I saw it was morning. I could tell by the light that was trying to leak in through the curtains. Marci was nowhere to be found. I got up, went into the bathroom, and took a piss. I had that terrible morning breath taste in my mouth. So I went to the medicine cabinet to look for some toothpaste. Before I opened the cabinet door, I took a minute to observe myself in the mirror.

"I don't know how you managed to luck out this time, but you sure did," I said to my reflection.

Then I noticed my bandage. I twisted slightly so I could see it all clearly. There were a few dried blood spots, but the gauze wasn't blood-soaked. So I figured it was all right. I opened the medicine cabinet and found a tube of toothpaste. I noticed the only toothbrush in the rack holder was already wet, so I grabbed it and brushed my teeth. After all, we had swapped a lot more than just saliva last night.

I walked back into the bedroom and found my pants. Forgoing my underwear, I put on my pants. I went to the bedroom door and opened it slowly. When I had it open about a foot, I looked out through the opening. I saw Marci busily working away in the kitchen. She had a radio on, and it was playing softly. The music was covering any noise I made so she didn't hear me. She was behind a counter. All I could see of her was from the waist up, which a T-shirt covered. I opened the door the rest of the way and walked out.

Marci obviously saw me come out of the bedroom. She looked up and smiled. "Good morning."

"A good morning it is."

"I trust you slept well?"

"Hard to tell."

"How come?" She had a quizzical look.

"Because I was asleep."

She picked up a dishtowel and threw it at me. It hit me square in the face. I could have ducked, and it would have missed me. She knew it, and I knew it. I caught the towel as it fell off my face. Marci was laughing, and so was I. I walked over and sat down on a barstool next to the counter. I got a complete view of her. She was only wearing a T-shirt, which was confirmed when she reached up to get something out of a cabinet. The back of the T-shirt lifted up enough so that sweet, lovely, naked ass was exposed. She turned back to the stove to make fried eggs, bacon, and toast. It was a simple breakfast, but my favorite. When she turned around, she had a cup of coffee in each hand. She gave me one.

She pointed to the containers on the counter. "Cream and sugar. Help yourself."

"Thank you."

I added lots of sugar and a little cream. While Marci was finishing up at the stove, she hummed happily.

"I fried your eggs over easy. It was strictly a guess, but you seemed like the over easy type." She sat a plate down in front of me, right next to a knife and fork. She set another plate down next to me by the other place setting. She came round the counter and sat down next to me.

"That's all right, isn't it?"

"It's marvelous. Thank you."

We ate in silence for a while. The silence seemed a little

awkward. I figured a little humor might help. "All that good lovin' and she can cook, too. What a woman."

"Multi-talented, that's me."

"You certainly are. You sure proved that last night."

She looked down a little embarrassed and slightly blushed. Then she gave me a sideways glance with just the impish of a grin. "I didn't hear any complaints from you."

"Complaints? Hell, Marci, last night was unquestionably the greatest experience of my life."

She poked her food a little and then turned toward me. "Jimmy, do you remember I told you how I've only been with two men before and you make three?"

"Yes."

Oh, shit. Here comes the brick to break my dream.

"Well, I'm very happy last night happened. I never … ah … I don't remember having …"

She was having trouble saying something. Judging by the fact that she wouldn't even look me in the face like she normally had been when we talked, that told me it was one of two things. One, she was embarrassed. Or two, it was something painful that I didn't want to hear. With my track record of luck, I figured it was the latter. Then Marci placed her fork down on the counter slightly harder than need be. That got my attention.

"Damn it, I've been practicing saying this for the last half hour. Now I can't get it out."

I set my fork down and took a sip of coffee.

What's one more disappointment? I'll get the rest of my clothes and get the hell out of here. At least I experienced one night that I'll never forget. I'll always have that.

"Jimmy, I love you! There. I've said it." She went right on and didn't give me a chance to interrupt. "I know you wouldn't let me say it last night because we were full of physical desire, but I've been awake for hours."

"Boy, I'm shocked. I sure wasn't expecting that one." I stuttered but managed to get it out.

I didn't know what to say. When I didn't say anything, it bothered her. I saw the look on her face change from one of determination to one of, "Oh, shit. I said something wrong."

She said meekly, "I'm sorry. I shouldn't have said that."

She started to turn away in embarrassed failure. I reached out and stopped her. She looked up at me sharply. I didn't really know what to expect.

"No, Marci, it wasn't the wrong thing to say. I feel very strongly for you also. It's my fault I don't know how to handle this. I'm very defensive and leery. When it comes to love and romance, I'm very negative. Love only happens in fairy tales. It happens to other people, but not to me. I truly don't understand how you can be so certain that you are in love with me. Granted, we did make love last night. Not just sex. I can understand being in lust this fast. Two people are either physically matched, or they're not. Not much gray area in between. But love is emotional, and emotions are so varied and complex that they are very hard to be sure of. Please tell me how you can be so sure so soon."

"You're right. Emotions aren't something easy to measure or describe. But when I look at you or when I don't look at you, you're constantly in my thoughts. I guess it all comes down to whether you believe in love at first sight. Until now, I didn't. Mrs. Wilkerson and I talked all afternoon about this very subject. She basically said the same thing you have. I don't even know you. How could I be in love with you? She said you could even be an axe murderer. My answer to her was, 'Then I guess I'm in love with an axe murderer.' But I know you're not. I can see that in your eyes. You might have been through a lot of crap, but you aren't a bad person. You make me feel warm all over. Physically, as we were making love last night, I kept getting this feeling as if a warm liquid were pouring down my spine. Mentally, you are like a euphoric drug being administered to me directly. You give me the reason for taking the next breath. Every part of me, both mentally and physically, yearns to the degree of pain to be with you. My happiness comes from you. The very essence of my being is you."

I swiveled on my barstool and easily rotated her so we were totally facing each other. I took her hands in mine. "Marci, there's so much I have to tell you about me that I couldn't tell it all to you very easily. I wouldn't even know where to start."

"How about at the beginning?" We both said simultaneously.

We both laughed.

I went on after a short while. "You are so very pretty." I spread her hands slightly. "And you've got a body that would make men go to war over. Helen of Troy had nothing on you. You are like an angel from God for me. I know I don't deserve such a lovely angel. But I've always believed not to look a gift horse in the mouth. I refuse to believe that, if we weren't meant to be, then we wouldn't have met."

She slightly wiggled her chest. "I'm glad you like."

"Oh, I do. I do. I'm very, very much in lust with you. I want to say it's more, but, right now, I'm so very overwhelmed. My heart is telling me one thing, and my head is yelling at me that it isn't possible. I don't want to hurt you, but I can't say more right now."

She got off her stool, stepped over between my legs, and put her arms around my body. I put my arms around her shoulders. She looked directly at my face. "Don't worry about me. I'm a big girl. I know the risks. Just because I haven't slept around a lot doesn't mean I don't know what it's all about."

"You sure knew how to give me every ounce of pleasure I could stand. Now granted, I haven't had many chances to experience the pleasures of a lady since my divorce. Or for that matter, before or during my marriage either."

"Well, Mr. Peterson." Marci brushed her breasts against my

chest. "You sure did a good job of completely satisfying and draining me of all sexual pleasures last night."

"I guess that was kind of selfish on my part."

"What do you mean?" Her look said she didn't know what the hell I was talking about.

"The more I watched you get turned on, the more I got turned on. Several times, I almost came just watching you reach orgasm. Of which there seemed to be several."

She got that embarrassed look again. "That, my dear sir, was your entire fault."

I grinned. "I know. I did it on purpose."

"I'll bet you did. And I loved every bit of it. I've experienced multiple orgasms before, but never multiple, multiple orgasms. Last night, I had so many and so often that the whole night was almost like one long orgasm." She gave me that little suspicious look out of one eye. "I want to know where you learned all that. I know that, if you would have done that to your wife, she would never have let you go." She sat back down and drank some coffee.

I laughed. "I don't think my wife would know an orgasm if it walked up and hit her in the face. She was from the old school that said women aren't supposed to enjoy sex. The only reason a woman has sex is for one of two reasons. One is to make babies; two is a wifely duty that she had to perform whether she liked it or not. So once a week or sometimes once every two weeks, on Saturday night, she'd come to bed naked. I'd do my thing to her without a lot of response from her. Then she'd get up out of bed and clean herself off. Afterwards, she put on a long, heavy nightgown, winter or summer. She'd get back into bed and go to sleep. That's been the extent of my sex life for over the last twenty years."

"You poor boy. Why did you put up with it for so long?"

"It wasn't really her fault. It was the way she was brought up to believe. For her, that was the way it was supposed to be."

"Did you ever cheat on her?" That one caught me by complete surprise.

"No, as a matter of fact, I didn't. I don't know why. Lord knows I had a few opportunities, but I didn't take advantage of those chances. That was the way I was brought up."

"So where did you learn all those wonderful things you did to me last night? They totally revised my idea of what a real orgasm was like."

"I just reacted off you. I paid attention to what appeared to stimulate you and what didn't. If it did, I concentrated on that aspect. If it didn't, then I stayed away from it. You made it very easy. It was extremely nice to have someone who wasn't afraid to exhibit her feelings."

"Well, I don't remember you coming across to many areas that didn't stimulate me. It seemed that, no matter what you did, it served to excite me more and more. You touched all the right spots."

"Believe me, I truly enjoyed watching you get off."

"You really mean that, don't you?"

"I guess I'm like a participating voyeur."

"Oh, sounds like my kind of man."

"I'm serious."

"So am I." She had the biggest shit-eating grin. Then she pointed between my legs. "Do you remember when I took you in my hands and said how beautiful you were?"

"Yes, I do."

"Just seeing how hard you were because of me made my juices flow so hard that I was dripping wet. That's why I say you're my kind of man. Sexually, I'm the same way."

"Speaking about that, when you had me in your mouth, you recognized I was about to ejaculate. You did something that made it stop dead in its tracks without turning me off any. Where did you learn that?"

She gave me just the slightest bit of a suspicious look. "You mean, if I had only been with two men, how could I have recognized when you were about to ejaculate and be able to stop it?"

"Well, ah, yes."

"Well, Mr. Smarty, I said I'd only been with two men. I didn't say I'd only had sex twice. That married creep had plenty of experience for the both of us. We had sex quite often. He taught me many things. Why? Does that bother you? I won't ever bring it up again if it does."

"No! It doesn't. That's an unchangeable part of your past. It's part of what makes you what you are today. If we are going to have any kind of relationship at all, I want us to be able to talk about anything and everything, no matter how embarrassing or personal. Last night, we did the most intimate thing two people could possibly do. So we should be able to talk openly about anything else that would be less intimate."

"Sounds good to me." She had a big smile.

"You could go along with me, saying anything to you without any problems?"

"There might be a few things that would embarrass me and make me blush, but that doesn't mean I wouldn't want you to say them to me. I believe the most important part of a good relationship is being the best of friends. If you can't be totally open and honest with your best friend, then you can't be open and honest with anyone or yourself."

I wanted to say something to her. "Something has me mystified."

"What's that?"

"We've said things to each other quite naturally, as if we were talking about the weather, that I never thought I could openly discuss with another human being, much less a female."

"That's what a real relationship is supposed to be like."

"I know. But it's like we've known each other for years, not just hours."

"Well, maybe we have."

"What do you mean?"

"We are so much alike that I feel like talking to you is like speaking to a reflection of me. And I've known me for twenty-four years. Maybe that's why we both find it so easy to talk to each other about anything."

"Boy, you sure are a lot more than physically different from my ex-wife."

"Thank you."

"You're quite welcome. Now considering we have the understanding that we can say and/or do anything, you'll understand that I have to go to work."

"Understand it? Yes. Like it? Hell no!"

"May I call you later?"

"May you? You'd better! What are you going to do?"

"Do you remember last night that I was on my way to investigate a clue when I got shot? I also promised the police officer that I'd make a written statement this morning. So I'm on my way to the police department."

"Are you going to be gone all day?"

"Well, when I'm on an investigation, I never know where things lead. I have some loose ends to tie up. I don't know how long it will take. It's Sunday. There's no telling how much can be accomplished."

Marci got up, picked up the dirty dishes, and put them in the sink. I think she purposely turned her back on me so I couldn't see her face. I got up, walked behind her, and put my arms around her. She leaned back into me and wrapped her arms on top of mine.

"I'll be back. You can count on it."

"Promise?"

"I promise."

"In that case, you can go. I'll miss you, but I'll be all right."

"You sure?"

She turned to face me and put her arms around my neck. I put my arms around her waist.

"You go do your job. I'm going to stay here and do all those little household things I need to get done."

"Come talk to me while I get dressed?"

"Sure."

Without another word, Marci followed me into the bedroom. I got dressed while she sat on the bed and watched. I took off my pants so I could put on some underwear. I noticed that Marci watched me intently, especially when I was naked. I took a little extra time before putting anything back on because I could tell she was enjoying watching me. She was sitting on the edge of the bed. Her legs were dangling slightly apart over the side. Her T-shirt had ridden up to about her waist. She wasn't wearing any underwear. She did nothing to pull it down. The sight of her was breathtaking. The first thing I did to get dressed was sit down on the first six inches of the chair, which I noticed no longer contained our outfit. I put on my socks. Then I sat up straight with my knees spread wide. I started talking about nothing in particular and everything in general. I noticed that Marci's stare was directed straight at my crotch. So I made sure I kept my hands out of the way so as not to block her view. She was sitting about six feet away. Because I was sitting on the front of the chair, my testicles hung down the front edge. So Marci had a good view of everything. At one point, I reached down and played with myself for a few seconds. Her eyes got wide, and her breathing got heavy. Keeping my ass cheeks in place on the chair, I leaned back in the chair.

"You really truly do enjoy looking at me, don't you?"

Her eyes came up to look at my face. "Yes, I do. Why? Do you find something wrong with that?"

"Absolutely not. It's just that I'm not used to a woman who will admit enjoying looking at the nude male body."

She looked back down. "Well, I don't really get a big thrill at looking at most naked male bodies. Occasionally, I'll see one that turns me on. But, oh, I do enjoy looking at yours. But I have to admit you are the very first person, male or female, I have ever told that to."

"I'm flattered."

I hated to end the show, but I had things I had to do. I reached over, got my clothes, and put them on. When I walked out of the bedroom and headed toward the front door, Marci followed closely. We were also back into that awkward silence again. At the door, I stopped and turned around. She was right there. I put out my arms, and she rushed to me. I experienced a small, stinging sensation in my left shoulder, but I ignored it.

"Call me later?" she asked softly.

"Of course."

"Please don't let anything happen to you out there."

"Don't worry. I won't."

"What do you mean? You've been shot already."

And beat up.

But I didn't say anything because she didn't know about that. I didn't want to add anything to her concern. I kissed her on the lips, reached under her T-shirt, and patted and squeezed her bare ass.

"See you later."

Then I was out the door in a flash.

CHAPTER 9

As I stepped down the steps of the brownstone, my heart rate was elevated. When I reached the sidewalk, my eyes were looking at everything within view. I wouldn't say I was paranoid but having someone take a shot at you tends to make you very cautious. This was the true feeling of déjà vu. Marci said she had looked out her window last night. I looked up. Sure enough, she was there. I smiled and waved. I was trying very hard not to show what I was feeling inside. She smiled and waved back.

I was extremely nervous until I was safely inside the car. As I stuck the keys in the ignition and turned them, I thought of the hoodlum crawling underneath the car in the parking lot. I quickly closed my eyes and tried to pull my head down between my shoulders. But the car's motor kicked to life. I heard nothing except the smooth hum of the motor. I opened my eyes and drove the hell out of there. Eventually, my heart rate returned to normal. I started to think straight.

I was mentally counting off what I was up against. *First, I can't see Benny right now. Second, it's the middle of the day. Third, he'd be holed up somewhere asleep.* Reluctantly I admitted to myself, *Well, I did promise Mike I'd tell him if I had anything concrete. But it is Sunday. I don't want to bother him on his day off. I'm supposed to file a report on last night's shooting. Hell, it could also wait.*

Home was the obvious place to go. I needed to change clothes and think this all out. So much had happened in the last forty-eight hours that it felt like I was returning home after a long-extended trip. Suddenly, the prospect of home seemed better and better. I then realized the same car, a dark sedan, was behind me. It had been there when I left Marci's place.

"Oh, shit!" I said quite loudly.

So far, all it had done was follow me. I tried not to panic, although I started to break out in a cold sweat. I tried to get a look at the license number, but mud or something covered it. I couldn't even make out a single number.

Well, this is a well-traveled road. Perhaps this is just my imagination at work. Well, let's find out.

At the very next side street, without any turn signal or warning, I made a last-minute sharp right turn and accelerated. I sped up the best I could. My car wasn't quite designed for Grand Prix operation. When I looked in my rearview mirror, there it was, bigger than life, squealing tires and all. The dark sedan appeared to growing larger as it was indeed accelerating to catch up with me. I made the very next left turn. I kept making every turn I could, alternating randomly between left and right turns. The sedan was faster and stronger than my car was, but, because mine was smaller, it was more maneuverable. I gained distance on the turns and lost distance between junctions. I was able to make enough turns to counteract the straight parts. He was still the same distance behind me. This went on for a good fifteen minutes. I was beginning to enjoy this game of cat and mouse until I almost hit a pedestrian. When I swerved to miss a young kid, I almost lost control and crashed. I came back under control just in time to miss a parked car. The sedan didn't even lower its speed at all. The young kid barely jumped out of the way in time. Apparently, the sedan wasn't going to slow its pursuit or swerve to miss the kid. At this point, I was beginning to get weary of this chase game and wanted a way out. After about another ten minutes, my break came. I went through an intersection just as the stoplight turned from yellow to red. The sedan had fallen just enough behind me that, when a car that had stopped for a red light on the right side of the intersection proceeded forward on the green light it had received, it pulled out into the sedan's oncoming path. In my rearview mirror, I saw the sedan try to stop, but it swerved sideways instead. It slammed directly into the other car already well into the intersection. I didn't wait around. I sped off. I made a few turns and breathed easier when I retained a blank rearview mirror. Amazingly, I never saw a cop the whole time I was in a high-speed chase through the city.

What is that old saying, "There's never a cop around when you need one."

The drive the rest of the way home was uneventful. But it did serve to make up my mind. I was going to pick up the notebook from home and then go see Mike immediately.

I lectured myself, "I don't care if it's his day off. This shit is getting out of hand. I'm an insurance investigator, not a private detective. There's a tremendous difference."

As I walked up to my apartment door, I felt something wasn't quite right. Then I noticed the door wasn't closed all the way.

That's not right.

I stood with my back to the hallway wall, really close to the door. I very easily pushed the door open about an inch or two. Then I listened. After two or three minutes of dead silence, I pushed the door all the way open. I flattened myself against the hallway wall with my back away from the door. When nothing or nobody flew through the door, I carefully peeked around the doorjamb into my apartment.

I sometimes got a little lazy and didn't pick up after myself, but what I now faced wasn't part of my poor housekeeping habits. The place was a total mess. It looked like someone had gone through every place and virtually ripped everything apart. The floor looked like the city dump. Somebody was either really pissed at me, or he had been looking for something. I walked in and then closed and locked the door behind me. I walked over the top of the rubble. There was no use being careful. Most everything was broken or torn open anyway. I went straight to the refrigerator. The door was partially open. Something was blocking it from closing all the way. I opened the door all of the way. A now-empty milk carton was lying on the floor in the middle of a puddle of milk. The container of bad corn was sitting on the shelf. It wasn't anywhere near the same spot I had left it. The lid was one-fourth of the way open, and the corn was still inside. But the smell coming from that container was enough to gag a maggot. I reached in, grabbed the container, went to the sink, and dumped the contents into the sink. Right there in the middle of the pile of stinky corn was the notebook, still wrapped in sandwich bags.

"What do you know? The old, smelly corn trick worked," I said aloud.

I turned on the water to wash off the corn from the plastic and sink and move it into the garbage disposal. I turned on the disposal while I removed the notebook from the plastic bags. The mess in the sink didn't matter because it matched the rest of the place, but the smell was about to make me sick. By the time I got the notebook out of the bags and had found the trash can tipped over and empty, all the bad corn was ground up and gone. I tossed the old bags at the trash can and turned off the disposal. I put the notebook in my back pocket, along with the letter Marci gave me.

I reached over and picked up the telephone receiver that was dangling from the cord, only an inch or two off the floor. I held down the reset button for a few seconds. When I released the button, I heard the dial tone. I dialed the twelfth precinct police department. Sergeant Lewis, the desk sergeant, whom I also know a little, answered the phone.

After a few pleasantries, I said, "I think today is Lieutenant Glosman's day off, but I'm not real sure. Do you know if he's in?"

"He was in earlier this morning for only a few minutes. He

mentioned something about having to mow his lawn this afternoon. You might try him at home."

"Thanks a lot, Sergeant Lewis. You take it easy."

"Oh, I will, and you do the same."

We hung up the receivers together. I found my phone book relatively intact and not far away. I didn't call Mike at home very often, so I didn't have it memorized. I knew Mike's phone number was listed so it didn't take long to find it.

After about six rings, his wife answered. "Hello."

"Hello, Sharon. This is James Peterson. How are you doing?"

I'd had dinner at their house several times over the years so I wasn't an unfamiliar voice or name.

"I'm fine. How are you doing?"

"Actually, I've been kept quite busy. I'm even working weekends these days."

"If you're working that hard, I know you don't have time to eat properly. Why don't you have Mike bring you by the house occasionally for dinner?"

"I'll have to do that. Thank you, Sharon."

"Don't mention it. I suppose you'd like to talk to him?"

"Yes, I sure would."

"Well, he's mowing the lawn out back. I'm sure he'll be glad for a reason to take a break. Hold on. I'll get him."

"Okay."

A few minutes later, I heard Mike pick up the phone. "Hey, James, what's up?"

"I'm sorry to bother you at home on your day off."

"That's okay. I could use the break."

I could hear Sharon chuckle in the background. I could imagine Mike giving her a dirty look. Then again, he wasn't aware of the side joke.

"I'm sure you won't mind even more when you hear what I have to say."

I could hear the sudden interest increase in his voice. "What?"

"I know it's asking a lot, but I'd rather not talk about it over the phone. You never know who's listening."

"Acting a bit paranoid, aren't you?"

"Remember when we were talking yesterday? And I told you that, if I had anything more to tell you about what I was asking you questions about, you'd be the first one I told?"

"Yes?" A questioning tone was in his voice.

"Well, I've got a lot to tell you."

"How soon can you get here?"

"Actually, Mike, that's not a very good idea." I could tell by the sharp suddenness of his voice sense he was really on alert.

"Where and when?"

"My place as soon as you can get your ass here."

"I'll be there in about thirty minutes."

We both hung up. I looked around, and I had mixed feelings. I was somewhere between anger that someone had violated the sanctity of my privacy and depression that everything I owned was trashed. Then the thought hit me.

Maybe I ought not to be in here. Someone is anxious to get what I got. They know where I've been and where I live. They are apparently keeping track of what I'm doing.

I went into my bedroom, which was equally trashed. With all that had happened lately the only thing I had that could have caused this kind of destruction was obviously looking the notebook. Because of good old smelly old corn I still had it.

I said proudly to myself, *Since the notebook is still in place They sure didn't find what they were looking for here. Else, they wouldn't have torn the place apart so completely.*

They even included my mattress, which was off the box springs. I trudged around until I found what I was looking for. I moved my dresser, so I could get to the back. I looked around until I found a screwdriver and removed a small square panel off the back of the dresser. I reached inside and pulled out my loaded nine-millimeter pistol, two extra clips fully loaded, a box of shells, and a shoulder harness. I kept it hidden like this because I didn't trust my landlady. I wasn't totally sure the individual I had bought it from had gotten it through a legal source. No serial number was anywhere on the weapon.

I was able to finally find some clean and unwrinkled clothes. I quickly got dressed, including putting on the shoulder harness with the gun, and got the hell out of there. I made it outside with about fifteen minutes to wait before Mike arrived. I stood in the entranceway of the building across the street, so I could keep an eye on the entrance to my building. I wasn't there more than three minutes when the same dark sedan drove up in front. Two men got out. I couldn't make out the driver very clearly. I had never seen any of the individuals before. The two who got out were both dressed similar in casual weekend-type clothes. Both looked average with brown hair and were of average heights. They went inside and came back out in about five minutes. The sedan came back. They climbed in and parked down the street.

Ten minutes later, right on schedule, Mike came driving down the street. I went out into the street. He wasn't going very fast. I assumed he was looking for a parking space. I didn't want him to park. Because he was moving slowly, I walked out in front of his car. It wasn't hard for him to stop in time. I walked around to the passenger side. He reached over and unlocked the door. I opened it and climbed in.

"Keep driving," I said as soon as I was inside.

He did as I requested. "Where to?"

"Right now? Anywhere. And see that black sedan?" I pointed it out as we went past. I turned around to watch the car in the rear window.

"Yes. What about it?"

"It may follow us."

"Why?"

"I'll tell you in a minute. I want to see if they do indeed follow us."

They did. After we passed them, they pulled out and made a U-turn. They were not far behind us.

Mike saw the whole thing in his rearview mirror. "All right, James. What's up?"

"Those may be the same people who killed Branning and took a shot at me last night."

"Yeah, I heard about that. How are you involved in all this? Are you all right?"

"I'm fine. It's just a flesh wound. Nothing serious. What are you going to do about those guys?" I pointed back at the dark sedan.

He grinned. "Not a problem. They picked the wrong person to fuck with."

He reached down and quite unnoticeably picked up the mike to his radio. He was driving his own personal unmarked car, but he did have a police band radio installed. After a few quick radio calls, he turned to give me a quick look.

"As long as they follow us for another five minutes, they'll be sorry they even got up this morning."

I soon learned what he meant. As we turned onto a major boulevard, four marked police cars suddenly appeared out of nowhere and completely surrounded the sedan as we drove down the street. With lights flashing, they forced the sedan to stop at the side of the road. We kept going.

I turned to Mike. "Aren't we going to see who they are?

"No, the officers will take care of that and let me know. Meanwhile, you and I are going to talk."

"You aren't kidding but take me back to my apartment first. I want to show you something."

He looked at me suspiciously but didn't say a word.

"Mike, listen to me. I might have a career maker for you here.

I think this is going to be a big one by the time it's finished. My only condition is that you not stop me from following up on my investigation."

"What investigation?"

"I'm about to tell you if you give me that guarantee. I won't make it a condition that you help me. That wouldn't be fair to you. But I will insist that you promise not to stop or hinder me."

I sweated through several seconds while he stuttered. "Okay, but I won't help you with anything illegal."

"That's a deal."

"Then what the hell do you have?"

"I'm going to tell it to you in the same sequence I found it out. So this may be a long story."

"We have plenty of time. So, start at the beginning."

"Late Friday afternoon, I was walking home in that nasty rainstorm. I passed by the exact spot where Branning was shot earlier in the day, although I didn't know it at the time. As I was walking along, I found this key lying on the sidewalk."

He looked at me incredulously.

"At the time, because I didn't know anything about the shooting, I didn't associate the key with anything. For some reason or other, I scooped up the key and put it in my pocket without thinking about it. Anyway, when I got home that night, I saw the news broadcast. That's when I first heard about the shooting, though I still didn't make much of a connection between the key and Branning. I came to see you the next morning. I followed a lead you gave me and checked further."

"What lead did I give you?"

"I went to see that secretary you told me about. Her name is Marci Ann Johnson." Just mentioning her name brought a rush of feelings all over me. "She told me they were good friends but nothing more, though she did confirm a lot of the other things you told me. She did say he used to flirt a lot with every woman he met. But she wasn't aware of any extramarital affairs. She said his wife kept very close tabs on him. You know about his office bets, but he also bet quite heavily at the horse track. He might have had some very heavy gambling debts. The morning before he was killed, he was at the secretary's place and reviewing some files. She was on vacation, and he was supposed to be leaving town that afternoon. Probably it couldn't wait until she came back to work. She said he took those files with him when he left."

"There were no files on him when he was discovered."

"I heard. I asked if she knew anything about any kind of place where the key I found might fit. Like a storage area. She said the only thing she knew about was his bowling locker. I went to the bowling alley. The key I found fit his bowling locker."

"How did you know it was his locker?"

"A nametag was on the bowling bag inside the locker. It had his name and home address on it."

We pulled up inside the parking garage of my apartment building, but we didn't get out of the car right away.

"Before we go up, I need to show you something." I pulled out the notebook and letter. I handed him the notebook first. "I found this in his bowling bag."

He opened it. I held my breath that he wouldn't notice the missing first page. He didn't because he looked completely through it very carefully.

"This is very interesting." He turned and looked at me. "Do you know who belongs to the names in this book?"

"I recognize some of the investment companies, but that's about it. Why?"

"I'm talking about the people who are listed."

"No. Should I?"

"Perhaps not, but I figure a few of them should have caught your attention."

"What's so special about them?"

"Listed in here are some of the biggest names in organized crime." He opened the book to the second page and pointed to one of the names. "Right here. A. Gionetti is Anthony Gionetti, the undisputed kingpin of this area. Several of the other names, I've had the distinct displeasure of dealing with them on a personal basis. Others I have only known by reputation. They're from another area. This book is not enough to bring anyone to jail. But I'm sure the IRS would love to have its hands on this."

I handed him the letter. "This arrived at the secretary's house yesterday afternoon."

He opened the letter and read it through twice. "You aren't kidding. This is a career maker. Do you have anything else?"

"Just a few more clues that I dug up while talking to some of the other people. I talked to his wife. Quite some lady, isn't she?"

He gave me a look that told me he was trying to figure out if I were speaking seriously or sarcastically. I wasn't quite sure myself.

"She reaffirmed his gambling tendencies and said he traveled a lot. She said he told her where he would be going, but she was never sure where he actually went because he wouldn't let her ever call him. In fact, she said she wouldn't always hear from him on every trip. This tends to make me think that he wouldn't always go where he said he would."

"The secretary also told me that closed-door meetings often happened at their office. Participants would be several businessmen with bodyguards."

"Bodyguards?"

"Yep, bodyguards. Several, big, mean-looking ones. She said Branning was always in on those meetings. He seemed to be their personal accountant."

"This is beginning to form an interesting picture." Mike flipped through the notebook.

"It gets brighter. After I left Mrs. Branning's house, I stopped at some grocery store to pick up something for dinner. When I came out, three, very tough-looking, young hoodlums were messing with my car. We scuffled a little, and they left. I checked over the car thoroughly and couldn't find anything wrong. I went home. I didn't think much of it. After I got here, and I was about to climb into the elevator, someone slugged me from behind. As I lay on the ground, I heard a voice say to stop investigating the Branning affair or I'd wish I'd get the treatment he got. I recognized the voice as belonging to the apparent leader of the three hoodlums who had just been messing with my car a few minutes earlier. Then last night, the secretary called me to say she had received that letter. She hadn't opened it and didn't know what to do with it."

"Why did she call you and not the police?"

"I don't know. Maybe she thought I was prettier. How the hell am I supposed to know?"

"Yeah, right."

I ignored his sarcasm. "As I was leaving her apartment with the letter, someone took a shot at me."

"I heard about that. Apparently, you're all right." He showed a moment of concern, but it didn't last for long. "But the reporting officer called me and said you refused to give a statement. You said you'd call me in the morning. James, you know that's not how it's done." All concern was gone from his voice.

"That's not exactly true. I told him everything I knew about the shooting, and that was absolutely nothing. As I was walking to the car, I never heard the shot, but I felt the bullet. That's all I know. I didn't see anything. But the secretary who had looked out the window said she saw a dark-colored sedan pulling away quickly after I went down."

"That vaguely fits the description of the car that was seen leaving the scene of the Branning murder."

"It also fits the car that followed me this morning and us just a little while ago."

"Yes, it does."

"There's one more piece to the puzzle."

"What's that?"

"Come with me. I'll show you." I got out of the car.

Neither one of us said too much on the way up to my apartment. I imagined Mike was deep in thought while analyzing the new information I had given him. I was deep in thought about Marci. I was reliving our sexual encounter from last night in rapid replay. I didn't know why I chose that moment to think about that, but I did. Perhaps that was why I didn't react as quickly as I should have when the elevator opened. There stood Puke Face and his buddies. Mike didn't know who they were, so he didn't know to react. But the three hoodlums sure did. The instant they saw me, they took off down the hall.

I came to my senses and yelled, "That's them!"

By the time I got out of the elevator, the last of the hoodlums was just ducking into the stairway.

I started after them until I heard Mike yell, "You'll never catch them!"

I slowed to a stop. Then I walked dejectedly back to the elevator. By now, Mike was standing in the hallway.

"Those were the punks who have been giving me problems. The one in front was Puke Face."

"Puke Face?"

"Well, I've been calling him that. He didn't seem to like it."

"I guess not."

We both had a short laugh and proceeded to my apartment. When we got in front of my door, I could see that it was partially open.

"I guess I know where Puke Face was."

I pushed the door all the way open and led Mike into the apartment. I walked to the center of the room and spread out my arms.

"Home sweet home."

"Hey, James, I know your housekeeping abilities were lacking, but I didn't think they were this bad."

"Smart-ass!"

"Whoever did this sure was looking for something." He left

me standing in the center of the room and looked in every other room. He came back. "And judging from the looks of the destruction, they sure didn't find what they were looking for."

"No, you have it."

"The notebook?"

"What else could it be?"

"Nothing I know of."

"Me neither."

"You must be on the right track somewhere. Else, somebody wouldn't be going to all this trouble."

"That's the way I figure."

"And where do you figure to go from here?"

"I'm not really sure. Maybe I could check to see if Branning had any real gambling debts. I could possibly follow up any leads that might come from those guys you had picked up."

"Speaking of which, let me check on that." He looked around and even kicked a few things out of the way that were lying around on the floor. "Where the hell is your phone?"

"In the kitchen."

He made his way to the kitchen phone and started dialing. After about three phone calls and ten minutes of heated conversation, he hung up for the final time and came walking toward me.

"That proved fruitless."

"What do you mean? Who were they?"

"A couple of out-of-town boys who didn't say a word until their lawyer arrived in record time after their one phone call. Then they were gone in less than five minutes. You can bet your last dollar that they won't ever be seen around here again."

"Who was their lawyer?"

"Very good, James. You're still as sharp as ever. Anthony Jones of Jones, Jones, and Scarpozi."

"Didn't Scarpozi represent that big mobster in last year's sensational trial of that crime family?"

"The very one."

"Now that's very interesting."

We both took a minute and looked around at the mess.

"I'm sure not looking forward to cleaning up this mess."

"Before you do, I put in a call to have some lab boys come over and take a look around. They should be here in a few minutes."

"What do you hope to find? There's no way I could even tell if anything is missing."

"Who knows? But it won't hurt. Besides, we definitely wouldn't find anything if we don't look."

"I guess that's true."

I quickly ran through my mental checklist to see if there was anything here I didn't want the police to find. I already had my gun removed and in my possession. I had the front page of the notebook, along with the airline ticket, in my wallet. I couldn't think of anything else, so I relaxed on that score.

Mike said, "We might as well wait out in the hall until they get here. That way, we won't disturb anything."

"Disturb anything! Hell, a bomb could go off in here, and you wouldn't be able to tell the difference."

He gave me a disgusted look and went out the door and into the hall. I followed right behind him and closed the door. We spent about ten minutes of useless chatter until the lab boys arrived. I gave them the key to my front door.

Mike turned to me. "Let's go, guy."

"Where?"

"Sharon made me promise to bring you home for dinner. She said bachelors don't eat right. So, are you coming with me?"

"But I have several things I have to get done."

I was thinking more of seeing Marci than anything else, but I didn't want to tell that to Mike.

"Look, I have to live with this woman. You're coming home with me if I have to place you under house arrest. Besides, you can't stay in this mess. We'll go to my house and talk further about this. You can get a hot meal and a warm bed, and you can attack this in the morning."

"But—"

"No buts allowed. I won't take no for an answer." He didn't give me the chance for an answer. He turned and walked out.

When we were downstairs, I got into my borrowed car and followed Mike home. Somewhere along the drive, I discreetly removed my gun and holster and hid them under the car seat. I didn't figure it would be a good idea to wear an unlicensed, concealed weapon into a police officer's house, especially because I had told him that I didn't have a gun. That wouldn't have been one of my brighter moments.

CHAPTER 10

The early Sunday dinner was indeed excellent. I had forgotten what a real home-cooked meal was like, even if it were just plain roast beef and potatoes. My taste buds were very grateful that Mike had insisted. But other parts of me were yearning to see Marci. Mike and Sharon's teenage son and daughter were off doing whatever teenagers do on a Sunday evening. The three of us were sitting around the dinner table and having a cup of coffee. We had all shared in clearing the table. Mike and Sharon had objected at first to my assistance, but they gave up and let me help when I insisted.

The sharp ring of the telephone interrupted the light conversation. Sharon got up and answered the telephone in the kitchen. She came back in about one minute.

"Mike, it's the station." She sat down as Mike went into the kitchen.

I liked and respected Sharon because, no matter what, she never acted overly concerned that I was all alone. She never tried to set me up with anyone or pushed me to find someone. I wasn't really that close to Mike and Sharon, but they were good friends. When I was still married and living at home, they had dinner at our house about once a month. Because of Mike and my jobs, once my ex and I split up, they kept our friendship. Because the relationship was based on Mike and me, they eventually lost contact with my ex-wife.

"Once again, Sharon, I want to thank you for that fine dinner. It was kind of you to think of me."

"You are very welcome, but it was nothing special. Just dinner."

"Well, it was delicious. If the offer still stands, I'm going to have to show up for dinner more often."

"Of course, it does. And you don't need an invitation. Just let me know ahead of time enough so I know I've made plenty for everyone."

"Okay. That's a deal."

"Good. Now that it's settled, I'll expect to see you a little more often than once every couple of months."

We were both chuckling over that one when Mike came back in the room and sat down. "They didn't find anything. But the lab experts say the place appeared to be professionally searched to include the food containers in the refrigerator."

I had just taken a drink of my coffee. It was all I could do not to choke.

"But they said they found an interesting empty hiding hole in the back of a dresser. Do you know anything about that, James?"

"Yes, as a matter of fact, I do." I made a rapid decision if I wanted to tell Mike about my gun or not. "I used to store a pistol in there when I lived with my ex-wife. She refused to allow any firearms in the house. I always felt the need to have one available. I used to keep one hidden in there. She never knew, and I managed to get the dresser when we separated."

"Was there a gun in there when they searched your place?"

"No, I didn't have the need to hide one there because I lived alone."

"Where did you keep your gun?" His eyes narrowed slightly as he watched my actions.

"I didn't. I had no one to protect anymore."

I could see Mike didn't quite believe me, but Sharon interjected before he could challenge me. "How about you?"

I looked at her sheepishly. "That wasn't necessary."

Mike said, "It may be necessary now. Think about it."

"Okay, I will."

I sometimes felt like a real scum bucket for lying. I didn't this time. I felt like it was required for several reasons.

"Well, now that dinner is over you, I have some work to do," Mike said.

I looked at him in surprise. "What are you talking about?"

He first looked at Sharon and then me. Apparently, he didn't want to say much in front of her.

The less she knows, the less that can hurt her.

"We're going to sit down and go over that book completely from front to back."

"Oh, great. Mike, I got other plans."

"Cancel them!"

Sharon started to say something. But the look Mike gave her stopped her dead. Suddenly, Friend Mike was gone and Lieutenant Glosman had taken his place.

"James, some very deep-reaching things are going on here. I'm not going to let it rest." His tone had slowly grown softer, but not by much.

I sat back in my chair and just looked at him. He just looked back. After a little while, I shook my head. "I guess I don't have much choice, now do I?"

"No, you don't."

"Mike," Sharon said.

He ignored her.

I asked, "May I use your telephone for a private call?"

Sharon answered. "Of course you can, Jim. You can use the one in our bedroom."

"Thank you."

I got up and went into the bedroom. I stopped by the door and listened. As soon as it shut, I heard Sharon jump all over Mike. I couldn't understand everything she was saying, but I could tell it wasn't pleasant. It was something about us being friends though. With a grin of satisfaction, I went over, sat down on the side of the bed, and picked up the telephone off the nightstand. I dialed Marci's number.

She answered after two rings. "Hello."

The very sound of her voice caused my heartbeat to accelerate. "Hi, Marci. This is Jim."

"Hi, honey!"

"What are you up to?"

"Missing you. Where are you?"

"I'm having dinner over at a friend's house."

Her voice got meek. "Friend? What kind of friend?"

It took an effort to choke down a giggle. After all, it had been a long time since someone had cared enough about me to be jealous.

"It's Mike and Sharon Glosman. They've been friends of mine for a very long time. In fact, I'm practically godfather to their children."

"Oh, did you have a good dinner?" The happy uplift was back in her voice.

"Yes, I did. It has been a while since I've had a real home-cooked meal."

"I'll just have to make sure you don't have to wait a long time again."

"I'll have to take you up on that."

"Am I going to see you tonight?"

"Based on what's going on, I don't think that's possible."

"What do you mean?"

"Sometime yesterday, my apartment was trashed."

"Trashed?"

"Yeah. Somebody completely tore my place apart while looking for something."

"What were they looking for?"

How much do I want to tell this lovely lady? I mentally counted of on my fingers as I applied a soft pressure on each finger of my right hand. *First, this concerns information that people are willing to kill for. Second, I'm dealing with a Swiss-numbered account that may or may not have a great deal of money. It's another great motivator for murder. Third, I don't know if the telephone line is bugged or not. I'm not worried about Mike and Sharon's phone, but, because Marci works for the company under question, I'm not sure what the thugs might be up to.*

"That's what Mike and I are going to try to figure out. We'll probably be up half the night attempting that."

"When you get done, call me and tell me good night. I'll feel much better that way."

"It might be in the middle of the night or wee hours of the morning."

"That's okay. I don't mind at all. In fact, I'm sure it will help me to sleep better if the last thing I hear is your voice."

"Okay, I will. I don't want to go, but I have to."

"I understand. I miss you, and I love you."

I hesitated a bit. "Me, too."

I heard just a short intake of breath as she realized I almost said, "I love you."

"I'll call you later. Sleep well."

"Oh, I will. Not as good as if you were here, but I will."

"Good-bye."

"Good-bye."

Apparently, she was waiting for me to hang up first, so I did. Then I sat there and thought about her. I wanted to pick the phone back up, call her, and tell her how much I really cared and missed her, but I didn't. Instead, I got up and walked out of the bedroom.

Mike was still sitting at the table. Sharon was watching TV in the living room. I sat down and saw that Mike had the notebook and a pad of paper in front of him. He was busily making notes as he closely examined every page. After a several minutes, he looked up.

"This is extremely interesting. If we can absolutely connect the Browning Investment Group with some of the names in this notebook, then we have a major case."

"Why? Are some really big names in there?"

"Are you kidding? Some of the names in this book are some of the very top names in organized crime. The rest are various members of the lower hierarchy. What a coup this would be if we could indeed connect all of this."

"No wonder my place was torn apart. If they knew of this book, then they'd go to any lengths to get it back." We spent the next two and a half hours dissecting, bisecting, and trisecting the book. We'd broken it down as far as we could to include a separate list of all the names in the book.

Mike said, "I'll take this into work tomorrow and run it through the computer. We'll see if there are any known connections between these names and the Browning Investment Group."

I looked at my watch and saw it was ten minutes after ten. "I think I'm going to take a little run out and check something."

"Where are you going this time of night?"

"I'm going to check out a source who might give me some insight on Branning's gambling habits. I want to find out if he was into anybody for a lot of money."

"Do you want me to come along?"

"I wouldn't mind, except that, where I'm going, these guys can smell a cop from five miles away. Then I wouldn't get anywhere."

"You're liable to get yourself hurt messing around with those types."

"No, I don't think so. I know a few of them. They somewhat trust me."

"But can you trust them?"

"I'll be fine."

"Let me give you a key to the front door so you can get in when you get back. I'll have Sharon leave out some blankets. Sorry, the only thing we have is the couch, but it's comfortable."

"You don't have to do that. I may be getting in quite late. I can find someplace else to stay for the night."

"I don't want to hear it. You're a guest here until you get your place cleaned up."

"Well, Mike, to tell you the truth, I do have somewhere else to spend the night. And she's a lot prettier than you."

"You old son of a bitch you. Why didn't you tell me?"

"I wasn't really sure until I talked to her earlier."

"So that's what the private telephone call was all about. Who is she?"

"Oh, someone I met. I'll introduce her to you sometime. I'm not sure yet if it's serious or not."

"It's serious enough that you're sleeping with her."

I got a little embarrassed. "Yeah, what the hell. Even an old fart is entitled to some companionship."

"Sharon will be glad to hear you have someone in your life. She's been a little worried about you."

"Don't say anything to her until I'm sure where it's going."

"All right, but she'll kill me if she finds out I knew and didn't tell her."

"I won't tell her if you don't."

CHAPTER 11

About ten forty-five, I pulled into a section of town I really didn't like being at this time of night. But I knew that, if I wanted to talk to Benny, I had no option. Also, I still had my gun. It gave me some comfort. I was in the very heart of downtown. Nightlife in this city was almost as busy as noon in most cities in America. The strip joints, bars, and liquor stores were all in full fling. At least two hookers were on every corner, and business was good. I wasn't a total stranger to this neighborhood. Many of my investigations had led me here before. A full sample of every race, creed, and lack of religion roamed the streets. I parked my car on a busy street and walked the block and a half to the pool hall. I wasn't bothered much, and only two ladies of the night propositioned me.

Immediately upon entering the place, I stopped to look around. Most of the people looked at me to see who I was. They must have realized I wasn't a cop because they went back to what they were doing, except for one huge, black man. He got up off his chair and walked straight over to me. He was so tall that the top of his head traveled through the cloudy layer of smoke that was hanging from the ceiling. I quickly but as casually as possible looked around the room to see if I could find Benny. Just before the behemoth got in front of me, I spotted him sitting in the back of the room. Benny was watching a pool game being played on the coin-operated table located in one of the corners of the bar. I knew he saw me when I came in. Benny never missed anything.

"Man, what you want in here?" I heard a deep rumble fall on my head.

"I want to see Benny."

"There ain't a Benny in here."

I looked up at him with the hardest look I could muster. "Then that person back there with the blue sweater will be awful angry when he loses the money I was about to place on his business."

He stared down on me with a menacing look that was hard enough to break concrete. I knew that, if I even flinched the slightest, I'd find myself thrown right out on my ass. I used every bit of self-control I had to just stare right back. The fact I had my pistol in my shoulder harness helped, but I somehow felt that, against this guy, it would only piss him off. Finally, without saying a word, he just stepped aside. Keeping with the flow, I walked on past without saying a word. I did breathe a sigh of relief after I was a few steps past him. The seat to Benny's left suddenly became vacant. I walked up to it and sat down. Still, I kept quiet. I could feel that several sets of eyes were watching me very closely. But I sat still and watched the game that was going on right in front of us. I recognized that Benny was intently watching every shot. I knew that, if I wanted him to talk to me, I dared not interrupt him while he was working.

I took the opportunity to look over Benny, a light-skinned black man in his mid-fifties. He was clean-shaven except for a pencil-thin mustache. He had relatively short hair. He wore a black derby-type hat. He had on a blue turtleneck sweater, a dark pair of slacks, and a very expensive-looking pair of loafer shoes. Four shots later, one guy sank the eight ball and won. There wasn't a lot of cheering, but several voices erupted in sudden conversation. A lot of money exchanged hands. Benny, of course, only collected, from about four different individuals. I very seldom saw or heard of him losing.

After the voices settled and Benny put his money away, he sat back. "James, my man, how's it going?"

"Same old shit. You know, just trying to stay ahead of the bill collector. It looks as if you're doing a good job of that."

"Never a problem if you don't owe anybody anything."

"Yeah, I guess that's true." I paused a second to make it seem like I wasn't pushing for anything. "Heard any good rumors lately?"

I saw him give me a quick glance out of the side of his eye before he sat back and gave a few signals to the previous winner on the pool table. A new victim proceeded to rack the balls for the next game.

"I heard a ten-to-one shot filly is running tomorrow at Santa Belina in the fifth. Word has it that she might have some good winds on her back." Benny and I had interacted enough over the years that he understood my hint that I needed some information from him.

"You don't say."

I recognized this as a request for ten dollars if I were to get any answers from him. I knew he didn't need the money. It was more a matter of principle to him that no one got something for free. I reached into my pocket and pulled out all my money. I tried to make it obvious that fourteen dollars was all I had. I had used the rest on gas for my borrowed car. I handed him ten dollars.

"Put this on the nose of that sweet, little lady."

"You're covered." He pocketed the money. "Come with me. I'll let you buy me a beer."

I got up and followed him to a door in the back of the bar. I felt several sets of eyes boring holes in my back as he opened the door. I followed him into the room. After I closed the door, I looked back. Benny was sitting behind a small desk. He didn't offer me a chair to sit on so I walked over in front of the desk and stood still.

"What kind of information do you want?" he finally asked.

I knew that every minute of his time I took was potentially taking money out of his pocket. I got right to the point. "I want to know everything I can about the gambling habits of a man named

Joseph Branning." He worked down town…" I started to tell him a little bit about who Joseph Branning might be, but I didn't have to.

"It's a shame he got his ass blown away."

"What do you mean?"

"The man must have made a big score. Rumor has it that he just paid off a big gambling debt and was in the clear. So why would someone want to burn him?"

"That's what I'm trying to find out."

"The way I understand it, he was up over fifty gees until the day before his body found some new ventilation."

"If he was paid up, why would someone want to kill him?"

I think I know the answer, but I don't want Benny to know I knew.

"Your guess."

"Who did he owe the money to?"

"Hey, man, you know that names aren't important down here in the streets." That was his way of saying he knew, but wasn't going to tell me.

"Yeah, I understand. Is there anything else you can tell me?"

He just shrugged his shoulders and smiled.

"Thanks, Benny. If you hear anything else, let me know." I reached inside my wallet and laid out a card on his desk. "Right now, all I have to my name is four dollars. I'll make it up to you later."

"You do that."

"Oh, I will."

Not another word was said as I turned and walked out of his office. I didn't get five feet into the pool hall before the behemoth stood in my way. He remained frozen there until Benny came out of the room and nodded that everything was okay. Then he quietly stepped aside and let me pass.

As I walked out of the pool hall, I felt many eyes still on me. This time, it felt more like respect because I was all right with

Benny. After all, I'd just had a private meeting with him. But I did feel a lot safer once I was back on the streets even though the street itself wasn't exactly a sanctuary.

I got back in the car and started to drive off. I had no idea where I was going, but I knew I was getting out of this part of town. I thought about what Benny had told me. Branning must have had a huge score if he could pay off a $50,000 gambling debt and still have enough money to skip town.

Once again I was talking out loud to myself. If anyone could see me they would think I was looney. Talking away with no one else in the card. "Why did he pay off a big debt if he were about to leave town and not come back? Unless the people he owed the money to were big and/or mean enough that he could never totally hide from them."

This created a disturbing thought. It wouldn't wash that he paid the debt because he was worried about them taking it out on his family after he left. Granted, they'd do that, but, if he were running out on them, then chances were that he didn't care enough about them to worry. A long time ago, I might have thought he would have cared, but, over the years, I realized there are some people in the world whose only concern is their own welfare. *It's another one of those pieces of the puzzle that just don't fit.*

I drove around for another ten minutes and let my mind just wander. Sometimes, by free associating like that, it would allow the pieces to fall into place. I'd see a better picture, but not this time. I finally decided I'd give Marci a call. It took a few minutes before I found a pay phone in a quiet business part of town. There weren't any people around this time of night. There wasn't anything but empty buildings, the pay phone, and me. I walked up in front of the phone and reached into my pocket. I then realized I didn't even have the change to make the call.

I turned to go back to the car and noticed a dark sedan coming down the street from my left. It was headed in my direction. Maybe I was paranoid, but I slowly reached into my jacket and took hold of my pistol. I casually pulled it out. As I reached the side of my car, I momentarily turned my back to the oncoming car, so the occupants couldn't see what I was doing. I checked the safety to make sure it was off. Then I cocked a round into the chamber. Then I took a few more steps so I was behind the hood of my car. I turned to watch the sedan approach. Sure enough, just as it reached the rear of my car, the passenger window came down. A short-barreled shotgun was pointed in my direction. I quickly squatted down behind the fender, aimed my pistol right at the shotgun, and pulled the trigger at the same time a very loud explosion of shotgun pellets flew past where my head and body would have been if I hadn't squatted down. I must have been more accurate with my shot because no more shotgun blasts came my way. The shotgun had jerked back into the car. I didn't stop with just one shot. I kept pulling off rounds as fast as my finger could pull the trigger. The sedan didn't stop during all of this, so I had to continue to aim further right as I shot. The driver must have suddenly realized what was happening as the car lurched forward and accelerated away. I continued to fire until I ran out of ammunition. The sedan then disappeared into the night.

I quickly jumped into my car to give chase, but it was of no use. The sedan was gone. I pulled over to the side of the road. I replaced the magazine with an already-loaded one. I started to reload the now empty magazine with more bullets I had gotten out of a spare box I put in the glove compartment. My fingers wouldn't quite cooperate as the adrenaline withdrawal reaction set in. My hands shook so much that I couldn't accomplish the task. I just sat there and shook for a while until I finally was able to get myself back under control. I didn't keep track of how long I sat there. It must have been a while. Finally, not only could I reload my pistol, I could drive safely. But my mind was still racing at top speed. I contemplated calling the police.

The old sports saying came to mind, "No harm, no foul."

I finally realized that, if there weren't anyone around to have heard the shots, no one would be calling the police. It also meant I was sitting there all alone. I started the car and drove off. After that, I didn't really remember what I thought about.

On instinct, I pulled into my parking space at my apartment. Still operating on automatic, I got out of my car and walked up to my apartment.

Shuffling along I thought, *Well, no little elves came by and straightened up.*

I double-checked to make sure my door was locked securely. Then I went over to the phone and called Mike. By now, it was close to one o'clock, so my call woke him up. He was a little grumpy until I told him what had happened. I was a little apprehensive about telling him how I had returned fire, but, if I had indeed hit someone, it might help them if any gunshot wounds were reported. He never questioned me about how and when I got a gun. He probably already knew. I hadn't told him the complete truth about the hiding compartment in my dresser. After about thirty minutes of conversation with him, we hung up. I then instantly called Marci. She answered on the second ring.

I heard her sleepy and throaty sexy voice. "Hello."

"Boy, you even sound sexy when you're asleep."

Her voice perked up as she recognized my voice. "I can't think of a better sound than your voice to wake up to."

"In that case, we'll have to make sure that happens more often."

"I'd really like that."

"Me, too."

There was a slight pause while I could hear her give a soft moan. I could picture her stretching the sleepiness out of her body. I had a visualization of her lovely body all tense. I had the picture of her lying on her back with her arms over her head as her perfectly shaped, large breasts stuck straight out.

I came back to reality when I heard her say, "Are you still there?"

"Oh, yes. I could tell you were stretching. I was picturing what you looked like in my mind."

"What did you see?"

"The most heavenly sight a man could be treated to."

"I don't know about that, but I'm all yours."

"You're still sure about that, are you?"

"Without a doubt."

"Miracles will never cease to happen."

"What do you mean?"

"Only that I'm a very lucky man to have you care about me."

"I feel very fortunate to have someone like you who could make me feel this complete. I sure do miss you. I wish you were here right now. I'd do things to you that would make you feel a whole lot more than lucky."

I let out a soft moan. "I sure do wish I could."

"Why can't you? Where are you?"

"I'm at home. I've got some work to do here before I can go to work tomorrow."

"That's not fair. I want you very badly." I swore I could hear the pout in her voice.

"So do I. But we both must go to work in a few hours. I have a lot of work I have to get accomplished tonight."

"I understand, but that doesn't mean I can't want you."

"I wouldn't have it any other way. I'd wonder if you didn't feel that way."

"Oh, I do. You can count on that."

"I definitely will."

"I'll hold you to that."

"Well, sweetheart, I need to let you go so you won't be too tired for work tomorrow. Considering it's Monday, I'm sure you'll have plenty to do."

"But I don't want to go. That means I won't be able to hear your voice anymore."

"I'll tell you what. How about we have dinner out tomorrow

night? Or should I say tonight? Then we can spend the entire evening together."

"You've got a date."

"Good. I'll pick you up at your place at six o'clock, if that's okay with you?"

"That will be just fine. I'm already looking forward to it."

"So am I. In the meantime, we both need to get some sleep. The quicker we do, the closer it will be until I see you again."

"Jimmy?"

"Yes, Marci?"

"Do you really care for me? I'm not just someone for you to get a few thrills with and then be on your way, am I?"

"I can tell you that it is very, very hard for me to say the 'L' word, but it's not hard for me to say that my feelings for you are genuine and very deep. It just scares the shit out of me. Excuse my language. It just scares me to death to think I really feel this strongly for you in such a short period of time. My head is screaming at me with all these warning lights and whistles that I'm just going to get hurt again. But my heart says, 'Screw you, head. She's the real one. Damn the torpedoes! Full speed ahead!' It's quite a conflict."

"Don't worry about it. I'm not going to hurt you. You mean too much to me."

"But what if I do something stupid and screw it all up? Then you'd have every right to dump me."

"First, you couldn't do anything stupid. Second, even if you did, loving someone means you forgive and forget. My falling in love with you may have happened virtually on the spot, but it's never ever going to go away. If you do something stupid, I may get very angry or very hurt, but I'll never stop loving you. You are in my heart, body, and soul to stay."

"How can you be so sure?"

"Because I know."

"Yeah, sweetheart, but nothing is forever."

"We are!"

"You can't know that."

"I know as well as I know that the sun will rise in the morning."

"Why are you so sure you will feel the same when that sun does rise in the morning?"

"Listen, buddy, I love you. I love you with every fiber of my being. Nothing is ever going to change that. I yearn for you every moment we are apart. When we are together, it's like time stands still. You are constantly in my thoughts. I can't eat, sleep, or think without you being the reason for that. At first, that scared the hell out of me. Then I realized it was only the result of being truly and forever in love. That realization gave me such a feeling of contentedness that I know this is forever."

"You say that now, but, when you come to your senses tomorrow, you'll realize I'm an old fart not worthy of such a lovely, young woman. Reality will set in, and we'll go our separate ways."

"Are you in love with me?"

"Ah ... I ... Ah."

She only let me stammer for a short while. "Are you in love with me?"

"So much so that it hurts. In fact, I'm so deeply moved that I'm scared senseless. I have never felt so completely helpless and out of control."

"Then you listen to me. I'm not going anywhere, and you aren't going anywhere. I'm a very loyal person. I get the feeling you are, too. So, it looks like we have no choice. We are stuck with each other. Do you catch my drift, mister?"

"Yes, ma'am."

"Good. Now I can get some sleep and have wonderful dreams of you."

"Good night, sweet lady. Remember the words of *Romeo and Juliet*. 'Parting is such a sweet sorrow till it be the morrow.'"

"That's us. Like Romeo and Juliet. True deep and absolute

love at first sight. I never before believed it could really happen that fast until now."

"I'm still trying to believe it."

"Well, believe it."

"I'm trying."

"Stop trying and just do!"

"That's easier said than done."

"In the morning, I'll still be here for you."

"I'm lucky to have you."

"Well, you do have me."

"Good night, honey."

"Good night, lover."

I hung up with a smile on my face. I stood there a moment and looked at the telephone as if it were still a link between us. Then I grinned, shook my head, and turned away. The grin disappeared from my face as I looked around and saw the mess that was my apartment.

"The hell with it. It's late, and I'm tired."

I cleared off the couch. I got a blanket and my pillow from the bedroom and lay down on the couch. With my pistol stuck under my pillow and my alarm clock set, I was asleep within five minutes.

CHAPTER 12

I awoke with a start. I had heard a noise in the hallway outside of my front door. I reached under my pillow and got my pistol. I quietly walked over to the door and listened. I heard very soft footsteps approach the door and then stop. After a couple minutes of not hearing the footsteps withdraw away from my door, I quietly unlocked my door. After I silently chambered a round into my pistol, I flung the door open as fast as I could. I crouched down and alongside the open door with my pistol pointing out into the hall. I must have scared the old lady out of most of the rest of her life. She screamed and almost collapsed. I quickly lowered my pistol and put it behind me. I recognized her as the person who lived down the other end of the hall.

"I am sorry…I didn't realize it was you. I have been a bit jumpy lately."

"Well, you ought to be sorry. Scaring a poor, helpless, old woman by pointing a gun at her. You should be ashamed."

"My place has recently been trashed, I have been shot at and…" I started to explain that, because of all that had happened, I had overreacted, but she wouldn't listen. She just stomped off down the hallway.

I shut my door, stood up, and scratched my head. Then I looked at my watch and saw it was eight forty-five. It was a perfectly normal time for people to be up and about in this building. I went into my bedroom. It only took me about ten minutes to find some clean clothes suitable to wear. Thirty minutes later, I was all clean-shaven and still wearing my shoulder harness with pistol. I felt I was looking the best I could. I headed out the door. I had no plan of attack. I didn't know what I was going to do. I had no further clues or names to check on. About the only thing I could do was to go back and recheck some of the things I already checked.

But who and where do I start?

I drove along, not really knowing where I was going, and tried to form some kind of a plan. I just couldn't come up with anything. After I had pulled through a fast-food place for a quick breakfast sandwich and headed for my office. I got there a few minutes later than I normally do every workday. My boss, Bill Harper, didn't say much. A lot of the time, the investigators were doing our jobs out of the office, except I wasn't working on any case right now.

I first went to the assignment secretary to find out if I had anything newly assigned.

"Hey, Julie. How's your Monday morning going?"

She was a young girl, fresh out of secretarial school. She tried hard and did a fine job. In the six months she'd been with the company, I had come to like her. We got along fine. She was engaged to a law student and had a lot going for her.

"So far, it's going fine, Mr. Peterson. How was your weekend?"

I opened my mouth to tell her how hectic it had been, but I thought better of it.

"Busy, but I'm still alive to tell about it."

She laughed. She thought I was making one of my usual joking remarks. But little did she know.

"Nothing to write home about, huh?"

"No, nothing I'd write home to Mom."

"Even if she were alive." I mumbled to myself. I added loud enough for Julie to hear, "Do I have any new cases assigned?"

"Not right now. It was apparently a very slow weekend. We

only had a couple of minor incidents reported, so I gave them to the new guy."

"Oh, you mean that guy the boss hired last month. Is he ready for a case already? What's his name? Sean Muller?"

"Yes. Mr. Harper said they were insignificant investigations and it would be a good way to get his feet wet."

"What were they?"

"Some lady had a tree fall on her storage shed. The second was kind of cut-and-dry. Some guy was shot and killed Friday morning. He had a life insurance policy for one million dollars."

"That's a large policy to give to someone new."

"I know, but the policy is over six years old and fully paid to maturity. Plus, the boss said it was just a formality because it was obvious he was gunned down in a drive-by shooting."

I tried to make it sound as if I were going to let it drop, but I knew I was going to check into this further. I knew I had to talk to her about something else first and then come back to what I really wanted to know about. So, I paused.

"Julie, would you mind if I ask you some questions totally unrelated to work? I'm trying to figure something out, and I could use your help."

"Sure. Go right ahead."

"Well, you're young and in touch with how people in your generation think these days."

"I'd like to think so."

"Is it possible for someone, say about your age, to genuinely care or even be in love with someone about my age?"

"Sure! Why not?"

"But that's a tremendous age difference, isn't it?"

"So what? These days, that's not really an issue. A lot of things that didn't used to be acceptable are commonplace."

"That's fine with society, but how about the differences between the two generations? Attitudes and ways of life have to be different."

"That depends on the individuals. Everyone is different. Who's to say a twenty year old and a forty year old have to be different? Besides, so what if they are? That doesn't mean they can't truly be in love. Are they happy together? If the two people involved are happy with the relationship, then it doesn't matter what everybody else thinks, does it?"

"No, I guess it doesn't."

She grinned at me. "Why? Have you found a someone younger than you that you like and are afraid to pursue because of your age?"

I looked at her somewhat sheepishly. "Yeah, I guess you could say that. It's just that I'm so apprehensive about how much older I am than she is. I mean, we get along great. We seem to be extremely compatible. I'm just finding it hard to believe that such a young girl who has so much life still ahead of her could really care for someone middle-aged who is already halfway through his life."

"That middle-age crap is all in your head."

"Yes, I guess it is."

"Have you talked to her about it?"

"Yes, she basically says the same thing you do."

"Then what's your problem?"

"I guess there really isn't a problem, is there?"

"Absolutely not!"

"Thanks a lot, Julie. I appreciate it. Oh, by the way, is Sean still in the building?"

"He should be in his office."

"Okay. I'll see you later. Thanks."

"No problem, Mr. Peterson." I started to walk away. "Enjoy what the two of you have. It may be something very special. That doesn't come along every day."

I looked back, smiled, and walked away. I found my way to Sean's little cubbyhole of an office. He was sitting at his desk and going through some paperwork. I knocked on his open door. When he looked up and saw me standing there, he almost knocked his chair over backwards while trying to jump up on his feet as fast as he could.

"Mr. Peterson. Hi."

"Relax, Sean. I just stopped by to see how you were doing with those two cases they gave you."

"Well, sir, I'm really excited at the chance. I'm going to try to do my best."

"I'm sure you are. First, sit down and relax. I'm just an investigator like you are."

"Okay, Mr. Peterson." He sat down.

"Second, my name is James."

"Okay, James."

"What have you got so far?"

"Well, the first one is a homeowner's claim for a fallen tree. It seems kind of simple. An old, dead tree fell and crushed an elderly lady's storage shed. It appears like Friday's storm knocked it down."

"Let me give you some advice. It's the ones that seem simple at first that usually turn out to be the most complicated."

"I'll have to remember that."

"What's the other case?"

"It's not quite so simple. Mr. Harper said it was an open-and-shut one. It was just a paper formality, but I'm not so sure."

"What do you mean?"

"Well, it's about some guy who got gunned down and perhaps killed by a mobster. I understand the police aren't even looking at his wife, the beneficiary. I guess it's just processing the paperwork. But a million-dollar policy isn't an ordinary claim. I'm a little bit leery about signing the paperwork and verifying that all matters have been covered."

"I'll tell you what. Why don't you give me the paperwork? I'll go over it, review them thoroughly, and make some notes. That way, I can maybe ease the workload for you a bit."

"That'd be great. Thanks a lot." He handed over a manila folder.

I quickly looked through it. "If you don't mind, I'd like to take this to my office where I can really lay it open."

"I don't mind at all. That would be fine. Thanks, James."

"Don't mention it," I said over my shoulder.

I walked out of his cubbyhole with the folder in my hand. I went straight to my office. I closed the door behind me and sat down at my desk. I took a deep breath before I opened the folder. I went over every piece of paper and form that was included. It took about an hour.

The claim was a standard life insurance policy drawn up a little over six and a half years ago. All premiums had been paid on time. It held a cash value of one million dollars, payable in one lump sum. Anne Branning was the sole beneficiary. Everything was correct and properly filled out. The more I went over it, the more I felt like something was strange about it. I just couldn't put my finger on it. I made a photocopy of everything in the file. I put the copies in one of my desk drawers and took the original file back to Sean.

I collected my paycheck from the boss's secretary and notified Julie that I'd be out for a while. After I cashed my check at the company bank across the street, I realized it was nearly lunchtime. I figured I'd drive over to the Browning Investment Group. This would serve two purposes. First, it would give me a chance to check out what the place was like. Second, I wanted to see if Marci might have lunch with me. Because I had time to think about what Julie had said, I realized I was truly feeling something serious about her and I wasn't going to let our age differences stand in the way of our relationship. I was extremely excited about this last decision.

The drive was uneventful. In fact, it was quite peaceful. The Browning Investment Group Building wasn't located precisely downtown. It was still in the inner city, but not in the middle of the heart of the concrete jungle. I found a parking lot in front. The five-story building was one of those modern, energy-efficient, mirror-looking glass cubes. I entered the building through the front door and saw that the directory said that the Browning Investment Group offices occupied the entire third floor. Several other companies were spread throughout the rest of the building. I took the elevator up to the third floor.

When the door opened, I stepped out into the reception room. I walked up to the receptionist's desk, the only piece of furniture in the room. They clearly didn't want anyone to be seated while they waited. The girl behind the desk gave me a smile that said, "We're so happy to see you." It was as phony as all the perfectly white teeth she had in her mouth.

"How may I help you, sir?"

"My name is James Peterson. I'm with the investigator's office. I'd like to speak to some of your company officers about the death of Joseph Branning."

The smile was suddenly completely gone as she started fumbling all over herself while trying to push the right button on her switchboard. Apparently, she finally hit the one she was trying so desperately to locate.

I heard her say into her mouthpiece, "A Mr. Peterson from the investigator's office is here to talk to someone about Mr. Branning." After a momentary pause, she tried to whisper into the same mouthpiece, "I'm sorry, sir, but he's standing right here in front of me."

She looked up at me with a weak smile. I could see by the look on her face that she didn't want to tell on me but this was the boss, and she couldn't lie to him. I kept my stare noncommittal, but serious.

"Yes, sir, I will," she said after listening to an apparent in-depth list of instructions.

She looked up at me with a big sigh of relief on her face that someone else would relieve her of the responsibilities of dealing with me. "Someone will be right with you."

I nodded and didn't move from my spot. The longer I stood there, the more fidgety she got. I was really enjoying this.

After a few minutes, I said, "Did you know Joseph Branning very well?"

With the first sounds of my question, she nearly jumped out of her skin. But she answered. "I only knew him as he came in and out past my desk."

"The way I understand it, Joseph Branning was quite friendly. Are you saying he never stopped and talked to you?"

"Well … ah … yes. Ah, occasionally, he would."

"And?"

"He was a very nice man," she stuttered.

But the relief showed greatly on her face when the door to her right opened. Through the only other door besides the elevator walked an obvious company official. He looked as if a Hollywood casting director had picked him out as an exaggerated characterization of what a typical professional businessman should look like. He stood about six foot tall. He had black hair with a dark tan. It was hard to tell if it were from a sunlamp or the actual sun. His suit probably cost more than I made in a month. Nothing on him or about him was even a fraction of an inch out of place.

He walked up to me and stuck out his hand. "Detective Peterson, is it? I'm Edwin Loach, vice president of public relations. May I be of assistance?" He presented himself with an air or arrogance that I suppose was meant to deter me from asking too many questions.

"It's Inspector Peterson." This wasn't exactly a lie. After all I was an inspector, just not a police inspector. "Only if you could provide me with the cooperation I'm seeking." I was already beginning to not like what little of this company that I was seeing.

"What cooperation would you like to receive? Other police

officers have already questioned everyone here. Several times, I might add." His nose actually rose slightly, just like the stereotypical manner of someone who was imitating smudginess.

"I'd like to take a look around Mr. Branning's office … if I might."

"I wish that were possible, but the police who were here over the weekend released his office. We have already removed everything."

I wanted to punch that self-satisfied smile right out the back of his face. "Why the rush?"

"No rush really. But surely you understand that business must be conducted, and life goes on." He had that same smile.

I was more convinced than ever that I didn't like this guy or the company he represented. "I'd still like to take a look around and perhaps talk to a few of his fellow employees."

"Is that absolutely necessary? After all, we're trying to run a business here."

"I guess I could require them all to come downtown and make an official statement." I paused just long enough for him to start to say something. "All of these people absent at the same time would create quite an interruption of your business day."

I stood my ground and tried to give him back that same smile he gave me. Fortunately, he didn't call my bluff. I had to remember to try that a little more often while playing poker.

His shoulders and nose dropped slightly. "Certainly. Right this way." He turned and headed for the door.

As he passed the desk, he nodded his head. I heard the slight hum of the electric lock being released just before he pushed on the doorknob. Obviously, Miss Fake Teeth had triggered the lock. I followed him into a very large room. Several desks were neatly spaced throughout what appeared to be the office secretarial pool. Some had computer terminals; some had typewriters. Some had both. All but a very few had people working at them. Most were women, but a couple men were there. Around the edge of the large room were several independent offices. As he led me through the room, I looked desperately for Marci. I couldn't find her anywhere. I looked at every female in that room at least three times, but she wasn't there. There were a few very good-looking women, but I saw none that was even close to looking anywhere near as good as Marci did. I recognized no one; no one recognized me. My only salvation was that perhaps she sat at one of the few empty desks. We finally got to one of the offices located in the back of the large room.

"This used to be Mr. Branning's office."

He opened the door. All that was inside was a plain empty desk and chair. I walked in and looked around. The walls were bare. I walked behind the desk, moved the chair, and pulled open several drawers. Not even a paper clip was forgotten. Everything was neat and orderly. I looked back at Mr. Congeniality.

"How wonderful it is to be remembered for such a long time after you're gone."

He totally ignored my sarcasm.

I walked up to him. "If you don't mind, I'd like to take a few minutes and talk to some of your staff."

"Well, sir, we are a very busy firm. Every lost minute of production is costly."

"So is the loss of a life," I snapped. "I won't use up much of your firm's precious time. I have only a few questions."

He momentarily lost some of his composure. "Please make sure that is all that you do!" Then the public relations smile was back. "I'm sure you can find your way out when you are finished." He turned and walked off to one of the larger offices.

As casually as possible, I walked up to the first desk. I continued to look around the room for Marci. "Hello. My name is Inspector Peterson. If you don't mind, I'd like to ask you a few questions about Joseph Branning."

The young lady stopped typing and looked up slightly

annoyed that I'd interrupt her work. But she answered politely. "Yes, sir. How can I help you?"

"Did you know Joseph Branning very well?"

A slightly sad look crossed over her eyes just momentarily. Then she smiled as if nothing was wrong. "Yes, he was a very nice man. I'll miss his good sense of humor."

The man was dead, and she only missed his "good sense of humor". I didn't want to talk to this ditz. I figured I wouldn't get much from the office personnel, but I desperately wanted to find Marci.

"One last question, and I'll let you go back to work. Do you know Marci Johnson?"

"Yes, I do. She's right over there."

I felt my heart skip a beat when I looked where she was pointing. Across the room, about halfway up the middle, a woman was sitting at her desk. She was busily typing away. She was sitting sideways at her desk but facing her computer. If she were to simply look up, she would have been staring straight at me. The hair color was right, but this girl had her hair up on top of her head and in a bun. She also wore glasses. Her dress looked very plain.

I looked back at the girl. "That's Marci Johnson?"

She nodded her head yes. "It sure is. Now may I get back to work?"

"Certainly. Please do."

I stood there for a minute and stared at the person she claimed was Marci Johnson. Suddenly I knew that what had been said was accurate.

If it seems to be too good to be true, then it probably isn't.

The Marci Johnson I spent the other night was too good to be true. I felt like my whole life was a lie. I went on to another desk and asked the next person the same questions. I basically got the same response about Branning and that same person was Marci Johnson. I was in total shock. That person wasn't the same

Marci. I absentmindedly walked up to a few more and repeated the same questions about Branning. I stopped asking to identify Marci. I didn't want to believe it. My whole world just crumbled. The most wonderful woman in the whole world was a lie. I made about three more stops as I made my way toward the desk that supposedly belonged to this Marci Johnson person. She was finally next. I hesitated because I really didn't want to believe it. After a few deep, heartfelt breaths, I started to think about the situation. The more I thought about it, the angrier I got.

I used that as a motivator and walked up to this phony's desk. "Excuse me a minute."

When she looked up and I looked into her eyes, I felt chills all over. It really was Marci. I'd know those eyes anywhere. The shocked expression on her face told me that it only took her a split second to recognize me. She quickly looked around to see who might be watching. Then as casual as she possibly could, considering she was totally unprepared for my appearance, she whispered for the benefit of the other people nearby who were indeed listening to us, but were pretending not to.

"Jimmy, what are you doing here?"

"Excuse me, ma'am. My name is Inspector Peterson. I'd like to ask you a few questions about one of your former fellow employees, the late Mr. Branning. Did you know him very well?"

The expression on her face told me that many mixed emotions filled her. By the way she fidgeted with her glasses, I could tell she was extremely nervous. She was glad to see me, but she knew what was going on. She was nervous about someone seeing her associating with an inspector.

She caught on quickly even though she stumbled through her answer. "Mr. Branning was a very nice man. Ah, he was always very nice to me during the times I conducted any office business with him."

"I see! You only knew him here at the office then?" I said loudly. I whispered, "How about lunch?"

"Yes," she said loud enough for the others to hear. Then for only my ears, she said, "Del Rico's at noon."

"Fine. Thank you for your time." I winked and went on to the next person.

I repeated my performance with a couple more people and got the same response. But I didn't care. Marci was really there after all. I finally headed for the exit door. I turned to take a quick look around. I just caught someone in one of the back offices quickly close his door. I was being watched. I casually looked around the room as if I were taking one last look around. The last place I looked was at Marci. She was looking at me over the top of her glasses as she pretended to shuffle some papers on her desk.

She very discreetly mouthed the words, "I love you."

I nodded my head slightly yes as if to the room. But Marci knew I meant it for her. I could tell by the quick, slight smile. I turned and walked out of the door. The same receptionist was still there. But a very large man dressed in a suit was standing off to the side of the open elevator. It didn't take a rocket scientist to figure out he was there to make sure I left. I nodded to Ms. Fake Teeth and walked into the elevator. I calmly put my hand under my coat and palmed my gun in case I needed it. But the big suit just reached into the elevator and pulled out the emergency stop button that had been pushed in. Without saying a word, he pushed the button for the ground floor. The door closed with only me on board. I kept my hand on my pistol because I wasn't sure what would greet me when I got to the bottom. I even stepped as far to the left side of the car as I possibly could. When the door opened, I peeked around the corner and through the open elevator door. I saw that no one was out there. So I walked out into the lobby and quickly walked out of the building to my car. I couldn't see anybody watching me in the parking lot. As I unlocked my car door, I quickly looked back at the third floor. I couldn't see in through the mirrored glass windows, but I knew someone was watching me. I laughed, let go of my gun, got in my car, and drove off. I pulled away and watched to make sure if anyone was following me. The best I could tell, no one was.

I drove for about five minutes before I found a convenience store. I pulled into the parking lot off to the side. I got out of my car and went inside. I went right to the cooler vault, got out a soda, and went to the cashier. The whole time, I kept a lookout into the parking lot. No one even drove by the store. I was confident someone hadn't tailed me.

After I paid for my soda, I asked the clerk, "Could let me look up a number in your phone book." She laid it on the counter without a problem or comment. I looked up Del Rico's. The address told me that it was only about two blocks from the Browning Building. I looked at my watch. Eleven forty. I had twenty minutes. I asked the clerk, "Would be all right if I left my car parked in front of the store for a couple hours?"

She answered, "Where are you parked?"

I said with as much phony niceness as she showed, "I parked off to the side, so I won't be blocking any customer parking in front of your store."

She only gave me the slightest look and said, "It won't be a problem if you don't leave it here very long."

I said as nicely as I could, "You got it sure thing."

I walked back to Del Rico's. It only took me about ten minutes to get to the restaurant. That left me about ten minutes to check out the place. I went inside and looked around. I got the hostess to give me a secluded booth in the back. But I could see the front door because I was expecting someone. I also told the waitress, who had come right over, that I'd wait to order when my other party showed up.

My world brightened at about five minutes after noon when Marci walked through the door. I noticed her very plain business suit skirt came down below her knees. Her suit top very definitely hid the fact that she had any breasts at all, not to mention the largeness of them. If I'd seen her on the streets dressed like this and didn't know her, I probably wouldn't have looked at her twice, especially if she had on those horrible glasses. She spotted me right away and came straight to the booth. As she got within a few feet, she removed her glasses. That was the only change from the office she had made. After she slid in beside me, she gave me a nice big kiss.

She said softly, "I certainly was surprised but happy to see you standing there in the office."

"So was I."

She gave me a quizzical look.

"I didn't recognize you. I had looked at everyone in that office several times before I had to have someone point you out. Even then, I still didn't believe it was you."

She looked down and even slumped her shoulders slightly. I patiently waited for her to answer. After a few moments, she finally looked up at me. I could see the embarrassment in her eyes.

"I told you that I'm actually a very shy person in public. The way you saw me today is how everybody knows me, ordinary and mousy-looking. I prefer myself that way. No one bothers to mess with me. So, if no one bothers to mess with me, I can't get hurt again. It's a lot less painful. I'm not quite the lady in the streets you were hoping for. I'm sorry if you are disappointed in me for only being the whore in the bedroom part of the perfect woman you are looking for." She even slightly pulled away from me.

I sat there for a few seconds and looked at her. It wasn't my intention, but I could tell that, the longer I kept quiet, my silence was deflating her even more.

I said something I knew I absolutely felt but didn't mean to say. "I could never be disappointed with the lady I love."

The second I said it, I wanted to slam my hand over my

mouth, but I was too late. For the few seconds it took her to realize what I had said, I thought that maybe she didn't hear me. I felt momentarily relieved. Then I realized she had.

Her head came up suddenly. She looked straight at me. "What did you say?"

"I did say what I think I said, didn't I?"

She slumped her shoulders slightly, but she kept looking at me.

I stuttered a few times. "Marci honey, my heart just spoke what my head has been trying to stop. Now that it has spoken, my head knows it is true. I love you."

She practically knocked me over as she literally jumped into my arms. I didn't think I could remember a woman ever hugging me so tightly. Then she started kissing me all over my mouth and face. I noticed that several people in the restaurant were looking at us.

"Marci darling," I said each word in between kisses. "People are watching. We are in public."

"I don't care. I know it's not very ladylike, but I love you, and you do love me," she said in between a few more kisses.

She stopped kissing, but she didn't stop hugging me. She looked me straight in the eyes with the happiest smile I had ever seen. I felt like I had just melted. My whole body, head to toe, vibrated from the warmth of her smile. I reached up and softly stroked her cheek. She leaned her head slightly into my caress. She momentarily closed her eyes and purred the sigh of contentment.

About that time, I heard a female voice from the outside of our table. "Excuse me. I'm sorry to bother you, but can I take your order now?"

I looked over at the waitress to let her know that I'd heard her. Then I turned back to Marci. "What would you like?" I saw the smile on her face and the gleam in her eye. "Besides that."

We both lightly chuckled. The waitress cleared her throat a little extra loudly to tell us that she wasn't there for laughs. We both got the message. Although Marci did release me from the hug and sat back, she didn't pull away. She did sit so our hips and legs were snuggled tightly together.

While she sat all prim and proper, Marci said, "I'll just have a chef salad with ranch dressing and an iced tea, please."

The waitress wrote that down. She looked at me.

"I'll have a BLT on toast and a large glass of milk, please."

Our waitress picked up the menus from the table that neither one of us had even looked at. She turned and left without even another word.

After a few moments of silence, I said, "So I didn't know that you wear glasses."

She didn't look at me when she answered quietly, "I don't." I didn't say anything. She continued softly, "Men don't make passes at girls who wear glasses."

"I've heard that."

"The glasses are just plain glass."

"Those assholes really hurt you, didn't they?"

"Very much so."

"Well, don't worry. It's not going to happen again."

She cuddled up next to me warmly. "Promise?"

"I do."

"I do. That sounds wonderful." I somewhat stiffened when I realized the implication of what she said.

Marci felt my reaction. "I'm sorry. I didn't mean to twist your words."

"Don't worry. I'll get over it. I'm a big boy."

"You certainly can be." I looked at her and saw that gleam in her eye.

"That, my dear, is your doing."

"Every chance I get."

We looked at each other and giggled like a couple of schoolkids. The people sitting near us looked over at us. By the look on their faces, I could tell they weren't sure what to make of us.

"So, Jimmy, what do you think of Browning Investment Group?"

"Something is very definitely going on there. Did you know that all of Branning's office had been completely cleared out?"

She became a little more serious. "Yes. I think it's terrible. All they would say was that business must continue."

"Shows you what kind of place it must be."

"Not a very nice place."

I stuttered a bit, "I don't quite know how to say this."

"Then just say it straight out."

I looked at her. "I don't think you should continue to work there."

"Why?"

"Marci, it's a crooked outfit. I don't want you going down the tubes with it."

"But a lot of very nice people work there. And it's my job. I have to have an income to pay my bills."

"With your abilities, I'm sure you could find a better job somewhere legitimate."

"Where?"

"Anyplace else."

"I don't know."

"Look at me, sweetheart." She did. "Browning Investment Group is going to be shut down anyway. It is better that you leave on your terms."

"What do you mean?"

I took a deep breath. "The police know about them. They are just taking their time until all connections can be made. Then they are going to shut down the place and arrest all who are responsible. I want you out of the way."

She seemed rather shocked at first. "If I were on the inside, I could find out more information and help nail those creeps that killed Joey."

"Joey, I asked a bit taken back. That sounds funny for you to call him by that name."

"Well it became a kind of secret nick name for him because when every we talked or spent any time together I saw such a kid in him. Just like he was a young man. He that it was cute but asked me to never call him that in public because it might not sound professional."

I kind of felt relieved but still not certain as I responded, "No, absolutely not! It's not worth you getting hurt over."

"But I just can't leave. I have a lot of things there that I don't want to leave undone."

"Honey, please quit the place. In fact, don't even go back this afternoon."

"I can't do that. I have personal things in my desk that can't be replaced." I grumbled a bit. She took a hold of my hand. "Look, lover, I'll make you a promise. I'll go back this afternoon, clean out my things, and turn in my notice."

"I don't want you going back there."

"I'll be all right. I won't stay any longer than I have to."

"You promise?"

"I do."

"Humph."

She looked up at me with little girl eyes. "What's the matter? You didn't think it sounded good when I said I do?"

"Well, yeah, I did, but—"

"I love you."

"I love you, too."

"It's really not easy for you to say that, is it?"

"No, it's not."

"Don't worry. I'll do things to you that will make it easier and easier."

I looked at her. She gave me that sexy look with her eyes. I just melted.

"All right. You go back there. Get your things and get out."

"Yes, sir. But what am I going to do to make a living?"

"We'll work on that later. I do know some people in this town."

About that time, our waitress arrived with lunch.

I said, "This evening, I'm taking you to dinner at a friend's house. He's a close friend who happens to be on the police force. I want you to tell him everything you know."

"As long as I'm with you, wherever you are is where I want to be."

The thought crossed my mind that Sharon was sure going to be surprised. We both ate our lunches with nothing, but bits of love talk in between bites.

CHAPTER 13

After Marci kissed me good-bye in front of the restaurant, she turned and headed back to her office. I didn't like her going back there. I had tried one more time to talk her out of it, but she wouldn't hear of it. There were some personal things there, and she wanted them. Reluctantly, I let her go after agreeing to pick her up at her place at five forty-five. The whole time I stood there by my car, watching her until she disappeared around the corner, I had bad feelings about it. But she had insisted. I could tell that, if I had tried to play Mr. Macho and demand she not go back, it would have caused an argument. So, against my better judgment, I didn't argue with her. I just said a little prayer that she would be all right. I got in my car and drove off.

As I drove off in my car, I decided it was time to do a little checking on Browning Investment Group. I drove downtown to the courthouse. I knew the old lady who ran the clerk's office was a real bitch. I wasn't looking forward to dealing with her, but I had to see what was on record for this outfit.

When I walked through the clerk's office doors, there stood Old Iron Shorts. She was in the process of giving orders to one of her young female employees. I couldn't hear what she was saying. Considering how the young girl snapped to and did what Old Iron Shorts told her to do without any hesitation, it told me that she was her usual Marine drill sergeant self. I always kept meaning to ask her if that was where she had learned her management techniques. However, because she and I never had the chance at a constructive conversation, I never got the chance.

About then, she noticed me heading her way. Her expression changed from one of hard coldness to one of pure rage. If any stranger had happened to come across this fifty-eight-year-old, gray-haired woman and she might have accidentally had a smile on her face, he would have mistaken her for someone's sweet, little old grandmother.

She dispelled that rumor as I walked up. "And what the hell do you want, shithead?"

"My, my, did someone put razor blades in your iron girdle during lunch?" I asked as sugary as I possibly could.

I knew it wasn't much of a comeback, but it was the best I could do on short notice and not totally insult her. After all, I was there to get some information from the files and records she kept.

"Look, I haven't got time to put up with pissants today. I know you wouldn't have your broken-down ass here if you didn't want something. What is it?"

I let that insult go by without comment. It was mild to the way she usually talked to me. "I need some help."

"Boy, is that ever an understatement. I've been saying that for years."

It was getting harder and harder not to go off on her. "I'm investigating the murder of Joseph Branning. You know the guy who was gunned down Friday morning?"

"Yeah, I know. I read about it in the papers. What about him?"

"He worked for a company called Browning Investment Group. I need any, and all information you could possibly have on that company."

"What do I look like? Your personal secretary?"

"No, but, no matter what you and I think of each other, I

know you're the only one who knows exactly where I have to look to find the information I need."

She looked at me with that skeptical look that said, "All right. Where's the con?"

But I didn't say another word. I just stood there patiently waiting. I could see the wheels turning in her brain as she tried to figure out what my angle was. After a while, she finally must have decided I was on the level. She gave out a few huffs and puffs of grumbling.

"What do you want? I haven't got all day."

"All licenses, charter documentation, or anything you might have that would show ownership, major stock holders, or the real controlling agents of this company."

Her expression told me that it would be easier to attempt to move the Taj Mahal here than accomplish my requested task.

I simply said, "Please?"

That shocked her so much that she almost dropped her dentures. But it did the trick.

"All right. I can have everything ready for you by tomorrow afternoon."

"I certainly do appreciate you doing that. However, …" That skeptical look came back. "There are a few people whose lives are very much in danger. If I stay and help, do you think we could get that done this afternoon?"

"Look, I refuse to have you hanging around here and getting in my way. You're a pain in the ass enough as it is without being here all afternoon. I'll make you a deal. Come back in about two hours. I'll have it ready for you."

"Thank you."

Then I surprised both of us by giving her a quick kiss on the cheek. I quickly turned and got out of there. All the time, I waited for something to hit me in the back of the head as I walked out. It never happened and I let out a breathe I had been holding.

I went out the front door and found a phone in the hallway. I called Mike at the police station. It took a few minutes before he came on the line. I finally heard him say, "Lieutenant Glosman."

"Hi, Mike. It's Jim."

"Hey, James. What's up?"

"I called to let you in on what's developed since last night."

"Okay. Shoot."

"Poor choice of words to someone who has been through what I've been through lately."

"Ah … Well, you know. You're a tough ol' bastard."

I chose to ignore that. "Branning had gambling debts over $50,000 before he was killed. The day he was killed, he paid them all off. And rumor has it that he was skipping town the next day."

"What do you mean? What about his family?"

"He was apparently going to leave them behind."

"Nice guy," Mike said sarcastically.

"I'd say Browning Investment Group thought the same thing. I went by there. Every single trace of his existence there has been removed. His office is an empty room with an equally empty desk sitting in the middle of the room. The people there say someone else will be moving in there by this afternoon."

"What else have you got?"

"Not much. I'm conducting some research on the company itself. I should have something back by this afternoon. What I'd like to do, if it's all right with you and Sharon, is to come by for dinner around seven. Then go over everything with you."

"I don't see how that would be a problem. I don't think we had anything planned for tonight. I'll give her a call and ask her to set an extra plate at the table."

"Well, you might want to have her set two extra plates. I'm going to bring someone with me."

"Who?" he quickly asked suspiciously.

"A young lady friend I've gotten to know lately."

"You don't say. Who is she?" he asked eagerly.

"Her name is Marci Johnson."

"Marci Johnson? The secretary who works at Browning Investment Group?"

"Boy, nothing gets by that steel trap mind of yours, does it?"

"All right, James. What gives here?"

"I just went to question her about the case, and we hit it off. We've spent a lot of time together these last few days. I'm bringing her with me for two reasons. One, she and I have been going over this case with a fine-tooth comb. I'd like you to hear what she has to say. Second, I like her a lot, and I plan to have her with me a lot of places I go in the future."

"Well, I'll be a son of a bitch. Are you sure you can handle someone half your age?"

"Kiss my ass. This old horse ain't dead yet."

"Dead, no. But can you still trot with the fillies? All right. I'll let Sharon know. Boy, is she ever going to be surprised."

"Yeah, I kind of figured that. Maybe you can kind of prepare her a little bit, so she won't trip all over her face when we walk in."

"That's not a bad idea."

"Okay, Mike. I'll see you then."

"Bye, stud."

I went out of the building, got in my car, and drove off. As I was driving along, I thought about how I didn't have any clothes that were modern and appropriate to wear tonight. I decided to buy a new outfit.

Why not? Women do it all the time.

I found a men's clothes shop downtown that wasn't too expensive. With the sales clerk's help, I walked out an hour later with shopping bags full of everything new from the shoes on up. I put them in the trunk of the car. I glanced at my watch and saw I still had thirty more minutes left before Old Iron Shorts said she'd have the stuff ready for me to pick up.

I mumbled to myself, "What the hell. Maybe she'll have it ready anyway."

So back to the clerk's office I went. When I got there, Old Iron Shorts was nowhere in sight.

I went to the desk and asked the clerk, "The lady that runs this office said she would leave me something. Is she here?" I didn't want to call her by my pet name for so I just made it as neutral and friendly as possible.

"No, sir. She's not here. Are you Mr. Peterson?"

"Yes, I am."

"She left this for you." The girl handed me a large, sealed envelope.

"Thank you."

"Yes, sir."

She went back to whatever she was doing. I took the envelope and went back to my car. I didn't open it until I was sitting inside. I lost track of how long I was sitting there, but I looked through everything. What I found really wasn't a surprise. A nondescript company out of the Midwest owned Browning Investment Group. Apparently, Old Iron Shorts took it a little further. Another company from the East Coast owned the Midwestern company. About five years ago, they bought an already-existing building, and they were in full operation within thirty days. All licenses, including SEC and stock exchange stuff, was taken care of prior to their opening.

I said to only me because I was the only one in the car. "Where do they do their banking? Maybe Marci would know."

It hadn't been that long since we parted. She should still be at her office. I got out of my car, went back into the courthouse to the same pay phone, and called.

"Branning Investment Group," I heard the cheerful voice of the receptionist say.

"May I please speak to Marci Johnson?"

"Just one moment, sir. I'll check to see if she's available." After about two minutes, she came back on the line. "I'm sorry, sir. She's not here."

"What do you mean?" I felt the pangs of anxiety rush through me. Then I shifted gears and said a little more calmly, "She told me only a couple hours ago to call her at work and let her know about some redecorating she had planned."

"I'm awfully sorry, sir, but she apparently never returned from lunch. No one has heard from her." Then her voice got a little softer, as if trying to confide in me. "Sir, if you are able to locate her, you might want to tell her to give us a call. Her boss is quite angry."

"I certainly will. Thank you."

I hung up and stood there in shock.

I said to the phone as if I expected a response, "Maybe she took my advice and didn't go back after all."

I called her home. There was no answer. I didn't have any place else to call. I tried to calm myself. She was probably out shopping. I wasn't very convincing to myself as I mumbled, "Now what am I going to do?"

I walked out of the building and headed to the car. As I was fumbling with the keys, I heard someone walk up behind me. My reactions were slowed because I was thinking about Marci, so I was late looking to see who it was. What I felt told me I wished I had looked sooner. He hit me with a solid punch to the lower back. As my knees started to buckle, he caught me under my arms. He easily lifted me up and spun me around, so I was leaning back against the car and facing him. He was very big and a total stranger. Another carbon copy of him was standing behind him. He was essentially acting as a lookout.

The guy who hit me got up very close to my face. He lifted me slightly off the ground by my armpits. "Miss Johnson is our guest for the next couple days. If you do not stop poking into the affairs of Joseph Branning, she will become the permanent guest of the local cemetery. Do you catch my drift?"

I could only nod my head. I had no breath to speak with.

"I hope so. She wouldn't look so pretty if you didn't."

He just opened his hands, and I fell to the ground in a heap. I tried to catch my breath and gather my strength to try to stand up to see what I could. But I heard their car speed off before I could get any further than my knees. Then the sudden thought of Marci being in the hands of those creeps propelled me to my feet. As I stood, the pain in my back made stars shoot before my eyes.

"This is getting ridiculous. I suffered more pain in the past seventy-two hours than I had in the last twenty-five years. I am going to have to put a stop to this shit! Right now!" I declared loudly and proud.

I very carefully retrieved my keys from off the ground from where I had dropped them and slowly climbed into the car. I drove directly to the police station. From what I could tell, no one followed me. Over several cups of coffee, I filled Mike in on all that had happened since I first kicked that damn key. But I did manage to kind of leave out the part about the Swiss bank account and the airline ticket. Something selfish in the back of my head made me keep that to myself. I figured it was going to be my reward for all of this as I thought, *But how am I going to explain it all to Marci?*

As Mike poured over the stuff I had gotten from the clerk's office, I walked around his office and tried to figure a way out of this.

I'd give it all to them if they'd give Marci back alive and unharmed.

I finally heard Mike. "I wish I could promise you that she'll be all right. But you know the score as well as I do."

I turned and started to take my frustrations out on Mike. "If they hurt her in any way, I swear I'll blow that fucking building to the ground with all of them in it."

He looked back at me. "No, you won't. You're not on their level."

I looked dead at him and said coldly, "Hide and watch." I even scared myself with my sincerity.

His tone changed quickly. "You must really care about her."

"You could say that."

"Then do you think she'd want you to go to jail for the rest of your life, if they don't execute you, for killing a lot of innocent people?"

"Innocent? Hell, they are all a bunch of sleazy shits."

"Marci worked there. Does that mean her, too?"

"But that's—"

"Different?" He finished for me.

That sunk home a bit. "Then I'd take out those responsible."

"James, calm down. We'll find her."

"You damn well better." He let that slide. He sat back and quietly just watched me. I finally settled my temper down. "I'm sorry, Mike."

"Forget it. I know how you must feel."

"Pretty helpless right now."

"I'll bet you do." His eyes followed me as I paced back and forth across his office. "I'm going to make a few phone calls and see if I can get some discreet action started to try to locate where she is."

"She could be anywhere."

"I know, but we have experts who handle this kind of thing all the time."

"Experts, my ass. Their guess is as good as anyone else's."

"James, cool it!"

"Yeah, yeah. I know." Something occurred to me. "Something is strange about all of this."

"What's that?"

"Every time I was threatened, it was to stop investigating Joseph Branning's murder. When they tore up my place, it wasn't a harassment tactic. They were searching for something. I'd have to assume they were looking for the notebook. But never once when they were threatening me did they ask about that damned notebook. If they were concerned enough about it to tear my apartment apart, then why try to kill me? That wouldn't get it back."

"It indeed doesn't make sense."

"No, it doesn't. But I'll tell you what does."

"What?"

"I'm going to do what I have to do to get Marci back to include trading that notebook to them for her."

"You can't do that!"

"Don't tell me I can't. She is worth a hell of a lot more than that damn book."

"I know she is, but you can't make deals with these people. They won't hold up their end of the bargain."

"Neither will I."

He looked at me strangely. "What do you mean?"

"I'll tell them I have it and even give them a sample just to let them know I do. They'll have to produce her. When they do, you and your friends here show up out of the woodwork. We won't catch anybody big, but we'll get Marci back."

"It could work. It's worth a try. How do you want to do it?"

"First, see if someone could find another notebook just like that one, and dummy it up. Next, make some photocopies of a few pages, just enough to show what we've got."

"That shouldn't be too hard. We can have that ready in a couple hours."

"Make it an hour!" I ignored the look he gave me. I looked at my watch. "I'll be back then."

I turned and walked out of his office. I heard him pick up the phone and start issuing orders as I passed by his office door. I very quickly walked out of the police station. I got in my car and drove around until I found a pay phone. I parked alongside the phone, got out of the car, and made a call.

"Browning Investment Group," the receptionist said.

"Hello, ma'am. My name is Stanley George. I'm with *Financial*

Times. I've been assigned to write an article on new and upcoming investment firms across the country. Browning Investment Group rates very high with the SEC. I'd like to set up an interview with your chief executive."

"That would be Mr. Crossinger."

I silently thanked her for easily giving me that name. "Would this afternoon be acceptable?"

"Just a minute. I'll check for you, Mr. George. Hold on," she said eagerly.

After a few minutes, she came back on the line. "I tried, sir, but his secretary says he will be in conference all afternoon. If you'd like, you can make an appointment for next week."

"Well, I'm pretty rushed for a deadline. You say he's in the office now and will be for the rest of the day?"

"That's correct. But he'll be pretty tied up. Those conferences usually last several hours."

"Well, perhaps I come by later and sit around and wait for him to finish. How late does he usually stay?"

"About six o'clock or so. Sometimes later, but not very often."

"Thank you, miss. You've been very helpful."

"My pleasure."

I hung up and got back in my car. I drove over to Marci's apartment. I wasn't really sure why. Perhaps I wanted to check and see if maybe she hadn't just gone home. I could have called, but I didn't. I wasn't really sure why I didn't.

When I got there, I found the same redecorator who had recently rearranged things at my place had also visited Marci. Her door was slightly ajar. I pulled out my pistol. From the side, I pushed the door open. When no one or nothing flew out at me, I carefully peeked around the edge of the doorway. The place was a shamble. With pistol still in hand, I walked in and looked around. When I entered her bedroom, I really got pissed. Amongst everything else, laying there on the floor in a crumbled mess was our outfit. I quickly picked it up and very neatly folded it and laid it on top of her dresser where I had cleared a space for it. I felt as if someone had violated our sanctity when he had touched our outfit. This meant war. Still fuming, I holstered my gun and walked out of her apartment. After I closed and locked the door behind me, I went straight back to Mike's office.

When I walked in, the first thing I noticed was someone else was in there with him. I recognized him as one of the police detectives I had seen before but did not know.

He looked at me. "Take off your coat and shirt."

"Why?"

Mike said, "Sergeant Britton is going to wire you for sound." He recognized the look on my face. "You don't think I'm going to let you go in there without some kind of security, do you?"

"No, I guess not."

Sometime during the wiring, another police officer brought in the dummy notebook and photocopies of the original notebook. I looked through the photocopies and saw Mr. Crossinger's name was indeed listed. A very large amount was listed by his name, but not the largest. That belonged to A. Gionetti. After I was wired up, I picked up just the photocopies.

"How are you going to do this?" Mike asked.

"I'm going to the Browning Building and play it by ear."

"Don't stick your ear too far out. It might get chopped off."

"Funny, Mike. Very funny."

"I'm serious. Be careful. Even if we are listening, things could happen too fast for us to protect you. Sure, we may catch who burns you, but it wouldn't bring you or Marci back."

"I know. Let's go."

Mike followed me out of his office. We separated at the front desk. I went out the front door and headed to my car. He went with a couple of other officers down into the garage and into the unmarked police van. I drove straight to the Browning Building. As I drove along, I thought about Marci being in the hands of those thugs. The further I went, the madder I got. By the time I got to the parking lot, I was furious. I needed the anger to keep up my courage for what I was about to do. Just before I got out of the car, I checked my pistol to make sure it was fully loaded with a round in the chamber. I already knew it was, but nerves and a bit of caution prevailed. I got out of the car, took a deep breath, turned, and headed for the front door of the Browning Building.

As I walked in the front door, I saw an open and waiting elevator and said to myself, *Perhaps this is a good sign.* Not that I believed in that crap. But what the hell I need every break I could get.

I stepped in and pushed the button for the floor I wanted. This ride seemed to take longer than the last time I made the same trip. The doors finally opened, and I walked out, right to the same receptionist. She looked up and recognized me when I was about five feet from her desk. I couldn't tell if shock or fear momentarily crossed over her eyes. It was one of stark recognition. She started to fumble with her phone as she tried to call someone and tell him that I was there. But she was one step behind.

About that time, I noticed out of the corner of my eye that someone had opened the door to the inner sanctum of offices. Before it could close, I pushed right through. I nearly knocked some poor typing secretary clean over.

I mumbled, "I'm sorry. I really am."

I headed straight for the office where I saw someone peeking out at me earlier in the day. I crossed the room and noticed the room of desks was full except for two. Obviously, one belonged to the secretary I almost knocked over and Marci. The same things were sitting on top of her desk as earlier, but her chair was empty and pushed up under her desk. My luck was still holding out. No big muscle brain appeared in front of me before I got to the office door marked "Daniel Crossinger."

Without hesitation, I reached down and opened the door. As I charged in, the older, distinguished-looking man who was sitting behind the desk was just putting his phone back on the hook. I hadn't the slightest idea if he were talking to the receptionist or someone else. Two younger and tremendously larger men were standing behind and to each side of the older man. They started to come out from behind the desk.

The older man simply said, "No."

They froze. I walked up to the front of his desk and stopped. "Let me make this very simple for you! You have Marci, and I have this."

I slapped down the photocopies of the notebook on his desk right in front of him. They very easily spread out, exposing about half of them. He barely glanced down. Perhaps it was just long enough to verify what he already knew. But I noticed he did not touch them.

"Are these photo reproductions supposed to represent something I should be aware of?"

I ignored his comment. "The originals are in safekeeping. I get Marci; you get the notebook."

"I assure you that I know nothing of Miss Johnson's location. Also, this notebook means absolutely nothing to me."

"Then I guess you won't have any problems if I turn it over to the police." I turned and headed for the door.

I detected just the slightest amount of panic in his voice as I reached out for the doorknob. "For just one minute, let's assume hypothetically that there is some connection between that notebook and Browning Investment Group. What would that have to do with Miss Johnson taking the afternoon off?"

I came forward and put both of my hands on the front of the desk. The large bookends started to step forward but stopped when I didn't go any further. I didn't remember ever being as totally angry as I was right then.

With a quiet but icy cold and threatening voice, I pronounced, "You will deliver Marci Johnson back to me safe and sound. Or the police getting their hands on the notebook will be the least of your worries."

"Are you threatening me, Mr. Peterson?" He smirked slightly.

"No," I said calmly. "I'm making you a promise!"

Then our eyes locked in one of those, male macho, ego bullshit stare-downs, daring the other to blink first. He only had his false sense of security, which I felt was beginning to crumble. I had the emotional backing of fighting for a cause. He lost. He blinked first. He ever so quickly looked down at the photocopies and then back up at me. He instantly realized what he had done. I gave him credit. He recovered quickly, but it was too late. He had given in first.

"Let us once again speak hypothetically, Mr. Peterson. Let's assume I could have some influence over those who are keeping Miss Johnson company. Let's also assume that this alleged notebook would be something they'd be willing to trade her, shall we say, companionship for. How would you suggest this occurs?"

I stood back up. I looked at my watch. "One hour from now, Marci is to be released unharmed at the foot steps of the downtown police headquarters."

"Are you nuts? The police department? No way!"

I put on my best shit-eating grin. "Fine. Your choice. Either Marci or the notebook will be delivered to the police department. I'll be located there so I'll be able to watch her walk safely into the building. Once I'm assured that she is safely inside, I will call you and tell you where you can find the notebook."

His look was one of pure fury. "You are a dead man."

"Fuck you. I have only begun to live." I turned and walked to the door. Before I went out, I turned back and looked at Crossinger. "Now you have fifty-eight minutes."

I left the office at the sounds of yelling and screaming. The whole time I was walking across the office pool, I had the emptiest feeling at my back. I was sure something was going to slam into me from behind. It was a long walk across that office. I finally made it without anything happening. I had to wait a minute for the elevator. I didn't want to appear to anxious, so I decided to try and play coy and wait. I was walking out of the building before I knew it. Making sure no one was following me, I drove back to the police station. I only had to wait a few minutes before Mike walked in.

I asked, "Were you able to get all of it?"

"Yeah, no problem. But there was nothing there that we could use in court. But you're right. They do have her. I'm going to enjoy putting this one away."

When an hour had passed and no Marci arrived, I was extremely agitated. There probably wasn't a swear or cuss word known that I hadn't used in the last five minutes. I was scared and angry. Mike just sat there and watched me. This seemed to piss me off even more.

"How can you just sit there and do nothing?"

"And what would you have me do?"

After mumbling a bunch of uncertainties, I said, "I know. I know. There isn't much we can do. But doing nothing doesn't seem right either."

"Well, as of now, we have nothing legally to pursue."

"What do you mean? We have the notebook."

"Yes, we have the notebook, but, without Branning, we have no corroborating witness. The notebook is hearsay evidence. But I'm sure the IRS would be very interested in its contents."

I started to say something with a lot of bluster and anger. But nothing came out. Instead, I turned and walked over to the window. Mike's office window overlooked the street in front of the station. For the thousandth time, I looked down onto the front steps. This time, I noticed something different. A lot of commotion was going on. Many people were gathered around one spot. Also, several other people were scurrying around. Without saying a word, I ran out of Mike's office door in a flash. Mike was right behind me. It seemed like it took forever to get outside, but I knew I was moving faster than I had ever moved before. I just knew Marci was going to be the cause of all the commotion and not for a good reason. I felt like a professional football fullback as I busted through the crowd to get to the center of the disturbance. The only reason some pissed-off bystander didn't bust my ass was because of all the police officers who followed me into the mass of people. As I got to the center, fear of what I might find made me hesitate just the slightest moment. When I looked down, what I saw brought a load full of mixed emotions. I felt a great deal of relief as I recognized the body on the ground as not being Marci's. But a seething wave of anger got a hold of me as I realized the body belonged to the late Daniel Crossinger.

CHAPTER 14

Pinned to the front of Crossinger's suit coat was a note. It was in simple, handwritten block letters. "The notebook or Marci Johnson is next!" A single bullet hole went through his forehead.

I heard Mike's voice in my ear. "Let's get you out of here. Someone may be watching if it's not already too late."

He gently led me by the arm all the way back to his office. Neither one of us spoke until the door was closed.

I broke the silence. "What the fuck are we going to do now?"

"First, you are going to calm own and think with your head instead of your muscle." He pointed at my crotch

"Look, Mike, I'm only going to tell you this one time." I was talking with such anger that I wasn't yelling, but I was literally spitting out my words. "Yes, there is a lot of physical lust involved between us. But I'm very much in love with her emotionally as well as physically. Do you understand?"

He just sat there and looked at me with that penetrating stare of his. But I stared back. Just when I was about to blow my top and storm out of there, it must have finally sunk in.

"All right, James. I guess you really are serious about her."

"You're damn right I am."

He reached over and picked up the telephone. "Sergeant, I want every single person past or present who has worked for Browning Investment Group brought in for questioning within the next five hours." He paused a few seconds while he listened to the reply. "I don't give a shit. You have five hours. Do you understand?" He slammed down the phone receiver. He sat there for a moment, slightly rocking back and forth. I sensed he was concentrating on something, so I sat quietly.

When he looked up at me, I could tell he was getting extremely angry. "I'm going to bring everyone who is even remotely connected with this case. We will find your Marci Johnson." He tapped his fingers on his desk. "Those sons of a bitch are going to pay for dumping a body on my doorstep."

Apparently, the other police took Mike very seriously when he got angry. Within two hours, the employees of Browning Investment Group started pouring into the police station. People being questioned filled every interrogation room and office. I had decided to stay with Mike. After another two hours of questions, the only thing we had learned was that most of the employees of Browning Investment Group were just that, honest employees. It was becoming quite apparent that only Crossinger and his immediate staff seemed to be guilty of any wrongdoing. Everyone else checked out. The only discrepancy was the two very large bodyguards and one of Crossinger's assistants. They not only didn't show up for questioning, but they weren't anywhere to be found. They were also not even listed anywhere on the Browning payroll. But I was sure they didn't work for free.

Mike and I went back into his office and shut the door. He sat down at his desk. I sat down on the chair on the other side of his desk. We sat in silence for a few moments. We both felt frustrated, but for different reasons. The love of my life was being held hostage, and I was helpless to do anything to try to free her. Mike must have felt as if he had been slugged and not allowed to hit back.

"Well, James, I guess we only have one thing left to do."

"What's that?"

"We need to start calling in all the names in that notebook, but I don't know how successful that will prove. Some of those names belong to some very powerful people with close friends in high places."

Something just dawned on me. "There is one person we haven't talked to."

"Who's that?"

"Mrs. Branning."

"The widow?"

"Look, something Marci told me about her the first time we talked has been bothering me ever since. It has just occurred to me what that might be."

"What's that?"

"She said Branning shouldn't have had any gambling debts because his wife had always given him plenty of money."

"From all indications of their lifestyle, there is no sign that she's wealthy. I wonder why she had control of the purse strings. He was an accountant. You'd think he'd handle the family finances. She told us that she was a housewife and didn't work."

"Marci said Anne Branning was around the office quite often."

"Wait a minute. Didn't Branning's letter also say his wife was part of the reason he was leaving so unexpectedly and secretly?"

With these thoughts brewing, we both sat and looked at each other.

I changed track slightly. "How about doing a little background check on Mrs. Branning as well as call her in to talk to her?"

"At this point, I guess it's all we've got left."

The ringing of Mike's telephone startled both of us. Mike picked up the phone and pushed a button. Only a few seconds later I heard his response to whatever was said at the other end of the phone line. I didn't hear all of what he said, but he basically ordered someone about getting a complete background check completed on Anne Branning, including reference to her maiden name, family background, and all the way back to when she was nothing more than a gleam in her daddy's eye. He shifted through some papers on his desk and came up with one.

"I suppose it's not too late to call her at home." He dialed the number that was on the paper.

Nobody answered. After a while, he hung up without saying a word and looked at me. "I wonder where she could be. I got no answer." He stood up. "Come on. I'll buy you a cup of coffee."

"Sure. I could use one."

We walked down the hall to the department break room. It was just a small cubicle of a room with a couple chairs and small table. A coffeemaker, Styrofoam cups, and cream and sugar were sitting on the table.

"You know, James, something about all this case is nagging at the back of my mind. It's just not sitting right. Sure, that notebook is worth killing over, and that should be enough, but it's like it's not quite the entire picture in focus. Do you know what I mean?"

The sudden thought of the Swiss account number flashed through my mind. *Is this what Marci's kidnapping being really all about?* I let that mull around before another group of questions popped into my already confused mind. *The money?* It couldn't be just about that. Neither Crossinger nor any of the hoods had even so much as hinted that there is a hidden Swiss bank account. At this point I felt as if I was mentally scratching my head before I started coming up with answers. *They only said they were pursuing the notebook and for me to stop investigating Branning's murder. Maybe it's because the account number is in the notebook. That only served to bring another question with answers. But how would they know that? You could bet your last dime they've never seen it. If they had, it would never have left their hands and probably would have been destroyed.* By this time, I was having quite a conversation with myself. "Plus, they would have seen the account number and gotten the money out of the bank. But I have no way of knowing if there really any money in this account is." I lightly shuffled my feet in frustration. I finally decided, "No matter, Marci's life isn't worth any hidden bank account, no matter how large or small. But how am I going to tell Mike about it without looking like I had withheld information?"

I had been so quick to swear that I hadn't. It still came down to if I cared enough about Marci's life. With that as a concern, there was no hesitation. "You know, Mike, there is another possibility here that hasn't been considered or brought to light."

"What might that be?"

"Perhaps there might be something more than the notebook they want."

"Like what?"

I almost had some money. I pacified myself with the passing thought that there was no guarantee that there was any money in the account to start with.

I mumbled to no one in particular. "Nothing gained; nothing lost."

Just as I opened my mouth to tell him about the account, Mike's phone rang. He held up his hand to signal me to hold on while he answered the persistent noise. He answered before I could say anything else. Whatever he heard over the receiver created a very definite change over him. He sat straight up.

"Say that again slowly so I can be sure I heard you right." He looked up at me. A slight grin crept across his face. "I'll be a son of a bitch. Thank you!" He hung up the phone, kicked up his feet on the desk, and put his hands behind his head. He just sat there and grinned at me.

I almost shouted. "What is it?"

"Mrs. Joseph Branning's maiden name is Anne Gionetti. Does that ring a bell?"

"It sure as hell does."

"She's the daughter of Anthony Gionetti."

He took his feet off the desk and picked up the phone receiver. After dialing a set of numbers, he said into the mouthpiece, "I want Mrs. Anne Branning picked up for questioning and in this station within thirty minutes or I'll have someone's head!" He hung up the phone. He had a real self-satisfied smirk on his face.

"James, me boy, this is going to be more than a career maker. This is also going to be a retirement fund all wrapped up in one."

"Yeah, maybe for you. I'll just be satisfied to get Marci back."

"So will I, James. So will I." After about two minutes of quiet, Mike asked, "What was it you were saying about something else besides the notebook?"

I had to think quickly. With this new development of Anne Branning, perhaps it wasn't necessary for me to say anything about the account number. "Would they know about the letter Branning wrote to Marci? It does say some incriminating things."

"Yes, but it's all hearsay evidence. None of it is admissible."

"Then perhaps they feel I might be some kind of a witness against them, so they might consider me a threat."

"I think that is quite obvious."

"Well, if they are what you say, then they probably know I'm friendly with members of the police force. M y silence must be guaranteed."

I felt a little ashamed that my greed would allow me to risk not getting Marci back. But I also felt that, by holding back on the account number, it was kind of like having an ace in the hole if I needed it.

Or is that just rationalizing a selfish motive?

Just a little bit left of a suspicious nature was left in the back of my mind. I wasn't 100 percent convinced that a young, healthy, and beautiful woman could love an older man like me.

No! I know deep down inside that I'd pick Marci over the money when it came right down to it, but not any sooner than I had to. I just hope that, if I must make that decision, I don't wait too long.

The next twenty minutes went by agonizingly slow. We could only sit and look at each other. Neither one of us wanted to say anything. For the second time, the ringing of Mike's phone shattered the silence. He glanced at me before he snatched up the receiver. He grumbled greeting and then listened intensely. I grew tense as I sat there and waited. He never said a word the whole time. He just listened.

"That'll be fine." He hung up. He looked at me and smiled. "They picked up Anne Branning. And listen to this. They picked her up at the airport."

"Where was she going?"

I first thought about the plane ticket and Swiss bank account number. But I didn't have time to get over that thought when Mike's answer rocked me.

"She was getting ready to board a plane."

"Where to?" It seemed like Mike was purposely dragging this out. I was beginning to get irritated because Marci's life was on the line.

He must have heard the anxiety in my voice. "Calm down. I'll tell you. She was booked on a flight to Switzerland."

The word "Switzerland" sounded like a large explosion. All the blood must have rushed out of my head.

"James, are you all right? You just turned pale white. What's wrong?"

I could almost feel the piece of paper that had the Swiss bank account number burning up in my wallet. I took a couple moments to catch my breath.

"Oh … ah … nothing. If she had made it out of the country, she would have disappeared and taken Marci's life with her, if she's not already dead."

"Now you don't know that."

"For what other reason would Anne Branning be skipping town?"

"We'll find that out. They are bringing her here."

CHAPTER 15

The interrogation room where Anne Branning was brought wasn't like the typical dreary room seen on most TV cop shows. This one was designed with comfort in mind. The theory was that those more influential or wealthy suspects who needed to be coddled would relax and open up. The two soft, padded chairs, sofa, and table were in pristine condition. The wallpaper, though a soft blue for mood, was still full of color. Even a faint trace of easy music was in the background. I knew they'd had this room for a while.

Looking around the room at the apparent new look of everything, it told me that they sure didn't use this place very often. Influential or wealthy suspects were at a premium. But Anne Branning must be considered one of those select few. She sat there and confidently smoked her cigarette. Also present in the room, besides Anne Branning and myself, was Mike. A female officer was taking notes and acting as a chaperone. Another male detective was Mike's backup, although Mike was the only one asking the questions.

"So, Mrs. Branning, tell me again so I'll understand. Why were you leaving the country?"

"I was simply going to take a few days off to get rid of the pressures of what's happened."

I started to ask something, but Mike shot me a glance that silenced me instantly. "Initially, you told us that you were leaving on business. Also, I find Switzerland a long way to go for a couple day's rest. It would take you a couple days alone to just get over jet lag. How are you able to afford such an expensive and short vacation?"

"I said I needed to get away from here with all the distractions in order to clear my thought process. It allows me to make sound business decisions about my husband's affairs. It was intended to be like a mini working vacation."

I didn't give Mike the opportunity to stop me. "Your husband hasn't even been buried yet. Won't you miss the funeral while you're gone? That's hardly the grieving widow!"

I paid no attention to Mike. He was huffing and puffing so hard and fast that it looked like he had just run a marathon.

Her answer took some of the fire out of his anger. "Well, I wouldn't have been missing much. You see, my husband and I weren't very close anymore. Our marriage had become more of a business convenience than a relationship."

"Now you don't even have that," I quipped.

She started to bluster.

Before she could put together any coherent sounds, I pushed on, "What kind of arrangements did your marriage have?"

The anger was now very evident on her face. But she got it together very quickly. "Look, I agreed to talk to you because I was concerned about Miss Johnson's health. You have digressed this to a personal attack on my late husband and me! I will not let you do that. There will be no further discussion until my lawyer is present."

I started to go after her. Mike stopped me. "James, that is enough."

I turned my anger on him. "What do you mean? Marci is still missing, and she knows something about it."

"How dare you imply I had some connection with that tramp's disappearance?" Anne Branning was shouting so hard that she was spitting.

Mike looked straight at me and pointed his finger at my face. "You sit there and keep your damn mouth shut! Not one word! Or you'll be sitting outside until we are done. Is that clear?"

"But she—"

He didn't let me finish. "Is that clear?" He almost shouted.

"Yes, Mike."

"It had better be." He turned from me and directed his attention back to Anne Branning. Gone was his hostility. Total cordiality replaced it. "Please excuse his enthusiastic outbursts. He is quite concerned about Miss Johnson's current location. He is not acting his normal self." I knew he heard me stir in my chair, but he went on unimpeded. "We were talking about you getting away from everything for a few days. I certainly understand how bad things seemed to have gotten lately for you. But I just wonder. Why Switzerland of all places?"

I wanted to hear the answer to this question. "For me, Switzerland offers great relaxation and comfort. I have been there a few times before while growing up. It is a place where I can mentally revert to better times. This serves as great therapy."

"I quite understand the need for that at a time like this. But there is the question of your husband's funeral."

He gave a look that said, "Shut the hell up."

"Are you indeed going to miss his burial?"

"Due to the late arrival of some out-of-town relatives, his funeral is being held up for a couple days."

Mike sat there for a few moments. Then he slowly sat straight up in his chair. "Mrs. Branning, a simple yes or no will do. Were you going to miss your husband's funeral?"

There was just the slightest hesitation. "Yes, I was." She paused as if to gather her thoughts. "No matter what you may have heard or think, I cared about my husband dearly. To watch over his funeral would hurt me deeply. Besides, he is to be cremated with a simple eulogy to be said. There will be nothing elaborate. After all, he didn't have a lot of family and very few friends."

I said, "Not according to the people I talked to. He was apparently quite a ladies' man."

"James!" Mike stated before Anne Branning unloaded on me.

"Just what the hell do you think you know about my husband? You know absolutely nothing. The only thing you know is what that insignificant tramp told you."

"Marci Johnson is more of a lady than you could hope to be in your wildest dreams, Miss Anne Gionetti."

At the sound of her maiden name, she went ashen and froze in position. I realized my dropping of her maiden name screwed up Mike's plan of attack. But I was pissed, and this bitch was the cause of it all.

Mike turned to his assistant. "Get him out of here now!"

"But, Mike, I have an interest here."

"I warned you. But you couldn't keep your mouth shut. Consider yourself lucky I don't have you arrested."

I didn't wait to be escorted. I stormed out of the room. I had no idea where I was headed. I just walked. I found myself walking out the front door of the police department and into the night. I went straight to my borrowed car and got in. As I drove off, headed for nowhere, I didn't know where to go, but I knew I had to find Marci, or it would be like losing my life. I drove around for quite a while and tried to figure out where to look. I went to every single person I knew who might possibly know anything. I questioned many people who I had used over the years as stool pigeons on some of my investigations that eventually proved to be an attempt to defraud the insurance company I worked for. And I found nothing. Nobody knew anything. I must have hit every bar, dive, and hole in the wall in the city.

I was sitting at a stoplight and wondering where to go next when I realized the sun was coming up. I looked at my watch and realized it was six thirty. I was getting quite frustrated. I had no more ideas. I had no place to go and no one to question. I looked around desperately. I suddenly realized I was sitting in front of the city hall building. The thought hit me unexpectedly. The city clerk's office would have all holdings of Browning Investment Group on record. But Old Iron Shorts had said she had already given me everything. But she wouldn't be in the courthouse for another ninety minutes. I had exhausted all other options, so I had no other choice but to sit and wait. I circled around the block and found a parking space as close to the front of the building as I could. I got out and put some money in the two-hour parking meter. I got back into the car, and I could tell that the first signs of morning traffic were beginning to be evident. I set the alarm on my watch for eight o'clock. Even though I knew that it would not do any good. The damn thing really didn't sound loud enough to wake if I really fell asleep. "But what the hell. Maybe it might work." I mumbled.

My watch alarm worked, or maybe it was the car horn blowing right next to me. I woke up at three minutes after eight o'clock. I shook my head a couple times to get the cobwebs loose. Then I got out of the car and put some more money in the parking meter. Without hesitation, I headed into the courthouse.

As I came through the doors to the city clerk's office, I realized my worst nightmare. Old Iron Shorts looked as mean as ever. I guess I had that disgusted look on my face as I slowly shook my head to the left. When she noticed me, she rolled her eyes back and turned away. Neither one of us wanted this meeting. But I at least had justification for pursuing the agony. The need to find Marci overcame my distaste for this woman. I quickly walked around to her front side.

"Look, it's important!" I hoped she might see the desperation in my eye.

"What do you want?"

"I need any and all further information that you can provide me on the holdings of Browning Investment Group."

"Look, Shit Face, I gave you everything I could find. There is no more!"

"There must be something else. That can't be all there is." My voice cracked both from the strain of Marci's disappearance and exhaustion.

She took a step back, tilted her head slightly, and gave me a side glance as she was trying to figure out my latest outburst. She finally made her decision. "Look, I'd like to help you, but, honestly, there's nothing else. Why is it so important?"

"Some nasty people who work for Browning Investment Group have kidnapped someone I care a great deal about. I don't know where they have taken her. I must find out before they really hurt her beyond what can be fixed." My meaning was quite clear.

"I don't have anything else." She paused for just a couple seconds. "But I do know someone who might be able to help you. It's worth a try."

I jumped at this like a man grasping at the last straw of hope. "Who? How? Where?" I was so desperate that I was blurting out one-word questions so fast that she couldn't answer any of them.

"Calm down, boy. You're spitting all over yourself. His name is Bill Warden." A smug smile came across her face. "He's my nephew. He works at the *Tribune-Herald*."

"What can he tell me?"

"He has spent the last five years as a crime reporter. If anyone in this town can find a connection, he can."

"Thanks. I owe you one," I said over my shoulder as I rushed out.

I didn't hear her response, but I knew she mumbled something as I raced out the door. It probably was something along the line that I sure did.

It didn't take me long to get over to the newspaper building, The Tribune-Herald. I broke all existing speed laws.

I entered the front doors. I approached the receptionist with great haste. I normally would have strolled slower across the lobby to enjoy this young lady's pretty smile a little longer. But under the circumstances, I was in no mood to waste time.

I amazed myself as I said to myself, "Boy, I must really be in love to pass up an opportunity like that."

As I stopped in front of her desk, her beaming smile turned to words. "Yes, sir. May I help you?"

"I'm here to see Bill Warden."

"Do you have an appointment?"

"If you'll just let him know that James Peterson is here to see him. Martha Trumble, his aunt, sent me here."

Just a little of her smile left. A bit of suspicion replaced it. "Just one minute. I will check. Please have a seat."

She indicated a small sofa-style chair that was against the wall and out of the way. I started to object, but soon realized it was useless. The receptionist had her head down, and she was talking on the phone. I stepped over to the sofa chair and sat down. I only had to wait about five minutes when a young male version of Old Iron Shorts appeared before me. There was no doubt about their family relationship.

I stood up and accepted his offered hand. "Mr. Peterson, I'm Bill Warden. What can I do for you? I just got off the phone with Aunt Martha. She said I should help you with whatever I can."

I never thought of Old Iron Shorts as an Aunt Martha. I started to express that thought, but then thought better of it. It was a good idea not to insult the aunt or one I was about to ask for help.

"First, you can start by calling me James."

"Only if you call me Bill."

"Okay, Bill. That's a deal. Now, I'm investigating in the murder of Joseph Branning."

"That's the fellow who was gunned down across town. There was an amazing lack of clues, or so the police told us. Is that correct? Or do you know something that the police don't?"

"No. I'd say the police know about the same amount I do."

"The same amount, but not the same thing?"

"Not exactly. I'm working very closely with them on this. There are things that have come up that aren't relevant to the case, and they don't need to know."

"Such as what?"

"I'd like to take some of your time with a few questions." His natural reporter ability didn't fall for this poor attempt of a side-track.

"James, withholding evidence from the police is a crime. It also leads to a hell of a good story."

I looked cautiously around and answered in a slightly hushed voice, "Right here is a little too public of a place to be discussing this. Is there someplace where we can talk more privately?"

We locked stares for a few seconds.

He finally answered, "I don't think that would be much of a problem. Please follow me. We can have some peace and quiet, along with privacy, in my office."

He led me down the center of a large, open office filled with desks everywhere. Only about a quarter of them had people sitting at the desk. Most weren't really doing a whole lot. He proceeded into one of the side offices, which had a glass front starting about waist high and reached to the ceiling. Below the glass was brown wood paneling. After we walked into his office, he closed the door behind us. He indicated the chair next to his desk.

I waited until he was seated in his chair behind his desk. "I'm trying to locate any or all of additional holdings that the Browning Investment Group might have besides the obvious Browning Building."

"Why have you come to me with this?"

I squirmed in my seat a bit on purpose and tried to give myself some time to come up with a viable answer. I finally tried the truth. I justified it to myself by thinking, *What the hell. It's worth a try.*

"Because your aunt said you might be able to supply me with answers to some questions that she didn't have."

He grinned and shook his head. "That sounds like my Aunt Martha."

I'd never get used to hearing her called Aunt Martha. The picture it conjured up was entirely different from the person I knew and didn't love.

"But if Aunt Martha couldn't answer you questions regarding that company, then I don't know how I can be much of a help."

I started to get up to leave because I thought he wasn't going to be much help. But he surprised me.

"What were your questions?"

"I'm looking for anything that would give me a lead as to Browning Investment Group's additional holdings. Do you know of anything other than the main building that they own?"

"You know, it's funny you should ask that."

"Why?"

"Only about six months ago, I was investigating of my own into the Gionetti crime family. I was to do a five-part story on them and their effect on the local economy and businesses."

After a noticeable pause, I asked, "Is it possible to get a copy of your final story?"

"No, it isn't."

I couldn't tell if the grin on his face was of smugness or sarcasm. I finally couldn't stand the silence. "Why not?"

"The final story was never written."

My mouth hanging open probably looked funny.

He chuckled lightly. "I always thought it was strange. I got close to the actual writing of the story. I was called into my editor's office and told I should bring all information I had compiled to him for review."

"Is that a normal procedure?"

"Absolutely not! But it has happened. Although, when it does, it is an extremely rare occurrence."

"Why did he ask for the information?"

"His story was so he could see if there was enough meat to the story for me to continue with it to print."

"Was there?"

He just stared at me. "Apparently, no, there wasn't. Several days later, he still hadn't gotten back to me. I tried to track him down. It was quite an effort. It soon became evident that he was trying to avoid me. I finally cornered him in the employee break room. He said the story had been killed and that was final. After several minutes of very hard pushing, he said the order had come from up top. He had no choice. He also never gave me back any of the original material I gave him."

"Did you give him all of your research?"

He grinned, just like the cat that swallowed the canary. "Not exactly."

"What do you mean?"

"I made a photocopy of everything before I turned it over to him."

"Does he know that?"

"No. In fact, none of it is here on these premises."

"Where do you have it?"

"It's in safekeeping."

"Can you remember any of it that might show a connection between the Browning Investment Group and the Gionetti family?"

"Are you kidding? The Gionetti family is the Browning Investment Group."

"Why don't the police know that?"

"The police in this town generally try hard, but they can't be everywhere and know everything."

"Why don't you tell them?"

He sat forward in his chair. "Let me tell you something. It

doesn't matter what town it is. The police don't like the news media. Sure, they use us when they need us, but, overall, they plain won't even talk to us."

"That figures."

He ignored my comment. "The Browning Investment Group is a legal front for the Gionetti's money laundering. Anne Gionetti-Branning is chairman of the board. The health of the old man, Nick Gionetti, became too frail to allow him to continue to run the family. His only heir, Anne, took over. He still sits on the throne but make no mistake. Anne runs the daily family business. Times have changed."

"That's all fine and dandy for tying in the Browning Investment Group with organized crime, but it doesn't help me with my main problem."

Being a reporter probably gave him a keen sense of people. He noticed my anxiety immediately, even though I thought I had covered it well. He sat forward in his chair.

"What seems to be your main problem?"

After a few mumbles and false starts, I was finally able to get it out. "My girlfriend is Marci Johnson." It still felt both strange and exciting to refer to Marci as my girlfriend. "She works as a secretary for the Browning Investment Group." He arched an eyebrow as he heard that. "She has disappeared." I took a breath to pause to get together in my mind how I wanted to proceed. "My investigation of Branning led me into some sensitive areas that seemed to worry the head groupies. Shortly thereafter, two huge, gorilla-type guys pounded on me and told me that Marci was their guest. If I didn't stop poking into Branning's death, she'd become a permanent guest of the local cemetery."

"What are you going to do?"

"Find Marci and find a way to put those creeps where they can't hurt anyone anymore. Ever!"

"That sounds like you mean something permanent."

"Whatever it takes."

"How can I help?"

"They've had to stash Marci somewhere, perhaps an empty warehouse or something. I don't know."

"No, too obvious. Let me think. It would have to be someplace that no one would think of looking."

"Someplace where no one could accidentally stumble across. Where there was absolutely no traffic. Where they could make enough noise to wake the dead and no one would hear anything."

His sudden reaction startled me. "What did you say? Say that again."

"Yeah, where there was no traffic—"

"No. No. The last part about the noise."

I looked at him suspiciously. I wasn't quite sure where he was going with this. So I started out slowly and then spoke normal halfway through.

"Where they could make enough noise to wake the dead and—"

"That's it!"

"What's it?"

"Where they wouldn't wake the dead." He saw the quizzical look on my face. "Don't you get it?" He puffed a breath of frustration. "Wasn't one of Browning's executives recently killed?"

"As a matter of fact, he was. Daniel Crossinger."

"I understand he was unceremoniously dropped on police department steps. There must have been a message there, but none of us in the media could figure it out. Because it was two people from the same office, we knew there had to be a connection. It's just that no one could put it together. The police are being extremely closed mouth about this one."

I put my hand over my mouth and faked a cough, so I wouldn't give away my grin as I thought of Mike and his handling of this case. I knew Bill couldn't have known about the note pinned to Crossinger. The police hadn't released that bit of information. I decided to give him a hint. "It was basically a message to me. I should drop my investigation, or they would kill Marci."

"It must have been a very important message for them to kill one of their own."

"Not really. He was about to take the fall for it all. But dead men don't talk."

"That's interesting."

"How so?"

"Well, you must be doing something right, or they wouldn't feel threatened enough to threaten you. After all, kidnapping is not their usual style. Murder maybe. Prostitution certainly. Gambling without a doubt. Even some drugs. But a successful kidnapping is very hard to pull off."

"So, what you're saying is that Marci is probably already dead."

"I didn't say that. I said it was hard to pull off, but not impossible. It would really have to be worth their while. You don't have something they want, do you?"

"Remember I said earlier that things had come up that weren't relevant to the police investigation?"

"Yes, I do." His eyes narrowed a bit. "This has to stay between us for the cause of the investigation. If you let this out, it could really cause a lot of harm. Can you do that?"

"Why should I?"

I stared at him. I suddenly didn't care for him. I stood up and started to leave without a word.

He blurted out, "Where are you going?"

"If you can't promise to keep this off the record and out of the press, then you can find yourself another source!"

"Hey, you came to me for help. I didn't go to you. If I were to help you, you'd have to figure that I'd expect you to assist me. What's in it for me?"

"God, is that the universal question? What's in it for me? I had hoped that, for once, I had found a reporter who was more interested in the betterment of its readers instead of the greed."

"Look, you don't investigate out of the goodness of your heart. I'm sure you get paid for what you do. This is how I make my living."

"All right. How about an exclusive story after all is said and done?"

"Will the police agree to that?"

"What's to agree? I'm the only one who knows the whole story. Or should I say all there is to know up until now."

"That sounds reasonable. It's a deal."

"I have your promise that not one word reaches any form of the news media until this is all over."

"I cannot promise for everyone else, but not a word will come from me. I will guarantee that."

I stared at him for a long minute and sat down. "Well, I guess I can't ask for more than that."

He turned to his phone and pushed made a short call. Apparently, he called some internal number as he suddenly said, "Pull up the files on Daniel Crossinger." I wondered why he didn't just pull up a phone book from his desk drawer or something. That thought was never answered Then hung up his phone and stared at me. I deduced that this was some kind of "Chicken game". Who would give in first. I was determined to not blink, figuratively speaking. I sat there and starred back. After a few moments his phone rang. He picked it up and listened. He took a few notes on a note pad and then hung up. He sat there and just stared at me.

I was just about to pee my pants in anticipation when he finally said, "Daniel Crossinger," He was more mumbling to himself than talking to me. "He lives on Sasmore Street."

He wrote everything down on a piece of paper on a notepad. He ripped off the paper, looked at it, and handed it to me. "This is his address and phone number. Check it out."

"How did you get this?"

"A newspaper never throws anything away. I don't normally have a phone book handy, so I called down stair to our research department and looked they looked it up. It is good to give them something to do to once in a while to earn the big dollars we pay them."

I shook my head and said sarcastically. "Amazing."

"I'd suggest you get the police to help you go to his apartment."

I tucked it into my pocket without looking at it. "They'd make such a big production out of it that the bad guys would see them coming and certainly kill her."

"But they are especially trained to handle those situations."

"Yeah, right. And I believe in the tooth fairy, too." I mumbled.

"What did you say?"

"Nothing important. Just thinking out loud." I said.

"Tell me. What makes you think she might be at Crossinger's place?"

"He's been dead only a matter of hours. He isn't married. So, no one has any reason to go there."

"He was murdered. Wouldn't the police have gone to his place to search for evidence as to his killers?"

"It's a possibility, but highly unlikely. First, they would have to establish probable cause to get a search warrant. He was the victim, not the murderer. Second, from what you've told me, they already have an idea who killed him. It's just a matter of trying to prove it. They might eventually go there, but not right away. Plus, if the kidnappers were caught there, who would the police blame for the kidnapping? Crossinger is dead, the perfect scapegoat."

"It's worth a try. I don't have anything else."

"If it doesn't work out, give me a call. I'll try to find if there might be somewhere else."

"Thanks, Bill. I do appreciate it."

I stood and shook his hand. All the way to the car, I kept saying to myself, "It's too obvious. This can't be possible. It's too easy."

But something made me head in the direction of Crossinger's apartment without delay. I stopped at a local convenience store and picked up a street map of the city and some gum. My mouth was exceedingly dry. Sasmore Street was a few miles across town in the suburbs. The distance in a big city wasn't really much. It only took me about twenty minutes before I turned down the right street. Five minutes later, I was pulling into the Sasmore Apartments complex. It was your typical apartment complex, six long, two-story buildings. Each building had six apartments each. I found Crossinger's building rather easily. It was near the rear of the complex. His apartment was on the ground floor on the end of the building near the rear.

By now, it was mid-morning. I was very surprised, but happy the complex grounds were very quiet, and no one was out and about. I parked my car in an empty slot not directly in front of the apartment in question. I left the keys in the ignition in case I needed to make a quick getaway. As I got out of the car, I carefully closed the door so as not to rise suspicion in anyone. I approached the building from the side. As I got near his door, I pulled my gun out of the holster. I cocked back the hammer. Making sure the safety was off, I felt as ready as ever. Although, I just knew the pounding of my heart was so loud that it could be heard in the next county. I crept past several bushes, carefully ducked under any windows, and arrived at his door. A slight alcove was in front of his door. It was kind of like a front porch. It was just like all the other apartments. There was also only one door to each little porch. So I felt safe that no innocent people would pop up.

As silently as I possibly could, I snuck up to his windowless door. A peephole was in the door, so I had to avoid it. I put my ear as close to the door as I could without touching. I listened. Voices were coming from the other side. The more I heard, the more I decided it must be the TV. That was confirmed when I heard the familiar jingle of a well-known pizza joint. I stepped to one side in case someone was to open the door as I listened. I kept one eye on the complex grounds. I didn't want anyone sneaking up on me while I was attempting this rescue. I suddenly wished I had a plan.

I knew this impulsive storm trooper technique leaves a lot to be desired. I said quietly to myself. "What the hell am I going to do next? Bust the door down? Rush in, kill all the bad guys, and save the damsel in distress? I doubt it. That only works in the movies. So, what should I do? I could knock on the door and shoot my way in." As usual I answered myself with what I wanted to hear. "No. What if I have the wrong apartment and kill innocent people? I wouldn't be able to live with myself. Not to mention the long prison sentence I'd receive."

I squatted down against the wall alongside the door. I tried to think of an answer. I had been squatting there about three minutes when I heard the door being unlocked. My instinct was to jump up and run. But my old man legs wouldn't uncoil as fast as I wanted them to. I felt sure that whoever was coming out that door would catch me. I was able to straighten up and stumble on weak legs and knees around the corner of the alcove before the door opened. Just outside of the alcove were big enough bushes that I was able to slide noiselessly behind one. It was my only option. I wouldn't have had enough time to make it around the building's end. I couldn't have made it to any other building before whoever would have come out far enough to see me running away. Although, this only choice put me dangerously close. It gave me the opportunity to see who was coming out of the apartment and possibly hear anything that might be said.

I tried to stay still and will my heavy breathing and beating heart to be quiet. I even stopped chewing my gum in case that might make noise. I heard the guy coming outside say something, but I could only make out what sounded like "be back in about thirty." I knew that voice, but I couldn't place it.

Then fear, anger, and hatred all flowed out at once as I saw Puke Face step out of the alcove. He didn't even bother to look around. He just stepped on out. He walked over to the side of the building and got into a car that was parked in one of the parking stalls in the open parking lot. I saw him look back at the building just after starting the car and before pulling out. I froze like a rock, praying he didn't see me squatting behind the bush. He apparently didn't. I was still as a stone until he was completely out of sight. Then I sat still for another couple minutes. I just wanted to make sure he wasn't trying to be tricky, go around the block, and sneak back. He wasn't. Or at least he didn't reappear.

I figured this was my best chance. If I knocked on the door, perhaps whoever was inside would figure Puke Face had forgotten something and open the door without question. I slowly climbed out from behind my bush. I didn't even bother to dust off the dirt or leaves I had gotten on myself. I was going to have to do something about these legs of mine. They felt a hundred years old. After a couple steps, the circulation was back. As I walked straight up to the door, I considered if I'd stand in front or off to the side. If I stood off to the side when the door was open, whoever was inside surely wouldn't be stupid enough to step out to see who had knocked when he saw no one standing in the alcove. He'd probably just shut the door and be alerted that something was up. So the direct approach seemed to be the only ploy called for.

First, I took the gum out of my mouth and covered the peephole. With gun poised in my right hand, hammer cocked back and ready, I stood squarely in front of the door. I had my ears attuned to any sound, both in front of me and behind. I was sure Puke Face was going to return prematurely. Then I'd be screwed. I took a deep breath and knocked on the door. I took the classic shooter stance, knees slightly bent with my left hand securely holding my right gun hand steady. I pointed my pistol about chest high at the closed door. I heard movement inside the apartment. The inside person must have tried to look out the peephole because I could hear him just on the other side of the door. I heard the door being unlocked, and I slightly shifted my weight onto my left leg so my right was free to use. As soon as the door started to open, I kicked it with my right foot as hard as I could. I could tell by the resistance on the door that it must have contacted the person on the other side.

I didn't hesitate. I rushed in and entered the apartment. I saw Puke Face's buddy bouncing straight back on the floor. He still held on to the gun he had in his hand. When he stopped bouncing enough to gain control of himself, he jumped to his feet and started to bring his gun straight at me. I was faster or maybe just a little more stable than he was. I pointed straight at him and fired. But so did he.

As I heard the gunshots, I also more felt and then heard the wood splinter right above my head. I saw a bloody hole open in his chest. I didn't really have much time to further evaluate the damage as, out of another room, came flying one of those gorilla-type guys firing his gun as fast as his fat fingers could pull the trigger. I didn't hesitate. I crouched low and let off two shots in his direction. I had no idea where his bullets went. I only knew that they didn't hit me. He wasn't so lucky. One round caught him in the stomach. The other opened a huge hole somewhere around his neck.

I suddenly understood that if anyone ever says gunshots aren't loud, then they hadn't heard them inside an apartment or watched to many detectives shows.

I felt as if I were standing inside multiple explosions. When the ringing finally stopped, the silence was deafening. I stayed crouched as I desperately looked around and constantly jerked my pistol everywhere I looked. I wanted to be sure there weren't any more assailants.

Finally satisfied that no one was going to jump out of the woodwork or anywhere else, I started my search of the apartment. The first place I looked was the room the gorilla had come out of. I had to step over his obviously dead body as it was lying in the doorway. As I entered the bedroom, what I saw scared me more than anything else that had happened so far. Marci was lying on the bed on her back. She was still as a board. Her mouth was gagged. A piece of tape was over her eyes. Both her hands and feet were tied. I could see no movement at all. Except for no shoes, she still wore all the same clothes she had on when I saw her at lunch. Her hair seemed to be very messed up, but I couldn't see any other sign of physical damage. I abandoned all of my concerns for others that might still be in the room as I rushed to her side.

As soon as I got near her, I said, "Marci honey, it's me. James. Are you all right?"

Before I could release any of her bonds, she started to squirm. Wave after wave of relief swept over me that she was still alive. I quickly pulled down the gag off her mouth.

"Oh, Jimmy! Oh, Jimmy!" She sobbed.

I very gently took the tape off her eyes. It took a few moments for her to focus, but I could see the tears that were already running down her cheeks. I kissed away her tears.

"Relax, baby. I'll untie you, and we'll be out of here."

I untied her feet first so that, if nothing else, she could be mobile if we had to make a quick getaway. She wasn't reacting much. She still lay there even after I had her feet free. I figured she was probably still suffering from shock. As I untied her hands, she did react. She threw her arms around me and hugged me tighter than a vise grip. I squeezed back and hoped to try to stop her shaking spasms.

She kept mumbling, "Oh, God, baby. Oh, God, baby. I'm glad you're here."

"We'd better save your prayers for later. We have to get out of here before Puke Face gets back."

This thought seemed to send more waves of fear through her. She shook even harder. I had a very hard time getting her up on her feet. I was finally able to half-carry, half-walk her out of the bedroom and over the top of the gorilla. When she first saw him lying there with blood all over, I thought she might lose control. But she only let out a small gasp and took a small involuntary step back. I reassured her, and she proceeded to step over the body. It was a big step. As we passed by the second body, I tried my best to shield her from seeing another dead person. Either I was successful or she didn't pay any attention because she went past without any hesitation.

When we came to the front door, I just knew we'd find Puke Face standing there. When we got there, the alcove was empty. I paused long enough to look and see that the complex grounds were as devoid of people as it was when I first got there. I quickly escorted Marci to my car. She must have been a sight if anyone had looked at us coming out of the apartment. I was practically carrying this woman, who must have looked like she was drunk. She only wore her stockings and no shoes. I put her in the passenger seat and swiftly ran to the driver's side. As I reached for the keys to start the car, I realized I still had my pistol in my hand, so I put it in my holster.

I kept my head on a swivel and looked around for Puke Face to return. I felt another big sense of relief as the car started on the first try. I looked over at Marci. She was sitting back in her seat, slightly slumped. Her eyes were wide open, and she was looking straight at me.

I reached over and grabbed her hand. "Relax, honey. Everything is going to be okay now. I'm not going to let them hurt you anymore."

She didn't say anything. She just lightly grinned at me. I put the car in reverse and started to pull out of the parking slot. I put my right arm on the back of the seat in order to help myself turn so I could see what was behind us. I saw a dark sedan pull onto the complex grounds. The car was too far away for me to clearly see who was driving. If it were indeed Puke Face, there was no way I could drive out of there without passing him in the opposite direction. I cussed the decision I had made to park where I was, right in front of the building with empty slots on both side of me. When I had arrived, I was so intent on Marci's rescue that I hadn't been aware of my surroundings and possible escape routes.

Only an amateur would make that mistake. Maybe I should have listened to Bill and involved the police. *I hope this mistake won't cost me dearly. What should I do? The only thing I can!*

"Marci, duck down!"

"What? What did you say?"

"Duck down on the floor. Puke Face is coming back."

Even though I was sure she didn't understand, she complied. I heard a couple of small whimpers as she struggled down onto the floor. She didn't show any signs of injury, but I wondered if she had some internal bruises. Because I had already started backing out, it would look pretty obvious if I pulled back in. If I were going to do this, I knew I couldn't delay any longer. I took a deep breath and backed all the way out. I tried to accomplish this as if nothing in the world was wrong. I slowly pulled back about a car's length and then swung the rear end to the right. I came to a complete stop before I put the car in drive.

"Please, God, don't let him recognize me or the car," I said about three times.

I pulled as far to the right of the double-slotted parking area as our two cars approached each other. I tried as casually as possible to keep my face covered with my left hand as I slightly looked to his right. I initially thought this might work. Because he wasn't really expecting me to be there, he might not know who I was. But as we passed, I could see in my mirror that his head was rotating around as he tried to take another look at me. Because he was only looking and not doing anything about turning around, I only slightly picked up the speed of the car. It wouldn't do to panic yet and give us away. He hadn't shown any signs of total recognition. I was getting close to the exit of the complex when I saw him pull into the parking stall directly in front of the apartment that we had just left.

"Oh, shit!"

"Jimmy, what's the matter?"

"I should have shut the door to the apartment. I'm sure he'll be able to see that it's open from the parking stall."

Sure enough, I no longer had gotten that out of my mouth when I saw him burning rubber while backing out of the parking spot. The race was on. My foot hit the gas pedal so hard that I thought it would go through the floor. My little borrowed car started to hesitate just a half-second, as if in shock, that such a request should be asked of it. Then all four cylinders opened up, and we were flying out of there.

I turned right on Sasmore. I barely missed a car that was coming down the street from my right on the opposite side of the street. I was sure the driver had some choice words about me. But I didn't care to stop and discuss it. I kept looking alternately forward as to where we were going and in the rearview mirror to watch for Puke Face. We were getting close to the first four-way intersection. He hadn't pulled out of the complex grounds onto Sasmore yet. I took a quick second to look down at Marci. She was curled up on the floor, but her look back told me that, though she was scared, she was relatively all right.

"Come on. Come on," I begged as the corner got closer.

There still was no sign of the dark sedan behind me. Just as I started the left turn around the corner and thought I could let out a small breath, in the mirror, I saw the front end of his car come screaming out of the complex driveway. The next block was an even shorter one. I was able to turn left before the sedan came around the corner. But I couldn't count on him not following us. I kept the gas pedal on the floor. I didn't look at the speedometer. I feared that it would scare me. I said a silent prayer that no one would step out in front of me. There was no way I would have been able to stop in time. Another intersection came up, and I turned left again. There was still no sign of Puke Face. I suddenly realized I was approaching Sasmore again. I turned left, and I was soon in sight of the apartment complex. I slowed down and turned in. If Puke Face wasn't behind me, chances were, he wouldn't look for us here.

"What's going on? Have we lost him?" I heard from the car floor.

"I hope so. I haven't seen him for a couple of turns."

We pulled into a parking slot in front of the office. I kept expecting our adversary to pull in behind us. But our luck was holding so far.

I shut off the engine and took the keys with me. "Come on, Marci. Let's go."

"Where?"

"Where there are some other people."

I climbed out of the car and ran to the other side. I opened her door. Marci was just barely uncurling off the floor. I could see she was still very stiff and sore. I tried not to look at her exposed legs because her skirt had ridden up quite high. But it was awful hard not to notice. Her beautiful legs always seemed to hold my attention. I assisted her the rest of the way out of the car. I put my arm around her waist. After a couple steps, she was moving better. I was sure her shoeless feet didn't feel too comfortable on that concrete parking lot. I was sure it would feel better once we were on the smooth sidewalk. I saw the open sign on the glass office door. That was when Marci realized where we were.

She stopped dead and shook her head. "No, no! Not here!" She even took a step backwards.

I hugged her tighter. "It's okay, honey. People are here. It's the last place he'd look. He wouldn't expect us to come back here."

"You sure?" She still stood dead-still.

I wasn't sure at all, but I tried to answer as confidently as possible. "Look, there are people inside and a telephone. My buddy, the cop, is only a phone call away."

With my arm that was still around her waist, I pressed her forward ever so lightly. She reluctantly took the first step. The rest came a lot easier.

The office door was unlocked. I opened it, and we stepped in. The young girl inside looked up from her receptionist desk and smiled. Then she saw Marci. Even though she wasn't showing signs of any physical harm, her hair, clothes, and makeup were a mess. Of course, another woman would notice. I saw many thoughts pass over her face.

Finally, she got her voice. "Is she all right? What's wrong?"

"She'll be just fine if I can use your phone."

"Sure, yeah. Ah, okay."

"Where is it?"

"Over there on the counter." She pointed off to the side.

"Please help her." I lowered Marci on to a chair.

I stopped by the office front door and locked it. On second thought, I turned the open sign around to show closed.

"What are you doing?" the young lady asked as she cautiously approached Marci.

"Calling the police," I said back over my shoulder.

I picked up the phone and dialed Mike.

He answered on the second ring. "Lieutenant Glosman."

"Mike, this is James."

"James, where are you? We've found out some things."

"Like what?"

"I can't say over the phone, but it's extremely important to the Branning case. You need to come in right away."

"That will have to wait. I found Marci."

"Where?"

"We are at the Sasmore Apartment Complex. Guess who lives here?"

"I don't know. Who?"

"Actually, who used to live here."

"Tell me already!"

"Some detective you are. You don't even know."

"James!"

"This is where Crossinger used to live."

"You mean the guy who was dumped on our steps?"

"Right on your very first try."

"What in the hell are you doing there?"

"It's where she was held captive."

"Are you there right now?"

"Not exactly. We are in the apartment complex office. Right now, a couple of other nonliving entities are occupying his apartment."

"You stay put. We are on our way."

I didn't even get a chance to answer as I heard him hang up the phone. As I walked by the door, I saw that the receptionist had bent down on her knees. She was talking to Marci. I hesitated just a moment to look at my love. She was a little wrinkled, but none the worse for wear. Her hair was a tousled mess. Her clothes were badly wrinkled, and her light touch of makeup was running down her face and smeared. Still, she was as beautiful as ever. On my best day, I couldn't even begin to look as good as she did on her worst.

I chased those thoughts out of mind as I proceeded to the glass door. I stood off to the side so as not to silhouette myself to anyone looking from outside.

I soon saw that there was no sign of Puke Face or any other bad guys.

The next five minutes drug by. I kept my eyes outside and my hand inside my coat on my pistol. Then I heard the sirens. *What a beautiful sound.*

It wasn't very long before what seemed like every cop car that the city owned turned into the complex. Some stopped at the office, but most went past the office back toward Crossinger's apartment. That struck me as odd.

I asked myself, "How did they know where to go?"

I took my hand off my gun and stepped out of the office. The first few cops out of the cars approached me cautiously with their hands on the guns that were still in their holsters.

I kept my hands in plain sight as I stepped forward. "And the cavalry arrives in the nick of time."

"Who are you, sir?"

"My name is James Peterson. I just got off the phone with Lieutenant Glosman. Who are you?"

"I'm Officer Danko."

"Well, Officer Danko, the kidnapping victim is behind me inside. Apparently, some of you already know where the kidnappers are."

"Yes, sir. We were dispatched here."

"Is an ambulance coming?"

"Yes, sir. It will be here shortly."

"When it gets here, send the attendants in here. The ones in the other building are long past needing their services."

"Will do."

CHAPTER 16

Marci and I sat and looked at Mike over the desk in the apartment complex's office. The EMTs had released her as physically unharmed.

That's when I heard Mike's voice.

Mike said, "So this is Miss Johnson. It is indeed a pleasure. Although I wish it could be under better circumstances.

"Thank you, Lieutenant Glosman. I've heard a lot about you, too. Jimmy speaks highly of you."

Mike looked at me with a quizzical smirk. "Jimmy, who speaks highly of me?"

I opened my mouth to answer. Before I could, Marci answered strongly for me, "That's right!" Then she softened as she looked at me with a fond smile and gently touched my cheek. "He's my Jimmy."

Mike coughed a couple times. I looked at him. I could tell he was tactfully trying to cover a smile or even a laugh. He was glancing down so as not to make eye contact with me. It helped him stifle his laughter.

"Look, Mike—" I started to bark.

But he held up his hand and raised his face. The laugh was gone. Only a smile appeared. He looked at me. "I understand. You ought to hear what Sharon calls me sometimes."

"Oh? I'll have to ask her."

"No, you won't!" He continued with a different subject. "So

how did this all come about?" He gestured at the surroundings with his hands.

"I did a little research. I couldn't find anyplace that seemed to be a logical place for them to have taken Marci. I talked to a contact at the newspaper. He suggested that perhaps I might try Crossinger's place. I thought it was weird at first, but I had nothing else to go on. You remember Puke Face?"

"Yeah. What about him?"

"Well, when I got here, he was coming out of the apartment. So I knew something was going on. I waited until he got in his car and drove off. Then I got close enough to the door of the apartment so I could hear something going on inside. This seemed awfully strange for a single, dead man's apartment."

"That might be."

"So I knocked on the door. When the guy answered, he must have recognized me because he went for his gun. I was just a little faster."

"You're trying to tell me that you drew your gun faster than he did, Wyatt Earp?"

"Not exactly. I already had my gun in my hand."

"Maybe that's why he drew his gun. He felt the need for self-protection. By the way, where did you get this gun that you previously told me you didn't have?"

Marci interrupted with deep anger in her voice. "I thought you were his friend. Whose side are you on?"

Mike looked at her and said very stiffly as he nodded toward me, "His side. But these are questions the DA will ask later if I don't ask them now. Better they come from a friend than a prosecuting attorney."

"Oh," she said softly.

"It's all right, sweetheart. He has to do this. I really don't mind."

Mike interjected, "If you don't mind, then answer the question."

"What question?" I asked.

"Did you draw first?"

"No, I didn't. I had the gun in my hand, but down at my side." I knew this was a lie. But the only one who could dispute me was now dead. So he wasn't going to contradict me.

By the look on Mike's face, I could tell he wasn't sure whether to believe me or not. I understood immediately what choice die he has? My version is the only one available.

After a few seconds of staring at me, Mike decided to accept my story so far. "We did recover a round in the overhead door-jamb that probably is about the same caliber as the first stiff's gun."

"I knew he shot at me, but I had no idea where it went."

"Now answer the second question."

"Which was?"

Mike was now very close to losing his temper. I thought it the better part of valor to not try to tap-dance his question this time.

"Where did you get the gun?" he asked through clenched teeth.

"Look, Mike, after all I had been through the last couple days, I felt the need for protection."

"Where did you get it?" He was really close to the edge.

"I had it stashed. It came from a case. I came across it a long time ago."

"You mean in another little hole, other than the back of your dresser that had nothing in it."

"Exactly."

"You're pushing it. You know that, don't you? You're really pushing it to the edge."

"Come on, Mike. Would I lie to you?"

In a fucking heartbeat.

"Only when I absolutely have to," I mumbled.

"What did you say?" He jumped on it quickly.

"I do what I have to do to survive."

"Like lie to your friends?"

"Friends? It seems to me like you're being more of a police detective than a friend."

"This one time and one time only will I be a friend when I should be a police detective." He reached out his hand. "Give me the gun."

I slowly pulled out the gun and handed it to him as discreetly as possible. It wouldn't do any good to have some other over-anxious cop think I was pulling a gun on Mike. Accidents had happened on a lot less than that. Mike first unloaded it and then looked it over.

"Is it traceable? I don't see any serial numbers on it anywhere."

"If it didn't have my fingerprints on it, you'd think it just now materialized out of thin air."

Mike looked it over one more time. "You say you found this lying on the ground after your last struggle with one of these guys?"

He didn't have to prompt me twice. "That is absolutely right, Lieutenant Glosman."

"That's what I thought you said the first time."

"It is."

Marci was just sitting there and watching us. I didn't think she fully grasped what had really just transpired. He turned and called over one of the uniformed police officers and told him, "Take this into evidence Officer." After the officer left, he turned back to me. "Now what about the second guy in the apartment?"

"At the sound of gunfire, he flew out of the back room with gun blazing."

"You're one hell of a shot. Three shots from your weapon and all scored bull's-eyes."

"I don't know, Mike. I kind of felt like I was a bystander on the sidelines, watching the whole thing in slow motion as if someone or something was guiding me through the whole thing."

"Lucky for you."

"You aren't kidding. It might have saved both our lives." I shuddered slightly with the thought of how close Marci and I had come to death. "After the second guy went down and no one else came flying at me, I started looking around until I found Marci. We didn't hang around for very long. I was afraid Puke Face would return."

"Apparently, he did."

"Yeah, but not until we were in the car and pulling out of the parking lot."

"Did he see you?"

"I don't think so. When he pulled up in front of Crossinger's apartment, he must have seen the dead body in the open doorway. He never got out of the car. He just burned rubber after leaving the area."

"Did he come after you? "

"I don't know. We had enough of a head start that we were able to circle around the block and come back here without him showing up. That's when I called you guys. I think you know the rest."

Mike turned to Marci. "Miss Johnson, did you hear them say anything during your captivity that might be related to the Branning case?"

She took a moment to think. She slowly lowered her head and slightly shook it no. "Not that I recall. They pretty much kept me locked up in the bedroom. About the only thing they said was something about doing what the head lady wanted."

I quickly looked at Mike, who had a slight grin. "What head lady?" I saw he was hesitating as if to savor the moment. I started to get angry. I wasn't in the mood for guessing games. "What lady?" But he wasn't going to be hurried. "What the hell's going on?"

"It's what I wouldn't tell you over the phone." He paused a little longer. I was about to explode with another outburst. "Anne Branning."

Marci looked up at him with a strange, quizzical look. "Anne?"

"That's right. Anne Gionetti-Branning." It came as no surprise to me. But the revelation stunned Marci. "Through the notebook you provided, we were finally able to connect the Gionetti family with the money laundering going on with the Browning Investment Group. Of course, the IRS or feds will probably be more interested with that aspect than we will. But it won't be hard to tie in Branning and Crossinger's murder with conspiracy. Ms. Gionetti-Branning's name is all over it. Her reign as the queen of crime will be short-lived. The A. Gionetti in the notebook stands for Anne Gionetti, not Anthony Gionetti like we thought at first."

"Where is she now?" I asked.

"She's still in custody."

"You mean you've got her?"

"Not really as solid as I'd like. We can connect her with the money laundering, but nothing yet ties her in directly with the murders and conspiracy."

"I'm surprised that one of the Gionetti hotshot lawyers hasn't got her out on bail already."

"Her attempt to flee the country during an investigation is giving us a basis for holding her."

"Don't forget Puke Face. He's probably the one who pulled the trigger."

"That's only a matter of time. We'll have him, too."

Marci interjected enthusiastically, "You mean it's over? I can go back to work and get on with my life?"

Mike let out a deep breath. "Yes, it is about over. But, no, you can't go back to work."

"Why not?"

"Because the feds will shut down Browning Investment Group."

Marci turned toward me. "What am I going to do? I'm out of a job, and I certainly won't want to use them as a reference toward a new one."

"Yeah, but you're still alive and healthy. We'll find you another job." I looked at Mike. "So what's next?"

"Just a lot of grind work connecting loose ends. Once we pick up your friend Puke Face and get him to talk, things should work themselves out."

"If you can get him to talk."

"When he's faced with either the choice of the death penalty or life in prison, he just might be induced to talk to us."

"Are you finished with us? Can we go?"

"Yeah, I don't see any reason that you should have to hang around here. As long as I can get a hold of you if I need to."

We got up and left. At first, Marci was still a little bit weak in the knees. I put my arm around her waist to give her support. After a few steps, she seemed to regain the strength in her legs. She was walking much better now. I kept my arm around her waist. She slid her arm back around mine. Even though the place was swarming with police, I still felt very uncomfortable and unsafe with the prospect of walking out in the open all the way to the car.

As we left the apartment complex office, I noticed Marci was walking incredibly tentative and I can't say I blamed her.

Her eyes were darting around everywhere across the parking lot. I still had my arm around her waist. She was snuggled up as tightly against me as she possibly could. Myself, I felt a very strong case of déjà vu. I was looking for Puke Face to show up. Alas, we made it to the car peacefully. I let Marci in the passenger side. I breathed a slight sigh of relief after I had her safely tucked into her seat with the door closed. I started to walk around the back to get in the driver's side. As I passed by the trunk on the way to the driver's side, movement by the office door caught my attention in my peripheral vision. I looked over and saw Mike standing there. When he saw me look in his direction, he grinned and gave me the thumbs-up sign. It helped to relax me a bit. In fact, I shook my head and laughed lightly. As I got around to the driver's side and opened the car door, I looked in Mike's direction, intending to give him the middle finger. But he wasn't there. I got in the car.

Marci was already belted in with her door locked. She looked over at me with a weak smile. I reached over and patted her on the leg. Because she still had on her work clothes, the bottom of her skirt came to below her knees. I would have liked to have felt bare leg or, should I say, almost bare because of her panty hose. But I somehow didn't think it would have been appropriate to reach up under her skirt right now. I just left my hand there for a few extra seconds and gave her a light squeeze. She looked up at me. With a little more warmth, she smiled and then looked back down at her hands.

"Marci, I do think the worst part is over. Now we can get on with us. If you want?"

She looked at me quickly. "What do you mean? I've never wanted anything more in my entire life." With every word she spoke, she seemed to gain more strength.

"Then let's get the hell out of here." I started up the car.

"Where are we going?"

"Someplace safe to talk so we can plan out the future."

"Our future?" The full meaning of her question wasn't lost on me.

"Yes. Where do you and I go from here as a couple? Also where do you and I go from here as individuals?"

"I couldn't agree more." She sat up straighter with a better air of confidence about her. It made me smile on the inside.

Before I knew it, we were traveling down the road, heading a long way from the Sasmore Apartments. It was suddenly a beautiful day. Marci had a smile on her face. I, of course, felt for the first time in a long time like I really was worth more than a piece of dirt. I was privileged to have the prettiest, sexiest, and sweetest woman I had ever met known or seen sitting next to me, and she was all mine. It didn't get any better than this. I felt a warm glow all over. It was like I had spent the first forty-nine years of my life in a damp, dark, and cold environment. Now I was living in the warm sunshine for the first time.

I heard to old saying many times but now I was truly beginning to understand the meaning, "If it seems too good to be true, then it probably is."

I reached over and ran my hand up under her skirt and along her inner thigh. Marci separated her legs slightly to give me better access. I stopped just past the top of her thigh, not quite all the way to her crotch. She reached over without looking and casually played with my inner thigh, too. Then I knew for sure that, *Oh, yeah! This is real!*

I felt like a cocky teenager. Instead of trying to keep a low profile, I hoped somebody I knew would see me driving around with my honey, especially if that someone would be my ex-wife or a friend of my ex-wife. I dismissed this thought quickly as just "Childish thoughts".

But it was the first time in a lot of years that my ego was working in the positive. In some respects, the drive was well too short. I soon pulled up to Marci's apartment building. We sat there silently for a few minutes. Both of us just were looking at the steps.

I finally broke the silence. "Shall we?"

"What are we going to do here?" Marci had the most perplexed look on her face.

"How about we go upstairs? You can pack all the things you want or need for the near future, as if you are going on a vacation. Then we can go to my place, and I can do the same thing. That shouldn't take too long. Then, because both our places are trashed, we can check into a hotel for a few days and decide what we are going to do for the rest of our lives. How does that sound?"

She didn't answer right away. She was looking at me as if she were trying to decide if I were serious. Then that sexy and sensuous Marci grin came back.

"Is that a proposition or a proposal?"

I fumbled all over myself, stuttered, and stammered. She had done it again. Of course, she didn't let me off the hook. She tilted her head slightly and raised an eyebrow as if to say, "Well?"

I took a deep breath and composed myself. I tried to muster up as suave a look as possible. "Let's go up and see."

It must have been good enough. I swore I could see her shiver. It must have been contagious. I felt what must have been the same warm, tingling sensation run up and down my spine.

Marci seemed to have a hard time speaking. But she managed. "Okay."

I got out of the car. As I started around to her side, it suddenly struck me. I hadn't paid much attention to our surroundings. Anyone could have followed us, and I wouldn't have noticed. I quickly looked around. Even though I was a relative stranger to this neighborhood, nothing seemed out of place. Nothing jumped out at me. Then again, nothing had when I was shot right here. I could feel the wound in my shoulder for the first time in days. Then I realized it was all in my mind. An occasional case of paranoia couldn't hurt too much.

It's probably a good thing to have when people are trying to kill me. It keeps me alert instead of driving around town like a damn schoolboy with his hormones working on high.

Satisfied that nothing was of danger in the area, I walked around to Marci's side. Now I was very much aware of my surroundings. I opened the door, and I kept my eyes and head on a constant visual scan. I was so intent on looking for monsters and bogeymen that I missed the beaver shot of Marci's legs. I was sure I would have seen that if I had been watching her get out of the car. But instead I was watching the surroundings. Who says chivalry is dead?

"What's the matter?"

Maybe, in her case, a bit of paranoia isn't so good.

"Nothing, sweetheart. I'm just being my paranoid self and checking out the area."

She quickly looked around. "Do you see anything?"

"No, not a thing. All seems to be okay." I hoped I sounded more confident than I felt.

Obviously, I did. Marci's body language seemed to relax just a bit. It took every bit of strength I had to not look back over my shoulder as we walked up the steps.

As we entered Marci's place, my heart sank a little as I once again saw the destruction that had been dealt on her private sanctum. Marci stopped just a few feet inside the door. I was right behind her with my hands on her waist. I could feel her body tremble, and I could tell she was about to cry. I hugged her from behind and then turned her around toward me. This made her look away from the mess.

Between sobs, I heard, "It's everything I own. What am I going to do?"

"First of all, it's, 'What are we going to do?'" She started to respond. "Second, let's wait until we are safely tucked away in a hotel room where we can relax and discuss this fully."

She looked up at me and smiled softly. She reached up and gently patted my face. Without another word, she turned and proceeded to dig through the mess for any of her possessions that still might be salvageable.

"Just get what you need that you can carry in a suitcase, as if you were going on a trip. We'll worry about the rest later."

"I have a couple suitcases in the closet by the foyer."

We turned to look in the closet's direction. At least they were still in the closet. The door was wide open. The contents were scattered everywhere. We eventually found one large suitcase and an overnight case still intact on the bottom of the floor.

About twenty minutes later, she had the large suitcase full of clothes. She was finishing up with putting her makeup and toiletries into the overnight case. I hadn't paid much attention to what she had been doing or packing. I had been on the phone to my office to let them know I wouldn't be in for a few days. They had been wondering where I was. In fact, the big boss, Mr. Wheaton, had been looking for me himself.

Julie said, "Mr. Harper was showing a lot of anxiety about your absence."

"Then put me through to him."

"But I can't right now, Mr. Peterson. He's away from the office. When we couldn't get a hold of you, he said he had an errand to run. He left about ninety minutes ago, and he hasn't returned."

"Did he say where he was going?"

"No, but wherever it is, he sure left here in a big hurry. Is there someplace he can call you when he returns?"

"No, not right now. I'll call back later."

"Okay, Mr. Peterson. I'll pass on the message, and I'll talk to you later."

After I hung up, I said more to myself than to Marci, "That's strange."

"What is, dear?"

When I looked at her, I instantly noticed that she had changed her clothes. No longer was she wearing her mousy-looking office outfit. Instead, she had on what I had first seen her wearing, jeans and sweatshirt. Plus, she had put her hair up into a ponytail. No longer was her large breasts and voluptuous figure completely hidden. I totally lost my train of thought.

"Come here." I held out my arms.

She happily and quickly came into my arms. We just embraced tightly. I could feel her breasts pushing against my chest. After a few moments, I raised back my head.

"Are you about finished?"

"Just about. I want to take one last look around and make sure."

"Please hurry. I'm anxious to get you alone and safe."

She pulled away and made a quick look around. I grabbed her large suitcase. She picked up her overnight case. We were out of there.

She wanted to stop and let Mrs. Wilkerson know she would be gone. But when she knocked on her door, there was no answer. We went on downstairs to the car.

As we exited the building, I cautiously scrutinized the neighborhood. There was still nothing as we put her cases in the trunk. We got in the car and drove away. As we pulled off, I noticed her looking back with misty eyes.

"Are you all right?"

"It's always sad when you leave someplace and you know you're not coming back." Then she turned toward me and smiled. "But it gets better when you look forward to where you're going."

The love that swept over me warmed even the coldest parts of my old bones. But there was the slightest tightening on my chest as I felt the cold clutches of commitment. Love's warm embrace won out as I felt the lifting of happiness take me to new heights. I reached over and held her hand. Because of the bucket seats, she couldn't sit close to me. Instead, she held my right hand in both of her hands. Thank goodness, the car was an automatic. I didn't think she was planning to let go of my hand to allow me to shift gears.

We filled the drive to my apartment with small love talk, as if we were just out for an afternoon drive. We quickly arrived there with no problems. As we approached my door, I realized that Marci had never been here.

"I want you to know, Marci. I admit I'm not the best housekeeper, but what you are about to see is even extreme for me."

"If you had the same interior decorator visit you that I did, then I won't hold it against you."

I pushed open the door. I didn't pay any attention to the door not being latched shut. I knew I hadn't gotten it fixed from the last break-in. When we got inside, I wish I had. There on the end of my broken-down couch sat Puke Face. Marci quickly jumped behind me. I started to take a step toward him, and he pulled a gun from somewhere and leveled it straight at my chest. Of course, I stopped instantly.

I summoned up all the courage I had left and spoke as confidently as possible. "It's all over. The police have Anne Gionetti. They know everything. This won't get you anywhere."

I didn't call him Puke Face. It wasn't nice to insult someone with a gun pointed at you.

"Maybe not. But I have nothing to lose and everything to gain by making sure you don't live any longer."

"What do you have to gain?"

"Satisfaction! Payback for you having fucked everything up."

"The girl has nothing to do with this. It's between you and me. Let her go."

"Oh, yeah! Right! Let her go? She's a witness against me for kidnapping and murder."

"The police already have an APB out for your arrest based on other evidence. Her testimony isn't needed."

"I'm supposed to believe you. If someone had a gun pointed at me, I'd say anything as well."

I knew he meant what he said about killing us. Now I had nothing to lose. Besides, I was getting mad with this shithead.

"Come on, Puke Face. Get real!"

"I've had enough of you and your Puke Face." He jumped to his feet.

He was more aggressively pointing the gun at me. I just knew his next move was to pull the trigger.

But, in his anger to jump to his feet, he didn't pay any attention to what was on the floor. He stepped on the table lamp that was lying on the floor. His ankle twisted, and he went down in a heap. The gun fired, but missed us both. Because Mike had taken my gun, I did the only thing I could. I jumped on top of him. Both feet landed squarely on the small of his back, about where the kidneys are located. I definitely heard the sound of something breaking. I didn't stop there. I kicked him as hard as I could in the head. It wasn't the most fancy of footwork, but it was effective. He was out cold. I kicked his gun away. I didn't want my fingerprints anywhere on it. I took the lamp cord that was still attached to the now-broken lamp and tied his hands behind his back. I went into my bedroom and quickly came back with some of my ties. When his feet were bound tightly together, I tied his feet to his hands and pulled them as closely together as possible. If I had broken his back or rib cage in his back, then he was going to be in a lot of pain or possibly crippled for life when he woke up. But quite plainly I remember thinking, "Serves him right!" He looked strange lying there. It was kind of like a reverse fetal position.

I found my phone and called Mike. It took a while to get patched through to him. Once I talked to him, it didn't take very long for the police to get there. I did have enough time to pack a grocery bag full of the stuff I wanted to take. I didn't have much left after my ex-wife's lawyer got finished with me. She didn't even leave me a suitcase.

Marci and I were waiting out in the hall when Mike and his fellow police officers arrived.

Mike came right up to me. "Where is he?"

I indicated at my door. "In there, all dressed up like a Thanksgiving turkey with the rest of the trash."

"Is he still alive?"

"I'm hurt to the quick." I placed my hand over my heart, feigning pain.

"Asshole." He passed by me and went into my apartment.

They didn't keep us long after they took Puke Face away in an ambulance. The EMT said something about broken ribs with a possibility of internal injuries.

I angerly said, "He ought to be glad that's all he has instead of a broken spine."

CHAPTER 17

After we pulled into the parking lot of the hotel and stopped the car, I didn't get out right away.

Marci noticed my hesitancy. "What's the matter, Jimmy?"

"I'm not sure how to say this. It's all kind of new to me."

She could tell my hesitation was from nerves, not fear. She had no anxiety in her voice or body language.

"After all we've been through together, there's something you feel uncomfortable saying to me?"

I giggled shyly. "Yeah, there is."

She unbuckled her seat belt and put her arms around my neck. "And what might that be?" she sexily whispered in my ear.

"Well, are we supposed to get separate rooms or just one?"

"Oh, baby, from now on until eternity, we sleep together in the same bed."

"Won't the hotel management object to an unmarried couple registering for the same room?"

She started to chuckle. Then she saw I was serious. "Boy, I've got to get you to move into this generation. They probably couldn't care less. But if it bothers you that much, then just register us as mister and missus."

"You could go along with that?"

"Jimmy, as long as it keeps us together, there isn't much I couldn't go along with. Besides, I already feel kind of like Mrs. Peterson."

The sweetness of her smile melted all my inhabitation. "Well, the mister and missus part is one thing we're going to have to discuss anyway."

"I certainly hope so."

"Come on. Let's go." I kissed her lightly and then got out of the car.

Other than a few funny looks at my high-fashion suitcase, check-in went smoothly. We were on our way up in the elevator to our room. I had insisted at the front desk that a bellhop wasn't necessary. I was sure they made some comments after we left, but I was being more paranoid than stingy. I just wasn't taking any chance on anyone following us to our room. The past few days hadn't completely worn off. I was carrying my paper bag in one hand and Marci's big suitcase in the other. So I let her unlock the door.

I hesitated before going in. "Aren't I supposed to carry you across the threshold or something?"

"Only when I become the real Mrs. Peterson." She teased me with a sheepish grin.

She went into the room. I stood there with my mouth hanging open. After a few seconds, she came back to the door. I was standing in the hallway, still in shock.

"Are you coming in, Mr. Peterson?" she said, emphasizing the "Mr. Peterson."

I slowly but obediently entered the room. Marci closed the door behind me. She took her suitcase from me and laid it next to her overnight case on the one king-sized bed. I laid my paper bag on the bed. She stepped back and attained that Marci pose, hands on hips and feet slightly apart with her big chest pointing straight at me.

"What do you want to do first, Jimmy? Unpack, talk, or what?" She said with a sensuous purr on the "or what."

I found my voice. "Why don't you unpack? I'll call down for room service. I don't know about you, but I'm really hungry. Plus,

I think we might need the nourishment to give us the strength to get through the rest of the night."

She tilted her head slightly. "I like your way of thinking."

"What would you like to eat?"

"I don't know. Oh, look. There's a menu."

She went over to the table in the corner of the room and picked up a pamphlet. She brought it over to the bed and sat down. I sat next to her. Marci held the menu so we could both read what was listed.

It didn't take me long. "I don't know about you, but a roast beef sandwich looks good."

"I think I'll take a chicken sandwich with a glass of iced tea."

I got up and went to the telephone to call in our order. It took a few minutes, but I had everything ordered before too long. They said it would take about ten to fifteen minutes. After I hung up, I turned to tell Marci. But she wasn't there. I noticed that, even though her suitcase sides were closed, the latches were open. Her overnight case wasn't on the bed. The bathroom door was closed. So my panic eased, and I walked over to the bathroom door.

"The food should be here in about ten to fifteen minutes."

"I'll be out shortly. I just want to freshen up."

"Okay."

I looked around for something to do. I decided to wait at least one or two minutes and unpack my paper bag. I went over to the dresser against the wall by the foot of the bed. Three drawers were on the left; three were on the right. I opened the top drawer on the left. Old habits were hard to break. A man's domain, whether dresser, bed, or closet, was always the one closest to the door. It had something to do with why a man always walked on the outside of a lady when walking down a sidewalk. It was some Freudian subconscious bullshit about protection.

The drawers were big enough. I had so little stuff that everything except a few toiletries and one or two hang-up things fit in the one drawer. A couple minutes later, I had what few hang-up things I had hanging in the closet on the side closest to the door. I was just beginning to wonder what was taking Marci so long when I heard a knock on the door. I looked out the peephole and saw a bellman with a food cart. I unlocked and opened the door.

He smiled. "Room service for you, sir."

"Fine. Just put it on the table, please. I'll take care of it from there."

"Yes, sir."

After he wheeled in the cart and put it by the table, I signed the room service bill and gave him a couple dollars. He quickly pocketed the money, smiled, and left with the bill in hand. I started over to the bathroom door to tell Marci that the food was here.

She beat me to it. From behind the door, she asked, "Was that room service?"

I turned to go back to the table. "Yes, it was."

"Is the bellhop gone?"

"Yes, he is." I reached the table and started to take the covers off the food.

I heard the bathroom door open. I turned and started to tease her about there was no reason for her to be shy and hide in the bathroom until everyone was gone. Instead, I never got a word out. I stopped short with my mouth hanging open before I could say a word. Marci was standing by the open bathroom door. She was wearing our outfit, the black miniskirt with the bodice that came up just under her big breasts. The suspenders that came up over the extremely tight, thin, white sweater emphasized the shape of her chest. She was wearing those same black high heels that gave her already beautifully sculpted, nylon-clad legs further muscle tone. Because I was now in love with her, she looked even better now than when I first saw her in those clothes. Her hair lay seductively on her shoulders. Once again, she had put on just a hint of makeup. The eye shadow magnified the intensity and deepness of her sky blue eyes.

She stood by the door for a few moments to allow me to totally enjoy the vision. Then she walked toward me as only a very truly sexy and seductive woman could. As she came toward me, because of the high heels and the very low V-neck sweater, I noticed the four inches of fully exposed cleavage bounce with every step.

Marci stopped behind a chair at the table and very sensuously gave me a sideways glance. I hustled over, pulled out the chair, and held it for her while she sat down. Of course, because I was behind her, it gave me the chance to look down the front of her sweater. What a wonderful view that was.

"Thank you, dear," she said.

"No, thank you!" I responded.

I picked up her plate with the chicken sandwich and the glass of iced tea. I placed them in front of her. As I turned to get my food, I felt her squeeze my ass. I wasn't expecting it, so I stopped moving.

"I always wanted to do that. You know, play with a cute waiter's butt."

We both chuckled. I got my food and sat down. The first few bites for both of us were without any discussion. We were both pretty hungry. I didn't think I took my eyes off her for a second. She had the prettiest face I'd ever seen. Her facial structure was totally flawless. Every part served to compliment the rest.

Marci must have noticed my staring. "What are you thinking about?"

"I was admiring you. Without a doubt, you're the most beautiful woman I've ever seen. I could stare at you for hours and hours and not get enough."

"I think you're just a little prejudiced. But I have to admit that I like that kind of prejudice."

"No, really. You are. I've been a closet voyeur for all my life. I've quite literally checked out thousands of gorgeous women."

"Oh, you have, have you?"

"Yes, I have. And not one of them can come close to matching you."

"I guess you talked your way out of that one. I guess I can live with you looking. As long as it is only a look and the last look is always at me."

"After looking at you, everything else pales in comparison."

"Boy, are you good. I think I'll have to keep you around. You're good for my ego."

"No. Really, I mean it. I'm very serious."

"I know you are, Jimmy." She grabbed a hold of my hand. "Relax, honey, I'm just teasing. I guess it's my defense mechanism. I'm not very good at receiving compliments."

"Why not?"

"My past experiences haven't left me much confidence. I kind of feel that, if you're complimenting me, it's only because you're trying to butter me up because you want something."

"All I want from you is for you to love me half as much as I love you. If you do, then that is twice as much love as I have ever known or can expect."

"Half! Let me tell you something, Mr. Peterson."

"Yes, Mrs. Peter—" I caught myself, although it did seem the natural thing to say.

Marci just smiled. "No one could love someone more than I love you! So don't give me this half stuff again."

"Talk about lack of confidence. I'm still finding it hard to believe you're really in love with me."

"A real fine pair we make."

"As a matter of fact, we make a very fine pair."

"I think so, too."

By now, we had both finished eating and turned away from the table. We were facing each other. It was hard as hell to keep my eyes off her body. I could only divert my attention upward because of those beautiful blue eyes, full lips, and her complete face. It was so nice to look at.

I momentarily looked over at the bed and then back into her eyes. "Before anything else happens, we have a lot to discuss and decide."

"Go ahead, honey. I'm all ears."

I looked down directly at her large breasts and then down toward her exposed legs. I stared in the direction of her crotch that her short shirt just barely covered.

I looked back at her face. "Not exactly all ears. But who's complaining?"

She just sat there, smiled, and shifted the specific body parts that had caught my attention as my gaze passed over them. But she didn't say a word. Her body language said plenty.

"Marci, will you marry me?"

It must have caught her completely off guard. She twitched as if she received an electrical shock.

"Oh, yes! Yes! Yes!"

She practically flew into my arms and kissed me all over my face, but mostly on my lips. Before I knew it, she was sitting sideways on my lap. Her right side was toward me. She went back and forth between kissing me and hugging my neck. My right hand quite naturally went up and held as much of her left breast as I could get my hand around. Then she started to cry.

"What's the matter? Are you all right?"

"I couldn't be better. You've just made me the happiest person in the world."

After several long and passionate kisses mixed in with many short and teasing kisses, we embraced. I realized that all her squirming on my lap was giving me an erection. Even though the desire was building, I wanted to settle some open matters first. I pulled away slightly. It wasn't completely, but I pulled my face away from her neck so I could speak.

"We still need to talk about a few things."

She started kissing me lightly on the lips. "What?"

I reached up with both of my hands and held her head. I gave her one long kiss. "Please, Marci, we have to discuss things first."

"Okay, sweetie." She got up, took me by the hand, and led me over to the small sofa that was in the corner between the bed and the rear wall. "We can sit here and be comfortable."

Marci turned sideways and faced me. She had her left arm along the back of the sofa, behind my back. She had tucked her left leg underneath her opposite butt cheek. Her right foot lay flat on the floor. Her right hand was resting on her thigh. She straightened her shoulders and arched her back slightly.

She grinned and looked me straight in the eyes. "Okay. Then discuss."

How in the hell can a normal, red-blooded male seriously discuss anything with a goddess of beauty and sensuality sitting next to him and smiling?

She just sat there seductively smiling at me while I squirmed in my own uneasiness.

I sat back against the sofa and faced out into the room. It helped, but I still knew she was there.

"Marci, I know Joseph Branning was a special friend of yours. But we also know he got mixed up with some very wrong people. In fact, he was married to one. Some of the things Joseph Branning did may not have always been the most honest of things." Without looking at her, I could feel the change in her body posture. I didn't look over at her. I might not have been able to continue with what I needed to say. "From everything you've told me, he was probably a very nice guy who just got caught up in something that was over his head."

I didn't really believe the last thing I said, but I hoped Marci did. Her silence was beginning to bother me.

"His wife was the monster that destroyed him."

I was trying to give her some reason to hold on to her good

memories of a friend. She still didn't say a thing so I risked a glance at her. Although she wasn't smiling, she wasn't crying either. She brought her left arm forward and put it around my shoulders.

"Go ahead with what you're trying to tell me. I'm all right," she nearly whispered.

"You only know part of the reason why he may have been killed."

"What do you mean?" She didn't pull her hand away.

"During my investigation, I found out something I never told to anyone, including the police."

"Go on."

"In the bowling locker where I found the notebook, I also found a one-way airline ticket to Zurich, Switzerland."

"One-way?

"Yep."

"What else did you find?"

I reached in my back pocket and pulled out my wallet. I opened up my wallet and withdrew the first page I had removed from the notebook. I held it so Marci could see it.

"Inside the notebook was this piece of paper."

I unfolded it and handed it to her. She read what was written on the paper in silence. When she looked up at me, she grinned. Something in that smile told me that I'd fucked up. I was right all along. A gorgeous, young thing like her couldn't really be interested in an ol' foolish fart like me.

The old saying rang loudly in my head, "There is no fool like an old fool."

Then she spoke without looking up. Her words were like bricks landing on my soul. "I knew you would find it if I waited long enough."

The instant depression hit me so hard I know I must have actually physically shrunk. I felt her touch my hands that were grasped together in my lap.

"Jimmy honey, what's the matter?"

I was in such shock that I know I didn't really hear her correctly. I was now confused. Real concern seemed to be in her voice. I slowly looked up. Marci laid the piece of paper down on the sofa behind her as she got up on her knees on the sofa and walked over toward me on her knees. She put her arms around me. She pulled my head snugly against her breasts.

"Baby, are you all right? You look like someone just sucked the life right out of you."

"What did you mean?"

"I meant the real reason he was killed. I knew it couldn't be over his gambling debts. Else, how would they get their money?"

I slowly brought my arms up and around her waist. When she felt them go around her, she held me tighter. Then she slightly leaned back her head so she could see my face.

"Why? What did you think I meant?"

I saw concern in her eyes and lowered my head in shame. Marci withdrew her arms from around me and sat back on her haunches. She kept her left hand on my right shoulder. With her right hand, she reached over. With ever so light pressure under my chin, she raised my head and turned my face so I was looking into those deep, beautiful sky blue eyes. Just the lightest trace of moisture was in them.

"Jimmy, I love you! I love you with every inch and fiber of my being. Tell me what hurt you so badly."

A real tear actually ran down my cheek. I looked away and back down. "I don't want to hurt you."

"The only thing that would hurt me would be for you to say that you don't love me. Is that it?"

I raised straight back up and turned to face her. "Oh, no! I love you so much that I feel like my soul is going to explode right out of my body."

"Then tell me."

"Are you sure?"

"Jimmy!" she said firmly but not harshly.

I took a deep breath and then blew out through puckered lips, like I was whistling. Only I didn't make much noise, just a blowing sound.

"Remember when you were talking about how your experiences caused you to have a lack of self-confidence?"

"Yes, I remember very well."

"Are you sure you want to hear this? It could hurt you."

She reached up with her right hand and stroked the left side of my face. "Loving someone sometimes means sharing the pain. Now, please, tell me."

"After I showed you the paper, I heard you say you knew that, if you waited long enough, I'd find it." I paused.

"Yes, I remember."

"My lack of confidence caused a very negative thought to cross my mind."

"What?"

"I thought you were waiting long enough to find that piece of paper."

"You're not serious?"

I bowed my head again. "This answered my original question."

"Which one?"

"Why such a pretty, young lady could be interested in me."

"I don't understand."

"Do you know what's written on that piece of paper?"

"Well, considering that Joe had a one-way ticket to Zurich with it, I'd guess it's the account number for a Swiss bank."

"That's right. A numbered Swiss bank account. The kind that has no name. Just an account number."

I couldn't tell what she was thinking or feeling. She just sat there, looking at me and appearing emotionless.

I said to myself, "What the hell? I might as go for broke."

"From the beginning, if you were only interested in the paper with the account number, how could you know about it? Unless you belonged to the Gionetti family and were planted on me to get that number back."

"What changed your mind?" She was still stone-cold.

"You did."

"I did?"

"I looked into your eyes. I knew you had been telling me the truth all along."

She just sat there on her feet and looked at me.

"See, I told you that you didn't want to hear my thoughts. It would hurt." I paused. "Oh, baby. I'm so sorry. I didn't mean it that way."

"I know that now."

"I guess we really should get married. We are a perfect match. Maybe together we can build some security and self-confidence."

"You mean you're not mad at me?"

"Of course not." She put out her arms. "Come here."

I got on my knees and went into her arms. What a sight we were, a couple of adults on our knees in the middle of the couch and in a tight embrace. We hugged and kissed feverishly. What gave out first were my knees. I had to sit down. I sat on the left end of the sofa. Marci snuggled up next to me. I put my right arm around her shoulders. She laid her head on my right shoulder. When she crossed her legs, her already short skirt crept up even further. I was delighted. She laid her hands on my right leg. I turned my head and kissed the top of her head. Then I lightly laid my chin on the same spot I kissed.

I asked, "So you understand what is written on that piece of paper?"

She disengaged herself from my side, long enough to reach over and pick up the paper. After she sat back and snuggled against me, she looked at the numbers for a minute.

"Because he had that airline ticket for Zurich, I'd assume ZNB stands for Zurich National Bank. The numbers then, obviously, are account numbers."

"That's right. So you know what that implies?"

I felt her whole body stiffen just a little. "There's a lot of money in this account. He was going after it. Because he had only a one-way ticket, he wasn't coming back. He was just going to disappear and live a rich man happily ever after."

"So it would seem."

"So they killed him for it."

"I don't think so."

Marci looked up at me. "What do you mean?"

"Same answer you gave me about why they didn't kill him over a gambling debt. Then they wouldn't get their money back."

"Unless they had already got the number somewhere else and/or got their money back."

"No, I don't think they have it. Branning didn't impress me as being stupid. This is probably the only place the account number is written down. In fact, I'd bet they don't even know it exists."

"Where did the money come from?"

"The notebook was a record of the money laundering and profits from their illegal activities. Remember Branning was an accountant. He more than likely skimmed a little off each account and hid it in this Swiss account. The Gionettis may have made so much money that they may have not realized some was missing."

"Then why kill him?"

"It's just a guess, but he might have felt he needed insurance to help him make his disappearance work. He may have threatened them with exposure of the book to the feds. This would have only exposed the money laundering. All through this, whenever Puke Face and his hoodlums would hassle me, they'd only ask for the notebook. They never mentioned anything about the money or account number."

"Why didn't he just keep quiet and disappear?"

"That's a good question. We may never know the real answer for sure. Maybe because of all their family contacts, they found out he was booked on a one-way ticket to Zurich. They wanted to know why. I'd imagine that crime families tend to be control freaks."

"They had to figure that he was going to Zurich for a reason."

"True, but remember Anne was arrested at the airport, ready to board a flight to Zurich. She said it was for her mental health. What if there is another account that belongs to the Gionetti family? Whenever he sent money to that family account, he just diverted some to his private one without their knowledge. Perhaps Branning tried hard in an attempt to get away. He may have threatened to divulge the notebook to the authorities if they didn't let him go."

"Bad mistake."

"Maybe. But what if it was all he had left to use to get away?"

"What do you mean?"

"What if he were pushed into a corner? They made him think they were going to kill him anyway. He may have tried to use the notebook in an effort to hold them off long enough to sneak away, get the money, and disappear."

We both sat quietly looking at the piece of paper in Marci's hand.

I said, "Is this small piece of paper with some numbers written on it so valuable that people are willing to risk their lives for it?"

At first Marci didn't answer but after a few minutes, she asked, "Do you think there really is money in this account?"

"That is one of the things that we need to discuss."

She looked up at me. I could fall hopelessly right into those eyes. They sparkled, and they were quite entrancing. She waited for me to continue.

"What if there is money there? Branning put it there. Apparently, no one else knows that it's there. Because he no longer can get the money, it's going to sit there forever. Not belonging to anyone."

"Unless we go and get it."

"Yes, then what do we do with it?"

When I first found the piece of paper, there was no question in my mind what I'd do with it. It was mine. Now that Marci was in my life, I wasn't sure the money was worth it.

"It's money derived from illegal activities. If we turn it over to the authorities, they will confiscate it as evidence. The whole thing will go to the government."

"Will they need it to prosecute those responsible for his murder?"

"Not from what Mike tells me. With the notebook, they have enough motive and evidence for all the murders and money laundering to put them all away for a very long time. And remember, it's very possible that the only ones who know about this account are you and me."

"And the Zurich National Bank."

"Yes, the bank. But to them, it's just numbers. They have no idea or care to have any idea of its source."

Marci looked back down at the paper. Then she said so softly that I barely heard her, "You mean, if we go and get it, we can keep whatever is in the account?"

"Could you live with that?"

She started to say something and then stopped. She was nervously picking at the corners of the paper. I waited and gave her plenty of time to think her answer through on her own.

When she looked up at me, moisture was definitely in her eyes. I could hear a definite lump in her throat. "After what those monsters did to me? No, after what they did to us, no amount of money could make it right. But those bastards should have to pay. They do owe us something. What about you? Would you want to keep it?"

"Back when I first found the notebook, you're darn right. That was the whole purpose of not turning it over to the police." I decided not to go into detail about how I had actually removed it from the notebook.

"And now?"

"No amount of money could ever change, good or bad, what we have. "

She turned and put the paper back on the sofa behind her. Then she turned back toward me and took hold of my face with both hands.

"What we have is very, very real. It is also very, very strong. No amount of money could ever change or destroy that. I have you; you have me. As long as we do things together, no matter what it is, we will stay together as one. You are my man. I'm your woman. Whatever you decide, I will totally support with my very life." She kissed me lightly, but she held it for several seconds. Then she looked me in the eyes from about a foot away. "All that matters is us."

Marci again kissed me lightly. But this time, instead of it lasting only for a few seconds, it slowly progressed into a long, passionate kiss. As our lips pressed together a little firmer, we both began to move our mouths. Then our lips parted, and our tongues became actively engaged with each other. Very slowly, Marci leaned backwards. I was right with her. Our lips never parted as I carefully lay on top off her. My weight rested mostly on my knees and elbows. My knees were on the outside of her thighs. My elbows were on the sofa just above her shoulders. I had my forearms around the top of her head. My chest rubbed her breasts, and my crotch was massaging hers. Her hands were under my arms and sliding up and down my back and ass. To say that both of us were getting very turned on would be an understatement.

I wanted this woman. I wanted her in the worst way. I wanted her so badly that, not only did my penis hurt from how large it had swollen, I yearned for her with every fiber of my body and soul. But I needed to breathe. So I took my mouth off hers long enough to take in some much-needed oxygen. I didn't stop the foreplay though. I feather-kissed her left ear and the side of her neck. Marci was moaning deeply within her throat.

Due to the throbbing in my rock-hard erection, I decided I

either needed to slow down a bit or to lose my load in my pants. I raised my hips slightly so I wouldn't be rubbing her crotch with mine. I opened my eyes and watched her face as I gently kissed all over it. She kept her eyes shut, but she exhibited several different facial expressions as wave after wave of passion must have passed all over her. When she finally noticed I wasn't totally lying on top of her, she slowly opened her eyes about halfway. She saw I was watching her. She smiled at me, and she purred.

She brought up her hands and put them around the back of my neck. "Oh Jimmy honey, I never, even in my wildest dreams, thought love could feel this good. I had no idea that anything could feel this good."

"Compared to this, I've never even been close to being in love before."

I took a hold of her hands from around the back of my neck and got off the sofa. I stood up and looked down at her lying there. Her hair was spread out over the cushion. Her hair color emphasized her slightly flush face. Her skirt was pulled up to about her waist. She didn't have any panties on under her skirt. In fact, the only thing she wore was a pair of thigh-high nylon type stockings. With her legs slightly spread, the little light coppery red muff of hair highlighted her pussy, just like her makeup did for her face. Everything about her was extremely pleasing to look at. I felt like she was watching me. I looked up at her face.

She asked, "Do you like what you see?"

"Oh yes. Very much." I got down on my knees and kissed her heavenly wet spot.

She was so wet that I came away with a wet mouth from just a kiss. At first, she gently held the back of my head. Then as I started to kiss and lick more and more, she put her hands alongside my head and carefully lifted up my face.

She looked at me through her half-closed eyes. "Please take me to bed."

I stood up and took hold of her hands. I gently pulled her first to a sitting position and then all the way to her feet. She came straight into my arms and kissed me passionately, but softly. I had my arms and hands around her back. She had her arms up over my shoulders. Her hands were wrapped around my head. She was very much involved with what she was doing. We kissed like this for several minutes.

I pulled my body away from her slightly, but I still continued to give her multiple little kisses on the lips. I reached up and slowly lowered both of the straps off her shoulders. She dangled her arms off to the side just long enough for the straps to fall off her arms to her side. Then instead of placing her hands back on my head, she placed them on my ass and started to squeeze and play with my butt. I reached behind her and found the zipper at the back of the skirt. I pulled down on the tab and unzipped her skirt. Marci pulled her hips away from my hips just enough for the skirt to fall to the floor. As she stepped out of the skirt, we didn't break our feathery light kissing.

I reached around and played with her ass for a while.

I dreamily thought, *What a nice ass she has.*

Her ass cheeks and breasts were almost equally fun to fondle. The real main difference was that her breasts had the extra advantage of having nipples to play with and suck. This made a big difference.

I reached up to the bottom of her very thin sweater and started to lift it off. I reached just under her arms. Marci held her arms straight up and allowed me to slide her sweater completely off. The sight of her nicely rounded, large breasts entranced me. Her nipples were swollen and pointing right at me. Marci laid her hands on top of her head, obviously aware how they helped tighten her breast muscles. I took a hold of the side of each breast. They were far too large for me to take each one completely in one hand. Even one breast for two hands would have been difficult. I took a hold of the side of each breast. I alternated sucking and tongue flicking between the two engorged nipples. Marci brought her hands down behind my head and pulled me on to her breasts. She was moaning with delight. The more she pulled, the harder I sucked and the more she moaned. I was sucking so hard that I felt I was trying to suck everything right out of them.

While I continued sucking on Marci's nipples and breasts, I ran my hands down her sides and around to her lower back. I slid them around to the back and squeezed her wonderful bare ass. I started to caress lower and lower on her ass and legs. As I got lower and lower, I had to leave much more than a mouth full of delight. As I got about mid-thigh, I had to get on my knees. I was eyeball to eyeball with her pubic area. Without taking my eyes off her most intimate womanly treasure, I reached down and removed her high heels one foot at a time. I stroked her calves and feet as I removed each shoe. As I reached up to take a hold of her thigh highs, Marci placed her hands on my shoulders for balance.

She said, "No, please leave them on. I love how they feel when you make love to me."

I stroked up and down the thigh high hose to about ankle height. As I did, I lightly kissed my way down each leg. I'd occasionally tickle the inside part of each leg with my tongue. I found that just behind the inside part of each knee was particularly sensitive. Then I stopped for a moment to look at that gorgeous pussy mound from close up one more time. I leaned forward and kissed her right in the middle of her pubic hair. She reacted with a deep sounding coo.

I stood up and embraced her. I kissed her as lovingly as I possibly could. After several long and passionate kisses mixed in with quite a few little hen pecks, Marci looked at me in the eyes, smiled, and proceeded to undress me.

As she unbuttoned my shirt, she kissed my chest as it became exposed. She kissed all the way down until she got to my belt buckle. She unfastened my belt, unbuttoned my pants, and unzipped my fly. She pulled off my shirt and threw it somewhere. She ran her hands all over my chest and kissed everywhere her hands had been. She occasionally licked and sucked. When she sucked and tongue-flicked my nipples, it totally surprised me at how good it felt. I wasn't ready for that. After all, it was something a man did to a woman, not the other way around. But it felt so good that I wasn't going to stop her. I just relaxed and enjoyed it. When she removed her mouth and moved down to kiss and tongue my stomach, I couldn't believe it. My nipples were swollen and hard. They weren't as big as Marci's got, but it was a definite change. I was learning more and more about sex between men and women. I was being brought into this generation.

Before I realized it, Marci was pulling my pants and boxer shorts down past my knees. My dick stood up just as hard as it has ever been. I wasn't that big, maybe six or seven inches when hard, but it felt like it was trying to stretch to at least a foot.

She stood up. As she kissed me, she put her hands on my waist and very carefully guided me backwards until the bed touched the back of my legs. She very gently coaxed me to sit down on the edge of the bed. I could see that her attention was riveted directly between my legs as she got on her knees. One foot at a time, she removed my shoes and socks. Next off came my pants and boxers. I was now bare ass naked than she was.

She stood up. "Lie down. I'm going to give you what I promised."

At first, I didn't understand what she was talking about, but I obediently scooted back lengthwise on my back with my feet near the end and my head just short of the pillows. I soon remembered what she had promised. She got on the bed on her knees. She got over next to my waist. She looked down at my stiff erection. I could almost see her salivating. She took me in her hands and very gently stroked me up and down the entire length of my cock. Marci started to bend her head down toward my crotch, but, because her hair was so long, it fell down and covered her face.

She straightened up. "Don't go anywhere. I'll be right back."

I said, "Like I might really go anywhere."

And she giggled as she ran into the bathroom. Five seconds later, she came back out with her hair in a ponytail. She climbed back on the bed along my right side. "Now we can both enjoy this whole lot better."

She walked on her knees with boobs bouncing, up to about my chest. She bent over and kissed me on the lips. She held the kiss for several seconds and then kissed me all over my face. Her right hand was gently caressing my chest and nipples. Her left hand was playing with my head. As she worked her way down my neck and shoulders, I brought my right hand around and could just reach and squeeze her left buttock. She was sitting on her feet, which were tucked under her. When she felt me take part of her ass cheek in my hand, she shifted the way she was sitting, just enough to allow me full access to her ass.

Just about then, her kisses were reaching the top of my chest. I remembered what she had previously done to my nipples, and I was silently hoping she'd do it again. She didn't disappoint. She must have felt the reaction in my nipples. They felt like they were getting erect. Apparently, they must have because she moaned a sound of pleasure as she kept sucking and flicking her tongue. I heard another deep voice moan and realized it was I. Prior to her, that wasn't something I did. Before I realized it, she had left my nipples, and she was kissing her way down my belly. As she got lower on me, she had to face more toward my feet so she could lean forward on her elbows in the direction of her attention. This movement allowed me to reach both of her ass cheeks with my hand. I squeezed, patted, and played alternately with both of those luscious mounds.

When Marci got to my pubic area, she stopped her downward movement on me and proceeded to kiss and lick all around my pubic region, along the top of my pubic hair, and the tops and inner parts of my legs. It was an absolute tease. It felt totally marvelous, but my hard dick wanted some attention. She was kissing all around it, but not actually touching it.

I was lying flat on my back with my eyes shut. I was so totally caught up with what she was doing that, when my fingers slid between her ass cheeks and met her anus, I didn't realize it at first. Marci sure did. She raised her hips slightly so her ass was all the way off her feet. With the muscles in her buttocks, she slightly spread her cheeks. Plus, another pleasurable moan escaped her lips as she continued teasing my dick by kissing everything around my hard penis and tight balls. I tried to be gentle as I slid my middle finger lengthwise back and forth across her anus. Every time my fingertip touched it, it relaxed and almost opened just a little, as if Marci wanted my finger to finger-fuck her asshole. Her anus was dry. I knew that, without any lubrication, it would go in very rough and probably be painful, not pleasurable. Still every time my fingertip slid past, it opened as if to say, "Come on in. I want you."

The situation took care of itself. Marci was beginning to rock her hips on my hand in time with my sliding finger. I still wasn't sure if it happened by accident or Marci did it on purpose. One time when my finger slid forward and Marci's ass slid back, one of us went further than before. My finger easily slid right into her sopping wet pussy, all the way in as far as it could go. I felt her shudder as it went in. As she rocked forward and I pulled back, my dripping wet finger slid back along her anus, leaving some pussy lubricant on her anus. The exact thing happened again, a finger in wet pussy and then back across her asshole. This time, neither one of us moved as much. My now very wet fingertip easily probed her anus. Gently at first, the tip of my finger entered her asshole. I pushed it in about the length of my fingernail. I took it very slowly. I was new to this. I'd heard of anal sex, but there was no way with my ex-wife. Marci's body reaction told me that what I was doing was the right thing to do. I pulled my fingertip almost out and then pushed it gently back in the same amount as before.

I opened my eyes to watch her. She had an absolutely sexual pleasure smile. While I continued the in-and-out stroking of my fingertip, Marci brought her hands around the base of my erection. While I was probing her ass, she rolled her head back in ecstasy. Then as I continued, she lowered her head and very teasingly kissed the head of my cock. After a few more light kisses all over the tip, she stuck out her tongue and licked the entire mushroom-shaped end as if she were licking a popsicle and didn't want to lose a single drop. In fact, I realized what she was licking up was the small amount of moisture that was leaking out the opening at the end of my dick. As she alternated between kissing and licking, she moved her right hand down and started to caress and play with my testicles. Her left hand stayed around the base of my cock in order to hold it steady for her mouth and tongue.

I progressively worked my finger further and further into her asshole with each inward stroke. Marci leaned her head to the right toward my legs. She started at the base of my pulsing cock, just above my testicles, and started licking up the length of the underside of my penis. As she ran her tongue teasingly up and down the nerve and muscle that ran along that underside, I thought I'd come unglued. I had no idea that it was that sexually sensitive because no one had ever played with it before. She alternated between licking and sucking on that underside, up and down, from just above the testicles to just below the end of my quivering dick. The way she tongue tickled and then sucked along the very sensitive underside was incredible. I didn't know or cared where she learned how to do that because it was to my benefit. And boy was I benefiting. By now, I was able to slowly but entirely push in and out the entire length of my finger in her anus. Marci was certainly enjoying it. I think she was ass fucking my finger as much as I was finger fucking her ass.

We were matched so well together that we both changed what we were doing to each other at the same time. As she reached the top of the underside, she kept going to the end of my penis. After a few complete licks of the end, she took the head of my rock-hard penis in her mouth and closed her lips around it. As her right hand that was playing with my balls slid under them and fingered my anus, she sucked on the head of my penis as if she were trying to suck a thick milkshake through a straw. Realizing my anus was also dry, Marci reached up and wet her finger from her saliva that was on my dick. Then she took that wet finger and placed it back on my asshole, just like I had done, at first just barely probing. Then she pushed her finger fingernail length deep in and out of my asshole. Now I knew why she enjoyed it so much. It felt great.

At the same time she had been doing this, I had removed my finger from her anus, slid my whole hand forward, and grabbed a handful of pussy and pussy juice. I brought it back and rubbed it on her anus with my thumb. I inserted my thumb into her anus once again slowly at first because my thumb was a lot bigger than my finger was. She greedily accepted it. I reached forward with my middle finger and inserted it in her vagina. Using a rocking motion with my wrist, I slid my finger in her pussy and pulled my thumb almost all the way out of her anus. Then I pushed my thumb back in and pulled my middle finger almost all the way out. One was all the way in; one was almost all the way out. I soon was able to match this rhythm with her hips and ass. It must have been effective though. Marci's hips and ass were soon gyrating so much that I could hardly keep the motion up without missing a stroke.

Meanwhile, her mouth and tongue seemed to be as turned on as her pussy and anus. She was really working over the head of my dick. And not once did she scrape her teeth. I felt nothing except pure ecstasy. Then she surpassed even that. She started to take more and more of my cock into her mouth. She was sliding me in as if I were entering her wet, warm pussy. At first, she slid me in slowly until all but about an inch or two of me was in her mouth and throat. I knew how much she had taken in because, when I felt it begin to happen, I looked down to watch. If I had seen any other couple doing this, it would have seemed pornographic. But watching Marci do this to me was beautiful and extremely erotic.

After she reached the point of as much as she was going to take in, she clamped just her lips around my penis and sucked hard enough to create a partial vacuum around my dick. This pulled on the skin of my penis, which intensified the feeling. Then still sucking and squeezing with her mouth, she raised her head. This rubbed her lips that were in contact all the way around my erection the entire length of my shaft, just like her wet and soft pussy lips would. When she reached near the end, she stopped before I came all the way out of her mouth. Just a half-inch of the head of my penis remained in her mouth. She relaxed her sucking and lips enough to break the seal, but not the contact. Then closing her lips back tight again, she pushed her mouth back down on me. This time, she only took about two-thirds of me in before she sucked to create the vacuum and slid back off me. As she reached the end, she repeated the process and started back down.

I remember thinking, Whoever said you can't fuck the face never had oral sex performed on them.

Marci's mouth was doing to my penis what her pussy would if we were having regular missionary position intercourse. She was mouth fucking my dick. I reached over with my left hand and took hold as much of her left breast as I could. I held the nipple between my thumb and fingertip. With her mouth, Marci must have felt the muscle on the underside of my penis start to pulse and throb. With me, this is the first sign that ejaculation is soon forthcoming. She rotated her head to the right just enough that her upper lip was directly rubbing up and down along that throbbing muscle. I could feel her vaginal and anal muscles contracting and relaxing on my finger and thumb. It was like the muscles were relaxing to let them in and then squeezing tight and not wanting to let them back out. As we both neared orgasm, Marci's head and hips both sped up to match my wrist rotation of finger and thumb fucking.

I took a quick look at what my hand was doing to her. I lost it. I exploded in her mouth and throat. I shot so much cum that

I didn't know how I didn't drown her. She must have climaxed along with me as her hips and ass went wild with gyrations. She somehow managed to keep up the motion of both ends as we simultaneously erupted into a nether world of pleasure and ecstasy. Time, place, or reality no longer existed. I had never seen so many colors and felt so many wonderful sensations that passed over me that eternal moment. I was quivering all over. I felt as if I were suddenly dunked in warm, pleasant water. I couldn't stop literally shaking from head to toe as my sperm glands continued to shoot load after load of massive amounts of cum into Marci's mouth. Once I began to cum, she kept her up-and-down motion with her head, but her lips never broke the seal around my dick. She sucked and swallowed every single drop.

Some time later, we both slowed down our motion and came to a stop. I removed my thumb and finger and then patted and gently squeezed her entire crotch. She withdrew my penis from her mouth, but she licked it clean entirely.

Then with what remaining energy she had left, she actually crawled up to lie and face me along my right side. She tucked her left shoulder into my right armpit and laid her head on my right shoulder. She reached over the top of me and placed her right arm across my chest. She was barely able to raise her right leg and drape it over my legs. I brought my right arm up and around her back. My hand went under her right arm and rested on the side of the base of her right breasts that were lying on my chest. Other than the hard breathing that was beginning to slow, neither one of us moved nor spoke.

Once again, I lost all concept of time. I had no idea how long we laid there like that. The only movement was the now slow rising and falling of our chest that our breathing caused. I had no desire to move at all. I just laid there, luxuriating in the feelings flowing all over my body. It was if I'd ruin the moment if I moved. So I didn't.

Minutes, hours, days, or who the hell knows how much later,

Marci moved her right arm enough so she could play with my chest hairs with her hand. I slowly rubbed the side of her breast with my right hand. She made little murmuring sounds. I turned my head to the right just enough to kiss her on the top of the head.

"Jimmy?"

"Yes, Marci?"

"You not only have reached all through my physical being, but you have touched clear through to the very heart of my soul. Just now while we were making love, I felt like we were joined as one spirit. We became as one." She lifted her head and looked at my face. "Does that sound silly?"

"No, it doesn't." I suddenly realized what she said was just what I was feeling. "In fact, I was just lying here thinking that very same thing."

She slowly turned over on to her stomach and propped herself up on her elbows in between my arm and the side of my body. Our sides were still touching each other all the way down to our toes. As she looked at me, she had a surprised smile on her face.

"Really? I thought it was because I was so turned on that I might have just imagined it."

"No, it wasn't your imagination. It was our reality."

Still lying on her stomach, she put her right arm over my chest and laid her head back on my shoulder. With her face looking across my chest, the view looking down her naked back at that heavenly ass was breathtaking. I brought my right arm back over her back. I couldn't reach her ass, so I stroked her back.

I thought for a moment. Then I put it into words. "You know our souls and spirit really did totally blend together very nicely. In fact, I think that, in some ways, they are still somewhat blended. And they will remain so forever."

Marci hugged me tightly. After a minute or two, I felt something tickle me about where her face was. At first, I thought it might have been her hair, but, when I bent my head over to the left for a better view, I saw a couple tears had fallen off her face and onto my chest. She was also smiling. So I laid my head back down and figured it was a woman thing and I didn't understand. So I left it alone.

I shut my eyes for a second to enjoy what I was feeling. When I opened them again, I realized I had been asleep. And Marci was still asleep. She had turned onto her left side, and she was facing me in a modified fetal position. Her right arm was over my body about the lower chest or upper stomach area. Her right leg was stretched out straight over the tops of my legs. Her head had slid down, and it was lying on the bed with the top tucked up under my armpit. The left side of her face was against my rib cage. Her slightly opened mouth and nose was pointing up just over my chest, and she was sound asleep. Her long hair covered the right side of her face. Carefully so as not to move my body and disturb her, I reached over with my left hand and brushed her reddish brown locks off her face. She kind of smacked her lips a couple times, but she didn't wake up. When most people sleep, they make some really weird facial expressions. I thought her facial expressions were cute. Still being careful not to wake her, I reached up and pulled a pillow under my head. I put my left hand between my head and the pillow.

I lay there wide-awake and in deep thought. I went back through all the highlights of the last few days, starting with finding that damn key in the rain. This was one of those times when I believed that things happened for a reason. So what was I going to do if there was a lot of money in that Zurich account? I felt Marci move slightly. I looked at her. She was still asleep. Here laid all the treasure I'd ever need or want. But if there was money there, it really didn't belong to the Gionetti family. It was obtained through illegal means. Plus, Joseph Branning had probably stolen it from the family. So who did it really belong to? If we turned it in, the Gionetti family couldn't claim it. They'd have to explain where they got it. They couldn't do that without self-incrimination. So the state would absorb it. Did it really belong to the state where some politician would find a way to shovel it into his pocket? There was no way it could be returned to the people who spent it on those illegal activities. They would also never admit to criminal behavior like drugs, prostitution, and gambling. Besides, if they blew it that way, did they really even deserve it back? Their willingness to spend it that way was what promoted the activity itself.

Marci was right. We did deserve something for all they put us through. But did we deserve a lot of ill-gotten money? I didn't know what I was fussing about. There probably wasn't anything in that damn bank account anyway. Then I'd never know unless I went there and looked. I could at least do that and then make a decision. With that semi-decision made, I felt a little of the pressure relieved.

Speaking of relieving, I felt the need to relieve my bladder. I didn't want to disturb my little sleeping angel so I lay there and quietly tried to not to think of taking a piss. After a while, I really had to go pretty bad. I looked down at Marci. I thought about it and decided that, if I rubbed her back with my hand and it didn't disturb her, then she was asleep deep enough that I wouldn't wake her if I got up and went to the bathroom. So I easily rubbed her back. She made a few groans. Then she proceeded to stretch her arms and legs, much like a cat does when it first wakes up.

She looked up at me and smiled with groggy, sleepy eyes. "So it wasn't a dream. You really are here." She snuggled up even closer to me.

"No, I'm no dream. Dreams don't have to wake up and use the bathroom."

"Okay." She wiggled into my side. Then she must have realized what I meant. She opened her eyes as best she could and looked at me. "Oh, you have to use the bathroom?"

"Yes, lover. I sure do."

"Okay. Go ahead." She reluctantly disengaged herself from my side.

I purposely climbed over the top of her instead of sliding off the left side of the bed, which was actually closer to the bathroom. As I crawled over her, she rolled onto her back and turned with me so our body fronts were in contact the whole way. I kept kissing her on the lips until I rolled off the bed.

When I got off the bed and started to walk around toward the bathroom, I was shocked at how sore I was. I wasn't used to all this physical stimulation. If I were going to marry Marci, I was going to have to get in better shape. From everything I had read and heard, a twenty-four-year-old woman hadn't even gotten close to reaching her sexual peak.

I plodded into the bathroom, turned on the light, and stepped up to the toilet. It was on the left side of the bathroom just past the sink. I lifted the lid and then broke the sanitized paper that was around the seat and threw it in the toilet. I lifted the seat and positioned myself in front of the toilet. I took myself in my right hand and pointed it toward the water. I placed my left hand behind my lower back. I stood there and waited for my bladder to release the urine.

Just as I felt the urine start to come out, I was startled when Marci came up behind me. It caused my penal muscles to tighten and stop the process. She put her right arm around my waist, laid her head on my left shoulder, and looked down at the water.

She reached her left hand around and gently held my penis. "Can I help?"

I looked down at the top of her head. "Are you serious?"

"Sure. I always wondered what it was like."

I let go of my penis and raised both hands in the air. "It's all yours. You have control."

Apparently because Marci had never held a urinating penis, she underestimated the strength of the pressure. She squealed loudly as I pissed all over the toilet as she desperately tried to aim in the right direction. I was laughing so hard that I was sure it helped with her not hitting the water. I didn't let it go on for long.

I stopped peeing. I reached down and took hold of her hand and my penis.

"I think you need to start with training wheels. Here. Let me help you."

She smacked me on the arm with her right hand, but she didn't let go of my penis. She laid the side of her head on my left arm and paid attention to what we were doing. After the stream ended, I shook the last few drops off the end of my penis. Marci shook it right along with me.

"Doesn't it hurt to shake it that hard?" She didn't look up.

"No, not at all."

She let go and hurried out of the bathroom. "I'll be right back."

She came back with the spare roll of toilet paper from the closet. We cleaned up all the stray urine, put the soiled toilet paper in the toilet, and flushed. After we washed our hands, Marci took me by the hand and led me back to the large bed.

We lay down on our respective sides and faced each other. We were only about a foot apart. At first, we just laid there and stared into each other's eyes. We were saying so much to each other with actually speaking so little. Her eye makeup was still well in place even after having been asleep.

She broke my trance. "I sure do love your beautiful brown eyes. I wish I had your long eyelashes."

"I wouldn't trade any part of your eyes for anything. They are just right the way they are."

"Really?"

"Absolutely!"

"I think they are too big and too far apart."

"Not at all. They are perfect the way they are."

"You're sweet." She leaned forward and kissed me. "Thank you."

I was lying on the left side of the bed. I had my head propped up on my right hand. Marci had her left arm bent and lying under head. She was using her right hand to play with my chest hairs.

That was becoming a habit with her. Up until now, I had my left arm straight down and lying on top of my hip.

Then her gaze dropped down to her fingers in my chest hairs. "Jimmy?"

Something was coming. I tried to keep it upbeat. "Yes, dear? How may I be of service?"

She still didn't look me in the eye. "If there is no money in that account, what are we going to do?"

I breathed a sigh of relief because it was still, "What are we going to do?"

"Relax, honey. I still have a job. Remember? Plus, if need be or you want to, I will find you another job. I still know a few people in this town." I reached over and stroked her hip and waist.

She looked up into my eyes and placed her hand along my cheek. "You're sure we're going to be all right? I have been all alone and taking care of myself for so long that it would be different to have to depend on someone else."

"Even if I weren't in the picture, you'd still be just fine on your own. Besides, you don't have to be dependent on me. A married couple should be equal partners. Whatever we do, we do together."

"Promise?"

"I do," I said with a wink and double meaning.

She smiled. "I do, too."

I leaned forward and put my left arm under her right arm and around her back. I kissed her lovingly. It wasn't necessarily passionate, but not necessarily light either. It was just lovingly. Our kiss grew into something more as our lips held on to each other's lips. I slowly rolled over on top of her. Marci embraced me above the shoulders. Our lips parted, and we slowly but meaningfully interlocked tongues. They danced wildly.

My hips quite naturally slid in between her legs, which she gladly opened to allow me in. We were in a tight embrace as we kissed. My penis was lying right on top of her vagina. Marci brought her feet up and around the backs of my knees. She hugged my legs with her legs. All this was causing my penis to massage her clitoris. It wasn't long before I had a hard-on and she was starting to lubricate. It didn't take much movement before the head of my dick very easily and quite naturally found the now-damp spot at the entrance to her hall of pleasure. I let my dick slide in about an inch before I stopped its penetration. Marci hugged my upper shoulders, neck, and knees just a little tighter as I could hear a small moan through our kisses. I brought up my hands along her sides and toward her breasts. Instead of stopping on her breasts, I just brushed by them and started to run my hands up to her arms. As soon as Marci felt my hands touch the underside of her arms, she started to raise them above her head. I wasn't sure what she was doing at first, but I decided to go along with her. She raised them straight above her head as if she were reaching toward the headboard. She didn't completely stretch them out, but her hands were above her head and together. I thought I knew what she wanted so I reached up and took a hold of each wrist with each of my hands. I then held them there as if I were pinning them to the bed. I soon realized that this was the right thing to do as she moaned loudly in pleasure.

Then using very short and very slow hip thrusts, I took a long time to fully enter her. That was how we made love for several, several minutes, slow, easy, and tender, not hard and explosive. But it was soft, intimate, and long as I had her pinned to the bed.

CHAPTER 18

I awoke to a beautiful morning. I had no idea what time it was, and I didn't care. Marci was still asleep, and we were tangled together. I was on my back, and Marci was mostly facedown. But most of Marci was flat on top of me. Except for her legs and hips, she was sort of lying on the right side of me. Her right leg was over the top of my right leg and then under my left leg. Her left leg was under my right leg. Her head was on her pillow and facing me. She was virtually breathing in my ear. Her left arm was straight out to the side away from me. Her right arm was across my chest and just below my throat. Perhaps that was what woke me up. The sheet had slid down so it barely came up to Marci's ass. My left leg and her right leg were also sticking out from under the sheet.

When I stretched the sleep out of my limbs and body, Marci stirred. I looked over at her face. First one eye and then the other half opened. She stretched and then realized I was looking at her. She grinned and slowly squirmed closer until she could give me a kiss. Then she snuggled closer and tucked her head into the crook of my neck.

I barely heard what she said. "This is the best morning I have ever woken up to."

Because my right arm was straight down along my side, she was lying directly on top of it. As I went to move it, Marci raised herself enough to allow me to slide it out past her. I curved it around her back and hugged her tightly.

I said, "I don't think I'm awake yet. This is too wonderful to be anything other than a dream."

Marci reached down with her right hand and completely covered my now-soft penis and testicles with her hand. "Let me tell you, Jimmy. This is no dream." She let go and brought her hand back up on my chest.

I brought my right hand down, rubbed her ass a little, and then lightly popped her on the ass cheek with my hand.

"This is real, too. I have to use the bathroom."

"Well, mister, you are on your own this time."

I chuckled. I pulled out from under her.

Forty-five minutes later, we were riding down the elevator to the downstairs restaurant. We had both decided that we wanted to get something to eat instead of having room service deliver. I had put on dress slacks with a casual shirt. Marci was wearing a nice, short-sleeved blouse and a skirt that came down to about two inches above her knees. She wore her hair down, and she had put on makeup with no glasses. Gone was the mousy office girl. This was the beautiful and sophisticated woman that Marci really was. She looked great. When we first got on the elevator, we were all alone. I pushed the button for the lobby and then walked to the back of the car. With my back against the wall, I faced the door. Marci stood right up against me. We were face-to-face, and we kissed a lot. About halfway down, we could feel the elevator slowing to stop at one of the floors. Marci moved to my right side, but kept her left arm around my waist. I put my right arm around her shoulders. Some other people got on and shared the ride all the way to the lobby.

The restaurant wasn't crowded. We were seated right away. Five minutes later, we were sipping on coffee while we waited for our order. I looked at Marci across the table.

"Marci, do you know how long it's been since I had breakfast with someone I had just spent all night with?" *Boy, it does feel good to have someone in my life.*

"I don't know how long it has been for you, but it's been forever for me."

"Yeah. I could get used to this."

"Because I'm out of work, it is possible for me. But what about you? Aren't you supposed to be at your office?"

"Oh, shit! I forgot all about work. I had better call the office and come up with something good. I'll be right back."

"I'll be right here."

I got up and went out to the hotel lobby to find a pay phone. Two minutes later, the phone was ringing at the office.

"Wheaton Investigation, may I help you?" I heard Julie answer.

"Hi, Julie. This is Jim Peterson. Is Mr. Harper in?"

"Where have you been, Mr. Peterson? He has been looking for you."

"Mr. Harper?"

"Mr. Wheaton. Mr. Harper has disappeared. Then so did you. Everyone is going nuts around here."

"Well, put me through to Mr. Wheaton, please."

"Just a minute. I'm sure when he hears it's you that he'll interrupt whatever he's doing to talk to you."

Barely sixty seconds later, he came on the line. "Peterson, where the hell have you been? And what's this all about?"

"What do you mean, Mr. Wheaton?"

"Harper left the office two days ago and hasn't been seen since here or at home. His wife is almost hysterical. Then you left. Until now, no one knew about you."

"Well, sir, I've been investigating a case. I've been working very closely with the police. You can check with them about where I've been. I haven't the slightest idea where Bill Harper has been."

"So are we to be honored here at the office sometime today with a status report?"

It wasn't really a subtle way to say I had better get my ass to work now.

"I'm tying up the final stages with the client right now. I should be in shortly."

"See to it that you are!" He didn't even wait for a response before he hung up.

I barely remembered the walk back to the table. Something was definitely wrong. The hairs on the back of my neck were standing up.

I sat down. Marci reached over and took a hold of my hand. "Is everything all right?"

"Yeah, sure. But there's one peculiar thing. My boss left the office the other day and hasn't been seen or heard from since. Something is not right with that. Whatever his problem is, I hope he gets it straightened out."

Our breakfast was delivered. We both dug in with a hunger derived from all the physical activity we had been experiencing.

While we were finishing our last cup of coffee, Marci asked, "So what have you decided we are going to do?"

She didn't have to go into detail with her question. I knew what she was talking about.

"Well, I think that, as soon as we can work out the paperwork for visas, passports, or whatever we need, plus airline tickets, then we take a little trip to Switzerland."

She lit up like a Christmas tree. "I always wanted to see Europe."

"Yeah, me, too." I felt slightly downcast.

"Jimmy, what's the matter? We're going to Switzerland. Isn't that great?"

"Yeah, great."

"All right, mister. Spill it. What's wrong?"

I looked at her.

I suddenly was getting scared as I wondered, *It has already started. How can I afford to take care of her?*

"The bank account may as well be sitting on the moon. I don't have a lot of money. I can't afford for us to go on vacation and see

Europe. I'll be lucky if I can come up with enough money for the airfare alone."

"Is that all that's bothering you?"

I looked at her. "Is that all? I'd say that is a pretty big all."

"Look, first of all, I have a friend who works for a travel agency. If anyone can get us low airfare, she can. She can also probably get us nice hotel accommodation at the lowest possible cost. I'm sure she'll know all about the passport procedures as well."

"But I still don't know if I even have that much money."

"Look, Jimmy, who says it is all up to you? I may be out of a job, but I have some money in savings that should be enough to take care of our trip there and back if necessary."

I started to object. "I don't want you to use up your savings. If this all falls apart, you may need it."

Then I saw anger in her eyes that I didn't know she was capable of. "Damn it, Jimmy!" A couple of the other nearby patrons of the restaurant looked in our direction. "Let me remind you that you said that a married couple is equal partners. Whatever we do, we do together. Or do you mean that only as long as you are in control?" Fire was in her eyes. I could almost see steam coming out of her ears.

"Might I remind you that we are not yet married?"

"That is small technicalities that we'll take care of soon. So are we equal partners, or are you a hypocrite?"

I started to fire back at her in anger. Then I realized she was right. But my male, macho, bullshit ego wouldn't let me give in quite that easily.

"No, I meant what I said. It's just that I didn't think I had the right to ask you for something that was yours before we met."

She softened a little. "Look, are you prepared to share with me whatever you already have?"

"Of course, although it isn't much."

"I don't have much either, but I'm ready to share whatever I have with you. What I share with you, I share with us. Get it? Us!"

I sat back, looked at her, and smiled. At first, she maintained the anger. Then it slowly melted, and I saw all her body language relax.

I simply said, "I love you."

She looked down at her empty coffee cup. Then she looked back up at me. "I love you, too. Now can we get out of here and start taking care of us?"

I paid the bill, and we were out of there. When we got in the car in the hotel parking garage, I hesitated a bit before I started the car.

"What?" she asked.

"I'm just thinking about what we are going to do next."

"What might that be?"

"I have to run by the office and make an appearance. When I called there a few minutes ago, the owner basically told me to get my ass in the office. He wasn't happy that Bill Harper and I both had not reported for work this morning."

"How long do you need to go in for?"

"That's hard to say. At least long enough for Mr. Wheaton to be satisfied. That's for sure."

"I'm going with you. I don't want to be alone."

I looked at her for a few seconds. "I guess I can tell him that you are with me as a witness to the investigation I'm on. That's not too far from the truth."

"Good. Then let's go."

When we got to my office building, I parked in my usual space. I was kind of surprised that it was actually vacant. I took it as a good omen. I held Marci by the arm just above the elbow as we entered the front door. Julie looked up and took about five seconds to recognize us and remember our conversation about age differences. I could see it on her face.

"Good morning, Mr. Peterson. How are you doing?"

"Just fine." We stopped in front of her desk. "Julie, I'd like you to meet Marci Johnson. Marci, this is our receptionist, Julie McMichaels."

"Hi, Julie. It's nice to meet you." Marci offered her hand. They shook hands.

"It's very nice to finally meet you, Miss Johnson."

Marci looked at me. I knew it was in reference to the remark about finally meeting her. I acted like Julie hadn't said it. Marci turned back to Julie. "Please call me Marci."

I looked at Marci. To look at her now, one would see a very attractive, classy, and upper-class woman. Only a few days ago, she was just a mousy-looking office pool secretary. I'd bet she could really relate to Julie. Also, their ages weren't that far apart.

"Okay, Marci. I will." I noticed the look Julie gave Marci. It really wasn't a look of appraisal, but more a look of "now I understand why he was asking those questions." Then Julie turned toward me. "Mr. Wheaton said to tell you that you were to come to his office the minute you got in. But he didn't quite put it that nicely."

"Okay. I will in a minute. Let me get Marci situated."

I turned and started to say something to Marci, but Julie interrupted, "Mr. Wheaton said not in a minute. Now!" I looked at her. She raised both her hands in surrender. "His words, not mine."

Marci giggled. Julie laughed. I looked back and forth between them.

Marci looked at Julie. "Is he really that predictable? Or is Mr. Wheaton that good?"

Julie answered with a scrunch of her nose. "I think a little of both."

"That's very interesting. It may be helpful in the future."

Julie responded, "Oh, there's a bunch about Mr. Peterson that could be helpful."

"This I've got to hear."

I felt a bit like a spectator at a tennis match as I looked back and forth at them.

"All right," I interrupted. "I give. You two can discuss me without me. Julie, would you mind showing Marci the break room?"

"I most certainly will do that."

I turned to Marci. "I'm going to have to see what he wants. If you don't mind, I'd better do this alone."

"That's fine, dear. Julie and I seem to have a lot to talk about."

I could tell Julie noticed Marci calling me "dear." But she didn't comment on it.

I said to Marci, "This shouldn't take too long. I'll be back as soon as I can."

I stepped forward and started to give her a kiss. I caught myself just a few inches from her lips. She had held still and smiled. She would have let me kiss her. And why not? This wasn't her office.

A little embarrassed, I turned instead toward Julie. "Thanks, Julie."

As I turned to go, Julie said, "Mr. Peterson?"

I stopped and looked back. "Yes, Julie?"

"A few messages are on your desk."

I looked at her with a questioning look on my face as I wondered, *Why would she stop me for that?*

Then she added something that explained the real reason she stopped me. Her eyes kind of glanced toward Marci and then back at me. "You did really well, Mr. Peterson. I'm very happy for you."

She didn't give me the chance for a response. She got up and took Marci by the arm. The two then almost skipped off to the break room. I stood there for a minute and watched them act like little girls with a secret. I turned and went to see Old Man Wheaton.

His secretary saw me coming. She buzzed him on the intercom

before I even got in front of her desk. "Mr. Wheaton, Mr. Peterson is here." She said into the handset, "Yes, sir." She looked up at me as I stopped in front of her desk. "You can go right in."

"Thank you, Betty." I headed for his office door.

Just before I got to the door, I mentally put on my best manners. I opened the door and went in. He was sitting at his desk. Julian Wheaton was a prototypical example of a business executive. He was in his early sixties, but looked like he was in his forties, even with his perfectly placed, dark, dyed hair. His posture was always rigid and straight. He reeked with the air of old money. Though he never really looked down his nose at his employees, everyone, even at first glance, knew he was in charge.

He was leaning back in his chair and watching every move I made. As I approached his desk, he indicated toward the chair in front of his desk. I walked over and sat down. With Marci in my life and the possibility of that bank account, I, for once, felt like I was in control, no matter whom I was facing, so to speak. So I sat there and waited for him to speak. Just as I was beginning to wonder if this was turning into a game of who would blink first, he spoke.

"I just got off the phone with the police."

This caught me a little off guard, but I didn't think I showed it. So I waited. Once again, he spoke first. That was when I realized that, sometimes when you are really the one in control, you would lead. That was what he was doing.

"I've been talking to a Lieutenant Glosman." He paused for effect. "You do recognize the name?"

"Yes, sir. I do." Once again I chastised myself, *Damn, I didn't mean to add the sir part. But old habits are hard to break.*

"I'm very interested in the case that one of our investigators is looking into. The Joseph Branning murder case. You're familiar with it?"

"Yes, I am." *Good. I didn't say "No, sir."*

"I checked. That case was assigned to young Muller."

"That is what I understand."

"Funny, the authorities are under the impression that you're the assigned investigator. Why might that be?"

Now it was his turn to sit and wait. Never breaking eye contact, I leaned back in my chair.

I proceeded to talk to myself instead of giving in and speaking first. "Fuck this shit. I don't need this! But I have no idea what, if anything, what is in that bank account. Plus, Marci might need me to need this shit if she were to need a job. Maybe I do need it a little, so I had better not burn too many bridges. I might get away with scorching a few, but completely burning them might be hazardous. Though, I am feeling pretty confident in my position."

Finally he caved first and said, "Well?" It wasn't much but it was just enough for me to feel as if I had not backed down.

I then proceeded to let the full cat out of the bag. "The case was assigned to Sean Muller. But independently of his investigation, I came across several pieces of information that I felt was prudent for me to fully develop."

He waited silently for me to either dig my own grave or build my own mountain. So I gave it to him.

"I discovered that Joseph Branning's murder was part of a conspiracy to silence him from divulging extremely incriminating evidence. It was evidence that would have sent many people to jail for a very long time. When I was last in the office, I was told that Bill Harper had assigned the case to Sean. He was told it was a simple mugging and he should do the paperwork and close the case. I knew that was wrong. But the case belonged to Sean. He's a good kid. Young and inexperienced, but still a good kid. I didn't think it was right to step on his toes, so I used my own time and energy to get all the facts."

"Did you?"

"I believe so. Then I turned everything over to the police," I said with a finality that said, "So it's over."

The look he gave me was meant to drill clear through me. But I refused to be intimidated. So I glared back.

With almost-clenched teeth, he asked, "What do you know about what Bill Harper has been up to?"

Inside I was a bit shaken because that came from left field.

"I haven't the slightest idea. All I know is he took off a couple days ago and hasn't been back." I looked at the stone-cold figure sitting across the desk from me. Then it occurred to me. He knew something I didn't.

"Why? What do you know about him that I don't?"

"The police have him in custody."

"What? Why?"

He was reading my reaction before answering. "Lieutenant Glosman wouldn't go into details, but it has something to do with Branning's murder."

I suddenly wanted to be out of there. I wanted to talk to Mike. I got really antsy just sitting there.

"Mr. Wheaton, I need to leave. I have to find out what's his connection with the murder. Depending on what it is, it could have a large effect on all our futures."

This penetrated his rock-solid façade. He actually squirmed in his chair. "By all means, go."

I got up to leave. Just as I got to the door, he stopped me with a single word. It wasn't so much what he said, but how he said it. "Jim!"

It actually sounded as if I meant something to him, not just someone who happened to be one of his subordinates for over twenty years. I turned toward him, but I didn't say anything.

"Please let me know what you find out. I do have a lot of influence. I can help you."

It was a genuine offer. It wasn't an order or demand. One of the things about great leaders was that they somehow always instinctively knew when to lead and when to let their subordinates stray out on their own. Mr. Wheaton was an expert at this.

I smiled. "Mr. Wheaton, you can count on it."

As I turned to go out the door, I heard him say, "Take all the time you need. Just let me know."

I didn't look back or speak. I kind of gave him a thumbs-up just before I shut the door.

As I passed by Julie's desk, she was on the phone. Marci wasn't there. When Julie looked up at me, I mouthed, "Where is she?"

She covered the mouthpiece. "In your office."

"Thanks." I headed that way. When I got there, I saw Marci sitting at my desk. She was just sitting there and drinking coffee. I closed the door and headed around my desk, en route to my phone.

Marci chuckled. "You didn't tell me you had a tiny box for an office." When I didn't respond, her mood quickly turned serious. "What's the matter?"

"My boss, Bill Harper, is in police custody."

"Why?"

"I don't know. It has something to do with Branning's murder." She went ashen. If the cup of coffee in her hand hadn't been more than an inch above my desk, it would have crashed down as she dropped it. She sat quite still as I picked up the phone and called Mike. I was transferred directly to him.

"Lieutenant Glosman."

"Mike, this is James. Tell me about Bill Harper."

"He's in custody."

"So I've heard. Why?"

"I'm sorry, sir, but I cannot comment on that at this time."

"What the hell do you mean? What the fuck is going on?"

"Yes, sir. If you'd like further information on that, please contact the public affairs office."

The lightbulb went on. I understood. "Is there someone else in your office with you?"

"That is correct, sir."

"Look, I need to talk to you about this. Will you be home by six o'clock tonight?"

"Absolutely. I'm sure they will be able to help you then."

"All right. We'll come by." I hung up.

I stood there with my hand on the phone. A million things were running through my head.

Marci interrupted my thoughts. "What did all that mean?"

"I don't really know. Apparently, Mike had someone in the office with him, and he was unwilling or unable to talk about Bill Harper. So we'll go by his house later."

"So what do we do in the meantime?"

"We have to check on flight reservations and passports. But I don't want to do that from here."

"Why not?"

"I don't know. Something in the back of my mind is telling me that it isn't the wise thing to do. In those kinds of situations, I've learned to trust my instincts and those little nagging feelings."

"Okay. The travel agency where my friend works is not too far from here. It's only a couple blocks away."

"Good. We'll go down there in a little while. I need to check on a few things around here. Will you be all right waiting here while I check?"

"Oh, sure. I'll be just fine. If I need anything, I'll ask Julie. She's a sweetheart. And by the way, she is very fond of you."

"What do you mean?"

"More than once, she casually mentioned that she wishes her father was more like you."

I turned to walk out. "Yeah, that's just like me. The fatherly type."

I didn't quite hear her answer enough for it to register as I walked out. I went down the hall to find Sean Muller. Suddenly, the puzzle I thought was solved had a few key pieces missing. The picture wasn't quite so clear. Luck was with me. Sean was in his office when I walked in. He started to stand up, but I signed with my hand to stay seated.

"Please sit." I plopped down in the chair alongside his little desk. He was probably the only one in the whole company with a smaller office and desk than mine. "Look, Sean, I'll come right to the point. How far have you gotten with the investigation of the Branning murder case?"

"Oh, I finished that a couple days ago and gave it to Mr. Harper."

"And what was your conclusion and recommendation?"

"I concluded it was a homicide that fell within the guidelines of the policy."

I lowered my head in thought. *If he recommended it to be payable, then why would Bill be in police custody? Anne Gionetti would have her money, and no one would be the wiser.*

Then Sean added something that changed the complexity of things. "But I recommended and signed the payment to be held pending determination of the person or persons responsible for his murder. I didn't want someone to profit from his death if he were responsible for it."

I slowly raised my head. I knew I had a smile on my face, but I couldn't help it. "What did Mr. Harper say?"

"He got quite agitated and demanded I sign off on the payment. He said I really was too new to know what I was doing. How dare I hold up the timely processing of a claim that was such an open-and-shut case."

"Why didn't you sign off on it?"

"I remembered what you had told me. I did what my gut feeling told me was right, no matter what."

"You know what, Sean? You did really well. You just might make it in this business. It's too early to tell if you'll make it big, but at least you'll like the person who looks back at you in the mirror in twenty years." Sean was beaming like a high-powered light.

A few of those missing pieces were falling back into place. If Sean had signed to withhold payment, then Bill Harper would have to stick his neck way out and draw attention to him if he were to go against an investigator's recommendation, even if it were a new investigator. He would have to have an overriding reason for reversal. More red flags would be waving than you could imagine. The investigation he was trying to keep very quiet and quickly completed would suddenly become very loud and the center of attention. Then he would have to explain to Mr. Wheaton why he gave such a large-dollar case to a new investigator in the first place. Then he would be hard-pressed to explain why, when he first gave the case to Sean, he told him that it was an open-and-shut case and he needed to process it as soon as possible. The investigators were supposed to feel free of any persuasion or inducements so as to remain totally objective and unbiased throughout the entire process. Bill figured that, because Sean was new, he wouldn't be eager to go against the boss's suggestions and be too intimidated to mention them.

But what would make Bill so agitated that Sean wouldn't sign off on the payment? Unless it would mean he would suffer dire consequences if the payments weren't going to be made. And guess who would be the source of those dire consequences? Anne Gionetti!

Obviously, they had somehow gotten to Bill. If that was indeed the case, then it explained why I was such a constant focal point for Puke Face and his friends. That would also explain why they kept threatening me to back off the case. It wasn't because of the notebook. It had come directly—or more likely—indirectly from Bill Harper. Now any sympathy I had for Bill's predicament turned to pure anger for what he caused Marci and me to have gone through.

I stood up. "Thanks, Sean. You've been a big help."

With the state I was in, if I had said anymore, it wouldn't have been very nice. I paid no attention to anything he might have said as I walked out.

When I returned to my office, Marci was patiently sitting and waiting at my desk. She noticed the change in my demeanor right away. "What did you find out?"

"Come on. Let's get the hell out of here. I'll let you know on the way."

As we came out of my office and headed for the front door, I noticed Mr. Wheaton was standing next to Julie's desk. We had to pass right by him to leave. So I purposely stopped at Julie's desk. It would be a totally rude snub if I didn't introduce Marci to Mr. Wheaton. Because there was no way we could have made it by him without his noticing, I gritted my teeth and did the proper thing. Mr. Wheaton instinctively turned to see who had just come alongside of him. He saw me first. He was going to return his attention to Julie when he noticed Marci. He definitely took a double take at her.

He flustered all over himself just to ask, "And who might this be?"

He hardly even noticed I was there, but I performed the introductions anyway. "Mr. Wheaton, I'd like to introduce to you, uh, my fiancée. Marci Johnson."

I surprised everyone, including me, except for Marci. I couldn't believe it came out of my mouth. I wanted to turn around and see if a ventriloquist had his hand in my back. Julie squealed with delight. Mr. Wheaton just about dropped his jaw on the floor.

"Marci, this is Mr. Wheaton."

Marci stepped forward and reached out her right hand to the stunned super executive. "So very nice to meet you, Mr. Wheaton. Jimmy has spoken very highly of you."

As he eagerly took her hand in both of his, his smile was bigger than I had ever seen. "Please call me Julian. And it's very nice to meet you." He fondled her hand. "I had no idea one of my employees had such excellent taste."

Marci bowed her head in just the proper amount of humbleness in acceptance of the compliment. "Thank you very much, Julian."

Wheaton reluctantly allowed Marci to withdraw her hand

from his as she stepped back beside me. I just stood there and watched this sideshow. I looked over at Julie as the boss and Marci exchanged pleasantries. Julie was grinning from ear to ear.

She looked at me and winked. "Congratulations, Mr. Peterson. I'm so very happy for you. She's a terrific lady."

I said sheepishly, "Thank you, Julie. You were the first to know."

"Oh, that makes me feel really special."

"Well, your advice helped me to decide."

She wiggled a little with happiness. I turned back to the Marci and Julian show.

I waited for a pause in their conversation. I said to Marci, "Excuse me, dear, but we do have that appointment."

Marci smiled at me. "We certainly do, honey." She turned back to Wheaton. "I'm sorry, Julian, but we must be on our way."

"Of course, my dear. I understand. Now that you are becoming part of our family, be sure to stop by here often."

"I will as often as possible."

Mr. Wheaton beamed like a schoolboy with a candy bar. I looked at Julie. She rolled her eyes and turned away to hide her laughter. It was obvious to her that Marci sure knew how to play the game, and she had Mr. Wheaton wrapped around her little finger.

As we were leaving the building and heading down the street, Marci was leading me toward the travel agency. We were walking side by side and holding hands.

I said, "The old man is something else."

"You asked me before why I dressed the way I did at work. I used to try to make myself look the very best I possibly could. But I just couldn't take it anymore. Between that married creep I slept with and every man who came within ten feet of me, constantly trying his best to get to know me better. All they really wanted was to get me to go to bed. My life was like a constant battle of me against the whole male population. They didn't care about me as a person. All they cared about was what I could do for them physically. Julian Wheaton is exactly the type I was trying to hide from."

"You certainly handled him pretty well."

"I've had to deal with his type all my life. It's really quite easy. I just got tired of having to fight them off constantly with no let up. Hence the disguise. So I wouldn't have to concentrate so much of my energy on defense."

I pointed at her. "So why is it different now?"

She smiled and walked just a little closer. "Because now I have you in my life. It is more important to me to look as good as I can for you than it is to hide from the male leeches of the world."

"But if I remember correctly, when you opened the door that very first time I saw you, I was pretty physically awestruck. I know you had to notice how I couldn't help staring at your breasts and other body parts."

"Yes, I noticed."

"So why didn't you hide from me? In fact, you did just the opposite. From the very beginning, you purposely showed me that part you hid from everyone else."

"At first, I'm not sure why." As we continued to walk, she snuggled up close to me. "Then I realized you were different. Yes, you looked at the physical me, but you didn't come on to me. You took the time to notice the person who was inside of my body as well. You weren't some male, hormonal, raging creep."

"Believe me, when I first saw you, my male hormones were raging pretty hard."

"I know they were. But you had enough self-control and respect for me as a person that you got to my heart real quickly. Once you had that, the rest belonged to you."

"I can understand why you'd be willing to show me the real you in private, but you are no longer hiding in public."

"You mean you're wondering why I'm not acting the lady on the streets and the whore in the bedroom?"

"No, not at all. You are very much the lady. I'm just wondering why you no longer feel the need for the disguise."

"Because now all those bastards can no longer get to me."

"Because you now have me to keep them away from you?"

"That's right. My knight in shining armor to protect me from all the demons and dragons."

"I don't know about the shining armor part, but anyone or anything is going to have to go through me to get to you."

She hugged my arm as we came to the travel agency where her friend worked. We walked in and saw a lady sitting at a computer monitor. She had a telephone headset, and she was busily typing away as she talked.

When we entered, she stopped long enough to point to a couple chairs beside her desk. "I'll be right with you."

I noticed the nameplate on her desk. "Dolly Winters." I assumed it was hers.

We both looked around the room. Many travel posters hung on the walls.

"Hi. May I help you?" I heard the travel agent say.

Marci said, "Hi, Dolly. How are you doing?"

The travel agent looked at her and said hesitantly, "I'm fine. And how are you?"

Marci chuckled. "Dolly, it's me. Marci Johnson."

The agent looked at her unbelievingly. Then I saw the recognition come across her face. "Oh my God! It is you. I didn't recognize you. You have done something different with your ... with your ... ah ... hair."

I giggled to myself. Not the best of recoveries, but not too bad. She probably only knows the mousy Marci Johnson.

Still in shock, Dolly asked, "What can I do for you?"

"First, let me introduce my fiancé. Dolly, this is Jim Peterson." That was the first time she had called me anything except Jimmy. It was a female thing that she didn't want Dolly to know me by Jimmy.

She turned to me. "This is Dolly Winters. We've known each other ever since secretarial school. I went to work for the investment company. Dolly went to work in the travel business." I shook hands with her, and we exchanged pleasantries.

Dolly seemed to be still surprised with all the changes in Marci's life so I got to business. "We are interested in taking a trip to Zurich, Switzerland. Can you help us?"

"Zurich?" I saw her look at Marci. The looks that passed between them were another one of those female things that I didn't even want to know about. Dolly recovered nicely this time. "Certainly. I can set you right up. First of all, when would you like to depart?"

"As soon as you can get us on a flight."

"I see. Do you both have passports?"

I looked at Marci. She shook her head no. I turned back to Dolly. "Neither one of us has one. This trip is something that has come up recently. You are our first stop. I figured you could take care of everything we need."

"Do either of you have a copy of your birth certificates?"

I said, "I have one on file at my office with my investigator's license."

Marci said, "Yes, I have one at home if I can find it."

Although Dolly didn't say, I knew her understanding of why Marci would have trouble finding it wasn't even close to the real reason.

"Well, as soon as you can find it, then you can take it with a passport photo down to the passport office downtown. You should be able to get a passport within, say, twenty-four to forty-eight hours. If you are willing to pay the exuberant express fees."

"Where do we get a passport photo?"

"Dozens of places can do it in less than an hour. That is no problem."

I said, "That seems to settle that problem."

"How long would you stay abroad?" Dolly asked.

I looked at Marci. We had talked all about going, but nothing about coming back. She looked at me and very lightly shrugged her shoulders.

I turned back to Dolly. "How about a week after we get there?"

"Fine. You will be requiring lodging?" It was actually more a statement than a question.

Marci said, "Yes, we will. Single room with a king-sized bed located somewhere in town, preferably around the business district. You know stores and banks. That kind of thing."

Dolly looked at Marci and then at me. Then she returned her gaze back to Marci. I couldn't read minds, but I swore she was thinking, "Boy, Marci, you have changed a lot more than your hair."

But she maintained her professionalism. "How about a rental car?"

"Sounds good."

Dolly spent about five minutes pounding away at her keyboard. She didn't say a word the whole time her fingers were pounding away at the keys. Every once in a while, she'd look at Marci, still in amazement. She finally stopped punching and looked at her screen for a while.

She turned toward us. "Considering the time it will take to get you passports, I can get you a flight leaving the day after tomorrow in the evening with a week's stay and a rental car."

I swallowed.

Here comes the hard part.

"How much?"

"Right around $3,500."

I stirred in my chair. I was speechless.

$3,500 is a lot of money.

Marci answered without hesitation, "That will be fine. We'll take it. Set it up."

Shocked, I looked at her. "What?"

She just looked back at me and grinned. "We'll take it."

CHAPTER 19

We pulled up in front of Mike and Sharon's house a little before six o'clock. We were a little early, but I was anxious. I came around and opened the car door for Marci. As she got out, I couldn't help but notice how nice she looked. Marci had changed into a sleek, somewhat low-cut dinner dress. It wasn't anything formal, but extremely elegant and very attractive. When she had first put it on I had asked her, "By arriving at the time we did, I'd be very surprised if they didn't insist on us having dinner with them. It is just like having dinner at a family or friends house. So there was no need to dress up for dinner."

Marci answered, "I somehow get the feeling that it's extremely important for me to make a good impression on your friends. From what you have told me about them, the way to impress Sharon is to present a stable, loving woman whose primary function in life is to take care of her man. The way to impress Mike is by being the sexiest damn female who ever strutted on the face of the Earth. The first time I met Mike, I wasn't at my best. This outfit is the best compromise I have to fit both roles."

I couldn't believe it. I hadn't really told her that much about Mike and Sharon, but she had nailed them right on the head. Plus, I was amazed she was going through such a public change based on what was important for me. Someone was actually putting my importance ahead of her own. I was learning more and more about what truly loving someone was all about.

Sharon had opened the door. Mike stood behind her. Marci's first impression had achieved the desired effect. Sharon took Marci by the hand. With a lot of girly chitchat, she led her off into the house. Mike just stood there with his mouth hanging open, watching every move Marci made as she passed him and followed Sharon into the house. As he turned to watch her go, I almost thought he had completely forgotten I was there. In fact, if I hadn't stepped into the foyer, he would have absentmindedly closed the door in my face.

"Yo! Mike! Anyone home?"

"What? What? Oh, hi, James. Come on in."

"For a minute there, old pal, I thought the pussy had gotten your tongue."

He blushed as he got my double meaning rib. "I'm sorry. James are you sure you're going to be able to handle that much woman?"

"Either that or I'm going to die a very happy man." I left him standing there and headed off in the direction that Marci and Sharon had gone.

Sharon had dinner prepared and the table already set for four. She wouldn't even hear about us not staying for dinner. Marci looked at me as if to say that she sure called the shots. Then we joined them for dinner.

Dinner was excellent. Sharon had really outdone herself. All through the meal, Marci and Sharon seemed to become better and better friends. As usual, Mike never talked business at the dinner table so he and I just chatted about useless bullshit. Mike and I occasionally added a few words to the women's conversation. Marci insisted on helping Sharon clean up after dinner. She had said it would give us guys a chance to talk business alone. Mike and I went into his study.

"All right, Mike. Give. What's the story with Bill Harper?"

Mike casually walked over and sat at his desk. He pointed to the couch that was against the wall. "Have a seat. We'll discuss it."

I sat down and waited. It was difficult waiting, but I knew Mike wasn't going to be hurried.

"Bill Harper is a very scared man." He paused to try to get me to blurt something out. I didn't bite. "He came in to the station and asked to speak to a detective. He spoke to the next one up for rotation. Thank God, it was Detective Carlson."

"Isn't he one of your better detectives?"

"He's probably the best one I've got. Anyway, he recognized instantly what Harper was telling him was big. So he shut him up. Then he called me, and I called the chief. Because we hadn't been getting a whole lot from your friend Jose Guappo, this was a big break."

"Who?"

"Jose Guappo is Puke Face to you."

"You're kidding?"

"Nope. Anyway, Harper was so scared that the Gionetti family was going to kill him that he has been spilling his guts so fast that it's hard to get it all straight."

"Why is he so scared? What have they got to do with him?"

"It seems this whole thing stems from Anne Gionetti's greed." Mike seemed to refuse to call her by her married name. "Apparently, Joseph Branning wanted out for whatever reason may forever be known only to him. He was using some form of blackmail in order to force the Gionetti family to let him go."

"The notebook!"

"That's our guess. But Harper has no idea. It seems Branning was going to skip town and disappear."

"Switzerland," I mumbled.

"What did you say?"

I thought quickly. "Wasn't his wife trying to go to Switzerland? I wonder if there was a connection."

"That's exactly the same question we are asking Mrs. Branning."

"And, of course, you are not getting an answer."

"Of course not from her, but Harper is telling us more than we are asking."

"Like what?"

"Like how he got mixed up in all this. He's desperately trying to save his ass. He's trying to tell us everything he knows, hoping that, once we know, the Gionetti family won't go after him."

"Why would they in the first place?"

"You're going to love this one. It seems your boss has a special affection for little girls."

"Bill Harper?"

"Yep. He likes underage prostitutes. He prefers them about thirteen to fifteen years of age."

"Bill a child molester? I would never have figured it."

"That's what he was hoping. But it turned against him when the Gionetti family decided to get rid of Branning before he could leave town or squeal on them. Anne Gionetti's family genetics got the best of her." He noticed the perplexed look on my face. "She knew about the life insurance policy on her husband. After all, she was the beneficiary, and she probably made the payments. But that wasn't enough."

"When is it ever?"

"Exactly. But guess who runs the prostitution in this town?"

I said softly, "The Gionetti family."

"Correct again. Harper has been visiting their young prostitutes for several years. They probably have had something planned for the use of Harper's habit for a long time. When the situation arose, they came to Harper and pulled in the line. They threatened to release photos of him and his playmates to his wife and the news media if he didn't go along with everything they wanted him to do."

"Which was what?"

"He was to ensure the policy was paid immediately upon Branning's death without any close investigation."

"That probably means they really did their homework and had this planned all along."

"Not necessarily. Crime families are notoriously paranoid, especially about non-blood-related members. Their backup and safety checks are so complex and numerous that no one person could possibly be aware of them all. So, an additional safety net that no one person could short-circuit was in place. They have something similar on every member to ensure compliance and loyalty."

"If that's the case, then why did Bill come crying to the police?"

"He said he figured he was already dead or close to it. So he had nothing to lose and everything to gain. In the witness protection program, at least he had a chance to live for a while longer."

"But they only threatened to blackmail him. Not kill him."

"Don't tell me Harper figured this out better than you. So you really think they'd let him live to possibly expose them after they got what they wanted? They just underestimated how quickly he'd run to us."

So that's why Harper gave Sean the case.

Mike brought my attention back. "Then you came into the picture. A dead husband and a million-dollar insurance policy was suddenly the subject of inquiry."

"No wonder they wanted me out of the picture."

I was actually happy they wanted me dead to stop the investigation. I now felt a lot more positive that they knew nothing about the bank account. All Anne Branning wanted was the money from the insurance policy and her husband dead. In fact, her husband's death was really only a means for obtaining the money quickly. She could have controlled him other ways. Or, if he had just disappeared, whether to Switzerland or off the bottom of a river, then she would have had to wait seven years of paying insurance premiums to have him pronounced legally dead. Then she could get the money. That would be too long and costly. I was ready to run out, grab Marci, and go to Switzerland tonight even if I had to swim across the ocean.

My obvious reaction puzzled Mike. "I have never seen anyone happy over the fact that a crime family wanted him dead."

"I'm happy because that means it's over for Marci. She is no longer an important witness. They will leave her alone."

"Except as a means of control over you. Other than that, she won't mean a hill of beans to them. Then, for that matter, neither will you. Because you are no longer able to affect the insurance claim, you become a nonentity to them."

"Ain't it great?"

"I'd think so."

"That also means the police or district attorney won't need either of us for testimony. We will be free to do or go wherever we want."

"Marci was kidnapped."

"But all of those guys are dead."

"Except for your Puke Face."

"But you have him on much more serious charges."

"Well, you're probably right. But they still might want to talk to both of you. So as long as I know how to get a hold of you, it shouldn't be a problem. Why? Where do you want to go?"

"Somewhere Marci and I can be absolutely alone. Mike, she has agreed to marry me."

"Holy shit! This really is serious."

"Extremely. We are very, very much in love."

"Sharon is going to piss her pants when she hears this."

We spent the next five to ten minutes going over the finer details of the case when we heard a woman's scream. It was a race to see which one of us went through the study door first. Mike had a head straight shot so he was a half-step ahead of me. It was a good thing. As Mike was going out the door, Sharon was coming in. They almost knocked each other over. Mike grabbed her. They were both shouting at the same time. I saw Marci standing just outside the room with a smile on her face. Now I was really confused.

Mike shut up long enough to hear Sharon say, "They're getting married. Mike, they're getting married. Isn't it wonderful?"

Mike looked at me.

I said, "You might want to check the diapers."

He started busting up laughing. Sharon ignored my remark and ran to me. She almost knocked me over with the hug she threw on me.

"Jim, I'm so very happy for you. She's wonderful. And she really loves you."

Mike went over and hugged Marci. I knew that wasn't a really hard thing for him to do. I was sure he enjoyed it.

CHAPTER 20

We got up early the next morning. We didn't have a lot to do, but we wanted all day to do it. Sometime during breakfast, we made a major decision. We decided to get married as soon as we could find a justice of the peace. I asked Marci, "Why do you want to get married so quickly and not have a big church wedding?

She answered, "I have two reasons. First, I love you so much that I want to marry you that quickly. Second, I want us to be married before we found out what was in the Swiss account so there would be no doubt in my mind that I married you for you and not the money. This way, we'd be married and together, no matter what we found. We'd be married because we wanted to."

Since there was no waiting period in this state, by noon, we were Mr. and Mrs. James Peterson.

Everything was going so well that I kept expecting something to go wrong. The passports were ready soon enough that we had no problem making our flight. Even though it seemed to take forever, and it was the next morning when we landed, the flight was very smooth and uneventful. We passed through customs as if it were a mere formality. After we had checked into our hotel, we headed for Zurich National Bank. The closer we got, the more nervous I got.

It was a little after noon on Friday when we found ourselves standing across the street from the bank. As we stood there looking, the piece of paper with the account number written on it felt like a lead brick in my pocket.

I turned to Marci. "Honey, I don't think it would be wise for you to go in there with me."

"Why not?"

"I don't know what kind of a reception I'm going to get. This is making me extremely nervous. I'd feel a lot better if you waited outside. If it goes bad for some unlikely reason, I'd be better off if you didn't go down with me. It wouldn't do us any good to have both of us confined or worse. I might need you free in order to help me."

"I don't like it. My place is with you."

"It is. But this is something I have to do alone. It's safer for the both of us. My main concern though is for your safety. Look, a café is back down the street." I pointed in the direction of a bistro we had passed on our way to the bank. "Go there and wait for me." She started to protest, but I didn't give her the chance. I handed her keys to the car. "If I'm not there in an hour, then go to the hotel. If for some reason you haven't heard from me in the morning, catch the first flight home. Then go straight to Mike and tell him everything."

"I won't leave you! If you don't come back, I'll look for you even if I have to tear the bank apart myself. I won't leave my husband behind."

"Marci, I love you. I want you safe."

"My safety means nothing to me if you're not in my life. You understand me? I won't leave without you."

I looked at her. I could tell she was going to be stubborn about this. I'd do the same thing for her. So I kissed her. Without a word, I turned and headed for the bank. As I crossed the street, I prayed she'd go back to the café and wait like I asked. I never looked back as I entered the bank.

Forty minutes later, I walked cautiously up to the café. At first,

Marci didn't see me. I saw her sitting alone at a table. I stopped for a moment to look at her. She was so lovely sitting there, young, vibrant, and so much alive. I could tell she was on edge though. The little things always gave a person away, like the nervous way she played with her coffee cup, the shifting in her chair, and the continual looking at her watch.

She noticed me when I was about ten feet away. She started to jump up and say something. I hushed her with a finger to my mouth and a hushing signal with my lips. She sat back down and waited while I pulled up a chair. I looked around to make sure no one was within earshot. What I was about to tell her was for her ears only.

She couldn't take it any longer. "Well, what did you find?"

I took my time. With as neutral of an expression as I could, I looked at her. "Ten million, three hundred and seventy-six thousand, four hundred and twenty-four dollars."

"What?"

"There was ten million, three hundred and seventy-six thousand, four hundred and twenty-four dollars in the account."

"What do you mean? Was?"

I looked around casually and as cautiously as possible. When I was satisfied no one was paying any attention to us, I reached into my coat pocket. "I took five thousand in cash and the rest in this." I opened a folded piece of paper for Marci to look at. It was a certified bank transfer made out to me for $10.3 million. "I told the bank manager that I wanted to donate the rest to the bank's favorite charity. After that, he was most helpful. He even helped me to locate a bank in the Grand Cayman Islands that would be very receptive to helping with all my future monetary needs with all the privacy such an account deserves without any United States IRS tax problems, as he put it."

Marci just sat there with her mouth hanging open and stared at the transfer. I reached over, touched the bottom of her chin, and lightly lifted her mouth shut. "Careful, dear, my momma always said that is how you catch flies."

She finally uttered, "Is this for real?"

"As real as real can be." I put the transfer into my wallet and put my wallet back in my pocket. "Well, Mrs. Peterson, are you ready to start the rest of your life?"

At the sound of me saying "Mrs. Peterson," she smiled. And all was well with the world.

CHAPTER 21

As our private charted jet taxied to a stop in front of the VIP terminal on a secluded part of the airport on one of the outer romantic Bahamas Islands, I was finding it very hard to believe how far I had come in the last few days. Just a very short time ago, I was walking down the street in that downpour of a rainstorm in a worn, ten-year-old suit. Now I was sitting in a leased jet in my black tuxedo with an ivory shirt that had a winged collar. I had very expensive gold cufflinks and diamond stud buttons that Marci had picked out and personally put in place for me. Shiny black shoes topped off my outfit. Everything I was wearing, including my boxer shorts, were brand-new and bought for just this occasion. At first, I had resisted the expense, but Marci had insisted that I was worth it.

I looked over at her for the ten millionth time since we had left our home. Marci had her lovely hair in a French braid. In her hair, she wore clips that had small diamonds that sparkled like the stars every time she moved her head and they caught the light. I luxuriated in her beautiful, huge expressive eyes, which the most captivating of eye shadow I had ever seen highlighted. It was a golden brown with little specks of dust that glimmered. She matched the eye shadow with mascara that made her eyelashes look incredibly thick and long. Her eyelashes were naturally thick and long, but the mascara just made them seem even more luscious. As Marci looked over at me, I could see the love and admiration that she felt for me. It was easy for me to see, as it was a reflection of what I felt for her. Her lips were very thick and a deep rich cranberry color, which made her teeth look incredibly white. She had told me that it was her favorite lipstick color. I had to agree. It was now my favorite, too. I had noticed she hadn't stopped smiling ever since we started this trip. So I knew beyond a shadow of a doubt that she must be very happy.

Because she was sitting very close to me, I could smell her skin, scented with the most beautiful perfume. There was the hint of cleanliness with the strong suggestion of sexuality. It was both captivating and stimulating.

I had often heard the expression that the clothes make the man, but, in this case, I felt Marci's outfit was so enticing that mere words weren't adequate to describe the angel of beauty who sat next to me. Her sleeveless dress came to the base of her neck. However, the solid black part came high enough to just barely cover her breasts. From there to her neck, it was very, very sheer. In the back, it was cut down to just about where her elbows were. Then from there, it was sheer until the material that covered her lovely little ass. It was made from the most wonderful of material. It shaped itself to every one of her curves, but wasn't clingy. It just moved effortlessly with every part of her body as she moved. Across her breasts were tiny, little black beads that caught the light with every movement she made. I could tell she wasn't wearing a bra under those beads, as her nipples just ever so slightly made an imprint on the material.

Before we got on the jet, Marci whispered in my ear, "I am only wearing a black thong under my dress." I smiled. She purred even more seductively, "I am only wearing those instead of no panties at all was because I know I would be continually wet the whole night and didn't want to mess up my gown." Her gown reached to the top of her ankles, but was slit up her right leg to about three inches below her thigh. Below that, she was wearing very sheer, black, thigh-high stockings. Her beautiful, black satin pump shoes was like the final touch that made her look the perfect picture of a women. She looked very elegant and extremely sensuous. She looked so very curvy. She was completely covered, but she looked very sexy. I absolutely loved her dress.

Finally, the door to the jet opened, and we exited. As we approached the waiting limo, I happened to notice that all the airport people who were present were looking at us. Then I realized they were really looking at Marci. She was so stunning that every person was having a double take whenever his eyes were fortunate to catch a glimpse of her. Marci either seemed unaware or unconcerned with all the looks, as she reached over and nuzzled my neck and lightly licked me just below my ear. She seemed so happy that she kept giggling. A tremendous sense of pride and happiness filled me because I was so very fortunate that the most sensuous woman in the whole world was on my arm and wanted to be there. I liked that other people couldn't keep their eyes off her. That was a tremendous compliment to both of us, but mostly to her.

I whispered, "Look, honey, you look so good that nobody can keep his eyes off you. Men in lust and women in envy"

"That might be true, baby, but I'm certain the ladies are checking out your tight butt."

As we got to the limo, the chauffeur opened the back door for us. Marci smiled at him, and it just seemed to fall all over himself trying to please her. I could see him practically melt from envy right there in front of us. As I stepped aside, took a hold of Marci's elbow, and assisted her into the limo, I noticed the few ladies were indeed looking at us. I felt assured that some may have been looking at my butt, but I was sure some were looking at Marci and wishing they were her right then. Not necessarily to be with me but because they wished they were as pretty and sexy as she was.

As Marci passed right by me, she whispered, "Have you ever had sex in a limousine?"

I just smiled at her as I climbed in next to her. The chauffeur closed the door behind me.

She said a little bit above a whisper, "But we can't right now because it's still daylight."

The sun was still up, but it was just setting and in that twilight between night and day.

"I've never seen a sky that looks like that. Look at all the corals, pinks, and reds streaked endlessly across the sky."

"I know, honey. It's like a crimson rainbow," I answered in awe. "But I hardly notice it because it pales to the beauty in you."

Marci momentarily looked down and then back up at me. "You make me blush."

Finally, the chauffeur came around and got in. We pulled away en route to our dinner location. Everything had been prearranged. He knew exactly where to go without having to ask or be told. We were sitting hip to hip, and we were mostly just talking about nothing in particular. Marci's fingers kept tracing up and down my inner thigh as she was teasing me.

I knew the chauffeur could probably hear what I said in a normal voice, so I whispered into her ear, "I love how your nipples have just gotten hard enough to be seen through your dress."

Marci's eyes got just a little wider. She looked at me. "You noticed!"

"Yes, of course I did. Plus, Marci, I really do know you."

"I know you do." With her now-patented purr, she asked, "Do you want something to drink, baby?"

"I'd like a little whiskey, but not too much. The restaurant isn't that far. What would you like to drink?"

"I just want a Coke, please."

As we left the airport and turned onto the street, Marci looked around. "You know, I didn't realize they drive on the other side of the road here."

"Yes, they do."

"That's too intimidating for me. I'd be afraid when making left-hand turns. If we drive anywhere, I hope you want to do it."

"That's why we have a chauffeur."

Marci smiled at me. I reached up to the bar and poured a Coke in a glass over a little ice. I poured myself just a little, maybe about one finger of Crown Royal over two small ice cubes.

I handed Marci her drink. She asked, "Do you want to toast us?"

I wrapped my arm with the drink around her arm with her drink and looked deeply into her eyes. "Loving you is the most right thing I have ever done. The happiness that comes from this will never be outshined by even the brightest star."

"I love you for real and endlessly."

We each took a small sip of our drink and then very lightly kissed. But as we pulled back a few inches and looked deeply into each other's eyes, the car hit a small bump. We came very close to spilling our drinks, but not quite. We both giggled at the moment, giddy with the high of love. Then we were at the restaurant.

Before we started to move to the door, Marci lightly grabbed my arm. "This is the most wonderful night. I hope this never ends."

"Marci honey, no matter what happens in the future, this night will live in us forever."

"Do you know what you want to eat?"

"Besides you, I will have to wait to see the menu."

The doorman at the restaurant hurried up and opened the car door. I stepped out, turned, and offered Marci a hand out. As she stepped out of the car, her leg stuck out of the slit up the side of her dress. Her leg was completely visible. My eyes were drawn right to her exposed leg. Her calf and thigh looked great. I caught just a glimpse of the top of her stocking and her bare, naked thigh. It almost took my breath away. In fact, my heart nearly raced through my chest at the sight of her bare leg. Then when she leaned forward to get out of the car, I could see the cleavage of her breasts. When she stood up, I could tell by the look in her eye that the entire show was done on purpose just for my benefit.

I said softly for just her to hear, "Nice breasts."

"Thank you." She had a mischievous smile.

"And your nipples are still protruding very lovely through the front of your dress."

"Well, the material is black so you can see the outline. I'm not wearing a bra."

But I noticed that, in the darkness of the night, her nipples were only just barely visible. Plus, the way the material was cut, it pulled in her breasts tightly.

"I'm hungry, honey. Are we going to go eat?" Marci asked.

"I'm thinking I can't wait to get my mouth on those heavenly nipples."

"Calm down, bad boy. You have to feed me first."

"Right now, food is the furthest thing from my mind."

"I can't wait until you run your fingers up along my stockings." She looked at me very demurely and purred, "First, how about some dinner?"

For the minute, I seemed to come out of my momentary stare, put my hand around her back, and guided her to the restaurant door.

As I pulled her closer, she said softly into my ear, "I like the way your hand grazes across my back, grabs on to my waist, and guides me with you. Very manly. It makes me feel very womanly."

As we approached the door, the doorman was right there to open the door. We went inside. We paused just a moment inside the lobby. Marci let out a slight gasp.

"Oh, it's beautiful!"

I noticed once again she was the showstopper. All the way into the very eloquent and classy restaurant entrance, every sound and motion stopped as we approach the maître d'. As we got closer, we began to hear the band playing softly in the background. A young, male voice could just be heard singing. I found the timing almost incredible in the words he was singing. I didn't believe in coincidences, so I almost had to believe in this song being played on purpose.

He sang, "Young and tan and so enchanting …"

"I love the band," Marci said. She hummed along.

The maître d' knew who we were without me saying a word. Money was a powerful tool.

He turned. "Right this way, Mr. and Mrs. Peterson." He led us into the restaurant.

Marci and I both ignored the looks and stares we got as we made our way. We owned the world, and we had each other. Both Marci and I felt the whole world only consisted of two.

The young singer continued in perfect unison with our pace.

Marci had this very happy, content smile on her face. It made me feel like the king of the world. I had a small strut in my step. The maître d' led us directly to an intimate and isolated dinner booth. We were soon seated and left alone for a few minutes to get ourselves comfortable.

Marci was all aglow with happiness. "This is very, very romantic. I love the way the candles glow."

We were sitting about ten feet from an open terrace door so that, when the band broke in between songs, we could hear the ocean and smell the salt air of the sea. Our extremely isolated table was in a very dimly lit corner of the restaurant, but several people were jumping to our service if at our slightest wish or whim.

Marci asked, "Could I please, please have my favorite beach drink, a strawberry-banana daiquiri?"

"Of course, sweetheart. Whatever you want."

I turned to look for a waiter. One appeared almost from thin air. "Yes, sir. What may I get you and madam?"

"The lady will have a strawberry-banana daiquiri, and I'll have a piña colada."

"Very good, sir."

Away he went.

We had been holding hands since we had left the hotel to get in the limo. Marci lifted up her hand and kissed my hand she held.

She looked me in the eye. "I like the way your fingers never let go of mine. They just dance and flirt with my fingers. You look incredibly handsome." We were sitting very close to each other in the booth, so close that our knees were in constant contact. "I like how our legs keep rubbing. I also like how I sometimes feel your chest rub against my breast."

I looked longingly into her eyes. She reached up with her left hand and softly stroked my cheek. Our faces were just inches apart. It was incredibly intimate. But we refrained from getting too intimate because our love wasn't for display. It was only for us.

Marci whispered in a sexy, throaty voice, "You're the most beautiful, wonderful man. And I can't believe I get to be here with you." She suddenly pulled back slightly. "Here come our drinks." I smiled lightly, leaned forward, and kissed her passionately, but lightly and quickly. "I love your lips." Her shaking fingers touched my lips.

The waiter waited patiently because he could readily see the love flowing between us. Then Marci realized he was standing there. She slightly giggled with embarrassment and then sat back in her seat. The waiter placed our drinks on the table and then stood back for a moment and waited.

I was speechless, but Marci recovered nicely. "I know what I'm ordering."

"So, what will you have for dinner, my love?"

The waiter stepped forward just a bit. "I'd like crab legs with hot melted butter, please. I'd also like soft, delicious dinner rolls and a baked potato with butter and cheese."

The waiter nodded.

"What are you having, baby?"

I leaned forward and whispered in her ear, "When I heard you say crab legs, all I could think of was your great legs and how I'd like to lick the butter off them."

Marci whispered back in my ear so close that I could feel her lips brushing my ear. It sent warm shivers up and down my spine. "That will be your treat later."

The waiter waited until there was a break in our conversation. "Sir, your order?"

"I'll have the escargot appetizer with the lobster tail for my entrée and baked potato with butter and sour cream." I saw Marci scrunch her nose up a little as I said "escargot." "But, honey, escargot is filled with vitamin E. Dipped in garlic butter, it is very, very good."

She looked at me. "And vitamin E is good for?"

"Libido!"

"Uh-huh. Well, then eat them up, sir. But the lobster tail does make me want to lick my lips."

The waiter had patiently waited through our chatter. "That is a very good dinner selection. Would you care for a dinner wine?"

I looked at Marci. She said, "Maybe a good Merlot."

I looked at the waiter. He nodded approvingly and disappeared.

Marci leaned close to me and giggled. "I'm afraid that, if I keep drinking, you'll get me tipsy and have your way with me."

"That sounds like a good plan to me."

She smiled very mischievously. "I'm having a wonderful time. When do you want to hit the beach in the morning? I bought an incredible new bikini."

"What does it look like?"

"You'll just have to wait and see for yourself. I want to see your face when you see it for the first time."

While we were waiting for our dinner to arrive, I heard the band play a very romantic and sensuous slow song. I turned to Marci. "Would you like to dance, my dear?"

"I'd be delighted."

I came around behind her and pulled out her chair as she stood up. I could hear her singing softly to the song being played. "Unforgettable … that's what you are … unforgettable … though near or far … like a song of love that sings to me … never before … has someone been more … unforgettable."

She stood and walked by me. She walked very close and just brushed me. The scent she left behind enchanted me. It lingered in the air like the ghost of Aphrodite. As we reached the dance floor, we were the only ones there, but all eyes were on us. Every couple could tell we truly wanted to be together. The women looked at us with a romantic smile at the beauty we were as a couple, and the men were all smiles as they fantasized they were I with Marci.

I put my arms around her waist. Marci put her arms around my neck.

Marci whispered very seductively in my ear, "I love the way your arms wrap around me. I love how our thighs fit together as we dance. God, you are so sweet."

My hands slid down and rested along the top of her ass. I held the front of her hips against mine. I whispered back into her ear with a little extra warm breath to stimulate her, "I love the feel of the front of your body against me."

"I like the scent of your skin," she blew back in my ear. She ran her tongue along the inside. "I like how your hands feel on me. I wish they could explore all of me."

It was hard to tell if we were dancing or gyrating. But I was so into it that I didn't hear the music stop. After a few steps (or shuffles and hip grinds), Marci brought me back to reality, even though she was a bit short of breath from the encounter.

"The song has ended, baby. Please clap now."

We both separated about two inches and lightly clapped. When we had stopped, we were standing pretty close to the bandstand. The bandleader, who had also been appreciating our closeness, looked at Marci and said, "Madam is there anything you want to hear." The bandleader had that kind of Tony Bennett/ Frank Sinatra look going.

Marci gave him a really big, flirtatious smile. "The Way You Look Tonight."

He grinned and turned to start the band. "Very appropriate song for the lady."

We began to dance as the music started. I pulled her just slightly back against the front of me. Our feet slightly shifted along the dance floor. The natural movement of our hips was very stimulating to both of us. We danced in love throughout the whole song. Our movement wasn't blatantly sexual so much as it was very sensuous and intimate.

When the song ended, we both just stood there for a few moments in a tight embrace. It was like we had both expended a lot of energy and spirit in the joining of our two bodies and souls in those dances. It was similar to how we often felt after we had very passionately made love and it took some time to return to the physical world. Both our mental and physical beings were momentarily drained of energy and required time to stabilize back to the here and now. The most unusual thing about it was that every person who could see Marci and I seemed to realize what was going on. The bandleader, all of the band, the people at their tables, and all the restaurant personnel sat or stood very still and quiet and watched us. Then as we came back to the present, we parted slightly enough from our tight embrace so we could kiss lightly. Without a word, hand in hand, we turned to go to our table. We were both stopped in surprise as everybody softly clapped for us in appreciation of our love of each other. Marci blushed, and I shuffled a few steps. We looked at each other and grinned. With all the eyes on us, it was a very long walk back to our table. But holding on to each other tightly, we eventually made it.

Once we were back in the security of our private booth, we

both felt a lot better. Soon after, we were snug and comfortable again as our dinner arrived. Even though we sat so close, as if our hips were glued together, neither one of us said much over the next thirty minutes or so as we devoured our dinner. I did not ever remember a time in my forty-nine years that even just one of my appetites had been as constantly starving as all were now since I had met and fallen in love with Marci. It was like I could not get enough of anything to fully satisfy any of my cravings. She had truly awoken all of me to the fullest. Looking back at life before Marci, everything seemed so boring and drab, almost dead when compared with what it was like now.

After dinner, we each had a small after-dinner liquor that helped settle everything as only it could. I took care of the check by a simple signature and helped Marci up with her chair.

I whispered in her ear, "How about a nice stroll on the patio that leads out to the beach?"

She leaned back into me slightly. "Sounds wonderful. Maybe the stars and moon will be out."

"Don't worry, my dear. It has already been ordered."

She giggled lightly. "You silly man."

"For you, nothing is too silly or out of the question."

I took hold of her right hand with my left hand. She almost wrapped herself around my left arm as we walked out the open door and onto the terrace. Instantly, the smell of the ocean salt air filled our noses. It was so thick that we could taste it. Marci took a deep breath and exhaled with her eyes shut as she luxuriated in the aroma. We walked to the edge of the open-air terrace and stared out over the ocean. The very big full moon was just rising above the horizon, and we could see its reflection in the crashing waves. It seemed to glisten like thousands of little diamonds in the blanket of water as it curled over in the small waves. As Marci stood there admiring the ocean, I came around behind her and wrapped my arms around her waist. She leaned back into me, and I rested my chin on her shoulder with my head slightly pressing against the side of hers. The front of my body pressed firmly against the back of her body. We just stood there and looked at the view. After a while, I looked up. All the stars in the crystal clear night sky, thousands and thousands of little pinpoints of lights, amazed me. I noticed and pointed out to Marci the few constellations that I knew, like Orion's Belt, the Big and Little Dipper, the Seven Sisters that was straight overhead, and a few others I couldn't really remember the name. There was the one in the western sky that looked like a crooked "W."

After several minutes of staring at all this natural wonder and beauty, Marci turned and rotated in my arms so we were facing each other. I still had my arms around her waist. Now she had her arms around my neck.

"Jimmy, you've shown me so many wonderful and enlightening things. I never knew that life could be so full and beautiful. I love you more with every beat of my heart. Every second that goes by fills me with wonder that I love you more than the last second. You are so intoxicating to my heart and soul that I feel as if I'm under a magical spell. But I know with my mind that it is nothing more than deep, head-over-heels love."

She kissed me once very lovingly and tender. She placed her mouth very close to my ear as she hugged me tightly. "Jimmy, please take me for a walk on the beach and make love to me in the sand. I've always dreamed of that. But until I met you, I never wanted to really do it. Oh, please fulfill this one fantasy for me."

After a few seconds, she withdrew her head from the side of mine. She looked me in the eye to get my reaction. I could see the excitement of her passion in her eyes, but also the uncertainty of my reaction. I kissed her once very lightly on the lips.

"Honey, nothing would give me more pleasure than to love you on the warm sand of the beach with the sound of the waves in our ears. Shall we walk down the beach, away from the restaurant?"

Neither one of us said a word as we walked toward the

opening of the terrace that led to the beach and ocean. We started down the four steps to the sand. Marci stopped at the next-to-last one.

"I had better take off my pumps. The sand wouldn't feel very good inside."

"Here. Let me help." I continued down the steps to the sand and knelt at her feet.

She placed her hands on my shoulders as I removed the first shoe and then the other. I stood up and handed the pair of black satin pumps to her.

"Don't you want to take yours off?" Marci stepped out onto the sand.

I hesitated. "Sure. Why not?"

I sat on the bottom step and removed both my shoes and socks. I also rolled the bottom of my pant leg up about six inches. I picked up my shoes, stood up, and joined her at her right side. As she switched her pumps from her right to her left hand, I took her right hand in my left. I held my shoes in my right as we walked out onto the beach. The sand felt still just as warm as it ran between my toes. We walked straight out until we were on the firmer part, where the tide had reached within the last few hours. We turned left and walked on. As we walked, we didn't say much. Nothing vocal was really needed. We were both content to have been in the other's company. After a couple hundred yards, we had wandered slightly closer to the water. The surf reached up far enough where our feet were actually in the water up to our ankles. I thought at first that Marci might have a problem because of her stockings, but she didn't say a word or make a move to leave the surf. A long while later, I looked back over my shoulder and could tell we had walked quite a long way. We were far enough away from the restaurant that we were totally isolated. Also, nobody could see us or wander onto us from the restaurant because we had walked so far. For all I could tell, we were on an isolated portion of the beach. Looking away from the ocean, all one could see was a high sand dune embankment. Other than us, no other sign of life was anywhere. I felt comfortable that we were absolutely alone.

I stopped walking and turned Marci back toward me. I could just barely see her face in the darkness. But there was enough illumination from the full moon that I could see just a glimmer of happiness across her eyes and the smile on her lips. Nothing had to be said. Marci and I both dropped our shoes. She came into my arms, and we kissed deeply. At first, we kissed with just our lips. They were busy lips, but they remained closed. Our bodies were pressed tightly together. Soon though, our lips parted, and our tongues danced their love dance in and out of each other's mouths. I never seemed to tire of kissing her.

After we had been kissing to the point that our tongues were tiring, we separated our mouths and tongues and held each other in a very, very tight embrace.

Even though Marci was out of breath, she managed to say in a throaty whisper into my ear, "Jimmy, fuck me right here and now on this beach. I want you to fuck every fiber of my existence."

My brain was so filled with the wonders caused by how turned on I was that it didn't register at first.

She started to take off my dinner jacket. She said it again, "Oh, Jimmy, please fuck me really hard right now! It has always been a lifelong fantasy of mine to have sex on a beach. It couldn't be any better than to have it with the man I love more than anything else in the entire world."

"Yes, baby. Oh, yes. I will fuck you."

I started to kiss her face and neck as I reached behind her and unfastened the connection that held up her top. When it came undone, her dress dropped straight to the sand and around her ankles. She stepped out of it just enough so she wasn't likely to step on or trample it. Now all I had in my arms was a lovely angel in nothing more than black thong panties. I took a minute to admire as much as I could see in the dark as Marci very busily unbuttoned my shirt. She undid it quickly, but was very careful not to lose any of the studs. My shirt now joined my dinner jacket, her dress, and our shoes on the beach. Marci soon started kissing and licking down the front of me before I had a chance to do anything. As she reached my stomach, she knelt down on her knees. She was about eye level with my belt buckle. She lost no time as she undid my belt and unzipped my fly. She pulled down both my pants and boxers all in one motion as if she were desperate to have me exposed. I was very soon very naked as she took both my pants and boxers all the way down my legs and off my feet and threw them in the general direction of the rest of our clothes. Then she eagerly took my now-hard cock in her hands and placed the head in her mouth. She kept both of her hands around the base of my erection as she aggressively sucked and licked the now-blossoming head of my dick. I reached down and placed my hands on the sides of her head. She left her left hand on the base of my dick, reached under my balls with her right, and started to stroke and massage the area in between my testicles and anus. Then she brought her hand forward and very gently played with my balls. She had my nuts in the base of her palm with her fingers wrapped around and gently caressing. Her index finger very lightly flicked and tickled that area behind my balls. I thought I'd lose it right there, but she kept a tight hold of the base of my penis in her left hand. I came close, but did not cross that threshold of ejaculation. I soon found myself pulling her head forward and then back, as if I were holding her ass cheeks, to match my hip thrusts. At first, we started slowly. Then I more rapidly pumped my hips forward and back as if I were literally fucking her face. The moans I could hear from her were sounds of delight. She seemed to like that I controlled her head with my hands and was vigorously fucking her in the mouth.

After several blissful moments of this ecstasy, she finally released me and stood up. Marci came into my arms, and we just held each other tightly for a moment. As I lowered my hands down her back to her ass cheeks, I realized she still had her thong panties on, but not for long. I lowered her thong past her hips to her thighs. Then gravity helped, and they fell to the sand. Marci easily stepped out of them and kicked them aside. Neither one of us seemed to feel any shame or remorse about standing on this beach completely naked and about to make love.

We started back up with light feather kisses as we held each other tightly and stood still. Then as our kisses grew in intensity, our bodies rubbing against each other grew in motion as much and in time with our kissing. We were soon tongue dancing and hip gyrating. Marci was having a very difficult time keeping her hands still as they roamed all over the back of me. We both seemed to want the same thing all at once as we both sank down and lay in the sand. Marci was on her back. I was halfway on top of her, off to her right side. My left hand was around the back of her neck, and my right hand was very busy fondling her breasts and exploring the dampness between her legs. She was so wet that she was gushing. My fingers easily slid in and out of her pussy. The base of my middle finger rubbed along her soaking wet clit. I could feel that her whole vagina was swollen and enlarged from her passion. But then again, so was my dick. I was so turned on that my dick was swollen to the point that I thought it would explode. Marci willingly allowed me to explore to my heart's content while she just kissed me and held on to me around my neck and head. Both of us were moaning and groaning so loudly that I was sure we woke the fish in the ocean, whose waves were crashing ashore merely ten feet away. I couldn't tell which was louder, the crashing of the waves or our own love sounds.

Then I felt her quiver with several little pre-orgasms. So I crawled over on top of her and slid in between her legs with my hips. I raised my head slightly and looked at her face. Marci slightly opened her eyes and smiled at me as she felt the head of my penis separate her pussy lips and slide through her wetness and into her warmth.